IF YOU

Need

ME

NEW YORK TIMES BESTSELLING AUTHOR
HELENA HUNTING

IF YOU Need ME CAST

DALLAS BRIGHT
BEST FRIEND TO ASH, ARCH-NEMESIS TO HEMI
TERROR FORWARD

SIBLINGS
MANNING, FERRIS AND PARIS

PARENTS
DIANA AND MATTIAS

TEAMMATES

ASHISH PALANIAPPA
HUSBAND TO SHILPA (TEAM LAWYER)
BEST FRIEND TO DALLAS

HOLLIS HENDRIX
BEST FRIEND TO ROMAN HAMMERSTEIN
-TERROR COALIE

FLIP MADDEN
BROTHER TO RIX
BEST FRIEND TO TRISTAN AND DRED

TRISTAN STILES
BOYFRIEND TO FLIP
BEST FRIEND TO FLIP
SIBLINGS: NATE AND BRODY

ROMAN HAMMERSTEIN
HAMMER'S DAD
HOLLIS'S BEST FRIEND, TERROR TEAMMATE

WILHELMINA REDDI-GRINST
(HEMI, WILLY/HILLS)
PR FOR TERROR, BEST FRIEND TO SHILPA

SIBLINGS
SAMIR (SAM) AND ISAAC

PARENTS
GEORGINA & SANDITA (SANDY)

BADASS BABE BRIGADE

SHILPA PALANIAPPA
(SHILPS)
BEST FRIEND TO HEMI
MARRIED TO ASHISH PALANIAPPA

BEATRIX MADDEN
(RIX, BEAT, BEA)
ROOMMATE TO HAMMER
SISTER TO FLIP MADDEN
GIRLFRIEND TO TRISTAN STILES

TALLULAH VANDER ZEE
(TALLY/TALS)
DAUGHTER OF TERROR COACH
IN SENIOR YEAR OF HIGH SCHOOL

MILDRED REFORMER
(DRED)
NEIGHBOR TO FLIP
PLATONIC FRIEND OF FLIP'S

PEGGY AURORA HAMMERSTEIN
(PEGGY AURORA, HAMMER PRINCESS)
DAUGHTER TO ROMAN HAMMERSTEIN
TEAM COALIE

HONORARY MEMBER
ESSIE LOVELOCK
RIX'S BEST FRIEND
LIVES IN VANCOUVER

ACKNOWLEDGMENTS

Husband and kidlet, I adore you. You inspire me every day and I'm so grateful for your love.

Deb, I adore you. Thank you for always having my back.

Becca, it is such an honor to know you, as a friend, as a badass fairy plotmother, as a strong, amazing businesswoman. Thank you for coming on this journey with me and helping me push myself with every single book.

Kimberly, thank you for all you do. It's been an amazing decade and I'm excited for what's next.

Sarah, I honestly couldn't do this without you. You've been such a huge source of support and friendship and I'm so thankful to have you on my side.

Hustlers, you're my cheerleaders and my book family and I'm so grateful for each and every one of you.

My SS team, your eagle eyes are amazing, and I appreciate your input and support.

Tijan, you're a wonderful human and I'm blessed to know you.

Shaye and Lindsey, you are amazing and I'm so thankful for you and Good Girls.

Catherine, Jessica F and Tricia, your kindness and wonderful energy are such a source of inspiration, thank you for your friendship.

Jessica, Erica, Amanda, Julia, thank you so much for working on this project with me, I know it was a beast, and I'm so honored to be able to work with you and helping me make it sparkle.

Sarah, Kate and Rae, thank you for being graphic gurus. Your incredible talent never ceases to amaze me.

Beavers, thank you for giving me a safe place to land, and for always being excited about what's next.

Kat, Marnie, Krystin; thank you for being such incredible women. I'm so thankful for your friendship.

Readers, bloggers, bookstagrammers and booktokers, thank you for sharing your love of romance and happily ever afters.

For all the badass babes who hold each other up and fix each other's crowns.

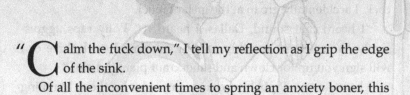

CHAPTER 1
DALLAS

"**C**alm the fuck down," I tell my reflection as I grip the edge of the sink.

Of all the inconvenient times to spring an anxiety boner, this sure tops the list.

"Open the damn door, Dallas." Willy rattles the knob.

"Ah, fuck me." I grit my teeth against the surge of desire.

It's pointless, though. I'm already picturing her pissed-off expression: rosy cheeks, fists on her curvy hips, full lips pushed out in an adorable, annoyed pout. My erection turns into a steel rod.

Wilhelmina Reddi-Grinst, referred to by the team as Hemi—but who I call Willy, mostly to ensure her attention is on me—is the public relations director for the Toronto Terror, the professional hockey team I play for.

She's also the woman of my dreams—has been for years. Unfortunately, she hates me. She has good reason. We've known each other since kindergarten, and I was a dick of the highest order growing up.

Even more unfortunate is the way my body responds to her every single time. Especially when she's giving me shit. People always bend over backwards to please me. But not Willy. Never Willy.

"I'll be right out," I call, panic layering on top of anxiety. This should not be happening. I took care of myself before I left the damn house. Twice. But here I am, battling yet another raging anxiety boner. In the bathroom of a pet rescue shelter. It's embarrassing.

And it's a new low. But handling my situation in here is better than having pictures of me holding a rescue dog while sporting a hard-on all over the internet.

Horrible decision made, I uncurl one hand from the edge of the sink, hating myself as I reach into my underwear to fist my cock. I accidentally groan at the instant relief.

"I heard that sound, Dallas. I heard it." Willy raps aggressively. "You better open this door by the time I reach three or I will sign you up for clown and sauerkraut pierogi detail."

I hate clowns. Probably because my older brothers, Manning and Ferris, made me watch *IT* when I was four. And sauerkraut reminds me of my great-grandma Helga's house, where my siblings and I sometimes had to stay as kids when my parents went away on vacation. I came down with the stomach flu after eating her borscht, and now the smell of cooked cabbage in any form triggers my gag reflex.

"I just need a minute!" I call back, stroking fast and hard. I slam my eyes shut, trying not to picture Willy naked and angry. It's difficult with her on the other side of the door.

"You've had ten. Your minutes are up." More knocking. "Three," Hemi's voice shakes with rage.

The fallout from this will be bad. So, so bad. She'll for sure make me pay for this. And the worst part is, I'll eat it up. Because it will mean her focus is exactly where I want it. On me. I know it's messed up to enjoy pissing her off. It's a problem, and I should seek therapy for it. But her anger is preferable to apathy.

The angrier she gets, the harder I get. It should be the opposite. I should *not* love getting under her skin the way I do. But at least I know I affect her, too.

"Two. Clown detail it is."

I can't do clown detail again. Public panic attacks aren't good for my image.

"I'm sending the email with your name, right now." The glee in her voice sends a shiver down my spine. *God, I love her.*

I'm so fucked when it comes to Wilhelmina.

And then I do something stupider than whacking off in a public bathroom.

CHAPTER 2

HEMI

The door swings open, and Dallas's arm shoots out. He grabs my wrist and yanks me into the bathroom. My boobs hit the door on the way in. He slams it closed behind him and turns the lock.

"Why am I in here with you?" I grimace at his sweaty, disheveled appearance. He's hunched at the waist, one hand on his knee. "Are you sick? Do you have the flu? You better not have the flu. You should have told me before you wasted everyone's time."

"I don't have the flu." He's panting. And still bent over. I don't know what's happening with his other hand, maybe cupping his junk?

"Then why do you look like...like this?" I fling a hand in his handsomely rumpled direction. Fucking Dallas. Such an annoyingly pretty boy, and a giant pain in my ass.

"I need a minute," he snaps.

I scoff and fist my hands at my sides so I don't give in to the urge to strangle him. He does this almost every time, and I firmly believe it's to annoy me. He was the most popular guy in our high school, always the center of attention. He should be used to it by now.

But getting angrier will only make me look unprofessional, not him. It's frustrating that nothing has changed since we were kids. I'm still the outspoken nerdy girl, and he's still the prom king. I take a deep breath and put on my nice-Hemi hat, because I need him to leave this bathroom and do the promo shoot with the adorable Chihuahua mix so I can go to yet another coffee date with a random online dude whose picture is hopefully not ten years out of date.

I have a high school reunion this summer. I can't go alone. Not when my ex-best friend and her longtime boyfriend will be there to rub their happiness in my face. High school wasn't the same fun time for me as it was for Dallas. I need to show them my life has turned out just fine—and that includes having someone to share it with.

"Dallas Mattias Bright, you are a badass hockey player." I stroke his overinflated ego. "Millions of people are cheering for you every time you take the ice. Adorable Chihuahuas are not a threat to you. You've done countless promo shoots before, and you know what you always do?"

"Make an ass of myself?"

"You always come out smelling like roses." I grab him by the shoulders and attempt to force him to straighten, but he resists. "Stand up straight."

"I can't."

"You can and you will unless you want to make balloon animals again at this year's Halloween Haunt fundraiser."

"Don't threaten me with that, Willy."

I grind my teeth at the horrible nickname he's used since I started working for the Terror.

He grimaces, like he's realized two seconds too late the mistake he's made.

"I warned you." He straightens.

And now I know why he was hunched over. Despite one hand being poised protectively in front of his crotch, it's glaringly obvious that he has an issue in his underpants. A seriously huge issue. "Why the hell would you pull me into the bathroom when you have a massive hard-on?" I slap him across the chest.

He groans. I really wish it didn't sound so hot.

"Do not make that sound while I'm in here with you! For the love of God, what the hell is wrong with you?" I tip my head up and stare at the ceiling rather than his dick print, which is clearly visible through his pale blue boxer briefs. I will never get that image out of my head.

"It's an anxiety boner."

"I don't want to know. Please make it go away." I continue to look at the ceiling tiles.

"I was trying."

I lower my voice to an angry whisper. "By masturbating in a damn bathroom?" I can't even.

"I tried to think of gross things, but then you started yelling at me, which made it worse, especially with the clown threats. You can't do that to me again."

I suck in a lungful of air and exhale my rage. I gentle my tone and pretend I'm dealing with one of the guys on the team who wasn't responsible for making my entire elementary-through-high-school experience a nightmare. "Take a deep breath, please, Dallas."

He gulps air like a dying fish.

"Come on, Dallas. In for the count of four, out for the count of four," I cajole.

He sucks in air as I count, then releases it as I head back to one.

"Better?" I ask when his color has returned to almost normal.

"Yeah. Thanks. Sorry."

I glance down, even though I shouldn't. The problem in his pants seems to have deflated. Thank God.

"Splash some cold water on your face." I check the time. We need to get a move on if I'm going to make my date. "Benita from hair and makeup is standing by to touch you up." I cross my arms and wait.

"Are you staying in here?" Dallas's gaze meets mine in the mirror for a moment before he does as I ask, then pulls a bunch of paper towels from the holder and dabs the wetness away. I do not appreciate the way the muscles in his forearms and biceps flex at all.

"You're the one who pulled me in," I point out. Again. It takes everything in me not to arch an eyebrow at him. I swear he'll be the reason I need Botox before I'm thirty.

"Look, I have to pee." Dallas runs a hand through his hair, making a delicious mess of it. "I swear I'll only be a minute. I won't even lock the door."

I say nothing, just stare at him.

His lip twitches. "Please don't get mad at me. I'll just end up with another anxiety boner, and then we'll have to go through this whole thing again." He motions between us. "I'm not opposed, but I think you might be."

"If you're more than a minute, I will come back in here and drag you out." Before he can say anything, I exit the bathroom.

Standing just down the hallway is Claudia the shelter director, Benita for makeup, the photographer, the cameraman, and two shelter volunteers. I smile and head for the group.

"Everything okay?" Benita asks through a practiced smile. She's attended many a promo op and knows what Dallas is like.

"Everything is fine," I assure her. I turn my attention to Claudia, dropping my voice to a conspiratorial whisper. "Dallas sometimes gets a little nervous before he's in front of the camera, but once things get rolling, he loosens right up."

Thankfully, Dallas appears in the hall. He peeks up at the group through his ridiculously long eyelashes and adopts a smile reminiscent of his last name. All the women, including Benita, also duck their heads and echo his smile. Dallas evokes the same reaction from pretty much everyone. It's exceedingly challenging not to roll my eyes.

"I'm sorry I kept you all waiting." Dallas tucks his hand in his pocket.

"It's totally fine," Claudia assures him. "We really appreciate your support."

"I wish I could have a dog, but my travel schedule makes that impossible. It would be one thing if I had a partner who could be there, but, uh, I'm still waiting for the right person to realize I'm the one," Dallas says as he falls into step with Claudia.

I choke on a cough. Dallas has never had a girlfriend as long as I've been with the team, so there being a someone is news to me. Especially since he's such a relentless flirt.

He glances over his shoulder and grins at me.

I drag my middle finger along my eyebrow.

"Is there someone special?" Claudia asks.

"Yeah, but she's not ready for me yet. She'll come around eventually."

His ego is ridiculous. Of course he believes he can charm anyone he wants into falling for him because it happens all the time at the bar. Whenever our crew goes out, he flirts his face off, giving some poor woman false hope, because he always walks away at the end of the night.

I check my messages while Benita tackles Dallas's hair and makeup. My date is still on. Conversation over the dating app has gone relatively well, so I'm hopeful this guy could be my date to this high school reunion.

Claudia and the photographer give Dallas a quick rundown. The only uncontrolled variable are the dogs. I know exactly how Dallas will act behind the camera, but puppies and rescue dogs can sometimes be skittish.

Claudia returns with the first dog, George. He's a cross between a Chihuahua and a cairn terrier. The result is a scraggly little thing with one tooth that pokes out of his mouth at an odd angle. He's adorably awkward. The second Dallas picks him up, he pees on him.

Dallas strips out of his shirt, putting his defined chest, abs, and arms on display. He's stupidly cut, and he knows it. The photographer snaps several pictures while the shelter volunteers bring him a wet, soapy washcloth and towel. Everyone fawns all over Dallas, and Claudia apologizes several times.

"I don't mind being peed on," Dallas says, probably to be reassuring.

Benita and Claudia side-eye each other.

"I mean, it's not a big deal. Not that I actually want—" George bites Dallas's ear like his favorite chew toy.

Claudia brings out the second dog as Dallas puts on a shelter shirt provided by one of the staff. Bernardo is a huge St. Bernard. He's so enthusiastic, he knocks Dallas to the floor, which is saying something since Dallas is six foot four and more than two hundred pounds of hockey player. Bernardo plants a huge paw on either shoulder and bathes Dallas's face with his tongue, covering him in drool.

"I love men who love dogs," Benita sighs.

"Especially hot, hockey-playing men who love dogs," Claudia adds.

I stand by and watch gleefully as Dallas tries to escape the tongue and slobber. "I hope you're getting this," I say to our photographer.

"Oh hell yeah. This right here is gold." He snaps away on his camera.

"I might need one of those turned into a poster for my office," I muse. It'll make the perfect dart board.

Eventually Bernardo stops making out with Dallas. There's another shirt change and makeup touch-up. The shoot takes a slightly X-rated turn when Bernardo decides Dallas's leg would be a good thing to hump.

"I wish I could do that," one volunteer whispers.

The other giggles.

I grit my teeth and keep my mouth shut.

Grudgingly I have to give it to Dallas; he takes the humping like a champ. An hour and a half later, we have plenty of video footage and photos for the shelter to use in their upcoming campaign.

Dallas makes the shelter staff fall even more in love with him when he writes them a check for $10,000 before we leave. I doubt they'd fawn over him if they knew him the way I do. Writing a check doesn't negate all the hell he and his friends put me through when we were growing up—like the time I heard the snick of scissors and my braid falling into their hands in elementary school.

By the time he's done, I have half an hour to make it to the coffee shop.

"You heading home or to the office?" Dallas holds the door for me.

"Neither."

"You meeting the girls?" he presses.

"No." I stop in front of my car. "If you must know, I have a date."

His lip curls as if in disgust. "A date?"

Same Dallas as always. I roll mine. "I realize I'm not a millionaire hockey player, Dallas, but I'm not an ogre, either."

"That's not—"

I cut him off. "Save it for someone who gives a shit. I'll be in touch once we have photo proofs and video clips." I unlock my car door and slide into the driver's seat.

"Willy—"

"Fuck a porcupine, Dallas." I pull the door closed and flip him the bird as I leave the lot.

I really hope this date is the one, because I'm running out of time.

CHAPTER 3
HEMI

My Badass Babe Brigade chat is full of messages.

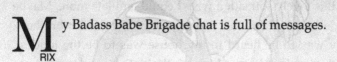

RIX

Good luck on your date!

HAMMER

Fingers crossed he's not like the last guy.

TALLY

Sending positive date vibes.

SHILPS

^^^All of this.

Shilpa sends me another message, independent of the group chat.

SHILPS

If this date doesn't go the way you want it to, the offer to take my cousin still stands.

HEMI

I love you, and the offer, but I love occasionally being your date to family events when Ash is away more than I want a date. Plus, Manreet is secretly in love with Sonali, trust me. Going in. Fingers crossed he looks like his profile pic.

SHILPS

I'll call you in twenty-five in case you need rescuing.

Shilpa Palaniappa, often referred to as Shilps, is my best friend and also the Terror's team lawyer. She's a strong badass, but she has this lovely soft side I wish I could emulate more. Maybe I struggle because I'm the youngest with two older brothers. The only way to be heard in my house was to be the loudest. As a kid, people told me I was intimidating, and sometimes unapproachable. It also made me a target for Dallas and his friends.

I scan the coffee shop before going inside. I chose this location because I don't frequent it regularly. I'm ten minutes early, so I'm pleasantly surprised when I spot Charles sitting in the corner, at a small table by the fireplace. I'm also relieved that he looks exactly like his profile photo. We're off to a good start.

His gaze lifts at the tinkle of the door. I hold my breath for a moment, waiting for his reaction as his eyes move over me on an assessing sweep. I don't fudge information on my profile. I know better than to take ten pounds off my weight, or inches off my height, or use a filtered picture that makes me look like I'm twenty-two instead of twenty-seven. He smiles, pushes back his chair, and stands as I cross the café.

His picture was accurate, but the height was not. I know this because I'm nearly five eleven when I'm wearing flats. Which I'm not. It's fine. So he wasn't perfectly honest about how tall he is. It's not a big deal.

He surreptitiously wipes his hands on his pants and extends one. "Hey! Hi! I'm Charles. You must be Wilhelmina."

"Hi, that's right. It's great to meet you." I slide my fingers into his palm. It's soft, and a little clammy. But he does work in advertising, so I shouldn't expect him to have calluses like the guys on the team. Their entire job revolves around being physically active. When they're not on the ice, they're in the gym.

"It's great to meet you too." Charles pumps my hand. "You look like your picture."

"I like to keep things real."

"Sometimes people use filters that make them look more attractive than they are." Charles's cheeks flush, and he rushes to backtrack. "Not that your picture was more attractive than the real you."

We're not off to the best start if this is his opener. I don't want him to give me a crappy rating on the dating site, though, so instead of telling him to fuck off, I motion to the barista. "Should we grab something to drink?"

"Yes. Absolutely!" He seems relieved.

He orders an oat milk latte with 750,000 modifications and an oat bar. I order iced coffee with a dash of sweet cream. We each pay for our own drinks and return to the table. I'm grateful for the takeout cup, because I have the feeling this date will be short and a little unpleasant.

"So you said you work in PR. How long have you been doing that?" Charles slurps his coffee.

I try not to be judgmental since he did order it extra hot.

"I've been working for the Terror for three years. Mostly, it's an amazing job." Except when I'm dealing with Dallas and his anxiety boners. *Do not think about Dallas's boner while you're on a date.*

"I don't really watch hockey. I'm more of a football guy." He takes a giant bite of his oat bar. Crumbs land on the table and likely in his lap.

"Did you ever play?" I ask.

"No, but my older brother did. He went to college on a scholarship. All the girls loved him." He rolls his eyes. "But now he's a used car salesman, and I run an entire department for my advertising firm."

"Nothing like a little sibling rivalry to motivate you to do better." This guy sounds like he needs a therapist, not a date. "What kind of advertising do you do?"

Charles launches into a fifteen-minute monologue about his job and how stressful it is to be the hardest-working guy in the office. Then he tells me he was passed over for a promotion last month that he totally deserved. This all seems like a red flag, and I'm just waiting for him to take a breath so I can escape.

But before that can happen, the conversation takes a swift dive into point-of-no-return territory. "How many children do you want?" he asks suddenly.

"I'm not sure." Do I want kids? I think so. I'm adopted, and I don't have information on my birth family. I've had genetic screening, but I'd want to have that discussion with my partner. If I were to have a family, I'd also like to adopt at least one child. But twenty minutes into my coffee date with Charles the Slurper is not the time to discuss that.

"I want five kids," he states emphatically.

"Is that right?"

"I think it's great that you're educated and you have a job now, but your first priority once we have kids is to be a mom."

That we've jumped from coffee to being the mother of his five children is a massive, flashing red beacon, on top of the flags from before. "That's an interesting perspective."

"Can you cook?" Charles asks. "You look like you must be able to cook."

If I wasn't sorely in need of caffeine, I would be tempted to throw my coffee in his face. "Thanks. And yeah, I can cook. Can you?" I fire back.

"I barbecue. I'm very traditional."

"It sounds that way." I can't wait to tell Shilpa about this guy.

Charles props his elbows on the table, his expression growing serious. "I'm looking for a wife, Wilhelmina. Do you think you're good wife material?"

"I am absolutely good wife material." But not for this guy. *What the fuck is happening right now?*

"You have great childbearing hips."

I think this is meant as a compliment.

My phone rings. Thank God for best friends.

"I'm so sorry. It's my grandma. I need to take this."

Charles frowns.

"Hi, Grammy, is everything okay?"

"How's it going?" Shilpa asks. "It's not too late to join me at the spa."

"Oh no! And they're locked in your car? Do you need me to come get you?" I mouth *sorry* to Charles.

"It's going that well, huh?" Shilpa sighs. "I'm sorry this one is another dud."

"Of course. No. No, it's no trouble. No, don't call CAA. I have an extra set just for this reason. Why don't you wait inside the diner? I love you, and I'll see you soon."

"I'll tell them you'll be here in less than ten," Shilpa says.

"Bye, Grammy."

I end the call. "I am so, so sorry. My grandmother locked her keys in the car again, and I have her set of spares."

Charles gives me a warm smile. "I totally understand. Maybe next time we can have dinner."

"I appreciate the offer, but I'll have to pass. Thanks for asking, though." What's the point in lying?

His brows pull together. "Excuse me?"

"You jumped straight to children on date number one. I get wanting goals to align but try to focus on the actual connection and a few more dates before you plan the next five years."

"You don't have to be a bitch about it," Charles retorts. "Any woman would be lucky to be with me."

I'm sure his mother would agree. "I hope you find what

you're looking for. Please excuse me. My grandma really does need me." I try for a soft smile because an angry man can be a dangerous one.

I can't get out of there fast enough. I speed walk the two blocks to the spa, where Shilpa is waiting. She passes me a glass of sparkling rose water as I take the chair beside hers.

"Sum up your date in one sentence."

"He told me I had childbearing hips."

She arches a brow. "You have great hips."

I sigh. "Back to the drawing board I go."

I've been on a ridiculous number of dates over the past several months, and the reunion is only a handful of weeks away now. I'm running out of time.

CHAPTER 4
HEMI

"It should not be this hard to follow protocol. I don't understand what the challenge is. Am I being unreasonable here? Like, are my expectations out of line?" I ask. The celebrities versus pros charity game is right around the corner, and dealing with rink availability for the women's team on top of this is exactly what I *don't* need.

Shilpa flips a pen between her fingers. "You're not being unreasonable."

She can't say anything else. Not in her position. Not when she's the legal representative for the team. When we're in the office, Shilpa always plays by the rules. When we're outside the office, she sometimes chooses to speak her mind. But only in an 'I am a lawyer, but not your lawyer' kind of way.

Topher Guy, the Terror's director of team operations, and I don't always see eye to eye. I can be direct when I need something, and sometimes I come off as harsh or cold as a result. But I'm efficient, and things get done in a timely manner. He doesn't always see my needs as important since they don't pertain to the actual game. But celebrities vs. pros is a huge event, and his ass dragging is a hiccup I don't need.

"I'm sorry this is so frustrating." Hammer's empathy is

written on her face. She's my assistant and the daughter of Roman Hammerstein, the team goalie. She's also dating Hollis Hendrix, Roman's best friend and another player on the team. She interned for me last season, and after she graduated, we were able to hire her.

"You don't need to apologize." I rub my temples. "I need to soften my approach sometimes." I was short with Topher the last time we spoke. He didn't love that and said as much. Last week he told me things would move faster if I wasn't such a ball buster.

Shilpa shakes her head. "You work with a team of alpha males. If you were a marshmallow, they would walk all over you. The issue is not you. Venting to us is fine, and completely understandable, but at some point, you may want to move this up the chain."

I hear what Shilpa is really saying. But it's a tricky situation. Topher has been with the team a long time. He's old school and struggling to catch up in a world where not all women are his subordinates. But I don't want to rock the boat, especially not with the success of such a huge event hinging on things going smoothly. Parts of my job require Topher's approval, and irritating him will only create additional issues.

I flop down in my chair. "I just need this last thing off my plate before I take my vacation."

"We have time," Hammer assures me. "And I'll be here while you're away, so I can make sure things go smoothly."

"I know. You are a freaking godsend." Hiring Hammer has made my job doable again. And I love having someone with fresh energy to bounce ideas off.

My phone buzzes with a new message from the high school reunion group on social media. It's from Brooklyn Bonner, my ex-best friend. It's a special brand of torment, knowing I'll see all these people in a handful of weeks. But not going isn't an option. "Fuck."

"Fuck, what?" Shilpa asks.

"Hold on." I don't even have to scroll for the newest content once I open the group. It's right there. Front and center. "No. No way. Those assholes!"

"What's going on?" Hammer asks. "Please don't tell me Flip is in trouble again."

"It's not about Flip." Flip Madden is the Terror center and my friend Rix's brother. He has quite the reputation as a partying playboy, but he's been so much better over the past few months. "It's about my freaking high school reunion. This can't be happening." I want to toss my phone across the room. But then I'll have to buy a new one.

"What can't be happening?" Hammer glances at Shilpa, who shrugs.

I probably sound ridiculous. I know I'm being extra about needing a date for the reunion. But I have my reasons. Mostly, I don't want to be remembered as the person I was growing up.

I haven't seen Brooklyn or Sean in person since graduation, which is a feat, considering the company Sean works for has a box at the Terror arena. But Sean loves to post every moment of his life on social media, so I've been able to avoid him whenever he's in town. That won't happen at the reunion, though. Huntsville High's graduating class is too small.

I decide to share at least part of the story, so my reaction makes sense. "I used to be tight with this girl Brooklyn in high school. I had a crush on this guy Sean, and I really wanted to go to prom with him. I thought he was going to ask me, but things went sideways, and instead he asked my best friend."

"Oh my God, what a douche," Hammer says.

"Yeah. Well, that wasn't the douchiest part, because Brooklyn said yes. We haven't spoken since." The humiliation did not end there, either. Not even close.

"I hope he got drunk and puked all over her dress," Hammer says darkly.

"Sadly, no." Afterward I heard from multiple sources that she lost her virginity to him. Which was a lie. She lost her virginity in grade eleven at a party. She made me swear never to tell anyone, and I didn't. "They're still together, and they just announced their engagement in the reunion group. And for sure Brooklyn will be waving her huge diamond around in my face. So now I really need a date to this thing." That's the kind of person she's always been, even when it was about getting invited to parties or anything else that made her feel important. Included. If she makes a comment about me still being single, I'll lose my cool, or worse, become my eighteen-year-old self again.

These days, I'm a badass. Here in Toronto, I'm appreciated by the team because I don't tolerate crap. Here I'm the person who gets shit done. But back in Huntsville, population 19,000, I'm the nerd whose best friend went to prom with the guy I liked. And now she's marrying him.

Shilpa taps her coffee mug with her nails. They're painted team colors. "This is your ten-year, isn't it?"

"Yeah."

"So they've been together for an entire decade, and he just put a ring on her finger *now*?" Shilps asks.

"Who just put a ring on whose finger?" Ashish appears, making a beeline for Shilpa. He bends to kiss her cheek. "I missed you, my love."

He's followed by Dallas and Hollis.

"What's this about a ring?" Dallas elbows Hollis. "Did you propose to Hammer?"

"Hollis has not asked me to marry him," Hammer clarifies immediately. "My dad needs more than a couple of months to adjust to this, and I'm twenty-one, so we don't need to jump on the married bandwagon anytime soon."

Hollis narrows his eyes. "Thirty-five is coming for me."

Hammer arches a brow. "Whatever, old man. That's a couple years away."

"Oh, I love that this is happening right now." Shilpa's eyes light up.

"We could have a long engagement," Hollis suggests.

"I think we need to let Rix and Tristan have first crack at the engagement game." Hammer gives Hollis a meaningful look.

"It's only a matter of time," Dallas agrees. "So who's engaged?"

"Just some people from high school," I mutter. "It's not important."

Shilpa arches a brow.

"It's still weird that you two went to school together." Ashish motions between me and Dallas.

"I call it fate." Dallas leans against the doorjamb.

"Are you going to the reunion this summer?" Shilpa asks.

I fire daggers at her with my eyeballs. She deflects them with her impenetrable lawyer shield.

"Yeah. Why not, right? It'll be fun to see everyone."

"That's because you were Mr. Popular and everyone loved you," I scoff.

"Not everyone." He pulls his phone from his pocket. "Is this for real? Brooklyn and Dr. Sean Sheep's Ass are engaged?"

I bite back a smile. Sean's last name is Ramsbottom. "It's for real."

"I can't stand those two." Dallas shakes his head. "They were a couple of douchebag attention whores back in the day, and nothing has changed. Good luck to her with that unfortunate last name," he adds.

Ashish looks between us. "So you're both going to this reunion?"

Hollis has taken one of the seats at the small conference table.

"Yeah," Dallas and I say in unison.

"Together?" Ash asks.

Why does he have to be so oblivious?

"No," I say quickly. "I am bringing a date."

Dallas snaps his fingers. "That guy you went out with the other day? After the shelter promo?"

Hammer snorts a laugh and tries to cover it with a cough.

"No. Not that guy. But I'll have a date. I am bringing

someone to the reunion." If I say it enough times, I will manifest a date into existence.

"We could go together," Dallas says—like it's the best idea he's ever had, like he hasn't totally fucked me over in the past. Need I mention Canada Day post grade eight graduation? He and his friend used my bike to do tricks then flipped it into the lake behind his parents' house. I had to save up for a year to buy a new one. It was preferable to my brothers going after Dallas and his friends, which would have only made my life harder.

At my lack of response, Dallas adds, "We can even drive up together."

I would rather eat sand than deal with Dallas and his buddies all weekend.

"That's a two-and-a-half-hour drive, isn't it? Hemi will murder you before you get there." Hollis's gaze jumps between us. "And while my girlfriend is great at her job, we still need Hemi in the office and not behind bars."

"Hollis is right. I can't go to prison. Orange is not my color." I smooth my hands over my blue dress pants.

And Dallas is not to be trusted. I learned that the hard way, and I've never forgotten.

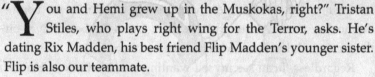

CHAPTER 5
DALLAS

"Y ou and Hemi grew up in the Muskokas, right?" Tristan Stiles, who plays right wing for the Terror, asks. He's dating Rix Madden, his best friend Flip Madden's younger sister. Flip is also our teammate.

We're at the Watering Hole, our favorite local pub. The owners love us, and the people who frequent the place mostly treat us like we're just regular folk. It's a lot easier in the offseason, although having won the finals this year makes us more popular than usual.

"We're on Lake Vernon. It's in a small town a couple hours north of here. Although it's become a popular retirement location, so it's growing." People will buy a piece of property on the lake and spend their spring, summer, and fall in the quiet there, then defect to warmer climates during the coldest months.

That Flip and Tristan were also born and raised in Ontario and play for an Ontario team is pretty rare. We all started our careers playing in other provinces or states, but there's something special about being able to play for our home team.

"Do you still talk to any of the people you grew up with?" Flip asks.

I shrug. "Sure. When I visit my family, I'll message to see if my high school buddies are around." Some of my friends went straight into a job, often working with their dads' small businesses in construction or landscaping. Small-town life can be like that. People like the familiarity of faces and the comfort that comes with a tight-knit community.

I went away to university, though mostly to play hockey and not because I'm an academic genius, and I also spent a couple of summers at the Hockey Academy. That's where I met Tristan and Flip, as well as Flip's archnemesis, Connor Grace, who plays for New York. We clocked a lot of hours on the ice, and it didn't leave much time for socializing outside of my teammates. The guys I play with have become like family over the years. They're my support system, along with my family back home.

I'm looking forward to seeing old classmates again this summer. It's nice to hang out with people who knew me before the hockey fame. Although back then, I was the best player on the team, and that came with its own notoriety.

Regardless, I can see myself wanting to settle back in Huntsville when I retire from the league. I've already invested in a piece of property on the lake. It's the perfect place to raise kids and get a couple of rescue dogs. But I've got years left in this career, and I plan to enjoy it for as long as it lasts.

"What was Hemi like growing up?" Tristan asks.

"The same as she is now. She was president of the debate team and the student council, and she ran the social justice and diversity and equity committee. She had a small group of friends she hung around with." Hemi has always been an intense, passionate person. She's all-in, one-hundred-and-ten percent, one-hundred-and-ten percent of the time. That's what makes her such a force in her role with the Terror. She's pretty amazing. But in the land of teenagers, being the smart, nerdy girl who didn't back down and always stood up for what she believed in, even if it went against the grain—especially then—didn't always win her points with the popular crowd. Which I was part of.

"That best friend of hers sounded like a real piece of work," Ash notes as he sips his pop.

"Brooklyn was more like a frenemy than an actual best friend."

"Who's Brooklyn?" Tristan asks.

Ash gives him the abridged version of the conversation we had in Willy's office.

Tristan's brow pulls together. "Why does Hemi even want to go?"

I glance over at Willy. She's sitting with the girls in one of the big round booths, laughing and smiling. She looks gorgeous, as usual. "She probably wants to prove she's above all the bullshit. Willy doesn't shy away from uncomfortable situations. Never show weakness is her motto." The anxiety boner last week was a new low in our relationship. I can't believe I pulled her into the bathroom with me and my hard-on. I'm surprised she didn't freak out more.

I doubt she'd be impressed with me if she knew how many times I've accidentally imagined her angry, sultry voice in my ear during my morning shower-and-whack-off routine.

"That explains why she wants a date for this thing," Hollis says.

"Yeah, maybe don't ever mention Brooklyn or Sean in front of her." My feelings of loathing for them have only grown over the years. Sean was a pompous douche, and Brooklyn was a nasty piece of work. She would talk shit about Willy behind her back. And what they did to Willy at the end...it was unforgivable. Just as unforgivable as what I did. It was one of those instances in which I unwittingly wielded my popularity as a weapon, and Willy got hurt as a result. That was the last thing I'd wanted to happen. She didn't come to prom because of it.

"It's too bad she's so opposed to driving up with you," Flip says.

He has no idea he's poking at wounds. Both hers and mine.

Of all my fuckups—and there have been many—this is the one I wish I could take back the most.

I force a smile and gulp my drink. "We have a few weeks. She might change her mind." *Wilder things have happened.*

"Good luck with that," Tristan says.

"Thanks."

Willy and me attending our reunion together would be a great way to put Brooklyn and Sean in their place and keep her safe from their assholery. They've been posting relentlessly in the reunion group about how excited they are to celebrate their engagement with everyone. I already despised those two. My tolerance for their bullshit has only diminished with this new development.

"As much as I'd love to stay here all night, Aurora and I are meeting Roman at the pool in an hour," Hollis says.

"Shilps and I are going to the movies," Ashish announces.

"Bea and I are staying in." Tristan rubs his mouth to hide a smile as he looks at his girlfriend.

Flip ignores him. "It's chess night with Dred. She always kicks my ass."

Ah, yes. Dred. Flip's neighbor, member of Willy's Badass Babe Brigade, and the one woman Flip truly has a completely platonic relationship with. He calls her his other "little sister."

We settle the tab, and all the paired-up people link hands and head out.

Willy hugs Shilpa and excuses herself to the bathroom. She doesn't even look in my direction. It's not surprising. Her disdain for me is warranted.

Ashish arches an expectant brow. "You coming?"

"I'll just finish this." I hold up my half-full whiskey on the rocks. I'm probably four drinks in. "And make sure Willy gets to her car." Then I'll call a ride for me.

Shilpa hides a smile in Ash's biceps. I pretend I don't see her and also that I'm not this transparent.

He claps me on the shoulder. "Have a good night."

"You too."

I take a seat at the bar and scroll through my phone while I finish my drink. My Willy radar goes off a minute later. She's halfway between me and the bathroom, talking to some guy.

The dude is gym fit with shoulders and biceps that pop, probably because he's half flexing. All white-toothed smile and fancy clothes, he exudes confidence. He'll need it with someone powerful like Willy. She could chew most men up and spit them out.

Her eyes dart my way briefly. I have a PhD in Willy's body language, and based on her panicked expression and the way she's crossing her arms, she's desperate to escape. That's rare for her. She's usually calm, cool, and collected—apart from when she's dealing with me.

I down the rest of my drink, slide out of the booth, roll my shoulders back, and head straight for her. As I get closer, I pick up some of their conversation. Her voice is pitchy; it's the same tone as her voice memos after I tell her I'm running behind for a promo op. She believes I do it on purpose, but typically it's a result of unfortunately timed boners.

Her eyes flare at my approach. "Dallas." Her smile is manic as her hand closes around my forearm and she pulls me to her side.

"Here he is! This is him." Her nails dig into my arm.

My dick is instantly rock solid. "Here I am."

"Dallas, this is Bert. Bert, this is Dallas. My boyfriend."

I'm already shocked that she's willingly touching me, so I'm pretty sure I imagined the words *my boyfriend*. I look down at her, waiting for the punchline, but her smile is wide, and there's real fear swimming in her eyes, as though she expects me to do something to embarrass her. Like deny it.

What she doesn't realize is that I've been waiting a decade for this very moment. I wrap an arm around her shoulders and pull her into my side. She's tall. Nearly six feet of curvy, perfect woman. "Luckiest man alive." I barely have to bend at all as I press my lips to her temple. She always smells like summer. This is the best moment of my entire life. "Bert, it's nice to meet you." I extend my hand. My smile feels like it could split my face in two.

He takes it, grudgingly. "Dr. Bert Cleaver."

"Seriously?" I ask. Whiskey lips have no filter.

"Yeah. I'm a cardiologist."

"Huh. Good for you." Why does Willy know a cardiologist? Is she having heart problems? Does all my bullshit cause her too much stress? She's definitely been stressed lately. More than usual.

"Thanks." His eyes move between us suspiciously. "How long have you two been a thing?"

"Oh, it's new. Very new. We just made it official." She looks up at me, imploring.

I jump in with both feet. "I can't tell you how awesome it was when she finally said yes to being my girlfriend." I kiss her temple again. Her nails dig into my ribs. My dick rejoices. "Gotta be honest, I've been trying for *years* to get the girl. And now, here we finally are."

"Wow. That's…" Bert swallows compulsively and smiles woodenly. "Well, I guess you turning me down for dinner makes sense."

I plaster a smile on my face. "How do you two know each other?"

"We went out a couple of times," Willy says.

"Four times. We went out four times," Bert clarifies.

"Four times. Right." Willy's cheek brushes my chest.

I hug her tighter to my side.

"Your dating profile is still active," Bert states.

"I need to take that down." Her voice rises three octaves.

I smile and stroke her cheek, tipping her chin up so I can kiss the end of her nose. "Always keeping me on my toes."

"That's me. The toe keeper."

Yeah. Willy's freaking out.

"Hey, Bert, can you take a picture? For posterity's sake? It's life changing when the woman of your dreams agrees to be your girlfriend. I don't have enough pictures of us together, you know?" I pass him my phone, not giving him the chance to say no.

"Uh, sure. Okay," he says.

I move to stand behind Willy and wrap my arms around her, nuzzling through all her long, wavy hair so I can rest my chin on her shoulder and press my cheek to hers. I'm in heaven.

"Oh my God, is that your dick poking me in the ass?" she asks through gritted teeth.

"Probably. Every part of me is super excited." I can't help myself. I kiss her cheek. "Smile for the camera, honey."

Her nails bite into my forearms, sharp stings that make my entire body sing with absolute fucking delight. Bert takes a bunch of pictures. I switch up the pose and wrap Willy's arms around my waist. Now my hard-on is inconveniently pressed against her stomach. I rest my chin on top of her head and smile my face off while Bert snaps several more pictures and Willy's talon nails dig into my back.

Bert passes me my phone.

"Thanks, man." I clap him on the shoulder. "You're the best. Can I buy you a beer?" I turn to Willy.

She shakes her head. "Oh, we don't need to do that."

"Sweetness, honeycakes, yes we do." Fake or not, this is a big moment, and I plan to celebrate the hell out of it. More whiskey will not do. Wilhelmina trusted me enough to let me help her out of a bad situation. It's huge progress. I call over to the bartender. "Marianna, a bottle of your finest champagne. Wills and I need to toast being madly in love. Isn't that right, angel?" I hug her to my side. "And a beer for Dr. Bert. You're probably an ultra-light-beer guy, right? Keeping the carbs down?" I point to his flat stomach.

"Oh, thanks, but I, uh…I should go back to the bar." Bert thumbs over his shoulder and then gives us the thumbs-up.

"Congratulations. Wilhelmina's an amazing woman. You're a lucky guy."

"Thanks, man. I appreciate that."

Bert fucks off. I turn back to Marianna, who holds up a bottle of prosecco. "We don't have champagne, but we have this."

"Perfect. Pop that baby."

"You don't need to do that, Marianna. Dallas is kidding." Willy tries to push my hand off her shoulder.

I squeeze tighter because Bert can still see us. "Isn't she so cute? She's just so damn cute, being all shy about how in love we are." I hold out my free hand as I approach the bar. "You can just pass me the bottle and the glasses. I'll do the honors. We'll tuck ourselves into the cozy table."

Marianna hands me the prosecco and two wineglasses. I guide Willy to the back corner and pull out a chair. She crosses her arms and glances at the bar, the stools are empty. "Bert is gone. You can stop the charade."

I pop the cork. "Who says it's a charade?"

Ever since I was traded to Toronto and Willy came on board, I've had to face my biggest fuckup, day in and day out. And I've fucked up a lot in my lifetime. But today is a new beginning. Today, she let me help her and didn't tell me to eat my own dick.

She rolls her big, beautiful brown eyes. They're the color of extra-dark maple syrup. Her lashes are thick and long, and her eyebrows are expressive and sharply contoured. And then there's her mouth. Good God, those lips were made for kissing. Among other, less appropriate things. But definitely for kissing.

"Ugh." She covers my face with her hand. "Stop looking at me like that. It's weird."

I cover her hand with mine and barely resist the urge to kiss her knuckles as I remove it. I would not put it past her to lay me out. So I hold back.

Instead, I pour two glasses of prosecco. "Went on four dates with Dr. Bert, huh?"

"Three of them were coffee. One of them was drinks."

"I was right about the beer, wasn't I?"

She rolls her eyes. "Close. Vodka and club soda. I've been trying to shake him for a couple of weeks, but he's not great at taking a hint." I try to hand her a glass. "What are you doing?"

"Celebrating. What does it look like?" I hold up both glasses. She gives me another one of her looks that makes me hard.

I clink the glasses together. "To progress in our relationship."

Gracefully, she gets up from the table. "Thanks for the save. If you rub it in my face, I'll put you on kids' camp check in with the aggressive parents every year for the rest of your career." She spins, hair furling in a glorious wave, hips swaying as she heads for the door.

"Honey, what about the prosecco?"

"Enjoy the headache tomorrow." She pushes through the door and disappears down the street.

I would chase after her if I wasn't already half in the bag and also fairly convinced she would cause me bodily harm.

I polish off the bottle of prosecco and take an Uber home. There, I get out the good scotch and pour myself a glass. Drunkenly, I wish I could make Willy my date to our reunion. I could pose as her boyfriend. I'd prove that I'm not just the asshole prom king who lucked into being good at hockey.

While I drink my scotch, I scroll through my photos. My smile is so wide I can feel it stretching my cheeks. In most of them Willy looks stiff. But in one of them she's smiling.

She's so damn beautiful with those expressive eyes and that stunning smile. I hold my phone to my chest and close my eyes. Drinking a bottle of prosecco after four whiskeys and following it up with scotch definitely wasn't my best plan.

Maybe I can convince Wills to be my date after all.

And hopefully I'll figure out how to keep her, too.

CHAPTER 6

HEMI

I grab my phone from my dresser as I roll out of bed and pad to my bathroom. I have five missed calls from Shilpa and one text message.

SHILPS

WHAT THE HELL IS GOING ON?

I sincerely hope things didn't happen last night that will make my job harder. Flip hasn't been as bad lately, but he still falls off the be-a-good-boy-and-don't-broadcast-your-extracur-riculars-to-the-whole-world wagon on occasion.

SHILPS

Call me now.

I dial her immediately.

"What the fuck is going on?" Shilpa demands.

"I don't know. I just woke up. Did one of the boys do something stupid?"

Silence follows.

"Shilps?"

"Look at Dallas's socials."

"What? Why?"

"Just look, and then we will discuss this," she replies.

I quickly pull him up, expecting that he was out with Flip or something after we parted ways last night. He wasn't sober when I left him with an entire bottle of prosecco.

My heart stops when I see his most recent post. Because it's so much worse than him making out with some random woman.

His arms are wrapped around my waist, chin resting on my shoulder, the widest, prettiest smile lighting up his face. His freaking boner was nudging me in the back. He'd said something ridiculous, and for a second, I'd smiled. For one freaking second. We both look deliriously happy.

But the caption he's paired it with is the worst part. In all caps. WITH THE LOVE OF MY LIFE.

"Oh my God. What was he thinking?" My phone dings with a new email.

"Is this real, Hemi?" Shilpa asks.

"What do you think?" I open the message, and my already-roiling stomach sinks. "Head office wants to see me this morning."

"What time?"

"In two hours."

"I'm coming over. I'll be there in twenty."

"Should I respond to the email?" My entire body has gone numb. I have no idea what's going on. Is this some kind of sick joke?

"Keep it simple and say you'll be there. If anyone else messages, ignore them. If it were me, I would put nothing in writing."

"Okay."

"I'll be there soon."

"Shilps, am I going to lose my job?" This makes it look like Dallas and I willfully went against the team's no-fraternization policy. And in a very in-your-face kind of way. While it's not impossible for relationships between people in-house to be sanctioned, there's a very clear process to follow, which includes paperwork and meetings with the head office *prior* to great public pronouncements.

"Not if I can help it. Try not to panic. I'll be there soon."

Shilpa ends the call, and I get dressed in a rush.

My roommate's door stays closed, which isn't a surprise. She works the night shift at a call center, and we rarely see each other. It works for both of us.

My head is spinning, and my stomach is in knots.

Shilpa arrives eighteen minutes later with two coffees in hand. She's dressed for work, her long, dark hair pulled up in an intricate bun, her makeup on point. I, on the other hand, am the conductor of the hot mess express.

She purses her lips. "Real or not real?"

"Not real."

"What happened yesterday to prompt this post from Dallas?" Shilpa hands me a takeout cup that I gladly accept.

Going into a meeting with the head office uncaffeinated seems like a bad idea.

Dealing with drama is part of my job as director of public relations for the Terror. These boys are fueled by testosterone, and sometimes they think with their dicks instead of their heads. So I handle it. I smooth it out. I help the guys make better career and personal life choices when I can. But I am not the reason for drama. So I'm at a complete loss as to what to do.

If any other player announced something like this on social media before bringing it to me and Shilpa, I would tear them a new one. I'll probably still tear Dallas a new one. But it's not just him on the line here; it's me, too.

I realize Shilpa has asked me a question, and I haven't answered.

She puts a hand on my shoulder. "Hemi, I am here first and foremost as your friend. But this is a direct violation of the team's policy."

"I know." The numbness is wearing off, and in its place is real panic. And fear. And anger at Dallas.

"There are channels we need to go through. We just did this for Hollis and Hammer," she says gently.

"I know this too."

"Management will want an explanation. Do you have one?"

I shake my head. "I have no idea what he was thinking, or why he believed it was a good idea to post that. He knows the rules." I swallow bile. "We're so screwed."

"I just don't understand *why* he did it." Shilpa blows out a breath. "Have you spoken to him this morning?"

"No. You're the only person I called."

"He's not an inherently malicious person, so understanding why could be helpful," Shilpa says. I put my phone on speaker and dial his number, but it goes to voicemail. "Dallas, it's Hemi. You need to call me as soon as you get this."

Shilpa raises a finger. "Hi, Dallas. It's Shilpa. Speaking as the team lawyer, check your email. And please, whatever you do, do not delete that social media post. Call me or Hemi when you get this message. Call only."

"What she said." I hang up. "What am I going to do, Shilps? He's put me in an impossible position. How bad will I look if we have to put out a public statement saying Dallas was joking?" Just kidding. I know the answer. I can't go to my high school reunion if that happens. I rub my temples. The humiliation would be too much.

The buzzer sounds, signaling someone at the door. I set my coffee on the side table and hop off the couch, rushing to answer. A minute later a flower delivery guy hands me an ostentatiously large bouquet of peach-colored roses. I tip him and set it on the counter.

I pluck the card from the bouquet and flip it over.

Shilpa reads over my shoulder.

Wills,
I'll be the best boyfriend you've ever had.
XO Dallas

"I don't even know what to say about this." *And since when did he shift from Willy to Wills?*

"Logically, you have two options. One, you tell the head office this picture was taken out of context and that you and Dallas are not involved, and he did this without your knowledge or consent."

"And he gets fined then traded."

Shilpa nods. "They won't give him a pass. Not when he didn't have your permission to do this."

"Which will negatively impact the entire team. Even if I'm the one in the right, the consequences of that will have a huge ripple effect. It'll stain both of our careers." Do I hate him for all the stupidity he and his friends put me through as kids? Absolutely. But being a jerk our whole childhood and ruining my prom is not the same as screwing over the entire team. They're like family, to me and to each other. And Dallas...he's beloved.

I'll never live it down. I'll have to leave Toronto and the Terror. I won't have Shilpa or the Badass Babe Brigade anymore. This is the first time in my life that I've really felt like I *fit* somewhere outside of my immediate family. Sure, there are a few people in the office who aren't my biggest fans, but I'm used to that. I don't want to lose everything else.

"Option number two, you play along. Dallas is your date for the reunion, and he owes you for saving his ass for the rest of his life."

"And if I go with option two, how do I spin it?" I wring my hands. I can't believe I'm considering this.

"You say you've been trying to stay on the right side of the line, but you've been spending a lot of time together, which is true. Dallas is involved in a lot of charity stuff, and you always go with him. You never send Hammer," Shilpa says.

"Because he's chronically late! And he needs managing." I sound defensive.

"Either way, he has promo stuff, and you always attend it. You spend an extraordinary amount of time together, so selling that you unwittingly developed feelings for each other should not be that difficult."

"But I loathe him."

"Hmm... Well, there's a fine line between love and hate, so we can sell them on you crossing that line, and for at least the next few weeks, you need to flip the hate coin and turn it into love."

I rub my temples. "This is a nightmare."

"It could be. But the only way this works is if you sell it and then live it, at least until you're through the reunion."

"Which means I have to lie to the girls, and the rest of the team, and my family."

Shilpa nods. "It's too risky otherwise."

She's right. No one else can know besides Shilpa and Ash. If the truth came out, it could be detrimental to Dallas's place on the team and both of our careers. "It's less than a month away. I can do anything for a few weeks." It comes out more like a question than an answer.

She points to my bedroom. "Now, let's dress you for maximum badassery. We have a head office to sell on your new boyfriend."

"Fake boyfriend."

"Not for the next several weeks."

CHAPTER 7

HEMI

Half an hour later, I'm sitting in a conference room with Jamie Fielding, the GM, Coach Vander Zee, and two other members of staff. Nancy, Coach's secretary, does nothing to conceal the disapproving look on her face as she regards me over her reading glasses. Shilpa is waiting to be called in later. Dallas is supposed to be here, too, but none of us have heard from him.

I try not to strangle my own hands or sweat through my blouse as Shirley, the head of HR, reads over the no-fraternization policy. Slowly. In excruciating detail. I want to die right now. How is it that Dallas has the ability, even ten years later, to embarrass me this badly? *And where is he?*

Shirley stops reading.

"Thanks, Shirley," Coach Vander Zee says.

Fielding taps his pen on the table. "I...don't understand. You know the policy, Hemi. We just went through this."

I can handle anger and frustration a lot better than the disappointed look on his face. I want to sink into the ground. I'd also like to bludgeon Dallas with his hockey stick and throw his body in Lake Ontario. And then maybe eat a pint of ice cream.

I hate lying, but I have no other choice if I want to save both of our jobs. There is solace in knowing Dallas will be indebted to me forever now. "We had a discussion last night, Dallas and I." This is the truth. We did. But not about me being the love of his life. "And I promise, we've kept it professional. We were planning to come in today to talk through logistics and sign all the appropriate paperwork." All this lying is making me sweat. "But I guess he got excited and jumped the gun." My mouth is horribly dry, and my palms are damp. I need a gallon of water and some deep breathing exercises.

There's a knock on the door.

"There's a meeting in progress," Fielding calls out.

Dallas pokes his head in. "Hey. Yeah, Shilpa said you were all in here. Sorry I'm late." His eyes slide to mine. "Wilhelmina." My name is laden with apology.

I'm not sure if I'm relieved to have him here or not. "I was explaining that we'd planned to come in today to discuss the progression in our relationship, but in your excitement, you preemptively shared it with the world by accident."

He slides into the chair to my left and covers my hand with his, squeezing. "I'm so sorry." Then he addresses the table. "I know protocol. This is absolutely my fault, and I'll take full responsibility for it. Wills was adamant that we wait until the offseason before we pursued this." He turns and gives me a soft smile. "And it's been so hard to be this close to her and not act on these feelings. But I wanted to respect Wilhelmina and the league, and of course, protocol and the no-fraternization policy. Which I fucked up royally by posting last night." He gives the table an imploring look. "We haven't even kissed. There has been no fraternizing. Just a lot of thinking about it. Like, so fucking much." He pokes his cheek with his tongue and nods, like all of this should make sense to everyone else.

His ability to lie convincingly is unnerving.

He squeezes my hand again. "I'm so sorry. I know we had a plan, honey, and I shot it all to shit." He returns his attention to the team and stretches his arm across the back of my chair, fingers skimming my shoulder. "Whatever the consequences are, make them mine. I'll do whatever it takes to make this right. It's just…I've known Wilhelmina for years, and then when we both ended up here, I had all these opportunities to get to know her all over again… How could I resist her, you know?" He smiles his famous smile.

Fielding looks like he's trying not to echo that smile.

Coach Vander Zee rubs his bottom lip. "Hemi definitely knows how to handle hockey players."

"Right? She's a badass. Wilhelmina is incredible." He motions to the people around the table. "You all know this. I know this. And last night when we talked things through and made the decision to try, I was just so stoked." He aims his megawatt smile at me. "All this time I've been waiting for you, and my patience paid off. It only took a decade." He has the audacity to wink, as if what happened in grade twelve was our inside joke, before he gives his attention back to Coach Vander Zee and Fielding. "But I posted without thinking, obviously, and that's my bad."

His bad? Like he forgot to pick up milk and bread. Like it's no big deal.

Fielding and Vander Zee nod like they completely understand. And once again King Fucking Dallas prevails, winning them over with all his goddamn charisma and charm.

Fielding shifts his gaze to me. "Do you agree with Bright?"

"I don't know about being incredible, but last night we did talk things through, and Dallas did express so much…joy. I wasn't there when he posted, so I'm taking him at his word for that part."

"If you were less capable and Dallas wasn't already prone to acts of thoughtlessness, you two would be in a hell of a lot more trouble. We need to get Shilpa in here with paperwork. And from here on, you'll need Hammer—" Fielding frowns. "Or do we call her Peggy? Or Aurora?"

Shirley calls Shilpa in.

"She's fine with Hammer when we're at work," I offer. "But

Aurora if you're introducing her to people outside the team. Roman is still a little stuck on Peggy." Our friends have a lot of nicknames, and we just roll with it. Her dad is the only one who calls her Peggy anyway.

"Got it. Thanks. Hammer should be the lead on any promo opportunities moving forward for Dallas," Jamie says.

"Wilhelmina is the best at keeping me level during promos," Dallas interjects.

"Hemi can be there, but we need another company representative," Vander Zee explains.

Shilpa arrives with the paperwork. She looks at me and then Dallas, but her expression remains neutral. The woman could be a professional card shark.

She takes the seat beside me. "I have the forms ready, as we discussed."

They're extensive. Shilpa reads the document, explaining the parameters, while Dallas and I follow along. Sweat drips down my back, and panic makes my throat tight. *This is really happening.* I'm committed to being Dallas's fake girlfriend for the foreseeable future. I have to steady my hand as I sign my name. We now have a legal, binding document that states that Dallas and I are in a relationship.

I think I might vomit.

In contrast, his eyes are alight with an unreasonable amount of excitement and satisfaction as he scribbles his signature on the last page. "It's official," he tells me. "You're mine."

CHAPTER 8

DALLAS

I surreptitiously rearrange my anxiety boner before I stand and pull Willy's chair away from the table. She's not expecting it, so it screeches obnoxiously across the floor. No one looks particularly stoked about this new development. Except for me. Internally, I'm delirious with joy.

I apologize again to Fielding and Vander Zee and gently press my fingertips against Willy's back as I follow her to her office. She closes the door and whirls to face me.

Her gorgeous face is a mask of rage. "Was this a ploy?"

"What?" I don't know what to do with my hands, so I mirror Willy and prop them on my hips, then think better of it and stuff them in my pockets.

"Did you post that so I wouldn't have a choice about being your date for the reunion?" She paces her office, heels clipping angrily on the floor. She's wearing navy dress pants, a burgundy blouse, and a matching blue blazer, buttoned at the waist, showing off her curvy hourglass figure. She pokes me in the chest with her pointy fingernail. "You better not humiliate me again. I swear on all that is holy, Dallas, if you screw me over again like you always have, I will make it my life's mission to destroy you, one humiliating promo op at a time."

Beneath the very real rage that causes her cheeks to flush, hurt and betrayal lurk in her eyes. It makes me feel like the giant bag of shit I am. My anxiety boner deflates, thank God. "It wasn't a ploy. I was drunk and not thinking clearly."

"Do you have any idea how fucked we would have been if I hadn't gone along with this? You would have been suspended then traded, Dallas, and I would have been the laughingstock of the hockey world. There's a good chance I will be anyway, thanks to you."

I frown. "Why would dating me make you the laughingstock of the hockey world?" I run a hand through my hair. "I'm in the top fifteen percent in the league."

"Check your ego, Dallas."

"That's based on stats, not ego. And dating me will be awesome for the reunion. We show up together, and no one will give a shit about Brooklyn and Sean." And I can keep her safe from their assholery. No one will mess with her if she's with me.

"Are you serious?" She gives me a disbelieving look. "How can you be thinking about our reunion? Do you not understand how this diminishes my credibility as a professional? I look like a bunny, Dallas."

Her words hit me like a slap across the face. "I'm not like Flip." I might flirt with women when I'm approached at the bar, but my family all keep tabs on me through social media. As if I want pictures of me doing inappropriate things floating around the internet for my brothers and sister to razz me about. Or my mom to lecture me over. *Shit*.

Wills pinches the bridge of her nose. "How people perceive you and how they perceive me is very, very different. I don't have the luxury of a double standard that works in my favor like you do."

"How so?"

"You can date whoever you want, and no one will pass judgment on you—except maybe to question why you ended up with someone like me when you could be dating a supermodel if you want."

"You're gorgeous." She sees herself in the mirror. She has to know this.

She rolls her eyes. She does that a lot with me. Willy props one fist on her hip. "How I look isn't the biggest issue, Dallas. I'm the team PR person, and you're a player. My salary and yours are highly discordant. You make millions a year, and I do not. I look like I got in bed with a player so I can skip my way down Easy Street. People will speculate, and it won't be in my favor. What you did yesterday goes against *everything* I'm trained to do. You created a shitstorm for me, so thanks. We also can't break up for a while or I risk even more damage to my reputation. And now I have no choice but to be your goddamn date to the reunion." She's back to getting in my face.

I wish my body's reaction wasn't to get instantly hard when she puts me in my place like this. She's a force, and I'm obsessed with her. It's not a new thing, but it has grown over the past few years since she came back into my life. I'm always game for whatever charity promo ops she has in the down months because it gives me a reason to see her. My infatuation verges on masochistic. I can't stay away from her, even though she hates me, and rightly so. Even when I wasn't an active participant in her torment when we were growing up, I didn't do enough to stop it. Not until it was too late. I can make up for all of it now, though. "I'll be an awesome date. The best date you've ever had."

She practically snarls at me. "Going alone would have been preferable than going with you. I refuse to be the butt of yet another one of your shitty childish jokes."

Looking at her now, I see the little girl kids made fun of, the outspoken preteen who didn't back down in the face of torment, and the teenager who held her head high even when it was hard. I didn't stand up for her the way I should have then. I was too fixated on fitting in, on being on top. But it got lonely up there.

No one was real with me. Except Wills. Always Wills. "I promise I won't fuck you over."

"Like I trust you."

"Let me prove that I can be exactly what you need. You want me to be the overly affectionate, doting boyfriend? I'm in. I'll keep you safe from Sean and Brooklyn."

She scoffs. "Like you kept me safe from *you*?"

"Wills…" I reach out, but she knocks my arm away and gives me a look that should have me six feet underground. It's the same one she gives me when I try to say anything that remotely resembles an apology. I hold my hands up in supplication, trying to find a way to appeal to the girl I broke all those years ago. "Let me be your wingman. For all the times you've saved my ass. Let me pay you back for—"

Her eyes flash.

I want to tell her how sorry I am. How I wish I could take every little thing I ever did back. When we first started working together, I tried often, but she always shut me down. So I stopped, not wanting her to think it was all lip service. She has never had a reason to believe I would be sincere. It seems she's still not ready for the truth. Not yet. Not now. I can see why she might not trust what I have to say. "We'll steal the show," I promise.

When her eyes come back to mine, I see the damage that was done when we were kids, how it sits inside her beautiful heart and weighs it down with hurt. And I let so much of it happen. I didn't save her every time I could have—should have. But I can now.

"How stupid do you think I am, Dallas?"

"You're brilliant, Wilhelmina." And I mean it. "You're the smartest woman I know."

"You'll just embarrass me again," she snaps, but there's a waver in her voice and a wobble in her chin.

I want to run myself over with a truck made entirely of

cactuses. "I won't. I promise. I will be a kickass date. I look great in a suit."

"Your self-love is unreal. Are you always your own first priority?"

"Your favorite color is royal blue, but you wear the lighter shades to support the team. You usually only drink club soda when we're out so you can keep an eye on everyone." I take a breath. "And your favorite band is The Hip, and it has been since you were a kid." The Hip, otherwise known as The Tragically Hip, is a Canadian band that is well loved, especially where we grew up.

Hemi blinks at me, her face a mask of confusion. "How do you know all this stuff? Why do you know all this stuff about me?"

I scramble for a reason that doesn't make me look like a complete creeper. I tap my temple. "My brother got the doctor brain, but I got the random-facts-that-are-good-for-dates gene."

Her phone buzzes inside her pocket; she fishes it out and exhales angrily through her nostrils. "Not today, Satan."

"Is everything okay?" I ask, stupidly. Clearly things aren't okay. I've accidentally forced Wills into being my girlfriend. As if she didn't already hate me enough.

"I have shit that needs to be managed, and I'm about five seconds away from strangling you, so it would be in your best interest to leave my office."

"Right. Okay. But we should iron out the details of this"—I motion between us—"over dinner."

She blinks at me.

"We can talk about it later." I'll make a reservation somewhere nice. I leave her office and am beyond relieved to find the hall empty. My phone has been vibrating against the head of my dick for at least half an hour. The fallout from this will be something else.

I duck into one of the empty conference rooms and drop into a chair. I remember scrolling through the pictures last night but not posting one. Although I did wake up on the couch this morning with a wicked headache and a bottle of scotch that was significantly emptier than I'd anticipated. It made my morning visit to the retirement village to crochet with The Crafty Crew less enjoyable than usual.

I open my messages and find I have more than a hundred new ones. My teammate group chat has been particularly active. I ignore it for now.

I have a single new message from Ash.

ASH

wtf bro GIF

I leave it for now. I'm sure he has no less than a million questions.

I also have a ton of messages from my family.

GRANNY BRIGHT

Why didn't you mention your girlfriend when you were here this morning? Why am I finding out about the love of your life on social media? Is she the reason you needed a peach pattern? Isn't this the woman who comes with you when you help with the church bazaar? She's a real spitfire. I knew there was something there.
Love, Granny

She ends all messages like they're letters.

DALLAS

Sorry, Granny. I'll pop by with an update and some cheesecake as soon as I can.

GRANNY BRIGHT

Bring her along when you do. Love, Granny

DALLAS

I'll do my best.

I doubt Willy will be enthusiastic about a visit to my granny, no matter how much she likes her. I move on to the next message, from my brother Ferris.

FIRE BRO

> Dude. You have some explaining to do. Last time I spoke to you, Hemi still hated your guts and now you're dating?

My oldest brother, Manning, has also messaged.

DOCTOR BRO

> Is this a publicity stunt?

I also have a message from my younger sister, Paris.

LIL SIS

> This is suspect AF.

I have many messages from my mom.

MOM

> Dallas Mattias Bright, you better call me the second you get this message.

> Why am I finding out about your girlfriend over social media?

> Why aren't you answering your messages?

> Granny Bright called me this morning. She's upset too. Especially since you were just there and one of the gossipy ladies had the info first.

> Your dad and I would like an explanation.

> We're happy for you, but this is not how I wanted to find out.

> You need to call me. All the women in my church group are asking questions, and I'm unable to answer them.

I have a single message from my dad.

DAD

> Your mom is already planning your wedding.
> She's also annoyed. Next time maybe tell her
> you've got a girlfriend before you go telling the
> whole world. I'm charging the flowers I bought
> to appease her to your credit card. You're
> welcome.

"Fuck." I run a hand through my hair.

I hit the call button, and my mom picks up on the first ring.

"Dallas, finally. Why am I finding out that you have a girlfriend through your social media? I'm excited about this, but I'm very hurt to be learning this at the same time as two and a half million other people—which is impressive, by the way. Your following just keeps growing." She layers in a compliment with her ire, it's her way.

"Thanks, Mom, and I'm sorry."

"You better be sorry. This is a big deal. You haven't brought home a girlfriend, or introduced us to anyone, or posted about anyone in years. Years, Dallas! How long have you been seeing each other? How long have you been hiding this from your family? From your own *mother*?" She *tsks* me.

My mom chose to set aside her own career so she could be a full-time mom. With three boys and one girl and only six years between the oldest and youngest, we were a busy household. Between getting Ferris and I to our separate practices, traveling for competitive sports away games, and Manning and Paris's extreme extracurricular schedules, my mom still found time to devote to her own volunteering. Fortunately, my dad is an oncologist and could financially support the family, making it easier for my mom to follow her heart and focus her energy on raising us. She jumped in with both feet and rocked the shit out of being the best mom possible. Even now, we're a tight-knit family.

Her hurt at finding out about me and Wills along with the rest of the world is likely pretty deep.

"It's pretty new, Mom." *Like a couple of hours now.*

"Do not lie to your mother, Dallas! The way you were smiling in that picture tells me this has been going on for a while!"

"I promise, it couldn't have been going on because of the no-fraternization policy with the team," I explain. "So we were trying to stay away from each other." Even that's a stretch. But, if I can be the boyfriend Willy never knew she wanted, maybe I have a chance in hell of turning this fake dating into real dating.

"Wilhelmina finally knows about the crush you've had on her since you were young, doesn't she?" She makes a little excited noise.

"Uh, I mean...we're dating so..." I clear my throat so it doesn't sound like my balls are caught in a vise. *Please don't have my year-book open.* "That was a long time ago, though. We don't talk about our childhoods much."

Mom has no idea what happened around prom, the nail in my proverbial coffin, and I'd like to keep it that way. She would be horrified by my actions.

"Since your dad and I are coming down for the charity game this weekend, we'll have a chance to get to know her better."

"Oh, uh, I don't know. She'll be pretty busy with the event."

"After the event we can plan a dinner for her. What kind of food does Wilhelmina like? Do you want me to stop and get you some of those butter tarts in Orillia on the way? The chocolate chip ones?"

"Uh, I, uh... Maybe you should let me check with her first."

"You're serious about this girl and you don't even know what kind of treats she likes? Dallas, I raised you better than that," Mom chastises.

"No, Mom, I know what she likes. Anything with peaches is her favorite. I'm sure she would love the butter tarts from Orillia." They're the best butter tarts in the world.

"Perfect. I'll hit the market today and make a fresh pie this afternoon." Mom's voice is giddy with excitement. Her pies win awards every summer.

"That sounds great, Mom, but—"

She cuts me off before I can express my concerns about the possibility of Willy murdering me over dinner with my family. As if the celebrity event isn't stressful enough.

"No buts, sweetie. We want to celebrate this new relationship. Don't you worry, we'll embrace her wholeheartedly, even though you didn't tell us before you told the rest of the world."

Yeah, she's stuck on that point.

"I really am sorry about that."

"I know. You're my impulsive one. I'll message when we're on our way down. Oh! And I'll bring Grandma Bippy's engagement ring!"

"Mom, we just started dating."

"You've been in love with her forever and it's important to be prepared. Besides, neither of your brother's even have a girlfriend, so there's no way they'll be proposing anytime soon. And your sister is too busy to date." She sighs forlornly. "Anyway, for the family dinner, I'll cook so it can be nice and intimate. I can't wait to see Wilhelmina all grown up! Love you. Bye, sweetie."

"Love you too, Mom."

She ends the call before I can protest. It sucks that I've gotten her hopes up to the point that she's bringing "the ring." Whoever gets engaged first is the proud owner of great-grandma Bippy's rare blue diamond ring.

"Shit." I run a hand through my hair. My hole keeps getting deeper. Wills is already pissed at me for being an idiot. I can't see her being thrilled about a meet-the-parents dinner date. We haven't even dealt with our friends, and now this. But there's no getting out of it.

I can soften the blow of an unexpected family dinner, though. I step out into the warm summer day and head down the street, stopping at the local florist to buy another ostentatiously large bouquet of pink and peach-colored flowers, complete with vase and heart balloon. My next stop is her favorite coffee shop. Treats and flowers are always a winner.

Armed with more flowers and food, I return to the office, but stop at my car to grab one more thing, tucking it into the takeout bag. Unsurprisingly, my raging anxiety boner is back in full force by the time I reach her office. I do some surreptitious rearranging and hope it isn't obvious as I prepare to knock.

My palms are sweating, my throat is tight, and my heart rate is elevated. Unfortunately, Willy's anger is preferable to the guilt trip my mother will lay on me if I back out of dinner. It's an impossible position, but Mom guilt supersedes even clown detail, which is saying something.

I knock on Willy's door and wait for her "come in" before I poke my head into her office. She fluffs out her hair. She was probably wearing it in a topknot. She does that often in the summer because her hair is so thick. I'm sure the back of her neck gets hot.

Her pen is clamped between her teeth, and she's wearing my favorite blue-light glasses. The frames are tortoiseshell with baby blue arms. She is stunning.

She removes the pen from between her teeth and glares at me. "Do you want to die today, Dallas?"

"I brought you lunch. And flowers, and I'm sorry." I envision her stabbing me with the pen in her hand when I tell her the news, which does nothing to calm any part of me down.

Willy frowns as I set the vase of flowers on the small conference table. I edge closer and set the latte and takeout bag on her desk, then quickly step back.

She eyes me with suspicion and crosses her arms. "What did you do now?"

"I didn't do anything per se." I back up several steps. I need a quick escape route, and I have the gift of speed on my side. "I thought your office could use a little pop of color." I motion to the flowers. "And I know you're busy with last-minute details around the celebrity hockey game this weekend, and you probably haven't taken a break for lunch, so I brought you something to eat and a latte for your caffeine fix." I take several more cautious steps backwards.

Willy narrows her beautiful brown eyes at me, then pries the lid off the latte. "Is this the lavender one?"

"Yeah. Half sweet with oat milk."

"That's my favorite." It sounds like an accusation. "Why are you being so nice?"

I swallow loudly. "I'm pre-apologizing through gifts." I know it will take a lot more than a couple of bouquets of flowers and a lunch or two, but it's a start. I back up another step.

When I reach the doorway, I rap on the doorframe and blurt, "My parents are coming down for the charity game and they want to have dinner with you after, and I'm sorry about that." I duck as she hurls a stress ball at my head. She only misses because my reflexes are so good.

"What the hell, Dallas? There's no way I'm having dinner with your parents. Tell them no."

"I can't. My mom's hurt that I didn't tell her about us before I posted on social media, which is not your fault, it's my fault. But she will make dinner happen, Wills. There's no getting out of it for either of us. She will corner you at the game and insist on making food for you while also reminding you that meals are important and everyone has to eat, and I'm sorry, but it'll be a great meal. I know you'll sign me up for clown detail, and that's something I'll have to live with. It'll be really casual. You don't need to bring anything, just your beautiful self. I'm gonna go before you kill me."

I book it down the hall, and another stress ball comes flying past me, but I'm fast, and she's wearing heels, so I outrun her for now.

CHAPTER 9

HEMI

I don't bother chasing Dallas down the hall. I'm in heels, and he's a pro hockey player, so there are zero chances I'll be able to catch him.

I glare at the bouquet of flowers sitting in the middle of my conference table. I refuse to have anything that smells this nice and looks this pretty in my office—especially when it was given to me by the person who has made my life a complete nightmare and seems intent on continuing this trend. I take the flowers across the hall to Shilpa's office. She's not there to say no because she has a meeting off-site. She and I have a date tonight to discuss the dumpster fire my life has become in the last twelve hours. I've put the group chat on hold until further notice. Hammer is out today with Flip and Ash at a pediatric hospital visit.

It's not enough that we have the celebrity hockey game in three days, now I also get to deal with the stress that comes with being Dallas's fake girlfriend.

I flop down in my chair and grudgingly sip the latte. Then I moan at how perfectly delicious it is. "That fucker." It makes me unreasonably angry that Dallas knows exactly what I like. He probably asked Shilpa.

My stomach growls obnoxiously. The only thing I've consumed today is coffee and water. I swear I can smell a peach scone through the bag.

I give into temptation and peek inside. I frown as I pull the item on top out. It's an inedible, adorable, crocheted peach wearing a little smile, complete with stem and a single crocheted leaf. His granny probably made it. I set it next to my family photo. It always garners questions since I don't look like my moms or brothers.

I return my attention to the bag. A delicious, frosted peach scone sits on top of a beet and farro salad. I carefully remove the scone from the bag and break off a piece, popping it into my mouth. The delicate taste hits my tongue, and I simultaneously sigh in contentment and groan in irritation. Now I'll forever associate my favorite scones with the world finding out I'm suddenly in a relationship with Dallas Bright.

My phone buzzes on my desk.

It's my group chat with my brothers.

SAM

I thought you hated Dallas Bright?

ISAAC

^^^this.

SAM

Mom and Ma are unimpressed that the hockey world knew about it before them.

ISAAC

^^^this. Also, Sam is annoyed that you didn't tell us either, but he won't admit it.

SAM

^^^he's the annoyed one. He also saw the post first and sent it to Moms.

ISAAC

Moms ran into Dallas's mom at the market
before I sent the post, so they already knew.
Apparently they want to plan a big family dinner
when you're home for the reunion, FYI.

SAM

Moms are coming for you, batten down the
hatches.

HEMI

Thanks for the heads-up. And fuck you, Isaac,
for sending them the post.

ISAAC

They already knew!

SAM

Not the point.

HEMI

^^^this.

My phone rings.

"Crap." I knew this was coming. I should've called my moms
first thing this morning. But the panic was real, and it's been a
tornado of a day. I can't be honest with them. Not now. Not
when Dallas's mom is already excited about it. And Mom is the
worst liar in the world. She has the most obvious, embarrassing
tells. Huntsville is too small a place, and everyone is in everyone
else's business. And if Sam finds out he'll unalive Dallas in
retribution. And then the team will really be screwed over. I have
no choice but to sell them on this. It'll be a feat considering that I
talk about Dallas all the time, and it's not with any kindness or
affection.

HEMI

They're calling.

SAM

Don't buckle under the guilt.

ISAAC

sinking into the ground GIF

I take a deep breath and hit the answer button. "Hey, Mom!"

"Hi, sweetheart, it's both of us on the line here," Mom replies.

"Hi, Ma." It's typical of them to call me together.

"Hi, Hemi, seems like you might have some news to share." Ma's tone tells me she's less than pleased.

"I hear you ran into Dallas's mom." No point in beating around the bush.

"We did. But it also seems to me like all of the hockey-watching nation knows about our daughter's love life before we do." Mom's nails tap on the counter. Based on the sound, they're in the kitchen. "I was under the impression you and Dallas didn't get along all that well."

That's because we don't, and currently I want to murder him all over again for making me lie to my moms. "Well, you know what they say about the line between love and hate. We've flipped from hate to really strong like. He does a lot of charity work."

As if that last detail somehow explains everything. Of all the guys on the team, Dallas volunteers the most. And honestly, the more obscure the charity, the better. For some of the guys, promo ops and volunteer work are also about visibility and helping their image. Like Flip. Sure, Tristan coaches hockey for kids with special needs with his brother regularly, but Dallas is the one who makes meat pies with grandmas as a church fundraiser.

"They do spend a lot of time together," Ma says thoughtfully.

"And you talk about him more than any of the other players," Mom agrees. "Although usually it's with disdain. I can see how that might shift over time, though, especially after he birthed that foal."

"That was so sweet, even though he did pass out," Ma adds.

"He is quite handsome," Mom says.

"And he knows it," I mutter. So does anyone who lays eyes on him.

"Well, darling, you are very beautiful, not to mention intelligent, driven, and successful. And I'm sure he sees the same things we do. It makes sense that he's smitten."

I'm thankful they can't see my face right now because my mouth is hanging open in disbelief.

"He's definitely smitten," Ma agrees. "He looks radiant. And so do you, sweetie."

"Yeah. I'm ecstatic." That my voice doesn't crack is a small miracle. I clear my throat into my elbow to muffle the sound. "We had to keep a lid on things because of the rules at work and the paperwork around it," I add. That's probably what I should have led with. "But we finalized all of it this morning."

"Of course. I wondered about that. Dallas's mom seemed just as surprised as we were by this development. Everything is okay with the head office? I would have had our lawyer look it over." Both of my moms are independent businesswomen. Mom is a general practitioner, and Ma is the CEO of an organic health product line. They supported each other and their career goals while each of them carried one of my brothers to term. Then they decided to adopt me. They've juggled careers and family and are incredible parents. I strive to have a love like theirs.

"I didn't have time, but Shilpa answered every question I had in great detail." Her duty is to the Terror, but she was exceptionally clear about what exactly I was signing.

"Of course she did. How are she and Ash?" Mom asks.

"Good. They're both good."

"Oh! And now you and Dallas will be able to go on double dates with them! How fun!" Ma claps.

"We're all going out tonight to celebrate." Dallas was not the partner I imagined for my double dates with my best friend, but I have to lean into it like Shilpa said.

"I'm thrilled that you've found someone who adores you, sweetheart," Mom says gently.

"Thanks. I'm sorry you had to hear about it the way you did. He wasn't supposed to post until after we talked to our families, but he's a little impulsive like that, and then the cat was out of the bag."

"Sometimes life just happens. You'll be going to the reunion together, then?" Ma asks.

"That's the plan." It's my only option now.

"That'll be a great opportunity for us to get to know him again, especially since he's the man who's stolen your heart. Are you excited?"

He's renting it, really. Temporarily. I'm his fake girlfriend without benefits. I have to really own it now. Lying to my moms is a cardinal sin in our house. Honesty above all would be on our family crest if we had one. But this is bigger than a fake relationship. This affects the whole team and my place with the Terror. So I try my best to be convincing because I need them to believe this. At least until we figure a way out of it. After the reunion. "I'm really lucky to have someone so committed and passionate."

The layers of complication keep growing.

"We'll figure out plans when we get closer to the date."

"Sounds good, Moms." I need to get off the phone. Being dishonest with my moms feels horrible.

We make plans to talk again later in the week, and I end the call. I take a moment to calm my heart rate. It's one thing to fool my moms into believing I'm head over heels on the phone, but it will be totally another to convince them in person.

The Badass Babe Brigade chat is taunting me as my number of unread messages keeps growing, and I cannot mute it forever. I scroll through, finding an excessive number of shocked GIFs and speculation. They must have gotten tired of my lack of response because they started planning our evening half an hour ago.

RIX

> Watering Hole at five. We need the deets on
> this new love story.

Looks like I get to start with my girlfriends. I really wish I had more than grade-eight drama class to rely on for my acting skills. I can't afford to have them question this.

It's already four. Where the hell did my day go? Down the drain, along with my freedom and my reputation, thanks to Dallas. I'm too amped up to focus right now.

I type out a text to my semi-regular hookup and put him on hiatus. Allen is a pharmaceutical rep. He was the first guy I went out with on my quest to find a reunion date. He travels often for work, and we realized quickly that we weren't relationship compatible, but we have great chemistry. So when we're in need of stress relief, we'll hook up. It's only happened a few times, and it's been a while, but if ever I could use some stress relief, it's this week. And now that's impossible. He's presenting at some massive conference on the weekend of the reunion, so he was out as a potential worst case scenario back up date.

There's nothing I can do about it, so I manage the last of my emails, make sure my checklist reflects all I've accomplished today, and create a new one for tomorrow. Only when I'm finished with my work tasks do I realize Dallas and the guys will probably end up at the Watering Hole too, and we need a plan.

HEMI

> FYI I'm meeting the girls at the Watering Hole at
> five to discuss the development in our
> relationship. We need our stories to align.

DALLAS

> Tell them I've been in love with you for years.

HEMI

> Seriously. *eye roll*

> No one will buy that.

DALLAS

No, no one would buy that you've been in love with me for years.

A picture of the two of us follows.

DALLAS

Does my smile not say madly in love?

HEMI

That smile says too much whiskey. I'm telling them you came to my place and professed your undying love.

DALLAS

thumbs-up Whatever story you tell, I will corroborate.

HEMI

You may live to regret that.

DALLAS

I survived the clowns and the sauerkraut pierogies—nothing is as bad as that.

HEMI

evil cackling GIF

You are so fucked, Dallas.

DALLAS

I know. See you at the Watering Hole. I look forward to whatever you decide to dish out.

I don't respond, just grab my purse and leave the office. Twenty minutes later, I'm tucked into a booth with Shilpa, Rix, Hammer, Tally Vander Zee, and Dred Reformer.

Tally's dad is the head coach of the Terror. She interned with me last year, too, and is heading to university in the fall. She's part of our Badass Babe Brigade, and we adore her. Dred lives in the same building as Rix's brother, Flip Madden. She works at the local library and has been folded into our group over the past year. Like me, she wasn't raised by her birth parents. Unlike me, she wasn't adopted and spent her childhood shuttled from foster home to foster home. It takes a while to get to know her—I'm still working on it—but she's a super interesting person.

"This is so exciting! I can't believe you and Dallas are finally a thing." Tally does an excited seat shimmy. Her dad was nowhere near that thrilled when I got called in to meet with upper management this morning. Coach Vander Zee can have a very intense face.

I try not to frown. "Finally a thing?"

She folds her hands together and props her chin on them. "We've all seen the way—" She flinches. "I mean, I'm just excited. Everyone is falling in love."

I glance around the table. Rix is rubbing her lips, and Hammer is biting hers together. Dred's eyebrow is arched, and Shilpa is doing a terrible job of suppressing a smile.

"We've all seen the way what?" I try to cross my arms, but we're sitting in the booth and my boobs are big, so it's impossible.

"The way you and Dallas look at each other, of course. It was only a matter of time with how much you're together," Shilpa says, helpfully digging me out of my hole.

"Oh, right. Yeah."

"I gotta say, you've done a pretty solid job of making everyone believe you can't stand him," Dred says, voice laced with what might be skepticism.

"Yeah, well, we were fighting the draw." That sounds ludicrous.

"Usually you want to murder him. When did that change? How did it change?" Hammer asks, apparently second command in the interrogation committee.

Although I'm grateful she seems more confused than hurt. We work together, she knows me, so pulling the wool over her eyes will be harder. I'm glad I don't have to do that with Ash and Shilpa.

"Mostly I was trying to convince myself that my feelings hadn't changed. But it's recent. The feelings changing. Very recent." *Like this morning recent.* God, I suck at this.

I mentally run through all the different promo ops I've done with Dallas. There are dozens to choose from. Once he had an allergic reaction, so I fold that into our origin story.

"He came to my place because he was stressing over one of his promo ops." He usually texts compulsively the night before. "He couldn't sit still, so he started cooking, because it calms him." This is good. I can filter in some truth. "I used to think he was sucking up when he brings sweets to promo ops, but now I know it's because he had a bake-off the night before." I'm rambling, and I need to get a grip. Too many details will make the lie harder to remember. "Anyway, Dallas was in the kitchen."

"What was he making?" Tally asks.

I scramble for a second. "Homemade cheese and potato pierogies, with fried onions."

"Those are my favorite," Dred says.

"I love the sweet cottage cheese ones." Hammer sighs.

"I like the ones with jalapeños," Shilpa says.

"I like the cherry ones," Tally adds.

"We should have a pierogi-making party," Rix suggests.

"Agreed," Hammer says and motions to me. "Continue with your story."

"I didn't have butter, so Dallas made do with oil. Except it was a bottled coconut oil blend, which he's allergic to." I discovered this at a church fundraiser. He had a reaction that required a boatload of Benadryl and a several-hours-long nap in my car. "He must have touched his face because his lip swelled, and then he broke out in hives." That's exactly what happened at the church. One second he was pretty Dallas, and the next he looked like something out of a weird horror movie. "He started to panic. He was dancing all over the kitchen, and I have a gas stove." I draw from another incident that happened in my building, several months back. "He bumped into the cookbook and his shirt caught on fire. I had to tackle him to the floor and smother him with a blanket."

"And one thing led to another, and you started making out?" Tally asks.

"Uh, no, that wasn't how it ended." Dallas is literally the last person I would willingly make out with, except for maybe Charles.

Shilps clears her throat.

"I can't believe we haven't heard this story before," Dred muses. I can't tell if I'm imagining her skepticism or not.

"Well, they were trying to keep it a secret," Shilpa explains helpfully.

A murmur of agreement comes from around the table.

"The fire alarm went off, we had to evacuate the building, and the fire department came."

"I love firefighters," Tally says.

"Same," I agree. "So we're standing outside, Dallas is wearing a half-burned T-shirt, covered in hives, and the fire department shows up. They do their thing, and of course we have to talk to them because it was my apartment. I was explaining what happened, and Dallas was boring holes in the side of the firefighter's head. I didn't know if he was just loopy from the Benadryl, but he went totally caveman."

"Caveman how?" Hammer's eyes light up.

I glance at the TV where two people are fencing and blurt, "He challenged the firefighter to a duel."

"No!" Rix throws her head back and laughs.

Dallas appears out of nowhere, a smile lighting up his stupid pretty face. "What's so funny?"

"Hemi was just telling us the beginning of your secret love story," Shilpa explains. Thank God for her fortress of a memory.

"You mean the time we went to karaoke and I serenaded you?" Dallas asks.

Of course he's going to screw this whole thing up for me. Sweat trickles down my spine. We're only hours into this charade and about to blow it all up. And my life. Worse than it already is. "No, that came later. Although your memory of the night in question might be a little foggy thanks to the Benadryl."

He nods slowly. "Because I had an allergic reaction."

"And nearly burned my apartment down. Then you challenged the firefighter to a duel when you thought he was flirting with me," I say as though I'm reminding him, not making this up on the fly. *Why is fencing on TV right now?*

I'm incredibly surprised when Dallas tucks a hand in his pocket, and gives me a sultry, impish smile. "I didn't think he was flirting with you, Wilhelmina, I *know* he was. And I needed him to know that despite the state of my face and how high I was on antihistamines, I was ready to fight to the death in your honor."

"You're giving the antihistamines a lot of credit." I prop my chin on my clasped hands and bat my lashes at him. I am more than happy to throw him under the bus and back up a few times. "But they were helpful in getting you to be open and honest with me about your feelings, considering you professed your undying love once we were back in my aired-out apartment."

Dallas's eye twitches. As much as I hate lying to my friends, there's immense satisfaction in watching him try to keep his expression neutral while I weave this outlandish tale.

"Well, I had been holding on to those feelings for a long time." He sighs and shakes his head. "It was a challenge. The allergic reaction, combined with the near-death experience, and that firefighter hitting on you—a man can only take so much. I couldn't hold back any longer. I had to tell you how I felt."

"You did, extensively and emphatically, and then you passed out with your head in my lap."

"I don't regret it. I could sleep with my head in your lap every day for the rest of my life and be a happy, happy man."

I don't have a chance to reply because Ash appears and slings an arm over Dallas's shoulder. "Not to be a party pooper, but the four of us really should get going if we're gonna make our reservation tonight."

Shilpa glances at her phone. "Oh wow, I didn't realize the time."

Dallas rolls with it, and so do I, glad for the escape.

I hug all the girls and slide out of the booth. I don't have a choice but to accept Dallas's hand and allow him to wrap his arm around my shoulder and pull me into his side.

He kisses the top of my head. I smile and try to laser beam him to death with my eyeballs at the same time.

"Are you staying at my place tonight, my little peach pie?" he asks as we move toward the exit.

"That's the first and last time you'll use that nickname if you don't want to end up at the bottom of Lake Ontario."

He nods. "You're so damn sweet, honey."

I dig my nails into his side, and he smiles down at me.

If today is anything to go by, the next few weeks will be an epic test of my patience. And my questionable acting skills.

CHAPTER 10
DALLAS

"Your parents get in okay?" Ash asks as we walk the two blocks to Tristan's condo. A bunch of us get together to work out in the offseason when we're in the city. We rotate whose gym we use, so people can never pin down our routine. We could go to the arena, but the condo gyms are sweet and not highly utilized during the summer.

"Yeah, they're settling in. We're going for brunch after the workout if you want to join."

"Do you want me to join?" Ash asks.

"Yeah. I could use the buffer." My mom can't stop talking about how excited she is to get to know Hemi better. I feel like a giant bag of shit, seeing as this whole thing is a lie from Willy's perspective.

Even my dad, who is pretty low-key about most things, is pretty enthused about this development. He also made an offhand comment about making sure I don't screw this up.

That comment stung, though it wasn't unjustified. I have done a lot of stupid shit in my lifetime. It doesn't help that both of my brothers and my younger sister have always been very focused on their goals and how they plan to reach them, with little in the way of distraction. Manning knew he wanted to be a doctor by the time he was five. And Ferris was set on being a firefighter by high school. Paris has loved every animal she ever met, so no one was shocked when she became a veterinarian. In similar fashion, hockey was it for me as soon as I picked up a stick. Unlike them, I was often more concerned with what was happening *after* hockey practice. I'd been so caught up in partying with the cool crowd.

"Are Hemi's moms coming to the charity game?" Ash asks.

"They can't make it." I know this because my mom already talked to her moms and they have to work.

"So you only have to handle one set of parents. That's good." Ash echoes the thoughts in my head.

I text Tristan to let him know we're standing outside his building. Hollis and Roman cross the street as he buzzes us in. They live in the building across from Tristan's. Most of us live within walking distance of each other.

We all give each other back pats in greeting as the elevator doors slide open, and Rix and Dred step out.

"Perfect timing!" Rix puts her hand over the door sensor and motions for us to pile in. "Tristan and Flip are at the gym. I'll get you up there before we head out so they don't have to come down."

"I just messaged Flip," Dred says, pushing her glasses up her nose.

"Dallas, Hemi said your parents are coming to the charity game tomorrow. I can't wait to meet them," Rix says.

"Same." Dred regards me curiously. "I still can't believe you and Hemi are dating. I feel like she owns your ass."

"That's not inaccurate," I concede.

She pats my arm. "It's okay to be a beta off the ice."

Rix looks up from her phone. "I think *golden retriever* is a more apt term for Dallas."

"Thanks?"

We step into the elevator and wave goodbye to Rix and Dred as the doors slide shut.

"Are all the girls getting together?" I ask without thinking. I should know this already if Willy is with them.

Hollis gives me a strange look, and Ash surreptitiously kicks my ankle.

"They're giving Hemi a hand at the arena this morning," Roman says helpfully.

"Right. Of course. I don't know where my head is." I give mine a shake.

"You have a lot going on right now." Ash claps me on the shoulder.

Roman rubs the stubble on his chin. "As much as I didn't see this coming, I kind of saw this coming."

I give him a quizzical look. "How do you mean?"

Hollis coughs into his hand.

The elevator doors open, and a couple steps inside. Their eyes flare in recognition. They side-eye each other, and their faces go red, but they don't say anything about the Terror.

Roman talks about the weather.

They stammer out an awe-filled response.

My phone dings with another notification from Dr. Sheep's Ass and Brooklyn, which mentions something about all the poor single folks missing out on a love like theirs. *Gag me.* I swear, if they didn't think Wills was my girlfriend, they'd find a way to ruin her weekend. That's one positive to come out of this mess.

Thankfully, we reach our floor before it can get awkward, and the couple doesn't follow us off. Tristan meets us at the door to the gym and ushers us in. We're the only people here now, as the commuters and diehard morning-workout people are long gone. Everyone fans out to their location of choice.

"Okay, back to the comment you made, Roman. What do you mean you saw this coming? What are you, the Love Detective?" I scoff. He's solving all the mysteries of the heart except when his best friend is in love with his daughter, apparently. In my fantasy world, Willy's hatred is a mask for her complete infatuation with me.

Roman looks around the weight room. "Raise your hand if you knew Dallas had a hard-on for Hemi."

All the guys raise their hands.

I cross my arms. "You couldn't *all* know that."

"Dude." Flip watches his reflection in the mirror wall as he does alternating hammer curls. "She gives you the most fucked-up promos in the history of the universe, and you never say no. There is no one else on the team who does half as much bizarre church charity stuff as you."

"The church stuff is mostly for Granny. And her friends and their friends." This is true, but also, Willy always accompanies me, so it's a double win. I get to spend time with my granny and give back to the community—like every other member of my family does every single day with their jobs—*and* I get Willy's undivided attention.

"Okay, but she always goes with you, no matter what," Flip counters. "I'm sure part of that is so you don't do or say something to cause her a headache, but that can't be the only reason. If that were true, she'd live in my condo, in my spare bedroom."

"What other reason would there be?" I wish I could be cooler about this, but I don't want to be alone in my obsession.

"She attends all this nonsense so she can spend time with you," Hollis says.

"The same way you started coming to the diner so you could spend time with my daughter," Roman notes.

"I came solely for their breakfast hash until earlier this year," Hollis replies.

"Uh-huh."

"Anyway." Hollis turns back to me. "Now we know why she attends even the obscure stuff."

"Did Hammer say something to you about it?" My sleuthing continues. If I have confirmation from my teammates that I am not alone in this, that changes everything.

Hollis gives me a disbelieving look. "Like I would share anything my girlfriend says to me with all of you."

"Rix has said something similar before," Flip pipes up.

"Is that true?" I ask Tristan who shoots death lasers from his eyeballs at his best friend.

"Don't see why Flip would lie about it," he mutters noncommittally.

I don't want to get my hopes up, but I've kind of gotten my hopes up. At least I'm able to focus on the weights and leave it alone for now.

After our workout, Ash and I meet my parents for breakfast at The Pancake House. They have the best eggs benny and great coffee.

"I'm so excited to see Shilpa tomorrow." Mom pours half a packet of sugar and a creamer into her coffee, stirs it, sips, and adds the rest of the sugar.

"She's looking forward to seeing you, too."

The adoration goes both ways between Shilpa and Ash and my parents.

Mom smiles and turns her attention to me. "I had Grandma Bippy's ring cleaned for you while you were working out with the boys."

I nearly spit-spray coffee in her face. As it is, I choke and sputter. I thought she was kidding about the ring. "Uh, it's a little early for that, Mom."

"Is it, though? You've known each other your whole lives. You've been working together for years," she argues. "Ash, when did you know you wanted to marry your wife?"

Ash looks like he swallowed a veggie sausage whole. "After the first date."

"And you two grew up together." My mom waves her spoon around like a weapon.

"Yeah, but we weren't really friends growing up, and we didn't run in the same circles in high school." I'm not about to tell her my friends tormented Willy in middle school and I stood passively by, which is just as bad as being the tormentor. She knows about the time I made student council posters for Willy, but she doesn't know why I did it, or how I accidentally fucked Wills over in the most unforgivable way right before prom.

"But you've been in each other's lives this entire time. And you can't tell me that her working for the Terror isn't fate bringing the two of you together." She tilts her head. "Besides, I can see how happy you are, Dallas Mattias Bright. You are head over heels in love. You can just hold onto it until you're ready to make her yours forever." She motions to Ash. "Don't you agree?"

"Being prepared is good," Ash says hesitantly and knocks my knee under the table while he gives me a look that tells he doesn't agree. At all.

"I just don't see the point in waiting when you have all this help and it's clear you're completely in love with her. You don't want to let this one get away, Dallas. Isn't that right, Mattias?"

"She's a keeper," Dad says from behind the rim of his coffee mug.

Being her boyfriend will protect from Brooklyn and Sean and the rest of the gossipy jerks at the reunion. But if she were my fiancée...then no one could question our relationship.

CHAPTER 11

HEMI

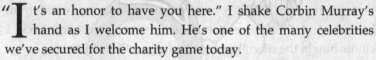

"It's an honor to have you here." I shake Corbin Murray's hand as I welcome him. He's one of the many celebrities we've secured for the charity game today.

"I'm stoked!" He smiles widely.

"So are we. If you're okay with it, we'd love for you to pose for a few photos, and then we'll have you escorted to the locker room to suit up." I direct him to the backdrop where the photographer is ready with the camera.

Tally takes his hockey bag as the next celebrity comes through the door.

"Hemi, it has been too long!" Eric Steele—his real name and not made up for acting—drops his bag and pulls me in for a warm hug.

"Hey! Thank you so much for agreeing to be here today." I give him an affectionate squeeze.

Hammer is standing to my right with wide eyes.

Eric is slow to release me. His fingertips glide down my arms in a familiar way, and his fingers curl around mine. His eyes are soft and so is his smile. "You look great."

I echo his grin and shake off the compliment. "You're making me blush."

"How are you? I saw that you're dating Dallas Bright. Gotta admit, I was kind of shocked, considering. I'm guessing things have changed a lot in the past couple of years."

Heat works its way up to my cheeks. Eric knows all about my disdain for Dallas. I scramble to make the lie sound convincing. "It's, uh...complicated. But yeah, my feelings have changed." Could I have asked Eric to be my date to the reunion? Sure. And I did consider it. But showing up with my ex, who also happens to be a popular movie star, would have felt like I was trying too hard. Now I regret not asking him, because showing up with Dallas is a whole different level of messed up. But it's too late now.

He nods, assessing me. "Well, he's a lucky guy."

"Who's a lucky guy?"

I go rigid as Dallas's arm winds around my waist from behind. And then his entire chest presses against my back. I elbow him in the ribs. "We've talked about PDA," I mutter.

We have *not* talked about PDA.

He backs off and holds up both hands. "Sorry, honey. I forget myself sometimes. I'll be on my best behavior." He moves to stand beside me and extends his hand. "Eric Steele, great to have you here."

"Thanks, man." Eric accepts his hand, and they shake it out for several seconds. "I was just saying you're a lucky guy to have snagged Hemi."

"The luckiest." Dallas wraps an arm around my shoulders and gives me a brief squeeze. "My dream woman is finally all mine."

"I should probably do the photo op and then get to the locker room. I'll see you out there on the ice, yeah?" Eric says, seeming slightly uncomfortable.

"Looking forward to it," Dallas replies.

He nods and looks to me. "Hemi, it's always good to see you."

"You, too."

Eric grabs his bag and makes his way over to Tally for photos.

"My sister would lose her mind if she were here. She lived in the T-shirt she had from his Fae movie franchise all through vet school." Dallas's eyebrows pull together. "How do you and Eric know each other?"

"We dated a while back."

"Dated? When?" Dallas props his fists on his hips. "How long ago is a while back?"

"Right after my undergrad. I did an internship in LA to get some experience, and he was a friend of a friend of a friend. We dated for a few months, and then I came back to do my master's and that was that."

"So you broke up because of distance?" Dallas confirms.

"It didn't work for a reason." He's actually jealous. Why would my fake boyfriend be jealous of my ex? Okay, famous ex, but still. "Why are you out here? You need to get ready for the game." I shove Dallas's shoulder, but he doesn't budge.

"More reasons than distance?"

"This is not a Hollis-and-Scarlet-Reed situation. Calm down. Can we discuss this later, when we don't have an audience and I'm not busy and you're not supposed to be getting ready for the game?"

He runs his hands through his hair and exhales through his nose. It's irritatingly hot. "Fine. I can be patient." He leans in and his eyes drop to my lips. *What the fuck is this fluttery feeling in my stomach all about?*

When the flash of a camera goes off, I put a hand on his chest and lean back. "What are you doing?"

"I need a good-luck kiss from my girlfriend."

"No, you don't. You are not allowed to put your lips on me when I'm at work. There needs to be boundaries. Gear up. Now." I point in the direction of the locker room.

His lip curls in a way that's all too familiar. It sparks a memory from our grade-eleven law class, one of the few we had together. He always wore that infernal smile when I got up in front of the class for debates. "What is this look?" *And why am I suddenly so flustered?*

His eyes heat, and he runs his tongue along his top lip. "I fucking love it when you order me around."

"Seriously. Go." I give him my death stare.

He mouths *so hot*, winks, and heads for the locker room.

I turn back to Hammer. "He's such a pain in my ass."

"He's obsessed with you," she says.

"He is not." But he sure is doing a good job of playing the jealous boyfriend and making a scene.

She arches a brow. "Why didn't I know you dated Eric until today?"

"It was a long time ago."

"But you stayed friends," she says.

I shrug. "There weren't any hard feelings about the breakup. I moved back here, and he was in LA. It was never serious."

"You are full of surprises lately, aren't you?"

"Sort of like you were full of surprises a few months ago, huh?" I tease.

"Yeah, falling for my dad's best friend was a thing there, wasn't it?"

"Yeah, but now that you're together, it's kind of impossible to imagine it any other way. Roman seems to be cool with things."

"Dad's definitely more relaxed. I think it helps that Hollis is pretty big on doting, and my dad sees it. Hopefully now that I'm settled in my career and have found love, he will too."

"He needs someone to take care of him for a change," I muse.

"He does. It's been me and hockey for the past twenty-one years, and with the backup goalie coming in more this season, he needs something else to focus on." Hammer sighs. "I'm just glad I still get to work with the team, you know? You're my family, and I can't imagine being anywhere else."

"I feel the same way." As much as Dallas being my fake boyfriend or people thinking I want his money is inconvenient, the alternative is far worse. If people found out it was all a lie, the embarrassment would be impossible to recover from. Not to mention the way it would impact the team. Which means I need to be extra convincing when I meet his parents. Too much is hinging on people believing in the lie of us.

When the final celebrity player has been checked in, we start to make our way to the arena, but Topher Guy stops me. "Hemi, there you are. I need to talk to you."

Because I don't have enough going on right now. I force a smile and turn to Hammer. "You go on without me."

"Are you sure? I can wait."

"It's fine. I'll be right behind you."

She heads down the hall, and I exhale my annoyance and give my attention to Topher. "What can I do for you?"

"We need to discuss your use of the primary rink."

"Sure. Why don't you walk with me? I need to check in with hospitality. Because the charity game is set to start in..." I find a clock on the wall. "Forty-five minutes. And I don't have a lot of time right now."

"You know, if you were a little less"—he motions toward me—"you, you'd be easier to tolerate."

I plaster on my fakest, brightest smile. "I need to be effective so that events like these run smoothly and bring positive press to our team, which is basically my job description. Now, what's the issue with the primary rink?" I walk briskly down the hall toward the VIP suite. I don't have time for this kind of shit today, especially not from Topher.

"You have it booked for the next four weeks for the women's team."

"It's the offseason, and there's no reason they should use the auxiliary rink when the men's team isn't on the ice. We've been over this before, so I'm not sure why we're discussing it again."

"That means it's not available for the junior boys' summer team."

"So they can use the auxiliary rink."

"I promised their coach they would have the opportunity to play there, so you need to move the women's team."

I come to a halt, and he skids to a stop, huffing with the effort of keeping up with me. "I'm sorry, what was it you said to me last month when I inquired about using the primary rink? That it was first come, first served and maybe next time I'd have my shit together?"

"Why are you always so difficult?" He tugs at his tie. "We could have done this the nice way, Hemi. Now I'll just have to go over your head." He storms off in the opposite direction. I take a deep breath and shake it off. Being nice about it means giving him his way, it seems. But I stand by my position, and he was never going to be nice about it with me anyway. I guess now he'll talk to one of the coaches and plead his case. He's been here longer than I have, and sometimes, his seniority wins out. But I will not be the one to break this news to Denise, the women's coach; that will be Topher's job, if he gets his way.

I check in to make sure our VIPs are taken care of before I head back toward the arena entrance. I find Hammer and Tally waiting for me with their clipboards in hand.

"Everything okay?" Hammer asks.

"Peachy. Thanks for asking. How's it going down here?" I look around the arena. Months of planning and this is it. It's a sold-out game, and it's being broadcast live. The ticket proceeds will go to two local charities, and afterward we'll have an online auction giving fans an opportunity to bid on signed jerseys, sticks, and special items donated by the players and celebrities.

"We're good to go. There was a minor hiccup on the second level, but we handled it. It's going to be kickass," she assures me.

"I love the jerseys for this," Tally says.

"It was a lot of fun to work with the design team on them," Hammer says.

"You know you're full-time in charge of that now," I tell her. Hammer has been helping the marketing team make deals with local designers so that the Terror brand stays relevant.

She nods. "I am one-hundred-percent good with that."

Rix, Shilpa, and Dred join us in the first row behind the bench, and we settle in to enjoy the game. Normally we're all up in a suite together. It's nice being this close to the action.

The players take the ice one at a time, and the crowd screams and claps their approval. This game is celebrities against pro players. It's all about fun and raising money for charity. I'm surprised when Dallas starts shit-talking and getting all worked up about the celebrities first goal, shortly after the game starts.

I knock on the glass, and he glances over his shoulder.

I give him a look.

He blows me a kiss.

But he keeps it up, scoring two goals in the first five minutes. Roman lets in two goals for the celebrity players to tie it up.

"What the hell is his deal?" I mutter. "This is supposed to be for fun."

"Seems like maybe he's a little jealous of your history with Eric," Hammer whispers.

"No." I immediately dismiss the idea.

Hammer shrugs. "He keeps stealing the puck from him."

It would make sense if we were *actually* dating and he had something to be jealous of. But we're not, and he doesn't. "He needs to settle down."

But he keeps up with the chippy playing and the aggressive moves on the ice, to the point that Ash blocks him from scoring another goal in the second period.

During a short break in play, the camera pans to one of the boxes, zeroing in on the last people I want to see today. "Oh for fuck's sake, why do they have to be here?" I mutter.

"Who?" Shilpa asks.

"Brooklyn and Sean." I shake my head.

The company he works for sponsors a box. Usually he attends with his coworkers, and I avoid him. There's no reason to seek him out. I also fully acknowledge I shouldn't care about him at all. But of course he's here with my ex-best friend today.

And of course they're kissing on the damn Jumbotron for the whole arena to witness. I'm an adult, it shouldn't matter. Except why does it feel like they're always rubbing salt in the wound?

This is my arena, my team, my people. I'm supposed to be safe here. They're not supposed to make me feel small when I'm in my domain, but God, they do. Sean probably doesn't even know I exist. But every time I see Brooklyn it feels like someone has sliced into my heart all over again. Every post, comment meant to needle, works it's way under my skin. I wish it didn't affect me, and I hate that it still hurts. I shouldn't even be fazed seeing them together, but they're my shitty insecurity kryptonite. I feel tiny and pathetic, like the stupid loser of a teenage girl who sat in the parking lot during senior prom after my best friend stabbed me in the back and cried until I puked.

The same friend who told me I should've been different in a thousand ways: less assertive, utilized my cleavage better, only smile, but never talk in case I made someone feel inferior. She told me a hundred times if I just listened to her, maybe more guys would like me. Worse was when she'd say other girls never wanted to be my friend, so I should be grateful I had her. *She was a bad friend.* Especially when I look at the amazing women I'm surrounded by now. They would never make me feel like that.

Romance and broken hearts might hurt, but losing someone I thought was my best friend left the deepest cut. In this moment, I wish for a thousand things. To be different. To not be so impacted by assholes from my past. To feel like being myself is okay. That being me isn't too much.

For a second, I feel the horrifying prick of tears behind my eyes—until a knock on the glass pulls my attention away from the Jumbotron. Dallas pulls off his gloves and makes a heart with his hands.

Ash slaps his shoulder and tells him to get his ass on the ice.

The Jumbotron catches it all.

I can't help it; I smile. Yes, he's a pain in my ass, but he also just reminded me people would kill to be me. Everyone thinks Dallas Bright is mine.

The players do their best to keep the puck away from Dallas during the last period, and the celebrities win the game by a single goal, which is how we always intend it to be, even if this time Dallas was single-handedly trying to make it otherwise.

At the end of the game, I lace up and take the ice, flanked by both teams, so I can thank everyone for being here. Vander Zee isn't much for speeches. We always end the charity games with a stuffie toss, which goes to the local children's hospital.

Just as the crowd has finished tossing the stuffed animals they brought onto the ice for the cleaners to gather in huge bag-lined bins, Dallas skates over.

I lower the mic and give him a look, which the entire arena can see. "What are you doing? Get back with the rest of your teammates."

"I just need the mic for a sec."

I don't like the look on his face one bit. I try to hide the mic behind my back, but I'm on skates and not a professional player with cat-like reflexes. Dallas nabs it and settles a hand on my hip to steady me.

"Seriously, Dallas, whatever you're thinking, you should stop now. Clowns are coming for you," I threaten.

"Don't worry, honey. I think you'll like this," he says before bringing the mic to his mouth. Sweat trickles down his cheek. His hair is wet at the temples, and his face is red with exertion. "Let's all give the love of my life a round of applause for putting together another incredible celebrity charity game!"

The crowd goes wild.

"I didn't do it by myself," I mutter.

"While she's quick to remind everyone she has a team of people helping her, I think it goes without saying that Wilhelmina is the glue behind that team. And she means the absolute world to me." He turns around, still gripping the microphone in one hand. But I notice the other is balled into a fist.

He drops to one knee in front of me, and the entire arena sucks in a collective gasp.

It takes every ounce of restraint not to reach out and throttle him.

"Get up," I whisper through clenched teeth and a tight smile.

This is not happening. He is not doing this in front of an entire arena. Whatever *this* is. At least we're past the televised part. *I hope we're past the televised part...*

"Wilhelmina Georgia Reddi-Grinst, you are the most incredible woman I've ever met. You inspire me every day to be a better man, and I know I'm forever a work in progress, but I want to be your work in progress. For the rest of our lives. There is nothing in the world I want more—not even another chance to hold the Cup—"

The crowd giggles, and a bunch of people cheer.

"Stop this now, Dallas. Clowns. Clowns forever," I threaten through the most extreme smile I can plaster on my face. It's one thing for me to lie to everyone I love about being his girlfriend, but if he's about to do what I think he is...the lies are about to get infinitely bigger.

"Ten years ago, I made the biggest mistake of my life not chasing after you. Be my person, Wilhelmina. Be my forever. Will you marry me?" He flips open the box he's had inside his fist.

Sitting on the black velvet cushion is the most beautiful blue diamond nestled amidst a halo of white diamonds. As far as engagement rings go, this one is exceedingly gorgeous. And I am so incredibly pissed off that Dallas, of all people, is presenting me with something so out-of-this-world beautiful in front of all of these people.

Especially because none of this is real. And the hole he's just dug for us has gotten so much deeper.

Dallas drops the mic. "Say yes, Wills. No one gets to fuck with you. We're going to rule. You and me. Be my badass queen."

I cover my mouth with my hand. I'm suddenly on the verge of tears. I'm angry. I'm sad. I have no idea what's going on.

"They don't get to win," he whispers. "Not now. Not ever. Let's show them how it's really done."

I fight back the tears and nod. However misguided, his intentions aren't evil. Or at least they don't seem to be.

He brings the microphone to his lips. "You gotta say the words, honey."

I drop my hand and cement this new lie. "Yes. I'll marry you."

His smile is radiant, and my heart feels like it's splitting in two.

We'll disappoint so many people when this charade ends.

His parents, my moms, our families, our friends—I'm already devastated for all of them. And most of all for me. Because the prom king just asked the nerdy girl to marry him, and it's all a tragic farce. Echoes of pain from all those years ago surface.

He slides the rock on my finger. It fits perfectly, and it's just so beautiful, and I'm just so angry at him. He doesn't love me. He doesn't want to marry me. It's just another game. Another win.

"She said yes!" He pushes to his feet and hands the microphone to Flip, who's standing beside me, mouth agape.

Dallas pushes my hair over my shoulder. I try not to react, to keep the smile plastered on my face as I speak through gritted teeth. "I'm going to kill you. You know that, right? You think clowns and sauerkraut were bad, just you wait." I want to punch that gorgeous smile right off his face.

"Can you stop giving me shit for a second so I can kiss you?"

"Wh—"

He cups my face in his palms and presses his lips to mine. I make a shocked sound and grab his wrists. His tongue pushes past my lips, not aggressively, but in the gentlest of sweeps.

My head swims, and fire rushes through my veins. It has to be shock. That's what this is. That's the only explanation as I fist his jersey and he tips his head. Every line of his hard body melds to mine. And it doesn't feel close enough. His lips meld to mine, so soft, and warm, and firm. Dallas's thumb grazes the edge of my jaw as he explores my mouth with a sureness that makes my knees wobble and the most embarrassing moan tumble from my lips.

"Damn, that's some chemistry," Flip mutters.

The arena is cheering and screaming.

Dallas breaks the kiss—thank God, because I clearly don't have the ability to make rational decisions. One corner of his mouth quirks up as his hot, knowing gaze meets mine. "I'm convinced."

With those two words, my bruised heart drops to my toes. *It's all just a show.*

He threads our fingers together and raises our hands in the air. "She said yes!"

I stand there, shocked beyond belief.

Dallas kissed me.

He kissed me.

And based on the way my body is reacting, that was the best kiss of my life.

This is really bad news for me.

Because he's not just my fake boyfriend anymore; now he's my fake fiancé.

CHAPTER 12
DALLAS

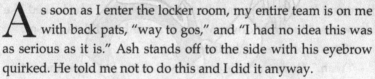

A s soon as I enter the locker room, my entire team is on me with back pats, "way to gos," and "I had no idea this was as serious as it is." Ash stands off to the side with his eyebrow quirked. He told me not to do this and I did it anyway.

We both know Willy will make my life a living hell for this. But I will absolutely take any and all of her anger because we just pulled the rug out from under Brooklyn and Sean's decade long power trip. They've been putting up passive aggressive posts lately. When Brooklyn mentioned something about it being "too bad" one of our classmate's partners cheated on them, I lost it. Those two assholes getting engaged isn't nearly as exciting as the pro hockey player proposing to his high school crush in an arena full of people. Petty? Definitely. But what's the point of all this power if I can't use it for good. Now no one can question the seriousness of our relationship. Not when my ring is on her finger. I'm running on a wicked adrenaline high.

"I just booked the Rose Room," Flip announces. "Everyone's invited for dinner, including your parents and whoever else wants to come." He drops his phone in his cubby and claps me on the back. "We need to celebrate the hell out of this."

"How did you manage that?" That place is usually booked weeks in advance.

"Connections. I have lots." Flip winks and heads for the showers.

I get additional back pats and hair ruffles as my teammates pass me, whooping it up. Nothing says celebration like booking one of the most expensive restaurants in town for the entire team.

I take my time getting undressed, and so does Ash. Neither of us says anything until we're alone.

"When we talked about the time being right, I didn't actually think the time would be tonight," he murmurs as he unclips his pads.

"I wasn't planning on it, but then I saw Willy's face when Sean and Brooklyn appeared on the Jumbotron." She looked like she wanted to throw down, which is something I'd pay to see.

"So you proposed," he finishes.

"Yeah." Was it a little impulsive? Sure. But fuck those two and their insidious behavior. I see their passive aggressive comments. I'll protect Wills however I can, whatever it takes. This is my penance in a diamond ring.

He purses his lips. "Think it might be a good idea for you to tell Hemi the truth about what happened back then?"

I've considered that several times recently. "She wouldn't believe me. Not yet. But hopefully I can change that between now and the reunion." If I'm being honest, I also can't force her to listen. Why would she trust my words now over my actions then?

"If that's what you think is best…" He sighs and claps me on the shoulder. "We should hit the showers. I'm sure your parents are freaking out. I'm sure Hemi is too."

An hour later, we've taken over the Rose Room, where an inordinate number of bottles of champagne are chilling. Wine, beer, and mixed drinks have been poured, appetizers served, and orders for dinner have been taken. The bill for this will be something else. Flip usually isn't an extravagant guy. He's the one who stops at the LCBO to pick up a six-pack of beer—always ultra-light—so he doesn't have to order room service when we're hanging out after a game.

Willy is across the room, holding a glass of champagne—although it could be club soda with a splash of something to make it look like champagne—surrounded by the girls. Shilpa is at her side, and has been the entire night. They're smiling and laughing, but I see the tension in Willy's shoulders. I wonder what kind of punishment she'll dole out for this major infraction. I'm already on the docket for kids' camp check in, the farmer's association prized pig ceremony, and another balloon animal rotation. I've been practicing for the last one.

It isn't until we're about to sit down for dinner that Willy enters my orbit again. Her hand slides up my back and curves around my shoulder, nails pressing into the skin through my shirt. She pushes up on her toes until her lips brush my ear. I can feel her breath on my neck. If I turned my head, my lips would touch her forehead.

"I hope you enjoy this party, Dallas, because it will be the last one you ever have," she murmurs.

I pry her fingers from my shoulder and link my arm with hers, leaning down so I can whisper to her while also breathing in her shampoo. "Careful, honey, you should know by now that threats just turn me on."

"Did you do this just to piss me off?"

I meet her stormy eyes. "I did it *for* you."

Her brow creases in confusion, but she doesn't have a chance to ask more questions because my mom approaches. She's over the moon. I've never seen her happier. If it were possible, her eyes would turn into hearts.

Her hand is at her chest. "You two are just the cutest."

"Thank you, Mrs. Bright. I can't believe this is happening," Willy says through a tight smile.

"Dallas is so smitten." Mom pulls Willy in for a hug, whispering something I don't catch. When she steps back, she takes Willy's hands in hers and inspects the ring. "It's the perfect fit. Do you love it? It was Dallas's great grandma's ring, passed down from her mother. I think it looks beautiful on you."

"It's stunning," Willy agrees. "I couldn't ask for a more beautiful ring." Her smile matches my mom's. If I didn't know Wills better, I would think she meant it. And maybe she does, but suddenly I'm hit with regret. I authentically want that ring on her finger, and I wish she did, too.

"When I gave it to Dallas yesterday, I had no idea he planned to propose right away, but I'm thrilled we were here to see it." Mom turns her smile on me. "Now, I know the credit card you gave me is supposed to be for Christmas presents and emergencies, but with your dad and me in town, we thought you and Wilhelmina would want a little privacy tonight. So I took it upon myself to book you a room at the Ritz. They have a beautiful honeymoon suite." She turns to Willy. "I know you work tomorrow, but maybe under the circumstances they'll be understanding, and you can go in a little late? That way you two can have a proper celebration." She winks and giggles as her cheeks flush. "Anyway, you don't have to worry about your dad and me. We'll be fine on our own."

"You really didn't have to do that," Willy says, a smile still locked in on her beautiful face. Although this one looks slightly manic.

If I'm alone with her tonight, I might die.

There are worse ways to go.

Mom shakes her head. "This is such a special night. And a once-in-a-lifetime occasion! Go out with your friends, have fun, and celebrate your love."

"Thanks, Mom. That was super cool of you. And thoughtful." It's her way, always thinking about other people, always wanting the best.

"So thoughtful," Willy agrees as her nails dig into my forearm.

I love the sharp bite it sends down my arm. I'm glad I'm wearing a suit and still have my jacket on, otherwise this boner would be pretty embarrassing.

We take our seats, and they bring out the first course, which is lobster bisque. Willy surprises me when she doesn't say no to a refill of her champagne. Clearly, the impromptu proposal is a stressor.

Between courses, I stretch my arm across the back of her chair and give in to the urge to finger the ends of her hair. It's soft and silky, and all I want to do is shove my face into it and smell her shampoo. I have to give it to her; she's playing the role of the happy fiancée pretty damn convincingly from the waist up. But under the table, her nails are digging into my thigh. I doubt she'd keep doing it if she knew what it does to me.

Dinner is a lavish affair, and again I'm surprised by how easily Flip seems to be letting us whoop it up on his dime. Unless he's going to pass me the bill at the end of the night.

Once the dishes from the second course have been cleared, Flip pushes his chair back and raises his glass, commanding the attention of the table. "While I don't think most of us saw this coming so soon, your love for Hemi is written all over your face, Dallas. And Hemi, as much as you ride my ass—in a professional way—"

The table chuckles. Flip ducks his head and shakes it for a second before he gives us a wry grin. "Sorry. Trying to keep it classy. Hemi, you are such an integral part of this team. You keep us in line, you give us opportunities to give back to the community, and you make us a better team. Seeing you and Dallas together is inspiring. Separately you're rockstars, but together you'll be a powerhouse." He holds up his glass. "To two of my favorite people finding once-in-a-lifetime love."

"To love!" Everyone echoes the sentiment as glasses clink.

A chorus of "*Kiss! Kiss! Kiss!*" follows. Willy's nails dig so hard into my leg, I wouldn't be surprised to find crescent-shaped cuts to admire later.

I turn toward her as she faces me. Her throat bobs with what I interpret as a nervous, or possibly rage-filled, swallow. But her eyes hold another set of emotions. There's indignation, but I swear, layered underneath that is a hint of anticipation. Or maybe that's me projecting, especially since the next emotion I see is fear. I don't know where it comes from, and I don't know how to fix it.

I don't want to force this on her, but I realize that by making her my fiancée, I've taken her autonomy. And a piece of her freedom. I'm relieved when she makes the first move, tipping her head, leaning in. Giving me permission.

I mirror the movement and stroke along the edge of her jaw with my thumb, trying to convey through tender touch that I know I've put her in a shitty situation. I'm still probably the last person she wants to kiss. But I swear I'll find a way to make it up to her, beyond shielding her from Brooklyn and Sean's vitriol.

Willy's nails retract from my thigh, and her hand slides over my chest to curve around the back of my neck. Once again, I feel the bite of her nails in my skin. It's a light press this time, a reminder that she can make me bleed if she wants, more than just physically.

My body is electric with anticipation. But we're in a room full of our friends, and Willy believes what's happening is all for show. But I still want it. I still want her.

We lean closer still, and when our lips have almost touched, Willy whispers, "Retribution is coming for you, babycakes."

"I fucking hope so," I reply. Her anger is better than her apathy.

I deserve whatever punishment she sees fit to dole out. Especially because I want this kiss to happen, regardless of the reason for it. Every single nerve in my body lights up like fireworks on Canada Day when her lips meet mine. A deluge of fantasies I've had about her over the past decade flood my mind at the soft, velvet press of her smart mouth.

I slide my fingers into her hair, sifting through those satin strands. If things were different, if this was real for her like it is for me, tonight we really would be celebrating—with her soft, curvy body under mine. She angles her head on the quietest, most boner-inducing whimper I've ever had the pleasure of hearing.

Her lips part on a sweet gasp, and her tongue sweeps my mouth. Shocked and fucking ecstatic, I let my tongue slide against hers. Willy's nails press harder into my skin, and I groan as those sharp bites make my cock swell further.

It isn't until the whistles and catcalls pierce the haze of lust that Willy wrenches her mouth from mine.

All I want to do is gather her in my arms and whisk her to the hotel room so we can do that all night long. Maybe with less clothes. Definitely with less clothes.

She reaches for her champagne glass, draining what's left.

While I've seen Willy red faced and angry, or delirious with glee over making me do something she knows I hate, I haven't seen her embarrassed—not in a lot of years, anyway. But based on the flush working its way up her neck and into her cheeks, she seems pretty damn horrified. This is unfortunate, because that was the second-best kiss of my life, the first being earlier today, after I proposed.

"That was some kiss," Hammer says from Willy's right.

"Agreed." Rix nods.

"I think we know what these two will be up to later tonight," Mom whispers to Dad in a not-very-quiet voice.

That elicits chuckles from the people close to them.

Willy hands me her empty champagne glass without looking at me. "Fill that, please."

"Of course." I kiss her cheek.

She grinds her teeth and side-eyes me.

This might be glass number three, unless she's been on the club soda, but I still refill it.

And I top her up once more during dinner. She rarely drinks, and definitely not this much, so I'm a little worried about her consumption, especially since she didn't eat much at dinner. Mentioning that seems like a bad idea, though, so I keep my mouth shut.

CHAPTER 13

DALLAS

After dinner, which to everyone's shock Flip insists on paying for, we all make plans to stop at home to change before we hit the club. Flip has booked table service at one of our favorite spots, all hyped up about celebrating our engagement.

Willy lives only a few blocks from me, so we drop my parents at my place first.

My mom opens the door and looks expectantly at me. "Aren't you coming up to grab an overnight bag?"

"We have to stop at my place. Dallas has clothes there," Willy lies smoothly when I start to splutter.

"Of course he does. You two have a wonderful night. We'll see you tomorrow." Mom kisses me on the cheek and gives Willy's hand a squeeze. Dad says good night and links hands with my mom, guiding her toward the building.

Willy watches them disappear inside with an unreadable expression on her face. "I really like your parents."

"They like you too. My mom thought she was doing us a solid with the hotel room tonight," I say.

"Yeah, I know. It sucks that we have to break her heart." Willy sighs, but anger simmers under the surface. "The fake engagement takes this lie to a whole different level."

"I'm sorry." And I am, but not for the reasons she probably thinks. I'm living my dream right now, but I'm making her live her worst nightmare. And isn't that a slap to the balls? I'm right where I want to be, and she's the opposite. But I keep putting her into positions she can't get out of. And I'm making us a PR nightmare. I keep tying her to me in ways that only get more difficult to untangle.

"I mean, as far as big news, our engagement definitely takes the cake," she grumbles. "I'm sure back home everyone's talking about it."

"It was an attention getter." I haven't checked my socials, but I'd be surprised if the news hasn't reached the reunion group.

"Oh my God." Wills's head drops against the back of the seat. "The shit is going to hit the fan when my moms hear about this, if they haven't already. I should call them. Actually never mind, I need to be fully sober for that conversation."

"I'm sorry."

"You keep saying that, but you also keep doing things that make my life complicated, Dallas. Your apology doesn't carry much weight."

I didn't consider much past adrenaline and the sweet taste of victory. Willy also has two older brothers, who will likely have things to say about her getting engaged right along with her mothers. I have no idea what any of them do and don't know about our tumultuous history.

"I wanted to take Sean and Brooklyn down a peg," I explain.

"Mission accomplished, I guess," she says.

I pull into the open temporary parking spot outside her building. When I cut the engine and start to get out, she holds up her hand. "You should stay here. I'll only be a minute." She hops out of the car before I can argue and disappears into the building without another word.

I let my head fall back and sigh. Sometimes I wish I wasn't so fucking impulsive.

Willy returns less than ten minutes later, wearing a royal blue dress that hugs her soft curves and strappy heels, looking like my number-one fantasy.

"Let's do this," she says as she slides back into the passenger seat. Her dress rides up, giving me a glimpse of creamy, bare thigh before she smooths the fabric down.

I clear my throat before I speak. "What about your overnight bag?"

She scoffs. "You're staying in that honeymoon suite by yourself."

"My mom will want pictures. And what about the girls? They'll ask about it, too."

Willy sighs. "Fuck. Fine. I'll go back to the hotel after we put in an appearance at the club. We'll take all the pictures you need, and then I will go back to my apartment and sleep in my bed. You can enjoy the comfort of the honeymoon suite."

The rest of the ride is silent. As soon as we're inside the club, Willy abandons me for the girls. She pours herself a drink, grabs Shilpa's hand, and hits the dance floor with Hammer and Rix. Dred was with us for dinner, but she works the early shift at the library and had to bail on club night. It's not really her scene anyway.

Roman puts his hand on my shoulder. "From a publicity perspective, I'm sure Hemi wants to murder you, but I will say, that ring is something else."

"Definitely matches the woman." I sip my whiskey. I may have to come back here in the morning and pick up my ride, but it's not far from the hotel, so I'll manage.

"So will this be a long or short engagement?" Hollis asks.

"Probably long, since I sprang it on her, and she's a bit of a planner." This lie tastes particularly bitter.

"Dude, how am I going to top that?" Tristan gripes.

"Top what?" I ask.

"That proposal. I'm planning to put a ring on Bea's finger before the end of summer. But I don't want her to think I'm only doing it because you did." Tristan crosses his arms, his frown deepening.

"We all know you're devoted to Rix. It's no surprise that you're planning to pop the question," I assure him.

"But you did it first, so now there's an expectation of grandeur," he argues.

Tristan has grown so much as a person over the last ten months. I've known him for a lot of years, and it's inspiring to see him work to be a better version of himself, on the ice and off.

"Rix would be happier with something less public, no?" Hollis adds.

Tristan rubs the back of his neck. "I'm just in my head about it. I want it to be perfect for her."

"What about you?" Ash turns to Hollis. "When are you popping the question?"

"I'd like my daughter to be at least twenty-five before she gets married," Roman says dryly.

"So technically, I can propose when she's twenty-three, and we can have a long engagement." Hollis gives Roman the side-eye. "When are you going to start dating?"

"When I'm retired."

"What if the right woman comes along before then and you let her slip through your fingers because you're too busy focusing on the end of your career?"

"Pretty sure I already found her a few years ago and lost her," he mutters, then turns his attention to Tristan. "You could give Rix a promise ring."

"Isn't that a high school thing?" Tristan asks.

Flip shrugs. "At least you get a ring on her finger, so everybody knows she's is yours."

"This!" Tristan points at Flip. "I need all those university fuckers to know she's off the market." Tristan laughs at how ridiculous he sounds, but I can understand the possessive draw to seeing your ring on that finger. "Jokes aside, mostly it's because I don't want to spend another day of my life without her being my wife."

"Shilps has been talking about babies lately," Ash muses as he rubs his chin.

Everyone's attention turns to him. "Seriously?"

"She's thirty, and I'm thirty-one. I've got a few years left on my contract, but I'd be kind of down with being a stay-at-home dad, if she wants to come back to work. Right now, we're just talking it out and doing a lot of practicing."

"I can't even imagine talking kids with someone right now." Flip drains the rest of his drink. "Then again, I haven't been in a relationship in years, so what do I know?"

Rix appears, downs a bottle of water, then grabs Tristan's hand and pulls him onto the dance floor. Hammer does the same with Hollis.

Ash elbows me. "We should get out there, too."

"I'll hang back. Go have fun." Roman tips his chin toward the action.

We weave our way through the crowd until we reach the girls, leaving Roman at the table. I've done this countless times, but it's different tonight. There's expectation in the air. I wish I'd done a lot of things differently, starting back in senior kindergarten when I pulled her ponytail standing in line, then lied and said it was Mortimer Fig, the quietest kid in our class.

Willy turns to me when I reach her side. Her hair is damp at the temples, her eyes are glassy, and her drink is mostly empty. She wraps my tie around her fist, her expression pensive. "Why do you have to be so pretty?"

"Why do you?"

She throws her head back and laughs. But there's no humor. It's bitter and angry and so many other things. She surprises me by clasping her hands behind my neck. The entire front of her body is pressed against the entire front of mine.

Everything goes haywire as I register her soft curves against me.

"Bet you never thought we'd be doing this, eh?" There's a bite in her tone, but there's sadness, too.

I wish I could erase it. Tell her the truth. I wish she'd believe me, but I know she won't.

She's right, though. I never thought I would be here, with her hands on me, looking so beautiful it hurts. I set one hand on her waist and give in to the urge to touch her face. I shouldn't. It's unfair. I've boxed her into a corner and allowed my truth to be turned into a lie. She believes it's revenge, when really I'd do anything to guard her heart.

I give her a slice of honesty, though I know she won't believe it. "You're the only place I ever want to be, Wilhelmina."

"I'm so mad at you." I can't hear the words, but I watch her perfect lips form each one.

I nod, my own smile wry. "I keep making messes for you, don't I?"

Her eyes slide closed, and she drops her forehead to my chest. I bend to kiss the top of her head. To everyone else this looks like a moment. And it is. But not the one I wanted it to be.

Willy's vulnerability is real in the way she's letting me hold her. Too bad it's because I've made her life a nightmare.

"I'm going to do right by you." I know the music covers my oath.

We close down the bar. By the time I get Wills into a taxi and off to the hotel, she's an absolute mess. I tuck her into my side as I guide her to the elevators, shielding her from prying eyes.

The last thing I want are pictures of a drunk Wills floating around on the internet for assholes to speculate over.

She stumbles through the door and melts into a heap on the floor. Her hazy gaze moves around the room, and her lips push out in a pout. She flails a hand toward the bed. "Look how nice this room is. This is supposed to be for two people who are really in love and want to spend the night boning each other's brains out."

"It is a nice room," I agree. If she wasn't totally wasted and she didn't hate me, I'd love to be boning her brains out. I crouch in front of her and hold out a bottle of water.

She knocks it away and takes my face in her hands. Her gaze drops to my mouth and then lifts to my eyes. Her expression is sad and angry and heated. "I fucking hate you," she whispers.

"I know. I'm sorry." After everything I've done, after what I've put her through, I deserve to feel like my heart has been punted into a swamp full of ravenous alligators. "I'll fix it."

"I really want to believe you this time," her voice cracks with emotion. "None of this is real."

"Some of it is real, honey," I counter.

"I can't stop thinking about kissing you, how pretty you are. And it makes me sick," she declares.

And then she throws up.

CHAPTER 14

HEMI

I t feels like there's a full twelve-piece band, complete with cymbals, playing out of tune in my head. My mouth tastes like ass. My head is throbbing.

I reluctantly crack an eyelid, only half committed to dealing with today. I'm momentarily perplexed by my unfamiliar surroundings. I sift through my brain, which feels like a bowl of congealed oatmeal, and try to figure out what happened last night to make me feel so horrendous.

I roll onto my back, taking stock of my surroundings. I'm in a hotel room. *The honeymoon suite Dallas's mom so sweetly booked for us.* I'd planned to stage some photos and a video walk-through so we'd have evidence of our romantic celebration. But I was not supposed to wake up here.

I glance to my right, and the horrible churning in my gut becomes overwhelming nausea. Lying on his back, head turned toward me, one hand lying palm up between us—almost as if he's looking for a hand to hold—is a very attractive, very passed-out Dallas. The sheet is pushed down to his waist, revealing his muscular, bare chest.

Oh fuck. Did we sleep together?

We better not have had sex. Especially not sex I can't remember. My stomach lurches. I throw off the sheets and roll out of bed, which is a terrible idea. The room spins, and my legs give out. I land on the floor in a heap. My anxiety reaches full-blown panic as I take in my attire. I'm wearing Dallas's T-shirt. And my bra and underpants. But that's all.

The room tilts perilously as I push to my feet and wobble-weave to the bathroom. I slam the door, the noise reverberating in my head. I make it to the toilet in time to unload a stomach of bile. I heave until there's nothing left. A full bottle of water sits on the vanity. With trembling hands I twist off the cap, rinse my mouth, then tentatively take a few sips.

I catch my reflection in the mirror. My mascara is smeared under my bloodshot eyes, my hair is a complete wreck, and my skin is pale and blotchy. I look rough. And based on my lack of memory, I'm guessing I was shitfaced.

A tube of toothpaste and an unopened toothbrush sit on the counter, with a second used one beside it. I remove the fresh one from the package, squirt a little toothpaste onto the brush, and scrub away the gross fuzz and horrible taste in my mouth. I brush far longer than necessary, mostly to avoid dealing with the man on the other side of the door.

Even the taste of toothpaste makes me want to throw up again, but I take a few deep breaths and steel myself as I open the door.

Dallas is sitting on the edge of the bed, wearing his navy and pale blue plaid dress pants, elbows resting on his knees, hands clasped. His head lifts, and his guilty expression makes my stomach lurch again. "Are you okay?"

I tug at the hem of his shirt. "How did I get into this T-shirt?" The black hole where the answer should be scares the hell out of me. Whenever we're out, I limit myself to one drink, two at the very most, and only on the rarest of occasions. Who knows what I could've said to Dallas last night. To anyone, for that matter.

He pushes to his feet and shoves one of his hands into his luxurious wavy hair, causing his biceps to flex and his abs to ripple. Despite how disgusting I feel, I appreciate how frustratingly attractive this man is. To this day he's still the embodiment of a prom king.

"Seriously, Dallas. I'm freaking out here."

He moves into my personal space. "I would never touch you without your permission, Wilhelmina. And last night, you were in no condition to give it." He holds out his hand. "Now, please sit down so I can explain without worrying about you passing out."

I let him guide me to a chair. He passes me a bottle of water and sits on the arm of the couch. "When we got back here, you weren't in the best form."

I cross my arms and try to keep my mortification from showing on my face. I can count on one hand the number of times I've been throw-up drunk in my entire life. I do not like to lose control. "That does not explain how I got into this shirt." My voice wavers with fresh anxiety. *What did I do last night? Did I throw myself at Dallas while I was drunk?*

Dallas's gaze lifts to the ceiling before dropping to meet mine again. "You threw up. Some of it got on your clothes. Which understandably made you upset. Then you took your dress off."

"I got naked in front of you?" My voice is dog-whistle pitched.

"Not naked. I stopped you before you got further than your dress. You were not in any shape to know what you were doing, so I walked you to the bathroom and cleaned you up as best I could, then took my shirt off and gave it to you." He runs his tongue over his eye-tooth but doesn't look away. "But in the interest of full transparency, your coordination was not great. You were having trouble getting into my shirt, so I had to help you with my eyes closed."

I cover my mouth with my palm. "Oh my God." The only time I've been more humiliated was senior year and yesterday when I got engaged. Ironically, those horrible situations also involved Dallas.

He rubs his bottom lip, expression full of empathy and regret. I want to believe it's real.

"I understand that I'm probably the last person you would want to take care of you. But I couldn't leave you alone last night. All I did was clean you up, help you get into my shirt, and put you to bed. I had your dress sent out to dry cleaning once you were settled."

"That's all that happened?" I croak.

He wets his bottom lip. "Yes. Mostly."

"Mostly?" I narrow my eyes.

"I was worried about you rolling onto your back in the middle of the night."

When he doesn't continue right away, I make a go-on motion. "Spit it out, Dallas."

"You kept trying to roll onto your back. Even when I put pillows behind you, you pushed them out of the way, so eventually I just spooned you."

"You spooned me?" I parrot.

"Yeah. I did what was necessary to keep you safe, and I won't apologize for that." He crosses his arms.

All that does is highlight his incredible muscles and defined pecs, which again, is a really fucking annoying thing to notice. Especially knowing he held me all night so he could protect me from myself.

"In the spirit of honesty, you move around a lot, and all that friction paired with the worry may have caused some... swelling."

I blink at him, and he blinks back at me. "You spooned me with a hard-on?"

He clears his throat. "I did my best to limit contact, but I had to stay close to keep you on your side."

There's a knock at the door.

"That's room service with breakfast." He hustles over.

I stand there, mulling over his words. It doesn't sound like Dallas got much sleep last night. He is absolutely correct; I'm a back sleeper. So the quest he was on would've been challenging, and rather ironic, all things considered.

A moment later he reappears, pushing a rolling cart with three silver-dome-covered platters on it. A bag from one of my favorite clothing stores dangles from his wrist.

"I called the office to inform them that you'd be in a little later this morning. Hammer said you didn't have any pressing appointments until the afternoon, so I let you sleep in. Dry cleaning will be up soon with your dress, but I ordered outfit options so you had something to wear to work. If you want to have a shower, I had your preferred brand of shampoo and body wash brought up. It's all in the bathroom, but maybe some food first will settle your stomach." He taps one of the dome lids.

I don't know how to handle take-charge Dallas, but food isn't a bad idea. I can't even imagine how much I must've drunk last night to feel this awful. I remember almost nothing after arriving at the bar. I have only the faintest inkling that I danced with Dallas.

I cross the room, uncaring that most of my legs are on display since Dallas has already seen me in my bra and undies. It's not much different than a bikini. I take a seat at the very beautiful dining table, complete with a vase of roses.

Dallas rolls the cart over and sets a plate and silverware in front of me. He even spreads a napkin over my lap before he transfers the covered platters to the table. He lifts the lids one at a time, revealing the contents. One platter contains a variety of seasonal fresh fruit and an assortment of muffins and pastries. The second contains strip bacon, eggs, peameal bacon, sausage links, and hash browns. The third holds French toast, pancakes, filled crêpes, and an assortment of toppings, including flambéed bananas and peaches.

Dallas runs his hands over his thighs again. It's a nervous habit. He does it a lot. Especially when we are at a promo op that makes him uncomfortable. "I didn't know what you'd feel like, so I got a little of everything."

"Thank you." He's being exceptionally considerate.

"I should've kept a better eye on you last night and traded a couple of those glasses of champagne for water." He fills my coffee cup, then passes me the cream and sugar.

"I wouldn't have listened if you'd told me to slow down."

"But you would've listened to the girls if I'd said something. I'll be right back." He leaves me to load up a plate and returns a minute later with a fresh water and a bottle of painkillers. "For your headache."

"Thanks." I pop two painkillers, down them with water, and start with buttered toast. It seems wasteful and unfortunate that there's all this beautiful food and all I have an appetite for is toast, but I don't want to end up back in the bathroom for the wrong reason.

Dallas takes the chair across from me and pours himself a coffee, then digs into the pancakes.

While he drenches them in maple syrup, I study his face. He has dark circles around his eyes. I can't believe he was up half the night making sure I had clothes for today and my work schedule was taken care of. Not to mention keeping me from choking to death in my sleep.

I don't know how to feel about being taken care of by him. He owes me for the cluster he's created, but this is different. He was legitimately worried. Everything he's done tells me that. I still hate him, and I hate being stuck in this situation, but he's also...really fucking thoughtful. It's conflicting. As is the memory of the kisses we shared yesterday. They were most definitely the catalyst for all of my bad decision-making around champagne.

My brain is functioning at about ten-percent capacity, and my tongue is probably barbed this morning, but still I state the obvious. There's no getting around it. "People are going to get hurt when this charade ends."

"I know. I'm sorry."

"Your mom was so happy last night, Dallas." She was beaming. And I like her. A lot. She's sweet, and kind and exactly the kind of woman I would want as my mother-in-law. If this were real.

"Yeah. She was."

"I'm wearing your grandmother's engagement ring." It's stunning. And it shouldn't be mine.

"I promise I'll fix this, Wills. I won't make this your cross to bear," he says softly. It's very clear that even though he continues to complicate my life with these media stunts, Dallas feels real remorse over how this has all played out.

"I'm not sure that's possible." Being his girlfriend was bad enough, but being his fiancée...

I push my plate away and stand. All I managed was two pieces of toast, a couple bites of egg, and one piece of bacon—but my appetite has disappeared. I leave Dallas looking forlorn and hop into the shower, wash off last night's sins, and get ready for work.

I'm incredibly surprised—though maybe shouldn't be—that the outfits Dallas had sent over for me are exactly my size. Option one is a pair of high-waisted, black dress pants, a pale blue chiffon blouse, and a white blazer. Option two is a teal dress with pockets. The fabric is soft, the cut is flattering, and it's the obvious winner. He even bought me a pair of shoes, with a kitten heel, as well as fresh underwear. They're nude, and seamless full coverage, but there are thong, bikini brief, and boy short options. Apparently, he wanted to cover all the bases for my booty.

By the time I'm ready, I feel less like garbage and slightly more human. "There wasn't a receipt in the bag, so let me know what I owe you for these and I'll e-transfer you the funds." He must've asked Shilpa about my sizes.

Dallas is still shirtless. This is funny, since he went out of his way to make sure I was fully dressed but didn't bother to get himself an extra T-shirt. Now he has to wear the one I slept in. He tucks one hand into the pocket of his dress pants as his gaze moves over me. If I didn't know better, I'd say it was an appreciative sweep.

"It's my fault you ended up in the state you did. The outfit is on me."

I narrow my eyes. "Does it come with any strings attached?"

"The string is that you're my fiancée for the next little while, Wilhelmina." He moves in closer, eyes on mine. "As your significant other, who makes several million dollars a year, I will buy you things, including clothes. It's my job to pay attention to you and your needs, and I failed at that last night."

I'm too tired and my brain hurts too much to remind him that I'm his fake fiancée, so those rules don't apply.

"I would like to drive you to work," he states.

I could deny him and take an Uber, but I'm not in the mood to be nice to someone I know, let alone to someone I don't know. "Okay, that would be good."

"Great. Good. Let me box up the food. The fruit and muffins you can take to work."

"What about the rest of it? Seems like a waste."

"There are a couple of guys down the street from the hotel who are unhoused. They might like the waffles and stuff."

I love that he has a plan in mind. Having worked with Flip the past couple of years, and having spent a lot of time with Rix, I'm aware that they often didn't have enough growing up. When Flip isn't helping Tristan coach kids with special needs or trying to keep his endorsement campaigns from being cancelled, he's all about giving back to the community. He donates to school programs and foodbanks.

I gather my personal effects, which consist of last night's panties, the dry-cleaning bag containing my dress, and a tiny clutch purse with my lipstick and phone. Dallas carries the extra clothes and takeout containers.

We leave the beautiful room that did not get the appreciation it should have and make our way to the lobby. As promised, Dallas gives two unhoused men our takeout boxes. The valet brings his car around—which means he somehow orchestrated getting it back here—and he drives me to the office.

When we arrive at work, I pause with my hand on the door handle. "Thanks for taking care of me last night."

"I'd do it a million times over, Wills. I'm sorry I stressed you out to the point that you drank too much."

"I'm responsible for my own actions, Dallas. At least Brooklyn and Sean's engagement isn't the biggest deal at the reunion anymore, right?" It seems so petty to even care.

"There's that." Dallas gives me a small smile. "I hope today doesn't suck too badly for you."

"Me too."

He looks like he wants to say something else, but I get out of the vehicle before he can make me dislike him any less.

CHAPTER 15
HEMI

I scroll through the email chain as I take the elevator to my office, my irritation level climbing by the second.

Subject: Arena Availability

Hi Topher,
Checking in on rink availability for the boys' team. We discussed dates, but you mentioned there might be some conflicts. Should I contact PR on this?
Best,
Bob Royer

Subject: Arena Availability

Hi Bob,
I'll check in with Wilhelmina and get back to you.
Best,
Topher Guy

Subject: Arena Availability Circling Back

Hi Topher,
Checking on an update.
Best,
Bob Royer

Subject: Arena Availability Circling Back

Hi Bob,
I'm pulling Wilhelmina into the conversation.
Best,
Topher Guy

Subject: Arena Availability Circling Back

Hi Bob,
Please see the calendar for rink availability. I'm linking it directly
for your convenience.
Based on the previous thread, it looks like there's a conflict with
your requested times and the women's team. Are your practice
times flexible? Otherwise, we can schedule you on rink B or C if
times and dates are firm. Just let me know and Topher or I can
provide you with an access code to book your own times.
Best,
Hemi

Subject: Arena Availability Circling Back

Wilhelmina,
Re-adding you back into the thread.
Topher

None of this surprises me, but it does frustrate me.

Topher responded to Bob only that we could see about over-riding the calendar and switching the women's ice time to a different rink so the boys' team could get in time on the main rink. That email was sent two days ago, and since then they've had a back and forth of six emails that didn't include me, with Topher insisting they could change the rink and Bob saying it wasn't a problem.

I take a deep, calming breath as I step out of the elevator. Instead of going to my office, I head for Topher's. I try to avoid face-to-face interactions with him, mostly because it's hard not to want to punch him in his asshole face. But this can't be helped. I knock on his office doorframe, and his eyes lift along with one finger. He continues to do whatever he was doing for an irra-tionally long time while I stand there. Waiting.

Finally, he gives me his attention. "I know what you're going to say."

"Please. Enlighten me with your mind-reading capabilities, Topher." I cross my arms and rest my shoulder against the doorjamb.

He leans back in his chair, sighs, and waves a hand in my direction. "This right here is your problem, Hemi. You're always..." He makes a face. "Aggressive."

"If I had a Y chromosome to go with my X, the appropriate descriptor would be *direct*. The women's team has been booked on that rink, on that day, for weeks. It's an experience the boys' team gets frequently and one that's new for the women's team. I understand that it's a change and sometimes that takes time to get used to, but dropping me from an email thread and under-mining me and the women's team does not help create an equi-table and inclusive environment, which is what the Terror strives for. I know you've been here a lot longer than me, and that I'm still green in your eyes, but I would appreciate it if you wouldn't undo all the strides we're making because you're used to doing things a different way."

"I've already switched the women's team to the other rink," Topher says.

"Are you planning to let Denise know about the change, or are you leaving that up to me?"

He folds his hands and smiles. "Up to you, Wilhelmina. Whatever you think is best."

"CC me on the email, please." He needs to clean up his own mess. I leave before I do or say something that will end up making this situation worse.

Dealing with Topher has become more difficult since the whole Dallas-and-me situation came to light. He didn't love me before I supposedly got involved with a player, and judging by his current attitude, this new development makes him like me less.

When I arrive at my office, I notice the crocheted peach sitting on my desk has multiplied, so now there are two nestled between my mug of pens and a family photo. I pick up the new one and flip it over in my hand. It's adorable with its little smile and brown eyes. Freaking Dallas and his sweetness. When the heck did he stop by and leave this here? I set it back where I found it and turn them both around so I'm looking at their bums and not their smiling faces.

I call the coach of the women's hockey team after Topher sends an email. Denise was more than understanding about the whole thing, even though she's pissed. Her pro team just got displaced for teenaged boys.

An hour into my day, I get a phone call I expected, but had also hoped to avoid. Possibly forever. I swallow the ball of anxiety sitting in my throat and answer on the third ring.

"Why am I seeing your engagement in the news before I'm hearing it from you?" Mom asks.

They hate any important news over text, but I should have escaped to video call them. I was just in so much shock. Now I'm being a terrible daughter all over again. Lying to them feels horrible.

"I'm so sorry, Mumma." I use the term intentionally because it always softens her up. "It wasn't planned. I didn't plan it. Dallas just did it, and I wasn't expecting it, and his parents were here, and it all happened so fast—"

"His parents were there to witness you getting engaged, and we were not."

The hurt in her tone makes me feel like a steaming pile of garbage. "Mom, you were on shift, and Ma was traveling back from that big vendor show in the States yesterday. Remember I invited you to the game, but you couldn't make it work? I know you would have attended if you could," I hastily tack on, so as not to make it seem like her fault. "And like I said, I didn't know it was going to happen. Dallas is a little impetuous."

She makes a displeased sound. "You just agreed to marry this man, and we haven't even met him."

Fuck me. "You've met him plenty of times. We went to school together from kindergarten to grade twelve."

"We knew him when he was a boy. That was a decade ago." She sighs. "It feels like we're missing all these important milestones. We just found out you were dating him, and now you're engaged. It's like you're living this life we know nothing about. I'm not used to being in the dark when it comes to you."

"I swear it's not intentional, Mom. It's a complicated relationship." The guilt really sucks.

She hmms. "Your ma and I, and your brothers, are coming to visit you this weekend."

"Wait. What? Doesn't Isaac have some big thing happening in New York? And how did Sam get a weekend off?"

"Isaac is CEO of his own company. He can take any weekend off he wants. And Sam is already off this weekend, so it works out perfectly. Your brothers were planning a hike, so now they're adjusting the location since Niagara has the Bruce Trail. We'll arrive early Friday evening. I'll bring everything we need for family dinner; you don't have to worry. But we are coming to see you. We want to get to know Dallas."

"Isaac and his older brother were in the same freaking grade."

"That's different. Besides, Sam didn't go to school with Dallas, and you were just kids back then. They only know *of* him —and, of course, what he looks like on the ice. They want to meet your future husband. And we would like to celebrate this engagement since we weren't able to be there last night."

"Right. Yes. Of course, Mom." Once she has her mind made up, there's no getting out of it.

"Great. It's settled. We'll see you Friday. Congratulations, sweetheart! I'm sure you're very excited. You can fill us in on everything this weekend!"

"So looking forward to it," I lie. Seems like my acting skills are getting a constant work out these days.

Mom ends the call, and the headache I'd finally gotten rid of comes back. Dallas is definitely going to regret this proposal. My brothers will make sure of that.

Two nights later, I've recovered enough from my epic hangover to spend time with the Badass Babe Brigade. Frankly, I need some girl time. My brothers have been messaging relentlessly since they found out about the engagement. At one point they started fighting about who gets to give me away. Which is sweet, but also, I'm not actually getting married.

"Thank you for hosting, Hammer." My roommate is home for the next two days, and the walls are thin. She doesn't need to hear about my relationship drama. I'm grateful she knows nothing about sports and has nothing to do with any part of my work life. Mostly we just say hi to each other in the kitchen, make small talk, and do our own thing. As far as quiet room-mates go, she wins first prize.

"It's no problem. It forces Hollis to spend time with the guys. And my dad."

"They seem good though, right?" Shilpa asks.

"Oh yeah. They're back to themselves again. And my dad has learned not to use his key anymore, so all is right in the world. But Hollis has a small social circle, and it's the offseason, so this means he has to find something to do that isn't me related. Also, it gives me a reason to use this place until the sublet is up."

Hollis and Hammer have only been openly dating for a few months, and the person who owns the unit she's subletting will be back in November.

"How many nights a week do you spend at his place?"

"Most. He would have me move in with him tomorrow if I said I was ready."

"But you're not?" Tally asks.

"Oh, I'm ready. We're trying to give my dad enough time to *also* be ready."

"I love that you take his feelings into account," Rix says.

"It's an adjustment." Hammer smiles and rubs her bottom lip. I can only guess what that's about. "Speaking of adjustments, how excited are you to move into university residence next month?" she asks Tally.

"Excited. Nervous." Tally flutters her legs. "Those top the list. I'm looking forward to an on-campus living experience for my first year. I know I could commute, but with so much rehearsal time on campus, it makes more sense for me to live there." We helped her set up a PowerPoint presentation for her parents to argue her on-campus-living case. "The apartment-style residence should be good. There will either be four or six of us, and we all have our own bedrooms and bathrooms, but we'll share a common kitchen and living room. The rooms are small, but at least there's freedom. And Rix will be on campus sometimes too, so that's cool."

"Once we get our schedules, we can organize lunch dates," Rix offers.

"How do you feel about going back to school?" Shilpa asks.

"Good. Nervous and excited, just like Tally. But this is my passion, so going back now makes sense. I can't wait to focus on nutritional facts instead of taxes. And Tristan is so excited for me, so that helps."

"He's really proud of you," Dred says.

"It's not the easiest adjustment to have a partner who can take care of me the way he can. He's suggested I quit my job at the firm, but they offered me part-time remote, so we'll see how it goes."

"In case you don't like the program?" Tally asks.

"It's more my personal feelings about not contributing financially, having to rely on somebody else to take care of my financial needs. I'm working on it in therapy. It's my own issue, and it doesn't have anything to do with Tristan or how much he loves me. I know he supports me, and will support me in whatever way I need him to. But I still need my autonomy. And he understands that, too."

"I love the way he loves you," I say.

"Me too. It's hard to believe he's the same guy who flew to Vancouver and turned around and got right back on the plane because he couldn't deal with his fears," Rix muses.

"He's come a long way." I agree. A year ago, Tristan was surly and could be a PR problem. But then Rix came along and turned his world upside down. Now he's so in love with her and committed to being the best version of himself he can for both of them. He's relentless once he decides he wants something. I see it every time he looks at her, like she's the beginning and the end for him. What I wouldn't give to have someone love me like that —who isn't a direct relative.

"How's Essie, by the way? Any word on when she's moving back?" Hammer asks. "Or at least coming for a visit?"

"Yes! Her company offered her a contract in Toronto and she could be back by the end of summer or early fall at the latest. I'm so excited that she's moving home. At least for a bit," Rix says.

"That's awesome. Our little group keeps growing!" Tally says.

"And pairing up! I know Dallas's actions lately have been pretty outlandish, and maybe not the easiest for the woman who prefers things to go smoothly, but he is clearly devoted to you." Hammer arches a brow. "I mean, the way he proposed..." Her hand goes to her heart. "That's the grand gesture to end all grand gestures. On the ice, in a place you both love so much, after you raised a ton of money for charity—so thoughtful."

"Yeah." I force a smile. "It's definitely hard to top."

"That post he made this afternoon was swoon city," Rix says.

"What post?" I can't deal with another media stunt. I've been avoiding his social media on purpose. Just because I know the crappy comments exist, doesn't mean I want to experience the firsthand.

"You haven't seen it, yet?" Hammer's eyes are wide.

Maybe I'll be better off keeping my head in the sand. "Will I have to run interference?"

"You shouldn't. Especially not after this." Hammer hands me her phone.

It's a photo of the on-ice proposal and it's captioned:

The Best Day of My Life and it's followed by a very sappy post:

Isn't she stunning?
I've been waiting a decade for this, and while I'm happy to shout my love for Wilhelmina from the rooftops, my bride to be tends be more lowkey. While our engagement was very public (that's on me), our relationship is ours. I've waited far too long to get the girl to mess it up with more public shenanigans. (I swear, Hemi, the proposal is the last shenanigan). We appreciate your respect for our privacy.

It's an incredibly thoughtful post. But I have no idea what the impetus is. Other than trying to get out of retribution promo. And the worst part is that everybody believes Dallas is in love with me. Even Hammer and Dred who were skeptical at first. Because he's an incredible performer.

It makes my heart hurt. I would give anything to find a guy who would do what Dallas has, including this sweet freaking privacy post, but actually mean it.

CHAPTER 16

DALLAS

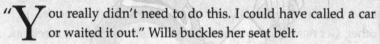

"**Y**ou really didn't need to do this. I could have called a car or waited it out." Wills buckles her seat belt.

It started raining half an hour ago, so I decided to pick her up from work. My timing was perfect, seeing as it's turned into a torrential downpour. "I don't mind." Besides, it gives me time to prepare for dinner with her family tomorrow night.

She checks her phone and sighs before shoving it back in her purse.

"Everything okay?"

"Yeah. No. Just my family inundating me with messages about this weekend. My moms were pissed about missing the proposal. Then there's been some shit with the rink schedules." Her head falls back, and she sighs. "I could really use some stress relief, but now that we're a thing, that isn't going to happen. It's making me salty."

"Why can't you get stress relief? Just schedule a massage. Or I can give you one." That's a brilliant fucking idea. I would love to get my hands on Wills.

She gives me a look. "I'm not looking for a massage, Dallas."

"What are you looking for, Wills?" I glance at her as I wait my turn at the stop sign.

She arches a brow.

I arch one back.

She sighs. "I have a friend."

"A friend? What kind of friend?"

Her expression tells me everything I need to know.

Jealousy makes my spine hot. "Like a fuck buddy?"

"Do not be judgmental. Women are allowed to have casual sex just like men."

"I'm not—you're not fucking him now, are you?" The steering wheel groans under my grip. I would like to lay out any person who ever touched her before me, but that's irrational and ridiculous.

"No. Of course not. We're engaged." She makes air quotes around the word *engaged*. "But typically when I'm feeling... exceptionally stressed, I'll reach out. If he's in town, we see each other. Get naked, get off, and get out. It's no strings, no feelings, all chemistry."

"No feelings at all?" This mystifies me. All my feelings are tied up in this siren of a woman.

"None. We're not relationship compatible. I want a long-term partner, and he doesn't. But he's hot, and he's good in bed."

I point to myself. "I'm hot and good in bed." What I would do for her if she gave me the chance. She would never need her hookup buddy again once I got on my knees for her.

"Seriously, Dallas, your ego needs a break." She crosses and uncrosses her legs.

I stop at the light. Traffic is stupid because of the rain. Normally the drive to her place takes five minutes, but we're crawling today. "I'm your fiancé. If you have needs, I will meet them."

"Oh my God, just stop." She crosses her arms. "We're not actually together."

"I'm serious, Wills. You need to get off, I will make that happen for you. However you want it to happen. You want me to finger fuck you to orgasm? My hands are yours. Wanna sit on my face? My tongue is ready. You want to ride my cock? I'm already hard." I point at my crotch.

She shakes her head. "You've lost your mind. I'm not going to have sex with you."

I make a right into her parking garage.

"What are you doing?"

"Parking." I pull into a visitor spot. "I got you into this mess. You can't see this fuck-buddy guy." Who I want to destroy for having her in ways I never will. Unless she takes me up on my offer. "Use me."

Her eyes move over me in a way that jacks me right up. I shift and stretch my arm across the back of her seat. "Please." I wet my bottom lip. "Let me be the one to make it better."

"You're actually serious," she murmurs.

"A thousand percent."

Her eyes roll up to the ceiling and she mutters, "I can't believe I'm entertaining this."

"Is that a yes? Can I get you off right now?" I slide my hand into her hair.

She bats it away. "Not here. There are cameras in the parking garage."

"Your roommate is on afternoons this week. We can go up to your apartment." I unbuckle my seat belt and hop out of the car, rearranging my hard-on as I round the trunk and open Willy's door.

"Why do you know my roommate's work schedule, Dallas?"

I shrug. "I just remember that shit." And I keep track of when she's home alone at night.

I grab her hand and tug her toward the elevator. We're not alone on the way up, so I behave myself. But the second we're inside her apartment, I take her face in my hands.

She covers my mouth with her palm. "We need to set some ground rules."

I back off. "Right. Lay them on me."

"No kissing."

I frown. "Why no kissing?" I must think about the two kisses we've shared at least a hundred times a day.

"Because I said no kissing. This is only about orgasms."

"Okay." I'll give up kissing for orgasms. For now. "What else?"

"Uh…" She runs her hand through her hair. "When I'm done you have to leave."

"Got it. Orgasms, then out. Anything else?"

Her tongue sweeps across her bottom lip. "I think that's it. For now."

"Cool." I step forward, and she steps back, bumping into the kitchen island. She grips the edge of the counter as I move into her personal space. "I can make you come now?"

It's all I want. I never thought I'd have the opportunity to propose getting her off, let alone be the one to touch her. I've dreamed of her pussy since I was fifteen. I have to concentrate to keep my hands from shaking.

"You can try."

I stroke her cheek, one corner of my mouth tipping up as I work a knee between her thighs. "Oh honey, I'm going to do a hell of a lot more than try. I'll have you screaming my name before we're done." I drop my head and kiss the edge of her jaw.

"No kissing."

"I'm not even close to your lips. I need to get you worked up first." I push her hair over her shoulders and ghost my lips along the column of her throat.

"I'm already worked up," she mutters.

"Should I find out if that's true?" I trail my fingers over her collarbones and cup her breasts, thumbs brushing over her nipples through layers of fabric. No one has better tits than Wills. So damn perfect.

"If you want to make this better for me, you should take your shirt off." She slides her hand under my T-shirt and runs her nails up my chest.

I reluctantly stop kissing her neck and lose my shirt, tossing it on the island. "Better?"

She sighs as her eyes move over me. "Fuck, you're pretty."

"And you're stunning. I can't wait to get my hands all over you." I grab her by the waist and lift her onto the counter. "Make you come all over my fingers." She looks incredible in her dress today. Professional, but so damn sexy. I slide my hands up her strong thighs, pushing them apart. I want to get her naked and worship every inch of her, but a bigger part of me wants all the things I missed out on with her in high school—like third base fully clothed. I resume kissing her neck, fingers gliding along the edge of her panties. They're satin and lace. Probably pretty and sexy. "I'm going to make you feel so good, Wills."

"Stop talking and start doing." She shimmies out of her panties and drops them on the floor, then grabs my hand and guides it between her thighs.

"So fucking bossy." I bite the edge of her jaw. "I love it."

I brush my fingers over her sex and slip one between her folds, skimming her swollen clit. "So wet." I slide my other hand into her hair and curl my fingers. Then I lean back, lips hovering an inch away from her mouth as I ease a single finger inside her. "So soft. So perfect."

Her eyes flutter shut on a sigh.

I withdraw my finger and circle her clit as I tug her hair. "Open your eyes, honey. I want them on me when I'm making you come."

"Less talking, more finger-fucking, Dallas."

"You mean like this?" I slide two fingers inside her and pump.

"Oh God." She grips my wrist. "More of that."

I curl again as she moves the fabric of her skirt out of the way. Her gaze drops to where my fingers disappear inside her.

"Such a pretty little pussy. You look so fucking good stretched around my fingers."

"The shit that comes out of your mouth." Her eyes roll up as I curl my fingers again.

"I bet you taste like honey, honey. Next time I'm going to fuck this sweet, tight pussy with my tongue."

She gives me a look that doesn't quite land since she also moans and rolls her hips. "Oh my God, stop running your mouth."

I shake my head. "I can't. You feel too good. So soft, and hot, and wet. I'm going to make this pussy weep for me." My fingers make a liquid sound on the next curl. "I love that sound."

"Seriously, Dallas." Her legs are shaking and she tightens around my fingers. "Your mouth is a problem."

"I think you like my dirty mouth more than you want to admit. But if you really want me to shut up, you have two options. You can let me taste this pretty pussy, or you can let me kiss your smart mouth." I add a third finger. "The choice is yours, honey."

She grabs the back of my neck, nails biting into my skin. "Oh God, that's it."

"Am I hitting the spot? You gonna let me see you fall apart?" I smirk at her annoyed expression. "I want my name on your lips when you're creaming all over my hand."

"Fuck it." She tugs on the back of my neck.

I let her pull me forward until my lips almost touch hers. "You breaking your own rules?"

She growls. I slant my mouth over hers. She parts for me on the softest mewl. Her hips roll as my tongue pushes past her lips. I kiss her to the same rhythm as my fingers moving inside her. She's perfect. She's everything I've ever wanted, and right now she's mine. Her pussy contracts around my fingers. I break the kiss so I can watch her unravel.

"So damn gorgeous, coming all over my fingers like a goddess."

She quakes and shudders, eyes fluttering, nails biting into my skin as my name tumbles from her parted lips. She's glorious, and now I'll have this memory—skin flushed, surrounded by the scent of her, and the knowledge that I did this, I made her feel this way, made her moan my name, made her come, gave her what she needs.

She sags and softens, chest heaving. I wait until she opens her eyes before I withdraw my fingers, and I hold her gaze as I suck them clean. "So fucking good." I groan.

Wills gapes at me. "Good God, Dallas, you're depraved."

"Next time, you're sitting on my face." I kiss her cheek. "I'll see myself out. See you tomorrow night." I wink, adjust my hard-on, and leave her in the kitchen, looking sated—and like she's not opposed to the idea of my return.

CHAPTER 17

DALLAS

"I 'll take these. Can I also have them gift wrapped, please?"

"Absolutely, sir." The woman behind the counter gives me a megawatt smile and retrieves her wrapping supplies.

I've been on the hunt for perfect gifts for my fiancée's moms since nine this morning. I've been to no less than twenty stores. Before I stopped here as a last-ditch effort, I stumbled into a café/bookstore to grab some caffeine and scarf down a couple of fudge oat bars. I also managed to find what seemed to be the perfect gift for her mom who is a general practitioner. And now I've finally found something I think will be perfect for mom number two.

I pull out my phone, surreptitiously checking the time. *Fuck.* It's already four. How have I been at this for seven hours? Willy specifically said that I needed to be at her place by 4:30. She hates it when I'm late.

The woman behind the counter—whose name is LouLou, according to her name tag—appears to be performing delicate heart surgery, not wrapping pretty jewelry. While I appreciate her attention to detail, I'm already behind. Every extra minute increases Wills's wrath exponentially. Most days I'm more than happy to take a tongue lashing from her. Before I became her fiancé, I loved it when she laid into me. Her ire was better than nothing. But now I want more of what happened last night. I want her to need me, to rely on me, to trust me to take care of her. It's a shift in my perspective—hence the gifts for her moms and not wanting to be late.

Seven years later, LouLou is finally finished wrapping the gift. She takes another half decade to put it in a bag and curl the matching ribbon. I thank her and rush three blocks to my car.

I message Wills to let her know I'm stuck in traffic, but I'll be there soon.

She sends a thumbs-up.

Which is as good as a middle finger. I'm so screwed. My anxiety rears its ugly head in the form of a stupid boner.

I park in the lot across the street from her building. I give my hard-on a rueful glare. "Dude, I took care of you three times this morning." And twice last night after I got home from servicing my fiancée's needs. I used my left hand and sniffed the fingers that had been inside her like the fucked up, obsessed man I am.

It takes three minutes for my dick to deflate. I hurry across the street to Willy's building, managing to catch the door as someone else is leaving.

I hop into the elevator and run my damp hand over my thighs.

Everything will be fine. I will not die tonight.

The doors slide open, and I walk down the hall, the memories of last night are still fresh. I lock those down, because they're not helpful or appropriate for meet-the-family night.

I take a deep breath and knock on the door. Three seconds later, it swings open. An anxiety boner inspired by an angry Wills would be preferable to what greets me on the other side.

At six foot four and two-hundred-and-thirty pounds, there is nothing small about me. But for some reason, Willy's brothers look like lethal fucking giants, standing side by side in the doorway.

Neither of them smiles. "Hey! You must be Wilhelmina's

brothers, Samir and Isaac, right? I'm Dallas, her fiancé." I extend a hand and pray it doesn't get broken.

Her oldest brother takes my hand first. The shake is firm, but not life-threatening. "You can call me Sam. This is my baby brother, Isaac."

"He calls me his baby brother because I make more money than him and his ego can't handle it." Isaac elbows Sam out of the way and takes my hand in a mildly bone-crushing grip.

My smile does not waver. "It's great to meet both of you. Wilhelmina talks about you all the time."

"Probably about how we annoy the hell out of her," Sam says with a grin.

"Or how loud we are. She took up debate in third grade so she could win arguments."

Suddenly, so much about Wills makes sense. "That sounds like Wills. I'm sorry I'm late."

Sam gives me an inquisitive look as he steps aside. "You're early, not late."

"Right. Yeah." I nod a couple of times.

Isaac smirks. "Let me guess, Hemi told you to be here at four thirty to ensure you'd make it by five."

I rub the back of my neck. "She might've done that." I'm already lying about enough stuff, and these two look like they're good at sniffing out bullshitters.

As soon as I round the corner, I'm engulfed by two women. Apparently, Willy's moms are huggers. Sandhya—who goes by Sandy—is a petite thing, at least a head shorter than her daughter. She's dressed in jeans and a T-shirt with waist-length dark hair pulled back in a complicated braid. I briefly wonder if her wife does it for her, and if Wills would let me braid her hair. I learned how to do it for my great-grandma Bippy after she developed arthritis in her hands. Her other mom, Georgie, is tall and willowy. She wears white linen pants and a flowy tank top. Everything about her screams poise and elegance. They're an interesting couple, and I love them already.

"Dallas! My goodness! The last time I saw you in person you were a teenager. You have definitely filled out!" Sandy smiles up at me and pats my chest. "Oh wow. You're solid."

"I spend a lot of time in the gym and on the ice."

"That is absolutely true, isn't it?" She laughs, and Georgie joins in.

"It's amazing what a few years of professional hockey will do." Georgie squeezes my biceps.

"Yeah, I'm pretty dedicated to the sport."

"We watch all the time," Georgie's voice pitches up dramatically.

Sam snorts a laugh. "You mean you watch the thirty second highlight reel on the news.

"That's not true!" Georgie's voice is so reedy she sounds like she's channeling a dog whistle.

Isaac smirks. "You're literally the worst liar in the world, Mom."

A minute later, Wills appears. Her lips curve into a smile, and she smooths her hands over her hips. She's wearing jeans that hug her curves and a Terror shirt. "You're early!"

"I couldn't wait to get here." I move toward her, wrapping my arm around her waist, remembering just how good it felt last night to finally touch her in ways I've fantasized about for years. I can't help myself; I drop my head to her ear and breathe in her shampoo. "Thanks for making sure I got here on time."

She smiles wryly. "I know what you're like."

Her gaze shifts to my mouth, and then jumps back to my eyes, like she's remembering last night, too. I quirk a brow, silently asking permission. Her tongue sweeps out to wet her bottom lip. It's all the encouragement I need.

I brush my lips over hers. It lasts maybe a second, but I feel that brief connection everywhere in my body—including very inconvenient parts that would like this kiss to escalate. I pull back, mostly so the hard-on I've been battling doesn't resurge in front of her family.

Post introductions, Willy pours us all drinks, and we move to the living room where artfully displayed appetizers sit on the coffee table. A cheese platter, various cured meats, some fruit, and a bowl of chakri are waiting for us.

Her brothers load up their plates, which are the size of my palm, and take a seat next to each other on one of the couches. Willy's moms take the love seat, leaving the barrel chair for Wills and me. If we were two average-sized people, the barrel chair would be fine, but I'm tall and broad. I take up seventy-five percent of the chair on my own, which means Willy either has to perch on the edge or sling her legs over mine. I pass the gifts to her moms and help make the decision for her by tucking my arm under her legs and arranging them so they hang over my left thigh. She hooks her feet around my right calf. I'm in fucking heaven.

"You didn't need to get us anything," Sandy says as she pulls the ribbon free from the small gift bag.

"I was out running errands, and I stumbled across them," I lie smoothly. No one needs to know I spent seven hours shopping and was almost late as a result.

Willy gives me a sidelong glance, but I just smile and rub her hair between my fingers, so I don't give in to the urge to stroke the side of her neck.

Sandy opens hers first, carefully unwrapping the small box. She lifts the lid and her eyes flare. "Oh my goodness! Oh wow. This is…" Her fingers go to her lips, and she looks like she's on the verge of tears. That is the opposite of what I wanted to happen. "How did you know?"

She lifts the earrings from the velvet cushion, and Georgie gasps. "Oh my! The resemblance is uncanny!"

I just sit there smiling, since I have no idea what the hell they're talking about.

"Hemi must've said something." Sandy passes the earrings to Georgie, who helps her put them on. It's an incredibly sweet moment between these two women. "This is so sweet. So thoughtful, Dallas."

"I saw them, and I thought they were perfect." It's not untrue. I did see the earrings and think they were pretty awesome. I was also running out of time and figured I should go big or go home.

Sam and Isaac both look confused.

Wills pipes up, probably to help me understand why everyone is so emotional about earrings. "Mom was looking for Ajji's earrings a couple of weeks ago and couldn't find them."

Sandy nods. "I don't know if I misplaced them or left them somewhere by accident, but I was heartbroken when I realized I couldn't find them. These look almost exactly the same as my mother's. They're beautiful." She crosses the room, and I untangle Willy's legs from mine so I can accept the motherly affection. "I can't thank you enough, Dallas."

"I'm glad you love them." I pat her on the back and avoid adding lies to the already huge pile I'm sitting on.

Georgie waits until Sandy is sitting next to her before she unwraps her gift. I worry it's going to fall flat in the wake of the accidental replacement of the treasured family-heirloom earrings.

"That'll be a hard one to top." Isaac smirk. "Ajji would be proud."

I swallow my anxiety, because the earrings were seriously some dumb luck. Maybe I overheard Willy mention that her mom had misplaced them recently, and that knowledge was sitting in the back of my mind when I bought the gift. It sure as fuck wasn't conscious, though.

"I'm sure it'll be lovely and thoughtful." Georgie gives Isaac a pointed look before carefully peeling the tape away to reveal the contents. "Oh!"

She flips the book over in her hands and runs her palm over the cover.

"It's signed by the author," I say.

"Are you kidding?" Georgie opens the book and caresses the page with the author's signature. "Oh my goodness! How?" Her mouth is agape, her eyes welling. "I can't even..." She shakes her head. "I was supposed to see her speak at a convention two years ago, but something came up and I couldn't make it. I thought I'd be able to attend another event and get a book signed. But then she passed and..." Her hand goes to her heart. "She is my favorite author, rest her beautiful, intelligent soul. Her studies on pollinators and saving the bees have inspired me so much." She sets the book on the couch and rushes across the room.

I untangle myself from Willy again—she automatically slung her legs over mine when I sat back down—and wrap my arms around Georgie, accepting another hug.

"Thank you. You're just so thoughtful. Hemi is so lucky."

"I'm the lucky one." I pat her back.

"I had nothing to do with these gifts. This was one-hundred-percent Dallas," Willy declares. I can see every single question on her face.

"With or without your help, these gifts are lovely. And they will absolutely be cherished," Georgie assures me.

My dumb-luck gifts seem to soften up Sam and Isaac a little. Isaac is some sort of CEO, billionaire guy. From what I glean, he basically owns half the world because he started an online business that millions of people use every day. I have no idea what Sam does, but I would not be surprised to find out he disappears people, either for fun or for his job. He's intense.

The ensuing conversation is loud. Willy's brothers talk over each other, her moms interrupt them constantly when they think they're saying something inaccurate, and Willy sits back and listens, occasionally giving her two cents.

In a handful of hours, I understand better why she is the way she is. Here, when she's surrounded by her family, she's the quiet one. But when she's in the Terror office, she's a different woman. She's the one people listen to; she gives the orders and tells us how things are. She's the glue for our team. She grounds us and reminds us to be humble and use our advantages for good.

I was already hopelessly in love with Wills, but seeing this side of her, how hard she and her family love each other, elevates those feelings to a whole new level. She has so much love to give. She'll make a great partner and a patient, determined mom —if that's what she wants.

"What?" She nudges me with her elbow.

I arch a brow. "Eh?"

She arches one back. "You're staring."

"Just admiring the view." She wouldn't believe the truth.

Eventually, we move to the kitchen. Like everything with the Reddi-Grinst clan, preparing dinner is a loud, boisterous affair. Georgie barks orders, and we all follow them. I mostly try to be helpful and stay out of the way.

At the end of dinner, I still have no idea what Sam does for a living, but I've heard a million stories about Willy's childhood. Her family is intense, and I feel like I've spent the evening with fifty people instead of five.

After dinner, I clear the table and help load the dishwasher, while Sandy and Georgie prepare dessert.

Willy gets started on the pots and pans while Isaac takes a call and Sam follows orders from his moms. I step up beside Wills, fingers grazing her lower back. "Why don't you let me handle the dishes? That way you don't ruin your pretty nails."

"It's okay. I'm getting them done early next week anyway." She blows a wayward strand of hair out of her face, but it sticks to her glossed lips. She puffs out another gust of air, trying to free it, but it doesn't work. She tries again with the back of her wrist but her hands are sudsy.

"Let me help you."

She turns toward me, lips pursed.

I use my sleeve to wipe the suds away, then free the hairs from her lip.

Her fingers graze the back of mine. The diamond catches the light, and I capture her hand. "I can't stop thinking about last night." I kiss her knuckle.

Her breath catches. I can't read her expression, but her lips part as her eyes find mine.

"You gonna let me take care of you again?" I trail the fingers of my free hand down her side.

"Dessert is ready!" her brother calls from the dining room.

"Maybe. If you can be a good boy." Willy gives me a sultry smile as she steps around me.

I would do just about anything to earn that privilege. I follow her back to the dining room, where everyone else is already congregated. They stopped by an Indian market on their way over to pick up Sandy's favorite sweet, burfi. Her mom used to make it for her on special occasions growing up.

Once again, the conversation is loud and boisterous, filled with laughter and good-natured ribbing. When dessert is over, her brothers get ready to head back to Isaac's condo. It's in one of the exclusive high-rise buildings overlooking Lake Ontario. Last I heard, the penthouses were going for eleven million because of the view and the amenities.

"Why don't you stay there instead of here?" I ask as her family stands near the door, putting on shoes, making sure everyone has their phones and purses, and that her moms have their gifts.

Willy shakes her head. "It's four-thousand square feet of minimalist-decorated penthouse. It's massive. I can't afford a cleaner. Also, it would be incredibly lonely and sterile. I like this. I have a roommate to share the load with, and our schedules make it so we're not in each other's hair all the time." She motions to her apartment. "It's cozy, it's the right price for me to keep saving, and I can walk to work."

I hear all the other things she doesn't say, like she can take care of this on her own, and it gives her the autonomy and independence she's so fond of.

Willy's moms hug me and thank me again for the gifts.

"We're planning to hit the escarpment first thing in the morning. You up for a hike tomorrow, Dallas?" Sam asks.

Willy digs her nails into my arm and mutters, "Say no."

So I do the opposite. "Bruce Trail?"

"You know it?"

"It's been some years, but I'm totally up for it."

"Awesome." Sam fist-bumps me. "Hemi can send your number over, and we'll make a plan."

"Sounds great. I'm looking forward to it."

I get a fist bump from Isaac as well, and everyone hugs Wills before they're out the door. She lets it fall closed and peeks through the eyehole for a second before she turns to me. "You should fake sick tomorrow."

"It's a hike. How bad could it be?"

"Isaac climbs mountains for fun. When he says he's going for a hike, he's not going for a leisurely stroll in the woods to enjoy nature. He'll turn it into an expedition, and you'll be hiking for hours."

"Babe, I'm a professional hockey player. I have stamina for days. I'll be fine."

"If you say so. And don't call me babe."

I try to wrap my arms around her, but she steps out of reach.

"Aren't you going to let me take care of you? I was a good boy tonight, wasn't I?"

"Save your energy. You'll need it for tomorrow." She opens the door.

"I want to give you an orgasm before I leave." I want the smell of her on my fingers and the taste of her on my tongue.

"Not tonight."

"Why not?" I stand in front of her, trying to read her expression.

"Because my roommate will be home any minute."

I nod. "If tomorrow goes well, I expect to end it with you sitting on my face."

"We'll see." She pushes me out the door, but she's smiling when she closes it.

CHAPTER 18
DALLAS

"Just in time for the sunrise. Look at the majesty of it all." Isaac stands with his hands on his hips, smiling away.

It's dark fucking o'clock in the morning, and I've already been awake for an hour and a half. The only time I ever willingly get up at this freaking hour is when we have an early flight for an away game. I'm highly undercaffeinated, and I need about three more hours of sleep and a thousand calories of food. But I'm bonding with Willy's brothers and winning myself bonus points. Besides, it's a hike on Bruce Trail, no big deal.

"Let's get a move on." Sam adjusts his backpack and speed walks toward the trail entrance. Issac falls into step behind him, and I take up the rear. I worry I'm slightly underprepared for this excursion. All I have is a small pack with two water bottles, a couple of energy bars, and a pack of gum. They have stuffed backpacks.

It's muggy, which isn't unusual for July in Niagara. According to the forecast, it promises to be balls hot. The escarpment is on the peninsula, which only compounds the humidity. We've hardly even started, and I'm sweating already.

I hustle to catch up with Isaac. Based on last night and this morning, Sam is the leader of this pack. He sets a quick pace that doesn't allow a whole lot of room for appreciating nature or the view.

I can feel Isaac looking at me, so I glance in his direction and smile. "Did you have a good time last night?"

"Yeah. It was nice. I wish Hemi would let us set her up in her own place, but she can be stubborn."

"Oh yeah. At work it's pretty much Willy's way or the highway." I rub my bottom lip, hiding a smile as I think about all the times she's made it abundantly clear that she is in the driver's seat, and I'm just along for the ride. Just call me Wilhelmina Reddi-Grinst's Passenger Princess.

"What about outside of work?" he asks.

"Eh..." I consider the shit I've pulled recently. "It's more divided." In my favor, although not because that's how Willy wants it. Thinking things through has never been my strong suit. On the ice it's different, because intuition guides me, but in real life...usually it means I fuck shit up.

Issac makes a sound I can't interpret. "You're not her usual type."

"She dates guys with PhDs." Like the cardiologist who started us down this path. I should send him a thank-you gift.

"But you're not *that* different from her PhD dudes in some respects," Sam calls from in front of us.

"I don't mean it in a negative way," Isaac reassures me. "She has a type she usually goes for, and you defy that. It's probably a good thing, to be honest. You have the same drive and ambition."

"She needs a challenge," Sam calls over his shoulder.

How he can still hear us is a wonder, considering how far ahead he is.

"Yeah. She's exceptionally driven," I agree. "It makes sense that she would want somebody who's equally as ambitious and intelligent as she is. Yet somehow, she's ended up with me." I laugh weakly. I don't like the unpleasant feeling in my stomach that has nothing to do with my need for about three breakfast sandwiches. Willy always dates highly educated, well-mannered men. I have manners, a good family, a great career, but university wasn't my jam. I passed the classes I took, but I had tutors and some professors who took pity on me.

"You don't need ten years of post-secondary education to be the right fit for her," Isaac says. "The two of you complement each other. And it's clear that you're head over heels. I mean, those gifts for our moms won you bonus points. I still can't believe you found earrings like my grandma's. Hemi's a sucker for a thoughtful guy, and that's a lot more than I can say for the last couple of dudes she ended up with."

"There was a cardiologist a while back," I note.

"That guy was a clueless idiot. Just because he has an IQ of one-forty doesn't mean he understands how my sister ticks, but you do." Isaac claps me on the shoulder. "Pro athletes have a different kind of smarts. You're good at reading people, you understand risk management, and you know when to set your ego aside for the welfare of your team. That's why Hemi wanted to work in this field."

"Come on, guys! Let's pick up the pace," Sam shouts.

An hour into the hike, I'm soaked with sweat, my balls are chafed, and my legs are rubber. I could really use a five-minute rest—or a five-hour nap—and I only have a quarter of a water bottle left. According to my smart watch, we've already hiked eight kilometers. I'm not sure how far we're going, but if we don't turn around soon, I'll have to cancel with Ash tomorrow because I doubt my legs will be able to handle squats. I might have to cancel regardless.

Three and a half hours, two rope bridges on which I thought I was going to die, and twenty kilometers later, we're finally back at the car. I guzzle three bottles of Vitamin Water and accept two sandwiches from the cooler in the back of Sam's luxury SUV.

My plan is to sleep all the way back to Toronto, shower off the salt, soak in the hot tub for an hour, and follow that with a three-hour nap (during which I will dream about their sister sitting on my face).

We pile into the car, and I'm grateful that my legs no longer have to do anything other than feel like Jell-O as I stretch out in the back seat.

"Next up is paintball!" Sam exclaims with more enthusiasm than anyone should have after a twenty-kilometer sprint-hike through the woods.

Isaac looks over his shoulder and gives me a thumbs-up. "You in? We know a great place."

I'm definitely not in. All I want to do is sleep for the rest of the day, and probably part of tomorrow, but I return the thumbs-up because I will not tap out on Willy's brothers. There's too much at stake. "I'm in."

Willy messages for an update.

I send her a thumbs-up.

She sends a frowny face in return.

I send heart eyes and kissy lips.

She sends a middle finger.

I follow it with the tongue.

She doesn't reply.

Forty-five minutes and a brief ten-minute nap later, I'm outfitted in paintball gear, holding a paintball gun, while Sam and Isaac do jumping jacks and knee-ups in preparation for whatever is about to happen. I still have no idea what Sam does for a living, but he seems to love paintball guns.

There are several things I am not a fan of, one being clowns, two sauerkraut, three heights, and lastly, but also most importantly, I am definitely not a fan of dark, confined spaces. And it turns out, that is essentially the whole point of paintball. I have a raging anxiety boner, the head of which is tucked uncomfortably into the waistband of my pants. My skin is gritty with salt. Places that shouldn't be chafed are really fucking chafed.

And to add insult to injury, we're surrounded by an exceptional number of teenage boys, who scream incessantly at each other, and a few girls who obviously got dragged along for the ride. I relate to their lack of enthusiasm.

We enter the paintball room. At this point, I'm just trying to hide, and maybe take a small break so my legs can stop feeling like overcooked spaghetti.

A gaggle of noisy teens is headed my way, their giggles and swearing giving them away. I'm forced to leave my protective cover as they draw closer.

Sam's booming voice echoes through the vast room. "Two o'clock! Light him up!"

Paintballs slam into my arms, legs, back, and chest. I aim shots in their direction, but I'm decidedly shitty at paintball, and every one goes wide. I don't think it can get worse, until one hits me right in the anxiety boner, taking me to the ground.

I curl into the fetal position and pray for death. Instead, Isaac's black-booted feet appear in my vision. "You all right, buddy?"

"That was a nut shot," I groan.

"Sam's dirty like that." Isaac extends a hand. "I should have warned you to wear a cup."

Who needs a cup for paintball? Apparently these guys.

I would prefer to stay on the floor for the rest of the day, even if it means being trampled by teenagers, but I really want Wills to sit on my face, so I let Isaac help me to my feet.

Thankfully, Sam eventually runs out of paintballs, and Isaac expresses how hungry he is. I'd be down for a giant buffet.

We change out of our paint-covered clothes—I would love a shower to wash away the grit, but that's not on the menu yet—and we climb back into Sam's car and drive to a restaurant. I order four appetizers and two meals and reluctantly share them with Willy's brothers.

I'm fantasizing about a large pizza and a nap when Sam says, "There's an escape room close to my place that I'm dying to try out. You up for that?"

I pause with my fork halfway to my mouth. He doesn't look

like he's joking. All I want is my bed. But again, I think about Wills and how much I want the reward that comes with her brothers' fucking approval. "Yeah, man, absolutely."

"Awesome!" Isaac gives me a thumbs-up. It seems to be his thing.

"Want me to see if some of the guys from my team are interested?" Ash loves these things, and Roman and Hollis would probably be down. I could also use a buffer from the intensity of these two. They're seriously high octane. I thought I had energy to burn, but these two are next-fucking-level.

"Seriously?" Sam asks.

"Yeah, let me send them a text."

I send a message to our group chat, meant mostly for setting up workouts.

> DALLAS
>
> With my fiancée's bros.
>
> You guys up for an escape room?
>
> *there is no "I" in team GIF*
>
> *falling off the side of a mountain GIF*
>
> *paint splatter GIF*

> ASH
>
> *shifty eyes GIF*
>
> I can make it.

> HOLLIS
>
> Same. But mostly because I want to see what her brothers are like.

> ROMAN
>
> ^^^ And also because Peggy is with the girls.
>
> I can come too.

> FLIP
>
> I love escape rooms.

TRISTAN

Bea is out so I'm in, too.

DALLAS

You're the best.

We finish lunch and drive to the escape room.

"Sam is a diehard Roman Hammerstein fan," Isaac shares as we pile out of the SUV.

"Shut the fuck up, Isaac." I'm pretty sure Sam is blushing, which is…entertaining.

"He's an awesome player and a great goalie," I agree. "The team will be sad to see him go at the end of next season." He's diplomatic, even keeled, and basically the team dad.

"He's had an amazing career," Sam notes. "There isn't a better goalie in the league."

We meet Flip, Tristan, Hollis, Roman, and Ash in front of the building. I stage a round of introductions, and Sam gets all pumped up. Dude is intense to begin with, but he seems to know all of Roman's stats and his entire career history. I'm just happy to have the attention off of me for a couple hours.

"Are you limping?" Ash asks.

"I'm fine."

"Liar. These two seem like a lot to handle."

I hold two fingers a hairbreadth apart.

"Sort of explains why Hemi is the way she is," he muses.

"Willy's perfect," I snap.

He pats me on the back. "Agreed. I'm just saying, if this is how her brothers are all the time, it gives a little perspective as to why she's such a boss queen, that's all. Sort of like how Shilps is the youngest of five and had to fight for her place."

"Yeah. That makes sense. They're awesome women."

We split up into two teams, me with Isaac, Ash, and Flip. Roman, Hollis, Sam, and Tristan form the other team. I'm grateful that it only takes Isaac half an hour to figure it out, with the help of mostly Ash and minor input from me and Flip. Sam doesn't seem nearly as bothered by the loss as I'd anticipated, but then, he's practically glued himself to Roman's side.

Afterward, we head to the Watering Hole for beers and dinner. This day feels like the longest of my life. And possibly one of the most painful.

It isn't until I'm lying on my couch—freshly showered with baby powder on my poor chafed balls, wishing for a new set of legs—that my phone buzzes with a message.

I swallow the lump in my throat as Willy's name flashes across the screen. I open the message with a stomach full of rocks. At least until I read the content.

WILLS

My brothers are in love with you. They can't stop talking about what an awesome day they had. Thank you. I've scheduled you a two-hour massage for tomorrow morning at 11 a.m. You're welcome.

DALLAS

Does this also mean I can finally fuck your pussy with my tongue?

WILLS

When you've recovered, yes.

CHAPTER 19

HEMI

HEMI

Please stop posting your anticipated location. It creates a shitstorm every time.

FLIP

But how will my friends find me?

HEMI

You text them individually, or as part of your bro group. You do not share your whereabouts with the world so every underage girl out there tries to get into the same bar as you.

FLIP

Shit. Good call. Changing locations now.

HEMI

Seriously, Flip, why is this just making sense now?

FLIP

I'm pretty sure I just saw Tally in a lineup with her friends. Or it's her doppelganger. Maybe text her.

HEMI

WTF? If it's her, why would you leave her there?

I quickly send a message to the Badass Babe Brigade asking for a photo update. Tally is the first to respond with a picture of her with her cat on her bed. The rest of the girls follow with pictures, but I have what I need. Tally is safe and not at a bar. She's like a little sister, and while she's grown up with the team, she's also—

FLIP

She's my coach's g daughter. She's the last person I should have photos with outside of a bar. And I don't want to get her in trouble.

HEMI

Because being in a bar underage wouldn't accomplish that?

FLIP

She's an adult. Also, photos with her could axe my contract with Milk, and I'd like to keep that endorsement since it's basically funding my parents' retirement.

HEMI

sigh That's fair and reasonable. Tally's at home, so that's her doppelganger.

FLIP

Thank fuck.

There's a knock on my apartment door. Maybe my roommate locked herself out. It's happened before. But she shouldn't be home for hours.

I open the door and am stunned speechless by the sight before me. "What are you doing here? How did you get up here?" Dallas is standing in my doorway, wearing a T-shirt and khaki shorts. It's nine in the evening. He looks exhausted.

"I followed some dude in. I've recovered," he states.

I cross my arms. "You look half dead." That he's still upright after what my brothers put him through is unreal. Isaac called me half an hour ago to give me a play by play of their day, and then Sam jumped on to talk about how cool Roman is.

"I'm fine." He steps into my apartment, closes the door behind him, and turns the lock. "Your roommate is on nights now, right?"

"Yeah, but—"

He takes my face in his hands and tips my head up, lips hovering an inch from mine, his eyes hot with desire. "I was a good boy last night and today, wasn't I?" He manages to make that sound like a command instead of a question.

"Yes," I agree, my body already heating from the contact.

"Good boys deserve a reward, don't they?" His tongue drags across his bottom lip. He looks like he's ready to devour me. It's ridiculously hot to have this huge, imposing, badass hockey player desperate to make me come. Every part of me craves more of his touch.

I sent him home the other night unsatisfied because I enjoyed the fingerbang a little too much for my own good. His willingness to service me, all that power...it's a little heady. Getting addicted to orgasms from Dallas isn't smart. Not when he's so good at it, and not when this is extremely temporary. But one more time couldn't hurt...

I nod and give in to the urge to run my hand over his chest. I might still hate all the shit he did to me when we were kids, but I can't deny the effect he has on my body. The hottest guy in school became the hottest guy on a pro hockey team and he's standing in my apartment, desperate to give me an orgasm. Teenage me is over the moon. Current me is on board for very different reasons. Heat floods my center, and my nipples peak under my shirt. "You were a very good boy."

He strokes my cheek and slides his fingers into my hair,

curling them at the base of my scalp. "You're going to sit on my face, so I can fuck you with my tongue."

"Your mouth is a filth factory." But I like it. The other night when he finger-fucked me on the counter, I only wanted him to shut up so I wouldn't come too fast. I had no idea if the experience was a one-off, and I wanted it to last—at first out of sheer vindictive glee, and then because it felt so good.

"I know. You'll be keeping it busy soon enough." He laces our fingers. "Take me to your bedroom."

I guide him down the hall. The moment he closes my bedroom door, he's on me. Hands in my hair, lips on my skin. "I'm fucking starving for you, Wills." He pushes my sleep shorts over my hips and drops to his knees. I'm panty-less. His hands move to cup my ass and he nuzzles into my sex, his groan vibrating over my sensitive skin. He presses a kiss to the apex of my thighs and his eyes lift as his velvet tongue slides between my folds. My eyes flutter shut as warmth pools low in my belly and desire takes over.

I grip his hair and tug, pulling his mouth away. "Get on the bed."

His grin turns lascivious as he pushes to a stand and crosses the room. He pulls his shirt over his head and stretches out on top of my comforter. His erection pushes against his shorts, and his eyes are hot with need. He extends a hand, reaching for me. "Let me take care of you."

There's something in the way he says it, paired with the hungry look in his eyes, that makes me feel...powerful. Sexy. Beautiful.

As soon as I climb onto the bed, he moves me into position, one knee on either side of his head. He kisses and bites the inside of my thighs, then grips my hips and pulls me down onto his mouth. His tongue glides through my sex, his deep groan making everything tighten. I grip the headboard as he devours me, tongue circling my clit before plunging inside me.

"So fucking good, Wills. I've been dying to taste you like this," he rasps.

I thread my fingers through his hair, holding his head as I roll my hips and…fuck his face. He grips my ass, helping me maintain the rhythm as my legs quake.

"That's it, come all over my face. Baptize me with your pussy juice, honey."

I can't even with the shit that comes out of his mouth. But it has the desired effect. He slaps my ass, and I grind down, reaching for the headboard again as the orgasm rolls through me. The world is a wash of stars as I come.

I don't even have time to recover before I find myself flipped onto my back. Dallas's broad shoulders push my legs wide as he just…keeps going. He makes desperate mewling sounds, like he can't get enough, like he'll die if he stops.

He slides a thick finger inside me, then another and another. "Let's see how long we can keep this going." He latches onto my clit, sucking hard as his fingers stroke inside me.

The waning orgasm fires back up. I moan and grip his hair, writhing under him as sensation spirals and expands, consuming me, burning me up from the inside. Eventually, it's just too much, and I push his head away, preventing him from coming back for more by shoving on his shoulder with my foot.

He folds back on his knees, chest heaving, eyes heavy with lust as he swipes at his chin with the back of his hand. Then he sucks his pussy-juice-coated fingers clean.

I close my legs before he gets any more ideas.

"Thank you." His voice sounds like it went a round with a gravel truck.

"You're welcome?" I'm still trying to recover from the twenty-minute orgasm.

He grabs his shirt from the floor, pulling it back over his head. He rearranges his very prominent erection. I'd love to offer to reciprocate, but I worry he'll convince me to let him fuck me, and that would be a very, very bad idea.

I'm already addicted to his tongue and fingers. I can't get addicted to his cock, too.

He leans down and kisses my forehead. "I'll be on my way, but don't forget to lock the door before you go to bed, honey."

CHAPTER 20
HEMI

I'm getting ready for work two days later when my moms call. They do this sometimes, video call first thing in the morning. They've made a wedding inspiration board already. I wish one of my brothers would settle down and take the heat off me.

"Hi, Mom and Ma. What's up?" I prop them on the vanity while I work on my makeup.

"Your mom and I were thinking it might be nice to look at a few venues while you're in town for the reunion," Ma says.

"We haven't even set a date, though." *And we never will.* And I'll have to break my moms' hearts when I tell them it's over. There's no way we're putting deposits down on things just for show. My guilty conscience can't take that.

"It doesn't hurt to look, though, sweetheart. Places book up quickly, especially in the summer months. June would be perfect, don't you think? Post buggy season, but before the really hot weather sets in."

"I think the reunion weekend will be pretty jam-packed," I hedge.

"Hmm… You have a point. Well, why don't we plan for your mom and I to come down for a weekend so we can start looking at dresses, at the very least! We'll book a few appointments. It'll be fun!"

Their excitement makes my heart hurt. "Can we get through the reunion weekend first? Or can we talk about it more when I'm home? There's just a lot going on right now."

"Are you nervous about the reunion, sweetie?"

I'm lying about enough stuff, so I go with honesty. "Yeah. I haven't seen Brooklyn face-to-face in years, and teendom wasn't the easiest time of my life."

"Oh, sweetie, everyone in high school was focused on themselves," Mom says. "You have a great career, wonderful friends, and a lovely fiancé. It'll be fun."

"Thanks for the votes of confidence."

"We love you, Hemi. We'll back off on the wedding details until the reunion is over," Ma adds. "Let us know if you need anything else, though. Okay?"

"Of course. I love you."

"We love you, too," they say in unison then end the call.

The web of lies I'm weaving is sticky, and I'm worried about getting trapped in it. I don't have time to fixate on that now, though. Not with everything else going on.

Half an hour later I'm sitting in my office with Denise, the head coach of the women's team.

"I love everything about this, Hemi." She's all smiles as she reads through the proposal. "Winter Marks will definitely want to be involved, so however we can include her would be fantastic."

"I designed it with her in mind, knowing her background and the Hockey Academy's role in her life." I met her a few months ago, but when we were chatting recently, she shared how the retired players at the Hockey Academy took her under their wing at a time when she really needed the support and the team family dynamic, and it had changed her life. "I love how passionate she is about this and that she had the guts to mention it to me."

"Honestly, I'm just amazed at how quickly you've pulled this all together. Getting the team involved with the local foodbank and soup kitchen is a beautiful way to give back to the community. And I love that this charity game you've set up includes a food donation. It's meaningful in the best way."

"They're such an outstanding group of athletes, and I know how much it means to them and other young women who are looking at this path. It's a great merging of community work and team commitment."

She smiles. "I absolutely agree. Thank you for taking this on."

"It's the offseason, so I have some time, and it's absolutely a pleasure. We can meet with the team next week, and I'll work on setting up a rotating schedule in the meantime. If there are other promotional opportunities you'd like help securing, I'm happy to assist."

"That sounds wonderful."

We lob a few more ideas back and forth, discussing the logistics, the team's schedule, and their availability before Denise thanks me and heads back to the arena for practice.

I've just started tackling my email when there's a knock on my office door.

Dallas pokes his pretty head in. "I hope I'm not interrupting."

He runs a hand through his hair. During playoffs, the guys always get a little unkempt. Some of the playoff beards—especially on the rookies—are pretty scraggly. Others use it as an excuse to forget what a razor even is.

But Dallas always keeps things neat around the edges, and as soon as playoffs are over, he loses the beard. But he hasn't gotten a haircut yet, so it curls at the nape of his neck and around his ears. I try desperately not to give in to the memory of how it felt between my fingers when I rode his face the other night, but it's too late. The image, the sounds…they've been living rent free in my head, and I've gotten myself off to them more than once. It's a problem. Especially with the way my body is already preparing for another round of baptism by pussy.

"What do you need?" I'm embarrassingly breathy. I grip the edge of my desk so I don't get up, lock my door, and offer myself to him. I'm at work, for fuck's sake. I'm already the topic of too much office gossip these days.

"I brought you flowers." He produces a bouquet of lilies. I dislike how much I appreciate them, and the fact that he's varied the type of flower. "And lunch." He holds up a bag from my favorite café.

I cross my arms. "Why? What did you do now?" I'm reasonably wary. Every time Dallas has done something nice recently—sexual favors aside—it's caused me an incredible amount of stress, not limited to, but including signing contracts, relinquishing my freedom, cutting out my fuck buddy, turning me into his fake fiancée, an all-out engagement dinner with our friends and his parents, and forcing me to trust him when his past behavior with me has been nothing but red flags.

"Nothing that I'm aware of. I just know you had a busy weekend with your family in town, and this week is more of the same. I was in the area, and I thought flowers might brighten your day and food might be welcome since sometimes you skip lunch in lieu of a bag of Cherry Blasters. No shade to Cherry Blasters, but they're not very satisfying. I got you the salad with sweet potatoes and candied walnuts. And the charcuterie board sandwich with peach chutney, and an iced latte, but with the sweet cream foam and no syrup."

I don't know why it still shocks me that he knows exactly what my favorites are. Especially with Shilpa around for him to ask. But instead of saying thank you like a normal person, I blurt, "Hammer will be here in a few minutes. We're going to the retirement village."

"Oh. Is it for something special?" If I didn't know better, I'd think he was hurt that I didn't invite him. But it's only been two days since my brothers took him on the longest hike in the history of the world, after which he came over and ate me like a starved man, so I was giving us some much-needed space. He's too damn good at getting me off. I want more, and that's a problem. Also, my hate for him is eroding because he keeps doing sweet shit, and it's making my life even more challenging.

I don't want to like Dallas or be addicted to his orgasms. He's only providing them out of obligation because he's turned my life into a circus. It's an obligation, not a desire. Considering anything different makes me feel vulnerable, and it's a slippery slope. I can't keep my feelings about Dallas out of the equation, and they're becoming a tangled mess.

"It's ballroom-dancing night—well, afternoon because they have dinner at four thirty and are in bed by seven thirty. I set it up for Flip because it's good for his image."

"He's been better lately, though, hasn't he?"

"Yeah. Definitely, but trade talks have started, and he gets antsy."

"They're not thinking about trading Flip, are they?" Worry laces his tone.

I wave a hand. "No. Of course not. I just want to keep him on an even keel for as long as I can." Anything could happen, so he needs to be on his best behavior.

His shoulders relax. "Okay. That's good. This year's draft was full of surprises."

"Agreed." There have been some interesting picks this year. Not to mention Quinn Romero, who was drafted years ago, but has never been on a pro team, just signed his first contract. It was a shock to everyone. Romero included. "Anyway, Hollis is tagging along, but I'm ninety-nine-percent sure it's an excuse to spend time with Hammer."

Dallas sets the flowers on my conference table, then moves closer and props his hip against the edge of my desk. He sets the takeout bag beside me and crosses his arms. I try not to notice how fantastic his forearms look. Or consider the memory of how good it looked when his hand was between my thighs and his fingers were filling me. I'm not super successful. So I focus on my computer screen instead of him and pull up my email.

"Can I tag along, too?"

I side-eye him. "Why?"

"A few years ago, when the date auction became a thing..." He rubs the back of his neck. "I, uh...I wanted to be able to get on the dance floor and not look like an idiot, so I took some classes."

"Huh." Dallas is always full of surprises. "You can come if you want."

"Knock-knock! Who's ready to get their dance on?" Hammer appears in the doorway. "Oh! Sorry. I didn't realize I was interrupting."

"You're not. Dallas is joining us on this adventure."

"Oh, awesome!" Hammer flops down in a chair at the conference table. "Hollis will appreciate the company. I don't think he's had a ton of ballroom-dancing experience, but apparently the idea of having to spend a full eight hours away from me is too much for him to handle." She fingers the petal on a blossom. "These must be from you." She gives Dallas a knowing smile. "They're beautiful."

"Just like Willy," Dallas says.

I give him the stink eye. I don't know why he still calls me Willy. Other than to annoy me.

I peek in the bag, unable to resist the smell. He's right, I have a terrible habit of skipping lunch and end up eating carrot sticks and freaking Cherry Blasters—the carrots are for balance and vitamin C—and regret it later when the hanger hits.

Whenever we do a retirement-village event, they insist on feeding us. Secretly I love it when they serve things like meatloaf or chicken pot pie. It reminds me of my grandma Grinst. But waiting until four thirty is a terrible idea. I haven't had anything since breakfast, and it's already one thirty. I pull out my paper plates and extra cutlery and share the food with Dallas and Hammer, and then Hollis, when he arrives.

Flip arrives a few minutes later and finishes the salad. He never says no to food. I pack up, and the five of us head for our vehicles. Dallas insists on holding my hand and driving with me. I don't want it to feel nice. I don't want to like the attention, or being doted on. Adding in the sexual servicing makes it feel... less fake, for some reason.

It's hard to process how he's different compared to our childhood. He has always loved pushing my buttons. Admitting that I'm scared of how I'll feel after this is all over, or even what it means that I'm trusting someone who is party to so many bad memories, feels like a weakness I can't afford. I don't want to get comfortable with him, and if he keeps being sweet, that could happen. The lines keep blurring, and when he's like this, it's hard to remember this isn't real. It's dangerous to like this version of him.

When we arrive, the little old ladies at the retirement home are dressed to the nines. "I love this so much. How cute are they?" I murmur to Dallas, who seems committed to staying by my side.

"So cute. I especially like the one in the red flapper dress." Dallas's lips are at my ear. His warm, minty breath breaks across my neck and sends a shiver down my spine. "Picking her as my dance partner. Don't get too jealous."

The room is a sea of sequins and loud floral prints. All but a few are wearing their orthotics. A couple of brave souls wear chunky heels. Their makeup is done, lipstick not always inside the lines, and a few women have on enough blue eyeshadow to make the eighties cringe. But they're adorable, and all the men are dressed in suits.

The afternoon starts with tea and cookies served by the players, followed by an hour of ballroom dancing. Even I get pulled onto the dance floor, and so does Hammer. I'm in the middle of a two-step with Dougie, a spry ninety-three-year-old with an exceptional amount of ear hair, when I notice Dallas crossing the room. He crouches in front of Hester. She uses a wheelchair and has been watching from the sidelines. Often, she skips these events and says she's tired.

Whatever he says brings a wide smile to her lined face. He wheels her into the middle of the dance floor and makes a complete spectacle of himself, shaking his ass in front of her. She's laughing and clapping and smiling so wide my heart feels like it's about to burst. Sometimes, I forget that under all that sweetness, he's the same guy who put a frog in my lunch box in fourth grade.

After dancing, we join the residents in the dining room. Dallas and I end up at the table with Hester. She lost her husband of sixty-three years this winter. I can't even begin to imagine how untethered I would feel if I'd loved someone that long and suddenly they were gone.

"Miss Wilhelmina, this is new!" Irina, another lady at our table, takes my hand in hers and examines the engagement ring. "Who's the lucky fella?"

Dallas wraps his arm around my shoulder and hugs me to his side. It's tough not to appreciate how good he smells when he's all up in my personal space. "That would be me."

Irina, who's a spitfire, gives Dallas an appraising once-over. "He's a real looker, isn't he?"

"He's quite pretty," I agree.

Everywhere he goes, people fawn over him. Even if they don't know he's a professional hockey player, they're immediately taken by his wide, infectious smile and his charming personality. It's been like that since we were kids. He has a wicked sense of humor, and he can be exceptionally kind—as I've recently learned.

But the fact that I'll have to come back here eventually for another one of these events and share the terrible news that we broke up makes my chest ache. None of this is real. Both times he got me off, he didn't even ask for reciprocation. Our chemistry adds another layer of complication. The lies just keep building, and it makes his casual affection harder to take. What will people think when I allow the prom king to hurt me again? How desperate will I look then? How pathetic? How much will I regret the memory of how good he made me feel?

I'm all up in my head, so I must miss the next question.

"Wills?" Dallas's eyes hold mild concern. He must see my confusion because he adds, "Would you like me to tell the story?"

"Oh. Sure." I don't think I can bring myself to share another fabrication about how we fell in love without losing it.

"Wilhelmina and I have known each other since we were kids." Dallas's thumb strokes along the skin at the collar of my blouse, sending another annoying shiver down my spine. "We went to school together all the way from kindergarten to high school."

Irina claps. "Oh! Childhood friends? That's one of my favorites!"

I laugh, because my disdain for Dallas and his friends started at a very young age. And it only grew. Now that those feelings have shifted, I like it even less.

"Oh no." Dallas shakes his head solemnly. "Wilhelmina couldn't stand me when we were kids. Not that I blame her. I was a jerk. But by the time we reached high school, I knew she was the one. I had a lot of growing up to do, though."

I grit my teeth, hating how good he is at this. It's nothing for him to weave a story any woman would love to hear, if it was actually true.

"So how did this happen?" Irina motions between us. The whole table is engrossed in his tale now.

"When Wilhelmina started working for the Terror, I knew it was the only chance I'd get to show her I wasn't the same jerk she grew up with. I signed up for every promotional opportunity I could to be near her. Over the past couple of years,

Wilhelmina has seen a different side of me." He smiles down at me. "A better side. She knows how to manage me better than anyone. And then, like I'd hoped, she finally stopped hating me. And here we are."

The girl I used to be, the one who didn't really fit, wants a love story like this.

"That is just the sweetest." Irina's hand is at her heart, and her eyes glisten with unshed tears.

"It really is." Another woman dabs at her eyes with her napkin.

Irina takes my hand in her soft, wrinkly one and squeezes. "You hold on to this one, sweetie. He's a keeper."

I plaster a smile on my face and I fight to keep my voice steady, to be as smooth as he is. "He's a gem, isn't he?"

Dallas kisses my temple. It's tender, and so unexpectedly sweet. "I'm the lucky one here. She puts up with a lot of crap from me, and she knows exactly how to keep me in line. Wilhelmina is the real keeper."

That I'm beginning to crave this kind of casual affection scares the hell out of me. I tip my head up, intent on communicating through my eyes that he's pouring it on a little thick. But I'm shocked by the look on his face. If I didn't know better, if this wasn't all a performance and he wasn't just practicing here to get back at the assholes we grew up with, I'd think he meant what he said.

"Kiss her!" one of the men calls out.

Everyone around us has stopped to listen to the story—even Hammer and Hollis, who are sitting at the table kitty-corner to us. Both wear soft smiles. Hollis's arm is draped across the back of her chair, and he drags a single finger up and down the nape of her neck.

Not for the first time, I'm hit with a wave of sadness. Hammer's one of my close friends, and here I am, lying to her face every day. And how convincing must we be that she buys it? What will they all think when they learn the truth? How hard will it be when it all comes crashing down? When they learn that this was all a ruse because Dallas got drunk one night and I refused to go to my high school reunion alone? That I let the boy who teased me relentlessly as a kid be my date to avoid risking both our jobs?

"No pudding for you unless you kiss! And it's chocolate marshmallow fudge, which is your favorite," Irina threatens.

She's not wrong. The pudding here is good.

Everyone around us joins the chant, calling out *kiss, kiss, kiss.*

"And make it a good one!" Irina orders.

The flutter of anticipation in my stomach is unnerving. As is the way Dallas's eyes heat as he turns to face me. His fingers drift from the edge of my jaw to my chin. I swallow the lump made of desire and anxiety as he tips my head up and leans down. At first, it's the softest brush of warm velvet. But it sparks need, stoking the coals and turning them into fire.

Even in a room full of old people, I want more of his mouth on mine. Of his hands on my skin. Of him showing up at my door, asking to take care of me. No matter how things seem right now, I know better than to wish for something real with Dallas Bright.

He cups my face in his hands, warm, rough fingers pressing into the hinge of my jaw. He angles his head so he can deepen the kiss, tongue sliding against mine. I grip his wrist, nails digging into the skin.

He groans low in his throat, and his tongue sweeps my mouth. Owning me. Possessing me. I want to climb into his lap and feel all the hard lines of his body against me.

But instead, he pulls back, and the spell breaks as the room bursts into a round of exuberant applause.

I turn away from Dallas, unable to handle the fire in his gaze. This chemistry between us is seriously inconvenient.

I blush and laugh, and roll my eyes when I'm offered not one, but two servings of pudding. But inside, I'm all over the place.

My heart is racing, my hands are clammy, and my lips are tingling. It's discombobulating.

I'm starting to believe in those kisses, in the soft ways he shows up for me. And that's dangerous and stupid. The last thing I want is to turn back into the girl he fucked over all those years ago.

The only way I'll survive this is to throw my walls up and stay strong. No more flirting. No more kissing. No more weakness.

CHAPTER 21
DALLAS

"**Y**ou can do this. It's not a big deal. Just ask. It's one question." I'vegiven myself the pep talk a dozen times in the last fifteen minutes. I don't know why I can show up at Willy's house and ask her to sit on my face, but this situation makes me anxious. Regardless, it's time to take action.

I pry my hands from the edge of the sink, mentally berating my boner, who is slow to get a clue. Eventually he's calmed down enough that I can leave the privacy of the bathroom. I walk down the hall of the Terror main offices, taking a deep breath as I approach Wills's lair.

I hear her before I see her. Actually, I hear her fingers click, click, clicking away on the keyboard. She's an exceptionally fast typist. I don't knock at first. Instead, I peek around the jamb, so I can gauge her mood. If I catch her at the wrong time, she'll say no, and I need her to say yes. Though I already know she won't be happy about it.

A slight smile tugs at the corner of her luscious mouth. I will myself to not think about how good it felt to make her come. How much I loved being the one to give her what she needed, how I want to do it again. Aaaand now it's too late. My brain rewinds to her bedroom, to being submerged in the scent of her, the taste. Her hands in my hair, my mouth on her skin. And the fucking sounds she made. Wills is a badass every moment of every day, but she's so pretty and sweet when she's moaning my name and coming on my tongue. Sexy and formidable. I shake off the hormone haze as I take in the incredibly gorgeous specimen of a woman sitting behind her desk. A navy blazer hangs over the back of her executive chair. She's wearing a pale blue blouse underneath, the top button unfastened, revealing a small heart-shaped locket. It contains pictures of her moms. I know this because once she thought she'd lost it and tore her office apart to find it. She'd been on the verge of tears when it fell out of the bottom of her shirt. Apparently, it had unfastened on its own and fallen into her bra.

"Why are you spying on me?" she snaps suddenly.

So much for discreet ogling. I don't know what happened, but I'm ever familiar with guarded and prickly Wilhelmina. Her bark might be as bad as her bite, but I don't care.

"I didn't want to interrupt if you were on a call." And I fully intended to run away if she looked unhappy.

She takes off her glasses and levels me with an impatient glare. "What do you need?"

To convince you that all of this is real and not just a farce, and to let me worship you for the rest of my life. "To take you on a date." If I can't go with the actual truth, I can at least go with direct honesty.

Her lips push out, and her forehead creases. "A date." Her tone makes it sound like I'm asking her to go on a murder spree.

"Yeah. You know, we spend the day together, do a bunch of fun stuff, finish it off with dinner at a nice restaurant, and a walk on the pier if the lake doesn't smell like a giant pile of dead fish." Sometimes, Lake Ontario has a not-too-pleasing scent in the summer. I shove my hands in my pockets so I don't keep running them through my hair.

"Why?"

I expect this question, and the confusion marring her lovely features, but it doesn't stop the shitty feeling that makes my stomach roll. Telling her I want to take her on a date, that I want to wine and dine her and treat her like a queen will only be met with a scoff and more disbelief. I know why she's this way. I've seen her mocked in moments of vulnerability. I've watched people be kind to her face and so awful behind her back, even at work. It was short-sighted to believe adding sexual favors to our agreement would make her see the truth. But there was no way anyone else would be taking care of my fiancée's needs. Especially not her fuck buddy. So again, I go with honesty she won't question, even though it sucks.

"Brooklyn's mom has been asking my mom for pictures."

Willy's head falls back and her eyes roll up to the ceiling. "Because we don't have any online."

"Yeah." I should've seen this coming. Brooklyn's mom is the town gossip. She's always in everybody's business, and she creates drama wherever she goes. The apple doesn't fall far from the tree. Brooklyn was the queen of spreading rumors in high school. Probably still is. It always surprised me that Wilhelmina was her friend. But they'd hung out since elementary school, and Wills is as loyal as they come.

"It's one giant headache after another, isn't it?" Wills rubs her temples.

Spending an entire day with her, just the two of us, is my fucking dream. But she wouldn't believe that's true. She'd assume I'm mocking her.

"You know what she's like. I explained that we were trying to keep things low-key so as not to create more PR drama for you, which my mom understands, but she'd like a few pictures. She's pretty excited about the whole thing." And there's a five-million-percent chance that she's also planning to make one of those photo collages to hang on the living room wall.

Wills heaves an annoyed sigh. "Fine. I guess you have a point about us needing pictures as a couple. How long do you think this would take? A couple of hours?"

"We probably need a whole day. Unless you want to spread it out over multiple dates."

She wrinkles her nose. "That sounds inefficient. Plus, your mom will want some variety, won't she?" Her nails drum on her desktop. "We should schedule a bunch of activities in different locations. And I'll bring a few changes of clothes so it looks like different days. Besides, it'll give us a chance to plan for the reunion. We can tick a bunch of boxes, and Brooklyn's mom can back the hell off."

Half of me loves that she's already in planning mode, the other half would like her to look at this as less of an obligation and a job. But getting a day in with her is the important part. The only way I can prove my feelings are real is to show her. And I can't do that if we're not spending time together—fingerbangs and face sitting aside. "How about Saturday? Would that work for you?"

"Let me check my calendar." She types away on her computer for a few seconds, a crease between her eyes. I want to run my index finger over the spot to smooth it out. "Saturday is free. I planned to run errands, but I can do most of it on Sunday."

"Awesome. I'll pick you up at eleven?" That gives me a couple of days to get everything organized. I'll make the most of this day together, and not because Brooklyn's mom needs photographic evidence of our relationship.

"I can just meet you wherever." She crosses her arms, as if she's daring me to challenge her independence.

"It makes a lot more sense for me to pick you up. Especially since we live three blocks apart."

She taps at her lips with a blue painted nail. *Lips I've had on mine recently*. I wish I could stop thinking about kissing her for five seconds.

Another deep sigh. "I guess you have a point."

"Awesome. I promise I'll make it fun."

"If you say so. I have a call in ten minutes, so unless there's anything else..." She lets the sentence hang.

"Nope. I got what I came for. Looking forward to our date." I give her a thumbs-up and grin as she levels me with the evilest of evil eyes. "Have a great rest of your day, Wills." I exit her office backwards, in case she decides to lob something at my head as I leave.

"I hope you step on LEGO while barefoot," she calls to my retreating form.

I smile as I whistle my way down the hall. *I have a date with Wills.* Now I just need to make sure it's the best she's ever been on.

CHAPTER 22

DALLAS

A message from Wills is followed by several photos of various wrapped boxes.

> **WILLS**
> What is this?

> **DALLAS**
> Gift boxes.

> **WILLS**
> Why are they here?

> **DALLAS**
> They're for you, obviously.

> **WILLS**
> Why are you buying me things?

> **DALLAS**
> Because you're my fiancée, and I'm taking you on a date, and I love shopping.

> **WILLS**
> I'm not sure if you've hit your head recently, but I am your FAKE fiancée, and this is a FAKE date.

DALLAS

You should delete that message. That's not something you want anybody else to see. If you don't want them, I can take them back.

The humping dots appear, disappear, then appear again.

DALLAS

Seriously. I don't want to make you uncomfortable, so if they really bother you, I will take them back.

WILLS

You don't have to do that. But how do you know my size in EVERYTHING?

DALLAS

WILLS

That only accounts for my panties.

DALLAS

I went through your closet when I was at your place for dinner with the family.

WILLS

You did not.

DALLAS

You're right. I didn't. I'm very good at guessing. If this hockey career doesn't pan out, I figure I can move to carnivals.

WILLS

But the clowns, Dallas.

DALLAS

Good point. Better not fuck up this career then.

WILLS

Aren't you glad I'm here to keep you out of trouble?

DALLAS

Immensely grateful. I'm happy to show you how grateful with any body part you'd like.

WILLS

Thank you for the clothes.

Obviously, she's ignoring my offer. Hopefully she'll let me come up to her place at the end of our date so I can get another hit.

DALLAS

Entirely my pleasure.

CHAPTER 23

DALLAS

I sleep like shit the night before our date, worried I'll do something to fuck the whole thing up. Then I accidentally hit snooze and sleep through my alarm, which means I'm running late.

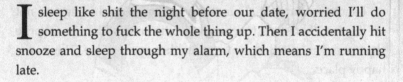

WILLS
It's after eleven. Where the hell are you?

DALLAS
On my way!

When I finally arrive, Wills looks more than a little annoyed as she exits the building. I want to get out and help, but she's already at the passenger side door, and I didn't have time to manage my anxiety boner, so all I can do is lean over and pull the handle. We're not off to a good start.

Aside from the murderous look on her perfect face, I notice she's wearing one of the outfits I bought for her.

She opens the back door. "You're twenty-five minutes late." She tosses her bag in the back seat and hangs the garment bag, closing the door with a little extra force before she slides into the passenger seat. "It's common courtesy to text if you're going to be late."

"I had trouble falling asleep, and then I slept through my alarm, and I forgot my suit and had to run back up and get it. I'm sorry I kept you waiting." As soon as she's buckled in, I put the car in gear and pull into traffic. I wait until the locks click before I say anything else. "I would have gotten out of the car to help with your bags, but I'm currently owning another inconvenient boner. I felt as though a public hard-on would make things worse—"

Willy puts her hand on my arm. I fully expect her nails to dig in, but the touch remains gentle. Instead, she does that thing where her voice gets all soft and sweet. "Take a breath, Dallas."

I suck in a lungful of air and try to focus on driving and not on the fact that she's touching me. She smells like her favorite shampoo. I inhale deeply. I can feel her eyes on me. This is my happy place.

"Good boy." She squeezes my arm and severs contact.

I groan. Loudly. Not on purpose, but any kind of praise from her lips, even if it's meant with a heaping side of sarcasm, just jacks me up. Especially phrases like "good boy."

She crosses one leg over the other and shifts so her body is turned toward me. "Talk to me about these anxiety boners."

"It's probably not a good idea."

"Because talking about it will make the problem worse?"

I nod once.

"Are you uncomfortable?"

"The angle isn't bad."

"How long do they usually last?"

"Depends on the situation." This one will likely last all day. My balls will definitely feel some type of way.

"How many times have you jerked off in a bathroom before a promo op?" I must be imagining the slight breathiness to her voice.

"Just a few times. Mostly I handle the situation at home." But sometimes even that doesn't work.

"Is this why you're chronically late?" she asks.

We've never talked about this. Not in all the years she's been working with the team. I just let her chastise me for my tardiness. "It's part of the reason."

"What's the other part of the reason?"

This is one of those rare cases in which being honest might earn me some grace. "I've done a lot of disappointing things when it comes to you. It was one thing to be an idiot when we were kids, and totally another when I'm putting your professional reputation on the line." Before Wills joined the Terror I wasn't all that concerned with promo ops. "I wanted to prove that I wasn't just a dipshit. That's when the panic attacks started. I'm sure it's hard to believe, considering all the shit I've put you through in the last little while, but disappointing you, or any company or nonprofit you liaise with, isn't something I want to do." I grip the steering wheel and slow down as we approach a stoplight.

Willy is silent for so long that I finally glance her way.

God, she's beautiful. Especially when she's wearing a sexy pout and one of her eyebrows is arched. She looks a little menacing, like she did when she straddled my face and rode my tongue. I should not be thinking about that right now. I look away so she can't see the thoughts on my face.

"You're serious," she murmurs.

"Yeah. I don't want to be a pain in your ass." I just wanted time with her. I'd sign up for something, then get nervous the night before and end up with a stupid anxiety boner which often resulted in me being late and Wills being annoyed. It became a vicious cycle I couldn't get out of.

"Hard to believe based on recent events," she mutters.

"Yeah. I know." I drive us out of the city, into the rolling hills of the countryside. It's pretty and scenic, the landscape dotted with fruit farms.

"Where are we going?" she asks.

"Currently we're heading to the Heartly Farm to visit my horse."

"Oh, so this is a day of self-flagellation, then, is it?"

I grin. "Would that make you happy, Wills?"

She makes a noise but doesn't give me an actual answer.

"I don't dislike horses. I'm just not a fan of the birthing process and seeing an animal in pain," I admit. "And I get that it's the cycle of life, but it's still unnerving to witness."

Willy huffs and pokes my arm. "Don't do that."

"Don't do what? Be honest?"

"Say things that make me like you." She turns up the radio.

I grin. Eventually we reach the Heartly Farm, where I witnessed the birth of Dallas Bright, a baby foal owned by a family with a son battling a serious medical condition.

I drive past the main house, all the way around back to the horse barn. Sariah greets me with a wide smile. "Dallas! It's great to see you! Todd is excited that you're here again so soon." She envelops me in a tight hug.

"How are his treatments going?"

Her smile turns soft. "Good. But he came down with a cold last week, so he can't ride. He'll come out a little later to say hi, though." She turns her attention to Wills. "Hemi, it's so nice to have you back."

"It's been too long."

"Come on. I was just getting the horses ready." She motions for us to follow her.

Wills falls into step beside me. "Have you been back here without me?" I can't read her tone, but she almost sounds...hurt.

"I try to come out once a month. I sponsor a couple of horses here, and I visit Todd. I couldn't always make it work during the regular season, so now I try to come every other week. When Todd is feeling good, he comes for a ride with me."

"I would have come with you if you'd told me."

"It wasn't about publicity," I say, somewhat defensively.

"I know." She bumps me with her shoulder. "You really need to stop trying to make me like you."

"Never."

We reach the barn, and Sariah introduces Wills to the horse she'll be riding. Thor is a dark brown steed, majestic and easygoing. Beauty is mine, a black mare.

I pass my phone to Sariah and ask her to snap a few for me while we groom the horses.

"What are you doing?" she mutters.

"Showing you how to do it properly." I get in nice and close, the curve of her ass pressing against me, my chest meeting her back as I guide the brush over Thor's flank.

"This is an excuse to rub my ass," she grumbles.

"Shh, The Sword of Destiny will hear you and rise to the occasion," I whisper.

She barks out a laugh. "Sword of Destiny?"

"Don't say his name, summoning him will embarrass us both," I say in her ear.

She laughs, and I grin.

"You two are so cute together," Sariah sighs.

Wills nudges me. "I've got it from here."

I reclaim my phone, and we finish preparing the horses and set out on the trail. We take a bunch more photos and meet up with Todd for a short visit once we're done. It's obvious the cold is taking it out of him, and he's frustrated because we have to keep our distance. All he's allowed is a fist bump, no hug. I promise him I'll be back in a couple of weeks, and if he's feeling better he can beat me at Crazy Eights.

Willy links her arm with mine as we walk back to my car. "I can't believe you've been coming here all these months," she says.

"Todd made an impression on me. So did Beauty, to be honest. And Bright Junior."

"Don't downplay it, Dallas. It's a big deal, and it clearly means a lot to him and his family."

I shrug. It's a small thing compared to what the rest of my family gets up to. My mom has spent her entire life volunteering and giving back to the community. My dad is an oncologist, and my sister and brothers are in the business of saving lives. I'm the one who stepped into a career where I make millions a year for chasing a puck down the ice. But I don't say any of that, because I don't like the way it makes me feel. "He's a great kid and easy to be around. Besides, I've developed a fondness for horses—outside of the birthing process, anyway."

Wills squeezes my bicep. "I love that you do this."

Her approval jacks me up even more than her ire, and I remind my body that we're in a public place and to settle down. "You're always welcome to join me, but I don't want to turn it into a promo op."

She smiles up at me, and it's so full of genuine warmth that my heart skips a beat. "This is a really special thing you're doing, Dallas. Thank you for sharing it with me."

She lets go of my arm, but her smile remains. And it feels like a huge win—like maybe she's starting to see the me who's been in front of her all these years, and not just the idiot kid who was too caught up in what everyone else thought to show her how I felt about her.

Our next stop is a fruit farm just a few minutes down the road.

We park in the back, and she trades her T-shirt for a tank top that dips low in the front and shows off her ample cleavage. I can't look away as she gathers her thick, wavy hair and twists it, securing it with a clip. My gaze skims the graceful slope of her neck and the softness of her shoulders. What I wouldn't give to kiss a path along that bare skin. She props her fist on her hip. "What?"

"You're beautiful." I pop the trunk and retrieve my duffel

bag. I pull the shirt I'm wearing over my head and toss it in the trunk so I can replace it with a fresh one.

"Dallas." Willy snaps her fingers.

I glance up. "'Sup?"

"Look pretty." She snaps several photos.

"Won't it look suspect if I'm changing my shirt?"

"There's no context. I can save it for when your socials need a boost." She smirks and tucks her phone back in her purse.

I run a hand over my abs and return the grin. "Wilhelmina Reddi-Grinst, were you objectifying me?"

"Yup. Absolutely. And don't think I didn't see you checking out my rack a minute ago," she notes.

"I like your curves," I confess as I pull my shirt over my head.

"I have a lot of them." Wills beckons me forward. "You've got something in your hair."

She slides a hand up my chest and curves it around the back of my neck. For a moment, our eyes meet.

"Bend for me," she murmurs.

I grin. "I always do."

Her nails dig into my skin, and my body instantly reacts as she tugs my head down. I don't resist. Especially not since I'm now looking down the front of her shirt into her glorious cleavage. I would love to end tonight snuggling on the couch, my head resting on her softness.

"Got it." The bite of her nails and the warmth of her palm disappears from the back of my neck. She holds a dandelion fluff between her finger and thumb. "Make a wish on three."

On three she releases the dandelion fluff. I wish, not for the first time, that she would see the truth and believe it.

She closes her eyes and her lips move as she makes her own wish, the fluff floating away on the breeze.

I almost lean in to kiss her pretty, tempting lips. But then I remember she's only on this date because we need photographic evidence of our fake relationship.

Once I've locked up the car, she falls into step beside me. She doesn't yank her hand away when my fingers graze hers, so I link our pinkies.

While we pick berries we talk about the reunion and iron out the details of our relationship. I pause to put sunscreen on her shoulders when they start to turn pink. Her lips push out into a pout. "You were just carrying that around with you?"

"I know you're prone to burning." I brush the back of my hand over her cheek.

She tips her head. "Are you always this thoughtful?"

"This isn't how you wanted to spend your Saturday, so I'm trying to make it bearable."

"I don't dislike being around you, Dallas. I just have a lot of feelings about the way you treated me when we were growing up."

"I'm sorry about what happened—"

"I said I had a lot of feelings, not that I wanted to talk about them."

And there's my favorite Willy. The one who says exactly what she means. But as much as I love her for it, the way she shuts me down also makes it impossible to have a real conversation about the past, or to apologize the way I want to.

We finish filling our baskets in silence. Then she changes her shirt again so we can take pictures in their flower garden.

We go to a theater in the park performance, followed by dinner at one of her favorite restaurants.

Dinner is easy. We avoid talking about the reunion and Brooklyn and Sean. Instead, she fills me in on the project she's working on with the women's team. She's animated and enthusiastic, and I wish, for the thousandth time, that I hadn't given her so many reasons to hate me before now.

At the end of the night, I pull into the fifteen-minute parking spot at her building.

She unbuckles her seat belt and smiles softly. "I actually had a good time today."

I stretch my arm across the back of her seat. "I could come up for a bit and take care of you."

Her eyes flare. "Oh, uh…my roommate is home tonight."

"We could go to my place instead."

Her bottom lip slides through her teeth as her eyes rove over me. "That's okay. I think it's better if we don't. Thank you for offering, though." Her hand is already on the door.

"Of course. Yeah." I swallow my disappointment.

Her eyes dart to my mouth, and for a moment I wonder if she wants me to kiss her. But this is Wills. The only reason she tolerated this day with me is so Brooklyn's mom will stop questioning the validity of this relationship.

She gets out of the car and grabs her bag from the back seat. "Thanks again, Dallas. Have a good night."

"You, too."

I watch her walk away. So much for that wish I made.

CHAPTER 24

HEMI

"I did something stupid."

"That is not a statement I often hear coming from your mouth," Shilpa says as she passes me another package of organza bags. We're making favors for her cousin's upcoming wedding. "What happened?"

"So you know I have a fun-time friend…" I fill another organza bag with Jordan almonds.

"The pharmaceutical rep?" Her eyes go wide. "Please tell me you're not seeing him on the sly."

"Of course not. I know better. The backlash would be horrible. It's bad enough that I'm in a 'relationship' with a player. I'd be raked over the coals if I was caught cheating on him." I let my head fall back against the cushions. "I may have mentioned him to Dallas."

"Okay…"

"And how I was minus a stress reliever."

"You have personal pleasure devices."

I give her a look. "It's not the same, and you know it."

Shilpa sits up straight, and a sly smile tugs at the corner of her mouth. "Oh, Hemi. Dallas offered his services, didn't he?"

I nod and bite my lip.

"And you took him up on it, didn't you?"

I hang my head in shame. "I did."

"Did you sleep with him?" she asks.

"No. No sex." Though my vagina clenches at the mere fucking mention, the traitorous bitch. "But I am now very aware of how talented he is with his hands and tongue. You know I've spent all this time loathing him for being a dick to me, and I figured, what harm could it do? He's nice to look at. And he owes me. So why not let him get me off, right?"

"Makes sense to me."

"So of course I set parameters and laid the ground rules."

"Of course you did." She hides her smile behind her mug of tea.

"But his mouth, Shilps. He just...doesn't stop running it. Ever. And he's so good with it. The chemistry is unreal. Last night, he offered to take care of me at the end of our date, and I turned him down. And in a few days, I have to spend an entire weekend with him. There's a very high probability that we'll have to sleep in the same bed. How the hell am I going to make it through the weekend? He'll offer again. I know he will."

"Why did you turn him down last night?" she asks.

"Because I can't get addicted. He's too good at it—like, so, so good at it." I shove down the memory of his head between my thighs. "And he was so thoughtful yesterday. And I had fun." I say this like it's criminal. "Letting him get his hands on me would have been a bad idea. But I don't know if I have the restraint required to say no this weekend, and it's messing with my head. He can't know how he affects me."

But it's more than that. He pushes every right button I have in the bedroom department, and that freaks me the hell out. We're ultra compatible between the sheets. Or at least he's compatible with me. I haven't put my hands on him, so that's speculation on my part. But both times he's been rock hard and ready to go when I've sent him home. The implications are... terrifying. What if I give in and have sex with him? What if it's just as amazing as I expect it will be? This arrangement isn't like the one with Allen—our life visions don't align, so that makes the casual easy to maintain. It's how I avoid any feelings. But I already have tons of feelings where Dallas is concerned. And some of them are shifting. I don't trust him. I can't be the nerdy girl who falls for the hot hockey player, especially not the player who hurt me a decade ago.

She smiles softly. "To be clear, every time he's serviced you—"

"Can you use a different word? *Serviced* sounds like I'm a broken washing machine."

Shilpa chuckles. "Have you orgasmed every time?"

"It was only twice, and yes. Both times. The second time it was the longest, most intense orgasm of my life."

"So don't you think he already knows he affects you?"

"But right now he thinks it was a hate-gasm! I need to keep it that way."

She leans back in her chair. "Explain why?"

Her phone chimes with new messages from Ash. I recognize the ringtone.

"Are you going to check that?" I would happily never speak of my life before university again if I could, except for memories with my family.

"In a minute. He can wait. Answer the question, Hemi."

I close my eyes and exhale some of my anxiety. "I don't know. They teased me relentlessly in elementary school. Gum in my hair, rotten fruit in my winter boots. It got worse in middle school and high school. They'd spread rumors about me. Like that I kept all my toenails in a jar or had a shrine to one of our teachers." And not one of the cute teachers. The old one with hair in his ears who smelled like cheese. "There were rumors that he and his friends used to deface my student council posters. They'd put shitty notes in my locker calling me names like Virgin Queen, or say I was a waste of big boobs. It was stupid and juvenile. I get that teenagers can be mean, but I was a target. And it fucking hurt. I know what doesn't kill you makes you stronger and all that, but it didn't make it feel any less awful at the time. He had so much social power back then, but he never did anything to stop them. He laughed at their shitty jokes like it wasn't cruel." I look to the ceiling. "He still has that power over people now. Everybody adores him. I'm supposed to hate him for every scar he left behind, but I don't think I do right now. This whole thing, this situation I'm in…I feel like I cornered myself. I protected him when I protected the welfare of the team and my own reputation. I never said anything to anyone about it, because I knew it would make everything worse. I don't feel like I have control over myself anymore." I spoon almonds into a bag. "And the worst part is, I'm attracted to him, Shilps." I cover my mouth with my hand. "Like, really attracted to him. I cannot stop thinking about his hands on me."

At this point, though, fantasizing about Dallas is the least of my worries. I have the reunion to deal with. When I visit my moms, I don't usually venture out much. It's easier to avoid running into people I know and having fake, awkward conversations on the street. But this is an event, and I was the class president. I can't hide from it, or the people who were shitty to me. More than that, I want to show them, and myself, that the crap I endured didn't hold me back. I'm already freaking out about it— being with the same people who called me terrible names growing up, becoming that girl again. But I can't back out, because if Dallas is right about one thing, it's that I can't let them get the best of me.

Shilpa sighs. "There's definitely chemistry between you. Can you be honest with him about how you're feeling?"

"Not a chance. He's never even apologized for what he did. I'm not going to open myself up like that."

"Has he ever tried?"

That gives me pause. He does try to bring it up sometimes. But… "I don't want to hear it if it's disingenuous," I tell her.

She nods slowly. "Which is what you assume it would be

because of your history with him. The version of Dallas I've known is different, but your fears are valid. It's easy to forget that everyone has their own experiences with people. Obviously, he's grown up over the past decade, but that doesn't take away the hurt he caused. You know what you can handle and what you need out of this. I get that you want to face down those demons, and attending the reunion will give you the peace you need to move past it."

I nod. Maybe that's exactly why I want this. Maybe I need to let go of all the hurt so I can leave that girl in the past and not let her follow me through the rest of my life. "Thanks, Shilps. You're always the voice of reason." I'm so grateful that I can be scared without judgment with her, but she always challenges me with a new perspective.

My phone buzzes with a message.

We both look at it.

"I'll check my message if you check yours," Shilps says.

We both pick up our phones.

"Oh wow," Shilps mutters as she reads.

"What?"

"Apparently, Dallas and Ash are on a shopping spree. One guess who he's buying things for." She nods to my phone. "Your turn."

> **DALLAS**
>
> Do you need anything from me?
>
> Like an orgasm?
>
> I can't stop thinking about the way you taste.
>
> Or how soft you are on my tongue.
>
> And how much I love the way my name sounds when you moan it.
>
> Haven't I been a good boy?
>
> When do I get a reward?

I cover my mouth with my hand. "He's sexting me."

"Because you turned him down last night?"

"Maybe." I bite my lips together. "He wants to know when he gets a reward for being a good boy."

Her eyebrows rise. "Sounds like you're not the only one affected."

"I'm so screwed this weekend."

CHAPTER 25

HEMI

Sitting in a vehicle, immersed in the scent of all things Dallas is torture. He smells way too good. I can't escape him, or his chiseled fucking jaw and his incredible forearms. There's this muscle at his elbow that resembles a half golf ball, and I can't stop staring at it.

My stomach knots as we pass the sign that reads *Welcome to Huntsville, population 19,000.* I grip the door handle and suck in a breath. And then another, but I still feel like I can't get enough air.

"Honey, are you okay?" It sounds like Dallas is in a tunnel.

I try to tell him I'm fine, but all that comes out is a horrible squeaky sound.

He takes the next exit and pulls onto the shoulder, shifting the car into park.

My vision blurs, and everything narrows to a pinpoint. This is so embarrassing. I think I'm about to lose it. That never happens. Not like this. I don't know what's going on, but I can't afford an emotional breakdown. Especially not in front of Dallas.

"Hey, hey. Is it okay if I touch you?"

I want to say no, but instead I nod.

Why the hell did I nod?

He unfastens his seat belt and unlocks the door. The strains of The Tragically Hip's "Bobcaygeon" fill the car. A few seconds later, the passenger door opens. Dallas leans into my personal space, releases my seat belt, and slides his hands behind my knees. It must be a sensitive part of my body, because that contact causes a jolt to buzz down my spine and settle in familiar places.

He adjusts my position so I'm sitting sideways, feet on the gravel. Dallas crouches in front of me so we're eye to eye. One hand stays on my knee, and the other moves my hair away from my face and curves around the side of my neck. It's intimate and gentle and so conflicting. I don't want to need grounding right now, especially not from him.

"Take a deep breath, honey." His thumb sweeps back and forth along the edge of my jaw.

"I don't know what's going on." I gulp air, but it doesn't fill my lungs.

"It's okay. You're okay."

He pulls me close, and I wrap my arms around him, holding on for dear life. Like he's a buoy. Like he can save me from whatever this is. "I—I can't breathe."

He lets me cling to him for a few seconds before he unwraps my arms and hands me his Terror water bottle with the absurd goose logo. "Drink this."

I grip it with both hands, but even then, it wobbles perilously. He helps me steady it while I take a sip. The ice-cold water is startling but refreshing.

"Good girl. A little more," he cajoles.

I refuse to acknowledge how that simple praise makes me feel instantly better, but I do as he says.

"That's it. You're doing great. You got this, Wills." His smile is as soft as his voice. He tips the water bottle again.

The cold liquid slides down my throat. My tunnel vision clears as the sensation that someone is gripping my throat eases.

He sets the water bottle back in the center console and wraps his wide, warm palms around my calves, squeezing gently. "Do you feel a little better?"

"I don't even know what that was." Embarrassment washes over me. "I felt like I was choking, and I couldn't take a breath, and my whole body went...numb? Did I just have some kind of medical episode? Do I need to go to the hospital?"

His expression shifts to empathy. "You had a panic attack."

I blink at him. "That's impossible. I don't panic."

"Normally, I would agree. However, I have some experience with panic, and everything you've just described fits into that category."

I frown.

"It's nothing to be embarrassed about. I've created a lot more stress for you around this reunion. I'm sure it feels like we're walking into the jaws of a lion. But I've got you, okay? I got you into this shit, and I won't let you go through it alone. Not ever again."

He's talking about a lot more than the reunion, but I'm afraid to put that much faith in him—especially since he's right; he is the reason we're in this mess. But if I take a step back and set aside our tumultuous history, he's been all-in since the moment we started fake dating.

"I can't have that happen again, Dallas." I'm not just talking about the panic attack. I'm talking about all of it, including what he did to me all those years ago.

He strokes my cheek and takes my hand, eyes brimming with emotion. "I won't let it. I promise, Wilhelmina."

I wish I could believe him. I pull my hand free and tuck myself back into the passenger seat. "I'm fine now. Thank you for whatever you did to make that stop."

He doesn't move yet. "If you need another minute, we can stop somewhere. Grab an iced latte."

I can't afford to be weak. Not with the shitstorm of a weekend ahead of us. Starting with Brooklyn and Sean's engagement party. "It's better if we don't. We'll run into someone." And

I'm not ready for that, clearly. I tap his knee, which is resting against my calf. "Seriously. I'm fine. Your magic worked. I'm good to go." I give him the thumbs-up.

He reluctantly stands and closes the passenger door.

I exhale a relieved breath. Having him that close, touching me, makes it hard to think clearly. The orgasm deal was a bad idea. I inspect my shaking hands as he rounds the hood. For a moment, I'm transported back to prom all those years ago. The way my body feels now is an echo of that night in the parking lot. It's the only time in my life I've lost it like that. It took forever to get myself under control again. But no one was there to witness it. And there was no one to calm me down, either. I cried so hard I made myself sick.

Dallas settles back in the driver's seat. "Wilhelmina?"

I can feel his eyes on me as I force a smile. "Really, I'm good. Let's get going. We only have a couple hours before their engagement party."

"If you're sure." Dallas checks to make sure it's clear before he pulls back onto the road.

I can fake it for a weekend. I will not break down again, not in front of Dallas and certainly not in front of our peers. I left this town for a reason. I'm a badass PR director who puts hockey players in their place on a regular basis. I can handle a bunch of former classmates.

It only takes a few minutes to get to Dallas's parents' house once we're off the main drag. Technically, there's enough space for Dallas and me to stay at my moms' place, but they downsized to a cozy two-bedroom a few years ago. Dallas's parents still live in the house he grew up in. It's a spacious two-story, five-bedroom home. I've only ever been inside it once, for a house party junior year that Brooklyn forced me to go to. It wasn't really my scene. Also, she disappeared into one of the bedrooms with some grade-twelve boy half an hour after we arrived, leaving me to fend for myself.

The front door flies open as we pull into the driveway.

Dallas's mom steps out onto the wraparound porch. Her hair is pulled back, and she's dressed in a pair of pink capris and a short-sleeved white top, which is covered by an apron that reads HOME IS WHERE THE CAKE IS. She is the quintessential Betty Crocker of moms.

Her smile lights up her face as Dallas parks behind his dad's truck. I'm once again submerged in guilt, knowing we'll eventually break her heart. And coming back to Huntsville once this fake engagement ends will be another challenge. I push those thoughts aside. We've made our bed; we have to lie in it. It's too late to go back now.

Diana rushes down the front steps, and Dallas wraps her in a hug, lifting her off her feet. My stupid heart gets all fluttery. The way a man treats his mother says a lot about him. Dallas adores his mom as much as she adores him. He always talks about her with respect and kindness.

I step out of Dallas's sports car as he sets his mom down. She rushes around the hood and folds me into her embrace. "I'm so happy you're here! How was the drive up?"

"Smooth like butter," I lie. "Thank you so much for opening your home to me."

"We wouldn't have it any other way." She squeezes my hands and looks over at Dallas. "Sweetie, why don't you grab the bags, and we'll get you settled in."

"You got it, Mom." Dallas rounds the trunk.

"Oh, I can carry my own bag." I packed like I was going away for weeks, not three days.

Diana chuckles. "I know you can, but it's okay to let people do things for you." I expect her to guide me toward the front door, but instead we round the side of the house. "We thought you and Dallas would appreciate a little privacy this weekend, so we set you up in the bunky."

"Oh, we would've been fine in the house." I look over my shoulder at Dallas who's wheeling my enormous suitcase and weekend bag, along with his own small duffel and our garment bags.

I widen my eyes at him, and he just smiles and shrugs.

"I'm so happy that you're finally together." Diana pats my hand. "He was always so protective of you when you were kids."

I frown. She must be thinking of someone else. The last thing Dallas ever did when we were kids was shield me from hurt. I don't correct her, though. Clearly her understanding of my relationship with Dallas is different than the truth.

The bunky is an adorable little cabin. The covered front porch faces the lake and has a wooden two-person swing decorated with cushions. The front door is painted butter yellow with a sign that says HOME SWEET HOME. Diana opens the door and ushers me inside. "It's cozy, but it's private."

"It's perfect," I say as I enter the small, one-room cabin. I'm impressed that my voice doesn't crack. There are two doors on the far wall, presumably leading to a closet and a bathroom. To my right is a kitchenette with a sink, a tiny counter, and a mini fridge. A bistro table and two comfy chairs sit to the right. And to the left is the bed. I don't even think I'd classify it as a double.

"We used to have bunk beds when the boys were young so they could have sleepovers out here, but I redecorated it when Dallas moved out, and now it's our guesthouse. There's a bathroom through there with a shower. And if you need anything, you just let me know." She squeezes my shoulder. "When you're settled, come up to the house and we'll have a pre-engagement-party cocktail." She winks and leaves me alone with Dallas.

He rolls my suitcase inside and drops his duffel on the floor before he hangs the garment bags on the coat hook and closes the door.

"What the fuck, Dallas?" I smack his chest.

"What did I do?"

I point to the bed. "It's hardly big enough for one person, let alone two! What size is that even?"

"I think it's a three-quarter bed. The frame belonged to my great-grandma Bippy, and obviously my mom couldn't bear the thought of parting with it, so she put it in here. In her defense, it fits the space well."

My stomach flips at the idea of having to lie beside Dallas in that tiny, tiny fucking bed and not give in to the chemistry raging between us. There isn't even enough room on the floor for his enormous body. And he smells so fucking good.

There are zero chances that our bodies won't touch in that bed. It's too small. How will I resist him when we're inches apart *all night long*?

CHAPTER 26

HEMI

"I hate to admit it, but it's a lovely party," Mom says through a practiced smile.

"It is," I agree.

It's also one of my worst nightmares come true. This weekend will be full of them. Everyone from high school is here, and their parents. It's like graduation night, but ten years later. Dallas is on the other side of the room, chatting with a bunch of guys from our year. I recognize all of them, and I'm sure they probably recognize me, but we weren't friends.

I can feel the judgy stares from across the room, where Brooklyn's friends stand in a semicircle, laughing and chatting. After prom, they all stopped talking to me. A few days later, I heard two of them in the hall saying I'd gotten what I deserved. That I was a pushy know-it-all, and they'd only tolerated me because of Brooklyn. I was too much, and they were glad they didn't have to pretend to be my friends anymore. I take a deep breath and shove those memories aside, because they still hurt, still make me feel small and insignificant. Even though I know I'm not. Or at least I usually know I'm not...

I stand between my moms, accepting another glass of champagne as the server passes. I'm on my second, and things are blissfully soft around the edges. More tolerable. And Dallas just keeps getting hotter.

"A plaid shirt and running shoes should not look that good on a man," I grumble into my glass. His shoes are custom made, and in team colors.

"He has interesting fashion sense. But it works for him," Mom muses.

"I know. Sometimes he wears plaid suits and sneakers and still manages to look put together." I sound more irritated than smitten, and at this point I'm not sure which is accurate. I'm stressed. I feel totally out of place, like the loser in the corner. I wish Shilpa was here. I wish the whole Badass Babe Brigade was here and I felt like part of something instead of being an outsider.

"It shows his personality, doesn't it?" Ma says thoughtfully.

I make a noise of affirmation. He's such an outdoorsy, northern-Ontario-loving guy. He's always smiling, even when I make him do horrible things he hates. He's been nothing but nice to me since we started this whole fake-relationship debacle. He's spent a ridiculous amount of money on clothes, gifts, and other things he thought I might need for dates and this weekend. Every outfit he's bought fits me perfectly and is exactly my style. And then there are the orgasms, which I will not think about right now. Shilpa's words about getting what I need out of this turn over in my mind.

They announce that the buffet is open, but I decide to wait until the initial rush has slowed, crossing my fingers there will still be a few of Diana's famous cheese biscuits left. She made several platters. They're such a simple thing—Rice Krispies, sharp cheddar, and cayenne pepper—but everyone loves them and always go back for more. Dallas sampled a couple before we left for the party, and Diana rapped him on the knuckles every time he tried to sneak another one.

My moms stop to say hello to Roland March, the town's primary real estate lawyer. I say hi, but when they immediately dive into business talk, I excuse myself and check out the buffet. I stiffen when I spot Brooklyn's mom. I haven't seen her in years, and I haven't spoken to her since graduation. Thankfully, Dallas's mom slides her arm through mine.

"Shall we grab something to eat together?"

"I don't want to miss out on your cheese biscuits," I admit.

She pats my hand. "I have more hidden in the freezer at home."

"Of course you do."

Brooklyn's mom's back is to us, so she doesn't notice our approach.

"What a surprise that Wilhelmina ended up with one of the players," she says sarcastically to the woman standing next to her.

Her friend laughs. "I guess now we know why she chose the field she did—access to all those rich men."

Dallas's mom stiffens beside me. "Ugly isn't a good look on you, Carla."

My eyes widen. I've never heard a harsh word out of her mouth until now. Mrs. Bright does not take anyone's shit, apparently.

The two women spin around. "Oh! Diana, Wilhelmina, I just meant—"

Diana holds up a hand. "I know what you meant, and Dallas is lucky to have found someone as special as Wilhelmina. She's exactly what he needs in a partner."

I squeeze her arm as I untangle mine from hers. "I'm going to use the ladies' room." I turn to Brooklyn's mom. "Congratulations. I'm sure you must be thrilled about Sean and Brooklyn's engagement. They truly deserve each other." I spin around before she can say anything else and make a beeline for the bathroom.

I'm only a handful of steps away from my escape when I almost collide with Sean and Brooklyn. I glance around, wishing one of my moms was with me, or even Dallas, but I'm all alone.

Adulthood has leaned out the soft lines of Brooklyn's face. I note, however, with a hint of petty glee, that Sean's hairline is already receding.

I force a smile and try to keep my voice steady. "Brooklyn, Sean, congratulations on your engagement."

Brooklyn's smile looks as brittle as I feel. Sean stands at her side, eyes moving over me on an assessing sweep. I mentally thank Dallas for picking out a dress that accentuates my curves and highlights my cleavage, but in a tasteful, not an in-your-face way.

"Wilhelmina!" Brooklyn's voice is all fake excitement. "It's so good to see you!"

She pulls me in for a wet-rag, limp hug. I pat her back and remind myself that after this weekend, I won't have to exchange more than a polite hello with her again for at least another decade—unless I get an invitation to her wedding. I'd consider giving myself food poisoning to get out of having to endure something like this again.

She steps back, severing the contact after a few painfully awkward seconds. "And congratulations on *your* engagement. I admit, I was a little shocked. You actually hooked Dallas." She shakes her head. "Who would've thought?"

"Right?" I laugh, and it sounds halfway to hysterical.

"I guess you're not holding a grudge anymore if you're here." Brooklyn glances around the room, like she's looking for an escape.

That makes two of us. "We're all adults now." I force a smile.

She hums her agreement and links her arm with Sean's. "Oh! There's Katie! We should go say hi." She turns her fake smile back to me. "Let's definitely catch up sometime this weekend."

"I should be so lucky." I hope this is the last conversation I ever have with these two.

Brooklyn guides Sean away, whispering as they go.

On shaky legs, I finish my trip to the bathroom, grateful that I cross paths with a server on the way. I grab two glasses of champagne, thank him, and continue into the bathroom. I'm grateful each stall has total privacy. I throw the lock, down a glass of champagne in two gulps, and drop to the toilet seat.

"This is the worst," I mutter. I take several deep breaths, determined not to lose my shit in a public place.

That I didn't punch Brooklyn in the face, or scream at her, or break down in a fit of tears, seems like a serious win. Except I'm finally ready to admit I haven't grieved the loss of Brooklyn's friendship properly. Instead, I shoved that pain into a box and tucked it away. Sort of like my adoption files. Time has taught me that she was never a good friend, but there's still a disconnect inside me. I wanted to be as important to her as she was to me. The way she hurt me caused a ripple effect that changed my life—*though probably for the better*, I remind myself. I moved to the city for university and vowed never to trust the wrong person to have my back again. And yet here I am. Fake engaged to the guy who watched his friends push me into puddles on the playground. I want to believe he's truly sorry for all the things that happened growing up. That he really is a nice guy, the kind I'd be happy to bring home to my moms. But we're just a big old pile of fucking fake, and I hate it.

I sip my remaining glass of champagne as I rummage around in my purse for my phone. My Badass Babe Brigade group chat is on fire today. The girls have been messaging relentlessly since I sent them a picture of the adorable cabin Dallas and I are staying in. I only showed them the outside.

But in my private chat with Shilpa, I included a photo of the very tiny bed. That chat is full of shifty-eyed GIFs. Again, I wish she was here. She knows how nervous I am about sleeping in a bed beside Dallas, particularly a small one. I leave my Shilpa chat alone, because there's potential for me to end up in tears if I'm honest with her about how I'm handling things. Instead, I open the Badass Babe Brigade thread.

There are several messages referencing a picture Dallas apparently posted, and everyone is all about the heart eyes and how hot I look. I quickly pull up his social media. The pinned post is a picture of me between my moms, smiling and laughing. He's captioned it with a cheesy phrase about how beautiful I am and how lucky he is to have me.

I return to the Badass Babe Brigade chat.

> **RIX**
>
> How's the engagement party? Is the groom already sloppy drunk?

> **HAMMER**
>
> That dress is 🔥 Do you and Dallas match? Is he in his plaid uniform?

> **DRED**
>
> Please tell me someone is awkwardly giving a play-by-play reenactment of something Dallas did last season.

> **TALLY**
>
> You and your moms are super cute. 🖤

> **SHILPS**
>
> You're a queen and we all wish we were there.

I compose a message in response:

> **HEMI**
>
> I got to congratulate the happy couple on their engagement. It was stupidly awkward, and if there's a twentieth reunion, I'm not going. This whole thing is a nightmare, and I want it to be over. What was I trying to prove by being here? I wish I was drinking margaritas with you and telling Rix not to eat the refried beans. I need a girls' night when I get back.

I'm immediately flooded with group hug GIFs and promises that we'll have a girls'-night sleepover at Hammer's when I return.

A new message from Shilpa appears in our private chat.

SHILPS

Do you need to talk?

HEMI

Later. I'm hiding in the bathroom chugging champagne. I grossly underestimated how awful it would be to see all the people who made me feel two inches tall in high school and apparently still do.

SHILPS

Oh babe. I'm so sorry. I wish I was there. They don't matter—they never did. Remember what a badass you are.

HEMI

I'm trying. And I wish you were here too. I should go. I'll message later.

SHILPS

Wonder Woman GIF

I use the bathroom for its intended purpose and not just a hiding place, then steel myself for more unpleasant interactions. Shilpa is right, yet trying to convince my brain of that feels insurmountable.

I barely make it ten steps back into the room when a body blocks my way. Broad chest covered in plaid. Smells like my favorite cologne. "Hey! I've been looking for you everywhere."

I fight to put my feelings back in the box, to hide all the hurt. To not show how out of place I feel. "I just needed the restroom."

His eyes search mine. "Are you okay, honey?"

I swallow the pain of this whole experience and struggle to form a smile. But he's all I have right now. He's my rock, and I've spent the last two hours watching him shine like he always does while I fight demons no one can see. "I'm fine," I croak.

He pushes my hair over my shoulders. "Wanna get out of here?"

I nod once and bite my lips together. I'm so on edge. I don't want to need him, but I do. So badly.

He cups my face in his palm and presses his lips to my forehead. I can't tell if he does it because he's sorry he left me alone, or he feels sorry for me, or to keep up appearances. Regardless, it makes my knees weak and my heart stutter. I want to curl up in a ball and cry my eyes out. When he pulls back, he tips my chin up, his normally carefree expression swapped out for intense concern. "You're the biggest badass I know, Wilhelmina."

"I don't feel very badass right now."

"Let's GTFO." He wraps an arm around my shoulder and guides us toward the door.

"Bright! Man, you can't leave yet!" calls one of the guys I vaguely remember.

"We'll see you tomorrow. I've got plans with my girl." Dallas keeps walking, nodding to our former classmates as he guides me to the door. He doesn't drop his arm even when we step out into the warm, dark evening. The sun has set, and the streetlamps cast a yellow glow over the sidewalk. Moths bumble around them, desperate to get close to the light.

"You want me to call a cab?" Dallas asks.

"Let's walk." I could use the air, and the time to mentally prepare for being trapped with him for eight hours in the small, romantic cabin, with only one tiny bed.

"Did something happen at the engagement party?" Dallas asks softly as we head back to his parents'.

"I ran into Brooklyn and Sean, which was to be expected, but I wasn't prepared for how it would make me feel." I don't have anyone else to talk to about this. Even Shilpa, who would gladly listen to me bitch and moan, can't truly understand what I'm going through.

"They're assholes. That hasn't changed in the past decade."

"It doesn't stop the hurt, Dallas. Brooklyn was my best friend. And yes, she was a shitty best friend, but she was one of the few people who liked me back then—or at least pretended to. I haven't seen or talked to her since graduation, and even then, she was standoffish at best. You have no idea what this is like for me. You made friends everywhere and everyone loved you. They still do. Now you're a professional hockey player. You're successful and accomplished and the most popular guy in our class. I was barely tolerated."

"That's not true."

"It is, though. I know I'm a lot. I know that about myself. I've certainly heard it enough. I wish I wasn't too much for most people. This whole thing is a reminder of how hard my teen years were. I wanted to come here and prove to everyone that I've made it, that I'm not still that know-it-all insecure girl, but here I'm like a bad joke, fiancée to the pro hockey player who routinely tormented me and ruined my senior year. I feel like an outsider all over again." I stumble over air and realize that on top of everything else, I'm drunk.

Dallas grabs my arm to steady me. "You're not a joke, Wills. And you are *never* a lot. You're perfect exactly as you are."

"It's easy for you to say from the pedestal everyone puts you on." I shake free of his hold. "I'm done talking about this. I don't want to say something I'll regret." If I get emotional on him, I'm liable to spill my guts, more than I already have. Ask him why he did all the things he did. In Toronto, I can usually ignore my past, but not here.

My mouth goes dry when we arrive at his parents and he ushers me into the cabin.

"I'm going to get ready for bed," I announce.

"Okay." Dallas tucks his hands in his pockets, looking lost and unsure.

I grab my nightshirt and toothbrush and disappear into the bathroom. I'm way drunker than I thought. I lost count of the number of glasses of champagne I consumed. I'm bleary-eyed and unsteady on my feet. I change into my nightshirt and nearly fall over. When I open the bathroom door, Dallas has already changed into shorts and a T-shirt. We trade places, and I stare at the bed for a few long seconds. It's so small. So, so small.

I turn off all but the bedside lamp and climb in, shimmying as close to the edge as I can. I pull the covers up and cross my arms, trying to make myself as small as possible, which isn't easy because I'm not small. This bed is *not* made for two adults.

I close my eyes and try to even out my breathing. The bathroom door opens and closes. The bed dips, and I swallow. Dallas's arm grazes mine. I should not feel that in sensitive places, but I do.

"I'm sorry tonight was hard." His fingers skim my thigh.

I make a noise but don't reply with words. The memory of how good he could make me feel is invasive and unnerving, because nothing would make me feel more vulnerable, which is terrifying.

"I could make it better. Distract you, if you want," he whispers.

It would be so easy to let him try. But I can't deal with physical contact. I have too many feelings tonight, and I can't manage chemistry feelings on top of all the other ones.

"'Night, Dallas."

He withdraws his hand. "'Night, Wilhelmina."

It's going to be a long one.

CHAPTER 27

DALLAS

I wake up to Willy's butt and back against my side. In her defense, this bed is really small, and there's a dip in the middle that causes us to roll toward each other. Not that I'm complaining. It's the opposite, actually. I'm living my dream.

I lie on my back, basking in the glory of this tiny fucking bed. My mom had a plan when she put us out here. My bedroom has a queen, and so do all of my siblings' old bedrooms. But out here in the cabin, we have privacy and closeness, which my mother believed we needed as a newly engaged couple. Bless her sweet, unknowing heart.

I have a crick in my neck from staring at Wills for the past half hour, but it's worth the pain to watch her like this. Her long, wavy hair fans out over the pillow, and she hugs another one to her chest. She kicked off all the covers at some point during the night, and her sleep shirt has ridden up, revealing a pair of dark blue boy short panties. They show off the incredible curve of her ass.

I continue to lie beside her until my morning wood demands my attention. I doubt she'd be impressed if she woke up next to me and my very excited erection after how last night ended. I have enough time for a stealth session in the bathroom, so I carefully slide out of bed. Wills immediately rolls into the center and snuggles with my pillow.

It does not take me long to handle my handle. Wills is still sleeping soundly when I emerge from the bathroom. I'd love a coffee, but I don't want to wake her with the noise. I avoid all the creaky spots on the floor as I open the door and step outside.

It's a beautiful July morning. The sun sits just above the tree line across the lake, its reflection forming a path across the surface of the water that ends at our beach. The lake is smooth as glass, a light fog caressing it. A few kayakers make the most of the morning serenity before the speedboats and jet skis come out to play.

This is my favorite time of day, other than nights spent in front of the campfire, making s'mores and enjoying the night lit up by stars. But nothing beats a summer morning. A humming-bird zooms around the feeder hung from the eaves. He's quickly chased off by another bigger hummer.

A lot of what Willy said on the walk home last night rang true in ways I hadn't considered before. In high school, I had friends in every group. Maybe they were more like acquain-tances, but people wanted to be around me. And my position at the top of the social hierarchy was important to me. Too impor-tant. Being the cool kid felt good, especially with a family like mine. Being popular gave me a false sense of importance, and I never wanted to lose that. I cared so much about other people's opinions that it took a long time for me to realize what kind of person it made me. It clouded my judgment.

I played on the sports teams, and everyone knew I had promise as a hockey player. It was too small a town for me to go unnoticed. But Willy's experience was the opposite of mine. She didn't fit in with a lot of the other girls in our class. She was strong willed, and she didn't back down. It made her a great class president, but a lot of people were intimidated by her, and guys didn't know how to handle her.

She's gone through so much bullshit to get where she is, and it makes me love her even more. But I hate how much I used to be part of that bullshit.

The door to the cabin opens, and a very rumpled, groggy-looking Wills appears on the front porch. She's still in her night-shirt, which skims the top of her thighs. Her nipples peak against the pale fabric. The front of her nightshirt boasts a cartoon of an angry coffee cup and lumps of sugar who appear terrified.

"Good morning, gorgeous."

"That's questionable." She grimaces against the sunlight, but trudges across the porch and drops down next to me on the swing.

"Did you sleep okay?" I have the gift of being able to pass out within seconds of my head hitting the pillow. But I woke up about an hour after we went to bed with Wills draped across my body.

She grunts and lets her head fall back. "My head is killing me."

"Let me get you something for that."

"I need coffee or heads will roll," she grumbles.

Despite the probability that she will retaliate by biting me, I lean over and kiss her forehead. "You are the most adorable gremlin in the morning."

"Ugh. I hate you." She groans. "But mostly because you're being so fucking sweet, and I'm so damn salty."

"Your saltiness is one of my favorite things about you." I pat her bare thigh. "I'll put the coffee on and bring you something for your head."

I push out of the swing and head for the door.

"Thank you," she mumbles as she stretches out, tucking a pillow behind her.

I set the kettle to boil and bring her a bottle of water and two painkillers.

"This view is incredible." Wills holds out her hand, and I drop the medicine in her palm.

"Right? It's why I love this little cabin and its tiny bed so much."

"Your feet hang over the end."

"They do. I'll be back with coffee in a minute." I disappear inside, use the single-cup press, and doctor her coffee the way I know she likes it. She starts to sit up, presumably to make room for me, but I raise a hand. "Hold right there." I set the coffees on the table beside the swing and tuck myself in the corner, adjusting all the pillows so she can lean into them.

"Is this even comfortable for you?" she asks as I pass her a coffee mug.

"Absolutely." I don't care if the armrest is digging into my side. I'm more than happy to end up with a bruise if it means being this close to her.

She sips her coffee and sighs. "This is perfect."

"Good. I'm glad." I stretch my arm across the back of the swing and sip my coffee, enjoying the hell out of this moment. It's probably only happening because she's too hungover to fight me.

"After coffee we can go for breakfast at Two Guys and a Stove."

"They have the best eggs benny," Wills sighs.

"With peameal bacon," I add.

"Yes times a million," she agrees. "But we'll probably run into people we know."

"That's inevitable. I won't leave your side today, Wilhelmina. I won't make the same mistake as last night."

"I don't need protecting," she snaps.

"I know you don't." I kiss the top of her head. Mostly, it's reflexive. "But sometimes it's nice to know someone has your back."

She gulps her coffee and pats me on the leg as she moves to stand. "I need a shower."

I want to offer to give her a hand, but she's turned me down twice now.

She disappears inside the cabin. I finish my coffee and hop into the outdoor shower. The cold water is a little hard to take, but I'll survive. I'm already dressed and ready to go by the time she comes out of the bathroom, wearing another outfit I bought for her.

She frowns at my wet hair. "Did you go for a morning swim? The water would be frigid."

"There's an outdoor shower," I explain.

"I bet the view is amazing."

"It is."

"Maybe I'll try it tomorrow."

"It's cold water only, so that's something to consider."

Her eyes widen. "You had a cold shower?"

"This place has a small water heater, and I didn't want you to run out. It's not a big deal."

She purses her lips. "Have you always been this sweet?"

I shrug. "You make it sound like that's a bad thing."

She blows out a breath. "You're making it extremely difficult not to like you, Dallas."

"Again, you make it sound like that's a bad thing."

I follow her out the door, all fucking smiles.

I reach around her to open the car door. She murmurs a quiet *thank you* and slides into the passenger seat. I round the hood and take my place behind the wheel.

Wills glances at the house as she buckles herself in. "Should we invite your parents?"

"They're not home. It's summer festival weekend, so Mom's already there helping set up for the pie-making contest."

"Oh wow. I totally forgot about that. I haven't been to the festival in forever." Every year, they shut down Main Street on the second weekend of July for a huge summer market and regatta. There are sailing competitions, loads of vendors, the prize pig event, and the pie-making competition.

"If you're feeling up to it after breakfast, we can stop by to check things out. If not, I can bring you back here and then head over to give my mom a hand for a couple hours."

"If I'm remembering correctly, you used to make pies with your mom. I swear I remember that—and you wearing an apron with flowers on it." She rubs her temples, clearly fighting the champagne headache.

"You're right. It's tradition. I've been in the bake-off with my mom since I was a kid."

"She almost always wins, doesn't she? Or she did when I was younger." Willy crosses her legs, and her dress rides up, exposing more of her creamy thigh.

"Until an out-of-town couple won two years ago. They were also professional chefs and a big draw for the summer folk."

"A little unfair that they tarnished her perfect record."

"She took it in stride and felt pretty good about coming in second."

I park in one of the many public lots, and we walk the two blocks to Two Guys and a Stove. It used to be our regular hangout between classes and on weekends. The decor is reminiscent of an old-fashioned diner, with red plastic bench seating and white tables with chrome edges. Chrome-and-red stools line the counter where regulars drink coffee and chat. It's busy this morning, which is to be expected with the fair and the regatta.

The place is full of familiar faces—even the hostess is the younger sister of a guy we went to school with. It only takes a few minutes for us to get a table, and Wills slides into the booth. I take the seat across from her.

One of the servers stops by our table to take our drink order and does a double take. "Oh wow! Hey, Dallas! I heard you were in town." She turns to Wills and gives her a shy smile. "I don't think we know each other, but my dad did some work on your moms' house last year."

"Oh! You're Vicki Cooper." Wills smiles. "Your dad and his crew did a great job on the new deck at my moms'! They eat out there almost every night in the summer."

"That's great!" Vicki beams with pride. "Congratulations on your engagement."

"Thanks." Wills stiffens before she shifts into the professional smile she wears when we're at a promo op.

Vicki glances around and drops her voice. "Brooklyn and Sean were all anyone could talk about until you two. It was so romantic. We were all watching the game, because you know what it's like around here. Having a Huntsville bred hockey player on a pro team, it's like, a huge deal, right?" Vicki laughs and rolls her eyes. "Of course you know what that's like, duh." Her cheeks flush. "Anyway, it was so cool to watch it happen on live TV. We all felt like we were part of it." She turns her attention to Wills. "Can I see the ring?"

"Of course." She holds out her hand, and Vicki leans in.

"Wow. It's just so beautiful. Like, the most beautiful engagement ring I've ever seen."

"Dallas has incredible taste in jewelry," Wills says, her smile firmly in place.

"He really does," Vicki agrees.

The door tinkles with the arrival of new customers, and someone calls Vicki's name from the kitchen. "Shoot. I should probably get back to work. Can I start you with coffee and water?"

"An intravenous drip of coffee would be stellar," Wills says. "But if that's not available, I'll just take your biggest mug."

"You got it." Vicki nods, and I request the same as she takes off.

Wills pulls her laptop out of her bag. "I need to take care of a couple of emails."

"Everything okay with work?" Offseason is low-key for me and the rest of the team, but it's the opposite for her. "Everything's fine. I'm working on a project with the women's hockey team. I don't trust Topher to handle things while I'm out of the office." Her fingers click on the keyboard.

"Is he giving you problems?" I've heard them having it out in the past.

"He doesn't always see the value in the other teams." She types away on her laptop.

"Bright? Dude, I wondered when we'd run into you!"

I look up as Brad and Trevor Wilson, two guys who used to play on the school team with me, approach our table. They were part of my core group. They weren't the worst of the jerks, but they weren't exactly nice to Wills. It's been a few years since I've seen them.

I slide out of the booth, though, because I'm trained to be nice to everyone. "How are you doing?" I glance around the packed restaurant. "You coming or going?"

"Coming. Might be a few minutes before we can get a table, though," Brad says. "Is it just the two of you?"

Willy's fingers pause on the keyboard, and she lifts her gaze. "Excuse my rudeness. I'm just dealing with a couple of work things, but you're welcome to join us."

"Are you sure?" Trevor asks, glancing between us.

I'm about to say we're having some quality time together and I'll catch them later when she speaks again.

"Absolutely." Wills gives them her bullshit smile as she slides over to make room. I take the spot beside her, while Brad and Trevor take the bench across from us.

"Brad, Trevor, you remember Wilhelmina." I slide my arm across the back of the seat. "Wills, do you remember Brad and Trevor?"

She hits send on the email and closes her laptop. "I sure do. It's been a few years though."

Based on her slightly stiff posture, I know their presence isn't all that welcome. I don't know why she invited them to sit with us.

"Congratulations you guys. Gotta be honest, kinda took us by surprise." Trevor's gaze darts to her hands, which are clasped on the table.

She turns toward me and adjusts her position so she can run her long nails down my neck. I expect her to dig them into my skin, but she just drags them back into my hairline. "High school was a long time ago, and people change, don't they, Dallas?"

"Yes, we do." After what happened at prom, I never wanted to hurt someone like that again. Vicki brings our coffees and rushes off to grab two more for Trevor and Brad. When she returns, she takes our orders, and Wills excuses herself to the bathroom.

Trevor glances over his shoulder as she strides across the restaurant. "Dude, she's still kind of intense, eh? Who brings a laptop to Two Guys and a Stove?"

I level him with a glare. "She's going to be my wife, so I'd watch yourself."

Trevor raises his hands. "I'm not throwing shade. I'm just saying, you've always been this easygoing dude. It's kind of surprising you'd end up with someone who sends emails over pancakes."

"She's the most incredible and driven person I've ever met." Not punching my former teammate in the face is taking all my willpower.

"Right, yeah." Trevor nods. "I can see that. She was the smartest girl in school, for sure."

"That you two ended up together after all the shit that went down is kind of mind-blowing," Brad adds quietly.

"I'm goddamn lucky," I agree. "I was an idiot back then."

The reality of the situation is sinking in. This will continue to come up, because based on what everyone believes, I intentionally sabotaged Wills. And everything before that. Our engagement is a shock to pretty much everyone. *Fuck.* So why would she believe me now, if I told her the truth?

Wills returns to the table, but before I can slide out, she sits down beside me and nudges me with her hip. I slide in farther and stretch my arm across the back of the seat.

"So how did this happen, anyway?" Brad asks, motioning between us.

Wills props her chin on her laced fingers and gives me a knowing, devious smile. "Do you want to tell that story, sweetheart, or should I?"

"Depends on which story you plan to tell," I counter, "the one where I almost burned your apartment down or the one where you had to save me from the clowns."

Her smile widens. "There are just so many stories to choose from. But I feel like nearly burning my apartment building to the ground is probably the most entertaining."

Brad laughs. "Sounds like something you'd do."

"We need to hear this," Trevor agrees.

"Go ahead, honey, give them the unabridged version." I press my lips to her temple. She deserves this, to weave these tales that make me look like the idiot I can be.

But instead of dragging me over the coals, she paints a very different picture—one where I'm not a clueless idiot doing clueless-idiot things. She makes me sound sweet and like a lovesick fool. Which, admittedly, I am.

Does she realize this isn't fake for me? Is she starting to see the truth? I never wanted to hurt her. I just wanted *her*.

Wills keeps Trevor and Brad entertained, showing glimpses of the girl I fell in love with, while we wait for our breakfast to arrive. She has an endless supply of stories, and surprisingly, not all of them are awful. Although it's clear she derives an incredible amount of joy from telling the story about Dallas Bright Junior, the horse named in my likeness.

"You do a ton of charity stuff," Brad observes.

"Mostly it was an excuse to spend time with Wills. She made me chase her." I kiss her temple.

She slides the hand on my thigh past the hem of my shorts and pinches me.

"You gonna get married in the city or up here?" Trevor asks.

"Not sure yet," Wills says.

Vicki stops by with our meals, ending that potentially awkward conversation.

Brad and Trevor take off after brunch, which I pay for, and I hold the door open for her as we leave the diner.

My fingers brush hers as I fall into step beside her. She doesn't yank her hand away, so I link our pinkies. "Why did you invite them to sit with us?"

"I don't want everyone to have the teen version of me as the only way they know me—unapproachable, cold, et cetera. No one likes feeling or knowing they're disliked. Trevor and Brad weren't openly mean to me. Mostly they were just people passing me in the hall," she says.

I nod, but don't say anything. I want to know more about what makes her tick. What she felt. What she wants. What matters to her.

"I had two moms in a time when two moms weren't commonplace in a small town. I have a hard time bullshitting, and I didn't play by the same social rules as most teens. I could have made it easier for myself by trying harder to quietly fit in, but I don't think it would have made the experience better, because then I wouldn't have been true to myself. In Toronto, I like who I am. I have a cool job and great friends. I'm doing something I love, and I get to give back to my community in meaningful ways."

"I think you're remarkable, Wills. I always have."

Her jaw clenches, and, again, for a moment I see the girl I made cry in the cafeteria. "You had a funny way of showing it."

I'm a second away from telling her the truth, but we're swarmed by a group of kids who recognize me, asking for photos and autographs. Wills immediately goes into work mode and pulls a Sharpie out of her bag. I sign for a few minutes until she politely lets them know I'll be around later this weekend, but I'm needed for pie duties.

We quickly duck down the alley behind the storefronts with her hand in mine. It's not particularly welcoming with the smell of hot summer trash, but at least we'll get to the pie-making area before the entire competition is over.

The contestants are already set up, the announcer counting down the minutes until the bake-off begins, when Wills and I slide into my mom's booth.

"Oh thank goodness! I thought I was on my own this year!" Mom says.

I kiss her on the cheek. "Sorry we're cutting it close. We had to take the alley to avoid all the crowds."

"Dallas is pretty popular around here." Wills pats my arm. "I'll leave you to it."

"I have an apron for you," Mom says. "I'd love for you to join us. Only if you want, though." Her smile is hopeful.

"Um, I don't want to slow you down," Willy hedges. It's rare to see her insecure. I want to wrap my arms around her and tell her she's incredible and has nothing to worry about.

"That's not a problem. Dallas and I will show you the ropes." Mom holds out an apron that reads *The Future Mrs. Bright* to me. "Help Wilhelmina with this, darling."

I take the apron and pull it over Willy's head. Her eyes are wide, her expression panicked, and her voice barely a whisper. "I can't even bake cookies."

"I've got you, honey." I wink and turn her around so I can tie the apron at the small of her back. I hold on to her shoulders when she starts to turn. "Let me manage your hair for a sec." I run my fingers through the loose waves and take the hair tie my mom holds out to me, carefully securing it in a loose braid. I'm not thinking when I lean in and press a kiss to the side of her neck.

"You two are so cute." Mom's phone is in her hand, her smile wide.

"Two minutes until the bake-off begins!" Howie Fresh, the town mayor, says into the microphone. All the kids are dressed up as their favorite kind of pie, except for his daughter, who's dressed as a math symbol. Basically, the entire town is here. It's one of the festival's most-attended events, and names are randomly selected for the pie taste test. The winner of the contest has their pie featured in the diner for the entire year. Mom always donates the proceeds from sales to the local foodbank.

Mom gives Wills a rundown of what to expect.

"I'm sweaty already," Willy gripes as the ten-second count-down begins.

"You've got this. We're a team," I assure her.

The buzzer sounds, and Mom starts peeling and slicing peaches.

While Willy carefully measures the flour and salt, I stand behind her, chest pressed to her back as I drop in the cubed butter and lard.

"What are you doing?" she mutters, nudging me with her elbow.

"Showing you the ropes, my future Mrs. Bright." I kiss her cheek and slide two butter knives into her hands. There are no electric mixers or even pastry cutters allowed for this event. I cover her hands with mine and start cutting in the butter.

"Your forearm porn is ridiculous," Willy mutters.

"You need them for stress relief, you just let me know," I whisper.

"The entire town is watching us, Dallas."

"I know. Just imagine what I'd do with these hands if we were alone right now."

She glances over her shoulder, glaring at me. "Seriously, your mom is right there."

I can't help it. I kiss the end of her nose. "Focus, honey."

She rolls her eyes but returns her attention to the bowl.

But she doesn't try to nudge me out of the way again. Instead, she lets me stay close. Once the ingredients are mixed, I split the dough into two pieces and show her how to form a ball.

"Do not say anything about my ability to handle balls, Dallas."

"Careful, gorgeous. My dick is listening and getting ideas."

She starts laughing, her ass rubbing against my cock. I step to the right to grab more flour, and she shuffles with me. "Only you could turn a community competition into foreplay."

"It's a skill." I groan as I kiss her neck.

Mom snaps her fingers. "Hey, you two, less flirting and more pastry making!" But she's smiling.

Wills doubles down, and we finish rolling out the dough just as Mom finishes the peach mixture. I flip the crust into the plate and pinch the edges.

"I feel like I should be doing something other than shielding your hard-on from the eyes of the public," Wills whispers.

"I'll need those beautiful hands of yours in just a minute." I kiss her cheek and pass the empty pie crust to my mom so she can fill it with the peach-custard mixture. I crack an egg into a bowl and press a whisk into Wills's hand. She takes over, and I step to the side so I can work on weaving the lattice top. Willy brushes on the egg wash, and I finish with a generous sprinkle of coarse sugar before we slide the pie into the oven.

I turn to Wills. "You get a gold star, honey."

Her apron is dotted with flour, and so is her face and hair. I brush some away and kiss the end of her nose, again. "And I meant what I said." I wink and wiggle my fingers.

She rolls her eyes, but the flush in her cheeks gives me hope.

CHAPTER 28
HEMI

I stare at the dresses laid out on the bed. Dallas is in the shower. We both needed one after the freaking bake-off. It makes perfect sense that he and his mom are uber competitive when it comes to baking the best pie. He was all smiles and excitement when they won. And he forced me to be in the pictures for tomorrow's paper. I was sweaty and disheveled and felt like I'd been more of a liability than an asset, but he insisted.

I should not have found pie making sexy, but now I can't stop thinking about the way Dallas kneaded dough like an expert along with the other things he can do with those ridiculously talented hands. "Get your head out of the gutter, Hemi." I roll my eyes to the ceiling. "Great, now I'm referring to myself in the third person."

I shake my head and refocus on my dress options. Mine is pretty, but the one Dallas laid out on the bed for me before he disappeared into the bathroom is stunning.

I try them both on and send pictures to the girls—still wearing the one from Dallas—asking for their opinion.

RIX

The second one.

HAMMER

I concur. Your curves are banging.

RIX

Option two is the winner.

TALLY

You look great in both, but the second one makes you look like royalty. QUEEN HEMI.

SHILPS

^^^Agreed.

A message in my private chat with Shilpa follows.

SHILPS

Dallas bought the royal blue dress, didn't he?

HEMI

Yes.

SHILPS

It's gorgeous. He has great taste for someone who wears so much plaid.

HEMI

He does.

SHILPS

How are you feeling about tonight?

HEMI

Do you have time for a quick call?

SHILPS

Of course.

I hit video call, and her beautiful, comforting face appears a few seconds later.

"You freaking out?" she asks.

"I'm so nervous, Shilps. So, so nervous. All these people...it's hard. And Dallas—we are sleeping in the tiniest bed, and we made pie today, and it should not have been sexy, but it was, and I'm so conflicted."

"Oh, my badass best babe, I'm sorry I'm not there to hug you right now."

"I'd probably get emotional, so it's better this way." I'm usually so good at staying in control of my emotions. But not today.

"What are you conflicted about?" she asks.

"I should hate Dallas forever—but he's making it hard not to like him now," I whisper.

"Will you tell me what exactly he did?" Shilpa asks.

"When I get home, I promise. I can't talk about it right now. I feel so raw, like it's a fresh wound all over again."

Her smile is soft with understanding. "Our hurts frame how we perceive past events, and you have a lot of feelings about the people you're seeing tonight."

"I didn't realize how hard it would be to deal with Brooklyn again. Like, I knew, but I didn't *know*," I admit.

"She was supposed to be your friend, and she hurt you. If you don't want to go, you don't have to. You don't owe anyone —not Dallas, not any of those people you went to school with. You've put yourself through so much to prove you could be there this weekend, but it doesn't matter. *You* matter."

"If I back out, I admit defeat. They win by breaking me."

"Can you be honest with Dallas and tell him why you're scared?"

I look to the ceiling, overwhelmed by the emotion of it all. "It's so hard to trust him because of the past, Shilps. And the way he looks at me when he lies about our relationship—I almost believe he's sincere."

Her expression grows sad. "Have you ever considered that's because he is?"

I laugh, but she doesn't laugh along with me.

"Why else would he be doing this, Hemi? I mean, really and truly think about it. You have the power to make his life a living hell if he fucks you over again. You literally could have let him be suspended or traded earlier this summer. He never says no to anything you throw at him. It can't all be penance."

"So you believe what? That he actually wants to be my boyfriend?" *If that's true, it changes everything. The story he told at the old folks' home can't have been real, right?* My body is on board with that idea, but my head and my heart are dragging their feet like there's a cliff ahead. The water stops running in the bathroom. "He's out of the shower; I have to go."

"Good luck tonight. You've got this. I love you."

"I love you, too, Shilps." I end the call and exhale a steady breath.

When the bathroom door opens Dallas steps into the room wearing a blue suit with plaid stripes. His tie, hanging loosely around his neck, is the same color as my dress. He looks stupidly delicious, and I'm so screwed. I have to spend the night with him at my side, touching me, being all affectionate and hot and sweet.

He did all of this to prove what? He allowed me to sign him up for endless torture at work and almost never balked—because...why?

I'm not ready for the answer to those questions. Not when my feelings are already on fire, and he looks this good.

"Good goddamn, Wills." He shakes his head slowly. "That dress was made for you." He glances at the one lying on the bed. "But you'd look just as good in the other dress, if you're more comfortable in it."

"Stop being so nice to me." I don't know how to handle his kindness. It makes me itchy.

Dallas frowns and moves into my personal space. His fingertips skim the length of my arms. "What's wrong?"

"Nothing."

He frowns. "You're lying."

I evaluate his earnest expression and view him through

Shilpa's new lens. These two small words feel like the biggest risk to trust him with. "I'm nervous."

He takes my hands in his. "I won't leave your side, Wilhelmina. Not for a second. Not unless you want me to. I won't let anyone fuck with you."

"Do you really mean that?" My heart is in my throat.

His brow furrows. "Of course I mean it. I know it's hard to have faith in me, but I'm trying my best to prove I'm not a stupid teenager anymore."

I nod once, letting his words sink in. "Just let me touch up my makeup, and then I'm ready to go." I need a minute to collect myself. I can't break down now. I disappear into the bathroom and make a final pass with my mascara wand, reapply my gloss, take a few steadying breaths, and then return.

Dallas is standing in front of the mirror, expertly knotting his tie. I step in and brush his hands away, though it's clear he can handle this task on his own. "I love the suit," I say to his chin.

"I love you." He fingers a lock of my hair. "—in this dress," he tacks on. "Do you like it?"

"It's perfect. Everything you've picked out for me is." I finish the double Windsor knot with shaking hands.

"I got Shilpa's approval."

"But you picked it on your own."

"Yeah."

I smooth out his lapels and meet his gaze. "If I didn't know better, I'd think you actually like me."

His smile is soft and maybe a little sad as his fingers wrap around mine. "I wish I could go back in time, Wills. What happened senior year—"

A knock on the door has his eyes sliding closed. "Dallas, sweetie, I have your corsage and boutonniere! I didn't want you to forget them!" his mom calls.

"She'll want to take pictures like a high school dance." Dallas's smile turns wry.

"That's fair. I didn't get prom pictures." My eyes burn

thinking about my eighteen-year-old self who longed for the Hollywood fantasy.

"You can come in, Mom!" he calls. "And me neither. I mean, I got pictures of myself, but I didn't have a date."

"Wanted to keep your options open?" I joke.

"Something like that."

He seems as though he's about to say something else when Diana opens the door. "Oh, now look at you two. Aren't you just the most perfect couple?" She crosses the room and hands my corsage to Dallas and his boutonniere to me. "Can I take pictures of you putting them on each other?" She directs the question at me.

"Yeah, absolutely."

"This night is a decade in the making," Diana says.

"What do you mean?" I ask.

"She never got to take these kinds of pictures at actual prom," Dallas explains as he opens the corsage box.

My heart stutters as Dallas carefully slides my corsage onto my wrist and kisses the back of my hand, his lips as soft as his smile. Awareness settles in the pit of my stomach. He'll probably kiss me tonight, maybe on multiple occasions. My hands are unsteady as I pin his boutonniere to his lapel.

Once we're ready, I slide my feet into the heels Dallas bought to go with the dress and grab the matching clutch. He holds out his hand, and I press mine into his palm, letting him guide me across the cabin and onto the front porch. We spend fifteen minutes posing all over the place, Dallas's body pressed against mine, his hands skimming my curves as his mom commemorates this moment. I'm hyperaware of every gentle touch, of the feel of his lips on my bare shoulder, of the light in his eyes and the warmth of his smile as he dips me with the lake as our backdrop.

This is what it should have been like. *And isn't that the mindfuck of all mindfucks?*

Photoshoot handled, Diana gives us a slightly teary hug and

kiss, and Dallas leads me to the car. He holds the door open and helps me into the passenger seat. My palms dampen as he takes his place behind the wheel.

"How are you feeling?" he asks as he pulls out of the driveway and turns right down the first side street. The high school is only a two-minute drive, but it's up two hills and I'm wearing heels, so driving is more practical.

"Cool as a cucumber." I'm reeling. And more nervous than I've ever been.

"Are you just saying that so I stop asking questions?"

I shake my head but give him the truth. "Definitely."

He pulls into the parking lot. Other than a new sign over the door, it looks exactly the same.

Dallas cuts the engine and reaches across the center console to squeeze my hand. "We're in this together, okay? You ready?"

"As I'll ever be." I open the passenger side door.

He moves with purpose to my side as I ready myself to get out of the car. When he holds out his hand, I take it. I feel like a high school senior again. I'm still that girl who didn't fit in— who knew what people said about her and struggled not to be too much for everyone. I was too direct, too intense, too passionate. I shake it off. *I can do this.* It's a handful of hours. And then I never have to do it again.

Dallas laces our fingers, and we walk up the front steps. We're greeted at the door by former staff. My political science teacher envelops me in a hug. The first fifteen minutes are a whirlwind of embraces and congratulations. Most of my teachers adored me. I was the girl who always volunteered to help, turned in my assignments early, participated in class discussions, and made the honor roll.

We have our photo taken under the balloon archway, and then we head down the hall toward the gymnasium. It's been transformed into a throwback to prom. For almost everyone else, it's a delightful trip down memory lane, but I'm seeing it all for the first time. The walls are lined with collages chronicling our time at Huntsville High.

"I was so short in grade nine," Dallas comments as we stop at the picture of the school hockey team.

"By the time you hit grade eleven, you towered over everyone." I tap the photo of the team two years later, where Dallas is a head taller than almost all the others. He's present in so many of these photos. He was part of everything, always the center of attention. Always wanted. Always belonging.

"I was so awkward that year. All limbs and no freaking coordination," he muses. "Should we go in? We can always make a run for it." Dallas inclines his head to the gym doors, which are framed by another balloon arch in school colors and a banner that reads WELCOME, TIMBERWOLVES!

"Let's do this." I'm ready to conquer my past and then leave it where it belongs.

We're spotted as soon as we cross the threshold. "Bright? Hey, my man! I was wondering when you'd get here!" A guy whose name I can't remember, but whose face is vaguely familiar, approaches.

I stand back while they go in for back pats.

"Wilhelmina?" Gentle fingers touch my arm, and I turn toward the familiar voice.

"Dorie?"

"Hi! It's been so long!" We throw our arms around each other. She's a life preserver in rough waters.

Dorie and I were on student council together all through high school. Most of our friendship happened inside these walls, as she lived forty-five minutes away by bus, and she and Brooklyn didn't get along.

She smiles at me with fondness as we part. "It's so good to see you. Congratulations!" Her gaze cautiously darts to Dallas who is now surrounded by at least half a dozen people, all chatting and laughing. "I have to admit, I was a little surprised by this development."

"I think we all were," I reply, forcing my smile to stay in place.

She's one of the few people who knew about my massive, years-long crush on Sean and how hurt I'd been when Brooklyn went with him to prom. "But you're happy with him?"

I nod, realizing it's the truth. "Absolutely. How about you? What have you been up to? You're a lawyer now, right?"

"That's right. I moved out to Midland and set up a practice there."

As we chat, more of my former classmates join the group. All the people I was on student council with come to say hi. I haven't seen most of them since we graduated. When I left Huntsville, I traded small town living for the city and went to university in Toronto, and I've only ever been back to visit my moms.

As promised, the only time Dallas leaves my side is to get me a drink. I get sucked into a one-sided conversation with a former classmate about astrophysics, and Dallas saves me.

"So sorry to interrupt, but this is our song," Dallas says with an apologetic smile. He holds out his hand, and I slip mine in his, excusing us.

He guides me to the dance floor, his lips at my ear. "Your eyes were glazing over."

"I was trying to stay engaged, but in my head, I was making a grocery list."

He keeps hold of one hand and the other settles on my waist. "So this is our song, huh?"

"Be glad it isn't 'Stairway to Heaven,' or you'd get to feel my hard-on for eight minutes instead of three." His eyebrows wag.

I roll my eyes. "You do not have a hard-on."

"You underestimate the power you have in this dress, honey." He pulls me tight against him, and I feel the evidence of his arousal.

"How long have you been like this?"

"Since the moment I saw you in it."

"That was hours ago."

"It ebbs and flows."

"That's a long time to be in such a heightened state." And frankly, pretty damn flattering. "Isn't that uncomfortable?"

Dallas shrugs. "It's pretty much my constant state when I'm around you. It's a small price to pay to have the pleasure of your company." He turns his head, giving me his profile, and brings my hand to his lips.

If that weren't true, why would he say it? What would he have to gain? I change the subject because it's the safe thing to do. "It's nice to see some of the people I hung out with in high school. Although my friend group was smaller than yours."

"Eh, I had a lot of acquaintances and not a lot of close friends who mattered in the long run." He sounds more resigned than I would have imagined.

"How do you feel about that? I thought you had all these close friendships. Best friends forever and all that."

"What I thought was important when I was eighteen isn't what's important to me now." His voice trails off as the song changes. "Have you seen our favorite couple tonight?"

I shake my head. "It's only a matter of time, I'm sure." We won't get through the night without at least one unfortunate interaction. Part of me wants to get it over with. But the part who still feels like that betrayed, heartbroken girl, is afraid of how much any real conversation with Brooklyn will make me hurt all over again.

"You won't have to deal with them on your own. I'll be right beside you." His expression is earnest.

"I believe you." Or at least, I'm trying.

I get lost in my thoughts as we move around the dance floor. Once again, my conversation with Shilpa comes back, and I wonder just how clueless I've been—stuck with my perception framed in hurt.

But I still don't understand. What was the purpose of hurting me like that? Tonight I'll ask him, once and for all.

The song ends, and a fast-paced one replaces it, so I step back and sever our contact.

A couple of Dallas's old hockey buddies call us over. I need a minute to collect myself, though. "I'll be right back."

"I'll come with you," Dallas offers.

"You can't follow me into the women's bathroom."

"I'll wait outside," he suggests.

"It's okay. I'll be fine for a couple of minutes." I pat him on the chest and press a kiss to the edge of his jaw. "Go talk to your hockey buddies. I'll be right back."

I make it to the bathroom without bumping into anyone unpleasant, but my luck runs out as I'm washing my hands.

"Wilhelmina! If I didn't know better, I'd think you were avoiding me." Brooklyn steps up beside me, her gaze trained on her clutch as she rummages around and retrieves her lipstick.

"Not avoiding you, Brooklyn."

"Aren't you, though? You didn't really even talk to me at my engagement party. It's like you're not even happy for me. It was a decade ago. And obviously you're over Sean. I mean, you scored yourself the hottest guy in our class, and he makes like millions a year. Sort of interesting that you two ended up engaged right after us though. Sean has always been proud to be with me, but Dallas only just confirmed your relationship." Her smile is fake and syrupy.

I'm done playing nice. It doesn't matter if it's safer. "Are you seriously trying to make this into a competition over boys? High school is over, Brooklyn."

She crosses her arms. "And yet you conveniently ended up with the most popular guy in our class who is seriously loaded now."

Is that all Dallas was to people? The one who came out on top? I rub the space between my eyes, frustrated by the stupidity of all of this. Now, I just want answers to the questions that have felt like slivers under my skin. "Why did you even hang out with me? Was it so you could feel more important? Did you want to make yourself feel better about where you sat on the social ladder? You were supposed to be my best friend. You knew back then I'd liked Sean for a long time, but that didn't matter to you. And I get that things happen, and obviously you and Sean belong together, but you should have told me you were going to prom with him instead of letting me find out through other people. That's what hurt. It wasn't a boy that was the issue between us. It was you."

Lied to by omission is still lied to. I was devastated. I felt betrayed and so very cast aside. Disposable. My moms have done everything to make sure I feel loved, but a tiny part of my heart will always wonder why I was given up in the first place.

"What was I supposed to say? It's not my fault he wanted to go with me more than he wanted to go with you," Brooklyn says defensively.

"You're right. I would never have stopped you from going with him. But you should have told me. All I wanted was for you to be happy, because that's what friends want for each other." *How did she not see that? How did I not see that back then?*

She clenches her fists and rolls her shoulders back. "Well, I guess I'm so—"

I hold up a hand. "I don't need your apology, Brooklyn, especially not when you don't mean it. We were friends long enough for me to know when you're lying. You were a shitty friend. You were cruel and mean. I don't know why putting people down makes you feel good about yourself. Whatever the reason you chose to handle that situation the way you did, I deserved better." Before she can speak, I continue, "Look, I'm sincerely glad you and Sean are happy. I truly want nothing but the best for you and, honestly, do hope you're well." And I do because a piece of me will always love her even though I shouldn't.

With that, I turn and leave her gawking after me.

I feel so much lighter, like I've finally let go of a weight that's been holding me down all these years. My heart is a little less broken walking away from her. I want to find Dallas and tell him, but on my way back to the gymnasium, I run into the *other* last person I want to see.

"Wilhelmina, how come this is the first time I've seen you tonight? You look great." Sean's words run together a little at the end. His gaze moves over me in a way that sends a shiver down my spine. "Sometimes, I wonder what would have happened if I hadn't listened. I should have said *fuck it* and asked you anyway. Your rack is hands down the best in our class."

I smile tightly and ignore the comment about my rack. Apparently, drunk and creepy is his current vibe. "Well, good thing you ended up going with the right person since you're marrying Brooklyn."

He looks around before he leans in uncomfortably close and drops his voice. "She was my runner-up. You were always my number one. I mean, that body." He winks, and his expression shifts, brow furrowing. "Wild that you and Bright ended up together. How'd that even happen? Especially when he was always such a dick to you. All the student council posters he and his hockey buddies trashed, and the notes they stuffed in your locker..." He tips his head. "They were pretty ruthless, weren't they?"

I believed that about the posters and notes, but I didn't have confirmation until now. And maybe Sean is just being a jerk because he can, but it makes the wounds fresh again. "We were kids, and Dallas did a lot of stupid stuff back then," I say as calmly as I can. "We all did."

I thought I was going to conquer it all—be this cool, new, fun Hemi, but I don't know if I can handle facing my past like this. Confronting Brooklyn was one thing, but this conversation is dismantling my armor with every harsh, painful memory dredged up by Sean's words.

"He really screwed you over, though. Came into the locker room and threatened to have the hockey team come after anyone who asked you to prom. Always singling you out like his favorite toy." He shakes his head. "But now he has money and he's famous, so I guess that makes up for it, eh?"

The hairs on the back of my neck stand on end a second before Dallas appears behind Sean. His face is a mask of rage, lip curled as he growls, "Who the fuck do you think you are, talking to my fiancée like that?"

His eyes meet mine, and I see his regret, as much as I feel it wrapping around me.

Sean startles and backs up a step but puffs his chest out. "What, you don't like the truth, Bright? Too real for you?"

"You don't know the first thing about the truth, Sean. Don't presume to know what my relationship with Wills is like. While you've been living in your time capsule, spamming the world with your bullshit, I've been atoning for my mistakes. Working to never be that selfish asshole again. I regret a lot of things, especially when it comes to Wills, but I sure as fuck don't regret telling you not to ask her to prom. You didn't deserve to even be near her then, and you don't deserve her now."

"And you think you do?"

"Not back then, no. I was a dick and focused on the wrong things. But I'm going to spend the rest of my life making up for those mistakes."

My head is spinning, and my heart feels like it's shattering all over again. Because as nice as it is to have Dallas stand up for me, it's gutting to have our tumultuous past thrown in my face all over again.

"I need air."

Dallas tries to grab my hand, but I shake him off and head for the closest exit, desperate to escape this pain.

CHAPTER 29

HEMI

I 'm reeling as I push through the doors and step out into the warm summer night. The soccer field lies ahead of me, the parking lot to the right. If I wasn't wearing heels and a dress, I might consider walking to my moms'.

Before I can pull my phone out to call one of them for a ride, Dallas bursts through the door after me. "Wills, honey—"

"Stop! Stop calling me that! Just stop!" I'm too wrecked, too raw, and too sad to handle any of this. But it's all happening. I can't escape history or the feelings that come with it.

I'm crushed all over again. Terrified that I'm about to endure the same humiliation I did all those years ago. And wouldn't I deserve it for being stupid enough to believe in Dallas's good intentions?

He stops when he's only a few inches from me. "My gorgeous fucking badass, I'm so sorry." He looks like he'd slay any dragon for me. But at one point in my life, he was part of the dragon that tried to ruin me.

My stupid chin wobbles. I should walk away, but instead I roll my shoulders back and do the one thing I never have. "Why? Why did you tell everyone not to ask me to prom?" Until this moment, I believed I knew the answer. He thought it was funny. He wanted to hurt me. Like everyone else, he thought it would be better without me. More fun.

I felt so small, so broken and unwanted. And being here makes me feel it all over again. It's rooted in my beginnings, and it's followed me through life.

Dallas's eyes soften, and his sadness is palpable. "Because I wanted to be the one to ask you, and I was buying myself time while I grew a pair so I could just do it already. I was scared to ask you. You had every reason to tell me to fuck off even if I was brave enough." He runs a rough hand through his hair. "Sean has been and will always be a douchebag. Worse, I couldn't stand the idea of him touching you, of getting to pick you up and hold your hand. Of spending the night with you the way I wanted to. He would make these gross, disrespectful comments —and I just couldn't handle it. Do you know what that would have done to me? To see someone so unworthy of you be the center of your attention? I would have done anything to be the one you wanted, but I was so caught up after everyone thought it was some big joke that I let the opportunity slip through my fingers. I always thought if I had just one shot to make a move, it would have been prom."

I'm slow to process his words. I'm so stunned that all I can do is echo him. "You wanted to go to prom with me?"

"Yeah, but I screwed myself over by not setting them all straight."

"You wanted to ask me to prom?" Why can't I say anything else? The world is tilting on its axis, whirling into orbit and taking me along for the ride.

He nods. "I did. So fucking badly."

"But...why?" It doesn't make any sense. He was the most popular guy in the school. Everyone loved him. Everyone wanted to be his date to prom.

"Why?" Dallas's eyebrows rise.

"Yeah. Why?"

"Because you're you, Wills. It's always been you."

"I'm intense. I'm bossy. I'm not always palatable."

He nods. "All of those things make you my favorite person in the world. You're powerful. The world doesn't deserve your soft parts. In school, you were a force, and that hasn't changed. You're brilliant and incredible, and I want to be close to you just to be part of whatever you're doing. That's how I felt even then. I was leaving for the summer, and I wanted you to be the girl I went to prom with. I wanted to bring you a corsage and pick you up in my dad's truck and spend the night dancing with you. I wanted you to see that I was more than just a dumb jock. Fuck, I was terrified you'd say no. But I shot that all to shit. Hurting you will always and forever be my greatest regret."

"I see." It's all I can say without losing it. Every breath in and out steadies me.

He gently tips my chin up. "Wilhelmina, I'm truly sorry for every time I never stood up for you. I'm sorry for letting people hurt you and not protecting you. I'm sorry for being more worried about people thinking I was cool than doing what's right. I'm so sorry I caused you so much harm growing up. You deserved so much better. You deserve so much better."

"Thank you, Dallas." I don't know if he realizes how healing it is to have him acknowledge and apologize for the way he treated me.

His smile is sad and hopeful. "Should we get out of here?"

I nod, dumbfounded, and he laces our fingers. "I can't believe you wanted to go to prom with me. Why didn't you say anything? Why not tell me the truth at any point over the last ten years?"

"I've tried a few times to bring it up, and you always shut me down. It was clear you didn't want to talk about the past. I knew you wouldn't have believed me. I don't blame you. But I want you to know, I'd just planned to tell Sean to back down. That's it. I'd gotten word he was going to ask you after school that day. We had gym right after him, so I cornered him in the locker room and told him not to. But half the senior class was in there.

A couple of the douchebags on the hockey team jumped in and started threatening everyone, and it sort of snowballed from there." He runs a hand through his hair. "And then Sean asked Brooklyn the next day, and that just made it worse. The last thing I wanted to do was hurt you. The very last thing." His expression is so pained.

"You had a crush on me in high school?" I clarify.

A blush brushes the tops of his cheeks. "Actually, it started in elementary school when you kicked everyone's butt in debate, but yeah, I wanted to ask you out all through senior year. I almost did right after winter break, but you told me to fuck off after English that day. Prom was my last shot." He rubs his bottom lip with his thumb.

"And when I joined the Terror, you never said no to a promo op, even if you hated it because..." I let it hang, still trying to get my head around it.

"I could make your job easier doing the things no one else wanted to. I got to spend time with you. I wasn't late on purpose. I was nervous, and my anxiety boners are really fucking problematic."

"You've really had a thing for me all these years?" I'm reeling in the face of these revelations.

He nods. "When we reconnected, mostly I wanted to fix what I'd broken, and I mean, I didn't really think through the boyfriend or the fiancé angle. But I'm kind of completely in love with you, and have been for a while." He chews his bottom lip, like he's waiting for me to reject him. Never have I seen Dallas this nervous. Not ever.

As terrified as I am, I believe he's telling the truth. But that's new to me, so putting my faith in him feels akin to jumping off a cliff into dark waters, unsure if there are rocks beneath the surface. Our entire history is in the process of reframing, shifting, so I do the only thing that feels right—I grab the lapels of his suit jacket and pull his mouth to mine. He makes a surprised sound, but his arm snakes around my waist and his other hand slides into my hair. He groans as I push my tongue past his lips and he pulls me tight against him.

This isn't like any other kiss we've shared. The anger and fear melt away, and that crackling energy between us explodes—like stars bursting and the world shifting back into alignment. It's raw and real and healing. Every wall I erected to keep my heart safe falls with this one perfect kiss. It's as though our souls are brushing up against each other for the first time. It's a promise of something new, feral, powerful, and earth shattering.

Dallas Bright, professional hockey player and grown up all-around nice guy, is honestly and truly in love with *me*. I feel that pouring into me, filling the holes in my heart, giving me the most incredible, unexpected balm of hope. All those feelings I've been fighting, the chemistry I've tried to shove down and suppress, are suddenly, viciously present.

I tear my mouth from his.

He growls, *fucking growls*, and tries to reclaim my lips.

"Wait."

He blinks twice and releases me. "Sorry. I'm sorry."

"What? No. Don't be sorry. Take me home now, please."

"Home as in…"

"Back to the cabin, so we can continue this not outside our high school where people can take pictures that will make both our lives more challenging, but mostly mine." I smile at him and realize this is what it must feel like to win the Cup. The world is mine, and everything I didn't know I needed is right in front of me.

CHAPTER 30

HEMI

The two-minute drive is fraught with an exceptional amount of sexual tension. All the time and energy I've spent hating Dallas, every time I organized a promo op specifically to torment him the way he used to do to me, now seems callous and vindictive. It feels petty and small. I spent years believing he'd set me up on purpose as a prank meant to entertain his friends.

"You never tried to explain," I say softly. My throat is tight, and my feelings are on fire.

He nods after a moment. "I realized that until I'd given you a reason to believe I was a different person now, it wasn't worth bothering with. I was a dick to you for a long time—too worried about the unimportant stuff, when you were always the only thing that mattered." He reaches for my hand as he pulls into the driveway. "And then more recently, it didn't seem like you wanted to talk about it. So I tried to communicate in other ways. I wanted to earn the right to be honest."

Every sweet thing he's done, every soft moment, every bouquet of flowers, crocheted peach, and coffee left on my desk were meant to *show* me the truth. That he cares. That he's sorry. That he isn't the asshole I've spent my entire life hating.

The walls I built around my heart are falling. The armor I wore dissolving.

He parks in the garage, but instead of passing by the house, he takes my hand and leads me down the path behind it so we don't get stopped by his mom asking how the reunion went. New energy crackles between us, no longer fueled by anger and vindication. My gaze stays locked on his profile as we navigate the uneven ground.

Low tones of music and laughter reach my ears, as though someone is hosting a lakeside summer party close by.

Dallas opens the door to the cabin, and I step over the threshold, tugging him along with me. As soon as the door closes, I grab his tie and pull his mouth to mine. His arm winds around me, one hand skimming my curves. I slide my fingers into his thick hair, gripping the strands as our tongues battle and tangle.

I can't get enough of the soft sureness of his lips, of the way his hands are all over my skin. We're a frenzy of desire as I abandon his hair and shove his suit jacket over his shoulders. I break the kiss long enough to say, "Get me out of this dress."

"You're my ultimate fantasy, Wills." He finds the zipper and tugs it down, a gentle counterpart to the frantic way I'm trying to rid him of his suit.

It's dark, and while my eyes slowly adjust, I feel my way through his buttons. As if he can read my mind, Dallas reaches behind him and flicks on the light over the sink, bathing us in a soft glow. Shadows dance over his face, and a shiver runs down my spine as his eyes move over me.

The sweet Dallas who stayed by my side all night merges with the alpha hockey player who will do anything to protect the puck. The same guy who doesn't hesitate to check someone into the boards is also the man who delivered a baby foal and let me dress him up as a clown, even though he hates them. He takes my hands in his and brings them to his lips. His calloused fingertips glide long the length of my arms until he reaches the straps on my shoulders. He hooks his fingers under them and reverses the motion. My dress falls away, sliding over my hips and pooling at my feet.

"Fuck, Wilhelmina." His fingertips travel the lace edge of my bra. "The number of times I've fantasized about being here with you is embarrassing."

"You probably shouldn't have told me that." I bite back a moan as his thumbs sweep over my nipples through the lace and satin.

His gaze lifts, and a deliciously devilish smile appears. "I hope like hell you make me regret it, Willy."

I narrow my eyes while I work his tie loose. "You call me that to annoy me, don't you?"

"It gets your attention, which I always want."

I pull his tie free. "You mean that, don't you?"

"This, right now, with you standing here looking like a goddamn goddess, undressing me? It's my personal heaven." He takes my face in his hands and slants his mouth over mine.

I've never been wanted this way, and it's a heady, addicting feeling. His hands move to my waist, and one eases lower while the other trails up my spine. He flicks the clasp of my bra open.

This time it's him who breaks the kiss and me who makes the displeased sound when I try to keep his mouth connected to mine.

He gently grips my chin. "Let me see you."

I slide my hands down his chest, and my bra drops to the floor. Dallas's nostrils flare, and he sinks to his knees in front of me. He presses a kiss below my navel and hooks his thumbs into the waistband of my underwear. "Permission to remove these very pretty panties?" he asks.

I run my fingers through his hair. "Permission granted."

He slides them over my hips and down my thighs, and I brace my hand on his shoulder as I step out of them. His hands go to my hips and his eyes stay on mine as he leans in and kisses just above the apex of my thighs. "I want to worship every inch of your perfect, gorgeous body."

"You're definitely starting in a great place."

He nuzzles into my sex, and I'm struck once again by how awe-inspiring it is to have this huge man on his knees in front of me, his expression and his touch equal parts reverent and greedy.

His tongue sweeps out to taste me, and my knees almost buckle at the deep groan that vibrates over my skin. He rises, hands sliding around to cup my ass as he lifts me. I wrap my arms around his neck and hook my feet behind his back as he carries me the short distance to the bed.

He climbs up onto the mattress and carefully lays me on the comforter, his hips dropping until I can feel him thought his pants, hard and thick against me. He captures my mouth in another searing kiss before he starts his descent.

"Wait!" I shout.

He stops immediately and pushes up on his arms, eyes wide with worry. "Am I moving too fast?"

"No. Not too fast. But I need you in less clothing. Preferably in no clothing." As hot as it is to have him so intent on getting his mouth on me, I'd love a spectacular view to complete the experience.

He looks down at himself and frowns. "Shit. Sorry. I'm on a mission."

I sit up, adjusting my position so I'm kneeling on the bed, too. "But I want to do this part."

His hands drop, and his smile makes my stomach and everything else clench. "Yes, ma'am."

As I unfasten the last few buttons on his shirt, Dallas's fingers explore my dips and curves. He kisses up the side of my neck. His other hand glides up the inside of my thigh.

"You're very distracting," I murmur as I push his shirt over his shoulders and tug it free.

"You're better at multitasking than I am, and I can't keep my hands to myself when you're naked and undressing me."

He nibbles my earlobe as I run my nails down his chest,

appreciating just how hard he works to be in this kind of physical condition. My fingers glide along the waistband of his pants,
and he makes a deep noise in the back of his throat. I unclasp his
belt, pop the button, and drag the zipper down. The temptation
is too much to resist, and I slide my hand into his boxer shorts,
wrapping my hand around his length for the first time.

"Fuck me." Dallas groans into the side of my neck. He cups
my face and pulls back, eyes dropping to my hand inside his
boxers. I free him, and he makes a guttural sound as I stroke my
thumb over the head. I can't take my eyes off his face, the overwhelming euphoria that softens his features, or the intense way
he watches my hand.

I have this effect on him. I make him feel this way. And I can't
believe it's taken me this long to see it. Him. How he feels about
me. It's so obvious, so devastatingly clear, and I've been oblivious, stuck in a past that colored my view of him. Because I
wasn't ready to believe anything else.

"Enough," Dallas barks. He pries my fingers from his thick,
swollen cock and brings my hand to his lips. "You can touch me
later, but first, I get to worship you."

Dallas guides me back down to the mattress and stretches out
over me, settling in the cradle of my hips. His erection presses
against me through his boxers. He kisses me, softly, tenderly, and
then works his way down my body, devoting attention to each
sensitive spot, his fingers gliding over my breasts, followed by
his lips. He continues his descent and settles between my thighs
on a contented sigh. Half his body hangs off the too-small bed,
but he loops his arms around my thighs, broad shoulders
spreading me wide. His gaze lifts as his tongue finds my most
sensitive skin. His eyes flutter shut as he groans. "Fuck, I've been
dying to taste you again."

His wide palms settle on the insides of my thighs, and he
holds me open as his tongue explores. All that soft, gentle sweetness evaporates, and the reverence with which he kissed his way
down my body turns into ravenous hunger.

Awareness seeps in that when he did this before, it came from a place of true desire. This entire time he's wanted me. I fist his hair and moan as sensation builds with every sure stroke of his tongue and curl of his fingers. The orgasm rockets through me, his name a scream on my lips.

"Yes," he groans. "That's it. Let go, honey. These are my orgasms, and I want all of them." He laps at my clit, soft strokes that make me shudder and whimper. "And that sound. I'll never get enough of it."

My pussy clenches around nothing, and the ache inside me expands. "I need you in me, please."

"I'm not done down here." He fucks me with his tongue.

"You can eat my pussy again later, but right now, I need you."

His gaze lifts and darkens. "I'm sorry, what was that?"

I don't quite understand the sudden shift in his demeanor. He bites the inside of my thigh.

"Cock. I need you to fill me with yours."

He gives my clit one last, soft kiss and prowls up my body, broad shoulders rolling, thick biceps flexing. "Say it again." He stops to suck each nipple. Somehow, during the oral-gasms, he must have taken off his pants and boxers, because he's completely naked now, and his glorious erection drags against the inside of my thigh as he kisses over my collarbones.

"Say what again?" I'm delirious with need, body in over-drive, anticipation making me a live wire.

"Tell me what you need." He braces his weight on his hands as he hovers over me, mouth an inch from mine, the head of his cock rubbing against me.

I cup his beautiful face in my palm and see the feelings he has for me swimming in his eyes. Everything I've missed. "You, Dallas. I need you inside me."

He leans over to the nightstand and opens the top drawer. A moment later, he produces a condom. I take it from him and tear the foil packet open. He shifts to give me better access, and I roll it down his length. And then he settles between my thighs again.

Our bodies align, and he shifts his hips forward, sinking into me, filling me on one perfect stroke. And the entire time he holds my gaze. Something passes between us, and for a moment, I feel as though I'm experiencing not only my first with him, but *his* first with *me*.

"Fuck, Wills." His eyes fall closed, and he drops his head, burying his face against my neck, lips moving against my skin as he groans, "Nothing has ever felt this good."

I expect him to lose control the way he did when he tasted me, but he just rocks back and forth, warm breath breaking across my neck. I run my hand down his spine, appreciating his hot-as-fuck body. When I reach his ass, I give it a tap, encouraging him to *just fuck me already*. But he continues with the gentle rocking. Sure, it feels nice. Yes, it's intimate, but I'm not ready for that the way he is. He's had years to understand his feelings for me, and I've had half an hour. So I turn my head and do something to rile him up, the way he usually does me.

With my lips at his ear, I whisper, "Booooo."

His hips stop moving, and he lifts his head, brows slanted in the most delicious scowl.

I fight a smile.

His brow arches. "Are fucking *booing* me?"

"What are you doing?"

"What do you mean, what am I doing? I'm making love to you." His expression is both incredulous and determined.

"Honey." I run my fingers through his hair. "You mess people up on the ice. You've promised me depraved things with your filthy mouth. And you just ate my pussy like a desperate man. So what I would really love is for you to channel some of that energy into pounding me into this mattress like the obsessed man you are, right now."

He pokes at his top lip with his tongue.

"Be a good boy and show me what you got," I taunt.

He strokes my cheek with his fingers, so sweet and gentle. "You're sure that's what you want?"

"To be fucked by you? Yes, I'm absolutely sure."

"Okay. I can do that." He kisses the end of my nose. "For you." His lips brush over mine. "Hold on, honey, you're in for the ride of a lifetime."

I start to laugh, but it turns into a gasp when he pulls out all the way to the ridge and snaps his hips forward. I slide up the bed and brace one hand against the headboard, gripping his taut forearm with the other. God, he has great forearms.

He cocks a wicked brow. "You want more of that?"

"Please, thank you, yes."

He drags his tongue along his bottom lip, and his hips retreat. I'm empty for one interminable moment. This time I'm ready, and I tip my hips up to meet his thrust.

"Oh my fuck," I groan at the fullness. The way his pelvis rubs against my clit in exactly the right way.

Dallas starts a fabulously punishing rhythm, and every thrust takes me higher, pushes me closer to the edge of bliss. It doesn't hurt that he's gorgeous, all tightly corded muscles, chiseled jaw, and intense expression. The bed creaks, and the headboard thumps against the wall with every stroke. And I'm so, so glad we have some privacy, because I can't hold back my moans of delirium. There's being fucked, and then there's being *fucked* by Dallas. He adjusts his position and hooks his arm behind my knee so he can change the angle and deepen his thrusts. His rhythm never falters, and he doesn't slow his pace. With every gasp and moan and bite of my nails into his skin, he fucks me harder. It's hands down the best sex of my life.

"Look at you, taking every inch of my cock like a goddamn goddess." Dallas caresses my cheek, a gentle contradiction to the way his hips slam into mine. "Am I fucking you the way you want?"

I nod. "So good, Dallas. Touch me right there again."

His lip curls into a satisfied smile that makes everything

below the waist clench. "You gonna be a good girl and give up another one of those orgasms for me soon?"

I grip the edge of the headboard to keep from sliding into it. "Keep fucking me, and there's a good chance," I pant. I'm on the edge, struggling to keep from falling off the cliff because I don't want this to end. But then Dallas has to go and open his big, beautiful, dirty mouth and tip me over.

"I can't wait to feel you coming on my cock, this perfect pussy squeezing me like a fist." Somehow, he growls that entire sentence.

And that's all it takes. A few dirty words and hard thrusts later, my entire world spins into a vortex of pleasure. My eyes roll up as sensation transforms me.

"Oh, no, no, no." Dallas cups my chin in his palm. "Open your eyes, beautiful. Let me see what I do to you."

I fight to pry them open and meet his gaze as wave after wave of bliss washes over me. I'm drowning in the intimacy of the moment. The emotions I catch and hold in Dallas's eyes take my breath away.

It isn't until I've crested the orgasm that Dallas allows his to take him under. He's beautiful as he unravels, body shaking, expression fierce.

He rolls us to the side and hooks my leg over his hip, keeping us joined as he kisses me, soft and slow.

"Hi." I run my fingers through his sweaty hair.

"Hey." He kisses the end of my nose. "I did good, eh?"

"At least a seven out of ten."

"Pfft. Your exuberance tells me you're a liar." He's all smiles, and it makes my heart flutter.

"Fine. You did good. But don't let it go to your head. Subsequent performances could drag your rating down, so you best stay on your A-game," I tease.

"I might need to tone it down to my B-game in the future, unless you can temper your enthusiasm."

"What does that mean?"

"You're kind of loud in bed."

I try to push him away, but he tightens his hold around my waist. "You're a jerk!"

"I'm kidding." His eyes are lit up. He's gleeful.

"No, you're not." My eyes flare. "You don't think your parents could hear all the way in the house?"

"Nah. Also, please always be that vocal. I fucking love it. And the nails, always try to stab me with your fingernail talons. Especially during sex. I wasn't kidding when I said it gets me going."

"Has everything you've said since we've gotten engaged been the truth?" I muse.

"I've never lied to you. Not once since we both moved to Toronto."

I trace his eyebrow. I have a lot of feelings I don't know what to do with. "You really want to marry me?" I whisper.

"Yeah." He nods, and his smile grows sad. "I know we're going about it kind of backwards, but would you officially be my girlfriend now, like for reals and not for fakies?" He swallows nervously, as though he's waiting for me to say no.

I kiss the end of his nose. "Yeah. I'll be your for-reals girlfriend."

"Thank God I brought my A-game."

He kisses me, and we start again, but this time I let him be soft and sweet. Because that's what he needs, and after everything we've been through, we both deserve a little tenderness.

CHAPTER 31

DALLAS

I wake up wrapped around Wilhelmina's gloriously naked body. She's warm and still asleep. I have no desire to leave the comfort of this bed, but today is a big day, full of amazing surprises, so I should really get a move on. Still, I lie there for another minute, basking in the glow that is my awesome life. The sex last night was transformative. The best sex of my life—especially round two when she let me make sweet, sweet love to her.

When my erection becomes a real problem and my need to relieve myself is too much to ignore, I carefully slip out of bed.

It takes me an irrationally long time to pee, and when I emerge, Wills is no longer in bed. Unfortunately, she's also no longer naked. But she's wearing one of my Terror shirts, and it skims the curve of her delightfully perfect ass. "What a gorgeous morning. Let's make coffee and sit on the swing." She stretches her arms over her head and yawns loudly. It doesn't register that she's already at the door until it's too late.

"Honey, wait." I hastily jam my legs through last night's boxer shorts and nearly faceplant into the corner of the bed. As it is, I stumble across the room just in time for her to throw the door open. My mom stands at the base of the front porch, a tray of baked goods and fresh fruit in her hands, wearing a huge smile.

But it's what lies beyond my mother that has Wills frozen to the spot.

One side of the yard is dotted with yurts, and the other side boasts picnic tables and a buffet full of breakfast foods. A huge shade tent has been set up near the water, and Muskoka chairs circle the fire pit, which still smolders. Shilpa, who's talking animatedly with my dad, is the first to notice us. Her eyebrows rise as she takes us in.

Mom's face lights up, despite our lack of clothing. "Oh good! You're awake!"

Shilpa climbs the steps and envelops Wills in a tight hug. "Surprise!" She releases her, but doesn't move aside, likely to shield Wills from everyone else's eyes.

"What the heck is going on? Why is everyone here?"

"It's your engagement party." She hands Wills a bag. "There's a shirt in there for you. Go put some clothes on and come join us. Then you can fill me in on last night." She winks and pushes Wills towards me.

I snake a hand around her waist and tug her back into the cabin. "We'll be out in a few."

I pull the door closed, and she spins around. "Shilpa's here."

"Yeah. Most of our friends made it, except for Dred. She had to work, but she sends her love. Rix's best friend Essie is here to do your make up if you want."

"Essie's here? She didn't come from Vancouver for this, did she?"

"I think she's looking for apartments because she's transferring back to Toronto." She's a makeup artist and has been living on the west coast.

"Right. That makes sense." Wills nods. "Who set this up?"

"My mom tossed around the idea of a party later in the summer, but your schedule is hectic, especially in August when you're setting up fall promo. And you've been taking on more projects with the women's team." I run my hands down her arms. "I knew the reunion would be hard for you, and I thought it would be good to end the weekend with the people who have your back and adore you the way I do."

Wills blinks up at me.

I'm pretty proficient at reading her moods, thanks to all the time I've spent obsessing over her, but I can't decipher her expression. "Did I get it wrong? Is having your Babe Brigade here the wrong move?" I wanted to alleviate her stress, not add to it.

She shakes her head and presses her manicured fingers to her lips.

"Are you upset? Tell me what's happening in your head." I settle my hands on her shoulders.

"I'm not upset. I just... I have a lot of feelings, and they're big," she whispers.

"I can handle big feelings. I want all of them." I make a come-on motion. I want to prove I'm the one she should trust, that I'll keep her heart safe. "Lay them on me."

She laughs, but drags her watery eyes to the ceiling. She props her hands on her hips.

"Seriously, I mean it. Bring on the feelings. I'll take everything you've got. Even the ones that bite me."

She blows out a breath. "I do not want to cry right now."

I wrap my arms around her and pull her against me. She fits so perfectly, all her soft curves melding with my hard lines. "You can cry on me. I don't care what kind of tears they are. They can be happy tears, overwhelmed ones, time-of-the-month tears, really-great-orgasm tears, or tears because your boyfriend invited all our friends to celebrate our fake engagement and you don't know what to do with all the feelings you have."

"Oh my God, you're ridiculous." She loops her arms behind my neck. "Thank you for inviting all of our friends. Fake engagement or not, it's exactly what I need."

"Good. I'm glad I got it right." I press my lips to the top of her head. "I want you to feel supported. I'm sorry this weekend was hard for you, and I'm sorry it took me until last night to be honest about what happened."

Willy leans back and looks up at me, eyes shining with unshed tears. "I'm sorry I couldn't see what was right in front of me."

I shake my head and stroke her cheek. "Don't apologize. We have a long history, but hopefully a future too."

She fingers the hair at the nape of my neck. One tiny tug, and I bend to her lips. It's a soft kiss, filled with years of apology.

My hands have a mind of their own and slide down her back to cup her ass.

Wills pulls back, eyebrows pinched. "Wait a second."

I arch one in question.

"There are yurts outside."

"Yeah." They almost showed up before we went to the reunion, but Ashish held them back until we'd vacated the premises.

"How long have our friends been here?"

"They started arriving after we left for the reunion," I say.

"So they were here when we got back last night?"

"Yeah."

"How come I didn't notice them?" The question sounds more like an accusation.

"You were a bit preoccupied with getting me out of my clothes."

She pinches my nipple. "Why didn't you tell me then?" Her eyes go wide with horror and her voice drops to a whisper. "I was loud last night."

"They were probably asleep already."

They weren't. I heard voices when we got back but chose to ignore them for obvious reasons.

She gives me a look.

"Honey." I take her hand and kiss the back of the one with the ring on it. "The only people who slept over last night are our closest friends. No one will be upset with you for enjoying my ability to give you multiples."

She gives me a look I'm entirely too familiar with, and it immediately makes me hard. "If you'd told me, I wouldn't have been so...vocal."

"I'm sorry."

She purses her plush lips. "You're not even a little sorry."

I shake my head and then change it to a nod. "Okay, that was a lie. I'm not sorry that I fucked you the way I did, but I am sorry that you're maybe a little upset with me for not spoiling the surprise." I can't resist those lips, so I don't even try.

"What are you doing?"

"Apologizing." I wrap my arm around her again. "With my lips."

She softens and parts for me when I stroke the seam of her mouth. Her hands slide up my arms, pausing to squeeze my biceps for a moment before they continue to my shoulders. Her nails dig in as our tongues tangle, and she makes a small plaintive sound, like she's annoyed with herself for enjoying it. Which makes sense, since there's a pretty solid chance our friends heard her screaming my name last night. To be fair, in the moment I'd been too focused on how unbelievable it was to finally be inside the woman I'd been pining over for the past decade to worry about what they could or couldn't hear.

When my hard-on pokes her in the stomach, she puts her hands on my chest to prevent me from claiming her mouth again. She glances between us, a sly smile curving her lips as she drags her nails down my chest. I watch her hand slide under the waistband of my boxer briefs and her gloriously warm, soft palm circle my erection.

She regards me with a knowing look. "Does irritating me excite you?"

"Everything about you excites me." It's the truth.

"Hmm... That's a vague, safe answer." Wills sinks to her

knees on the wooden floor and frees my erection. "Be a good boy and push your boxers down, Dallas."

Our friends can definitely wait. I'd like to ask her to take her shirt off. I'd also like to offer her a pillow so she's not kneeling on the floor, but then she'd have to stop touching me.

Her tongue drags across her bottom lip, and she leans in. Her warm exhalation breaks across the head. My cock kicks in her fist. I groan as she turns her head and rubs her cheek against the shaft. There's something so intensely sexy about seeing this badass, take-no-shit woman on her knees, nuzzling my cock like a happy cat. I want to bury my face between her thighs and make her come for hours as a thank you for being so amazing.

"You are so damn beautiful," I grind out.

"Are you going to do exactly what I say?"

Anything. I love when she's bossy. "Yes, Wills. Whatever you want. You can have it."

Her lips brush over the tip, and my knees nearly buckle. "Too bad you didn't tell me to temper my enthusiasm last night, otherwise I'd be inclined to help you with your problem." She presses her lips against the head and then parts them, her actions contradicting her words as she applies brain-melting suction. The head disappears between her lips, and she swirls her tongue.

I almost embarrass the shit out of myself and come on the spot. One second her lips are wrapped around the head of my cock, and the next she's tucking it back into my boxers and pushing to her feet.

"Why are you stopping?"

"Everyone's out there waiting." She pats me on the chest. "Don't worry. My mouth isn't going anywhere, and this will give you time to think about all the ways I'm going to use it on you later. A little punishment never hurt anyone. We should get dressed and go say hi to our friends." She pinches my ass and tosses a saucy wink over her shoulder as she disappears into the bathroom and flips the lock.

CHAPTER 32
DALLAS

"So, things have obviously developed over the past few days," Ash says as we sip our coffees on my parents' lawn a little later that morning.

Roman, Hollis, Tristan, Tristan's middle brother Nate, and Flip are playing a game of horseshoes. I'm always shocked by how shitty Flip is at anything other than hockey.

The girls are sitting at one of the many picnic tables set up in the yard close to the beach. They're all wearing their Badass Babe Brigade shirts and Wills's reads Queen of the Badass Babe Brigade. Her smile is bright and beautiful, and every time I look at her mouth, I get hard all over again. I'm very much looking forward to being tormented later. Although, I have a feeling I'll have to wait until we're back in Toronto since she works tomorrow morning.

"I told her the truth."

"Finally." He rubs the scruff on his chin. "Obviously that went over okay."

"Yeah. It was a long time coming." It's a weight lifted, but now I have a new one. I glance around to make sure no one can overhear our conversation and drop my voice. "She's agreed to be my girlfriend, officially."

He nods. "What about the engagement?"

"Hopefully she'll agree to make that real too, eventually."

I want her to be where I am today—elated as hell to be surrounded by all our family and friends, celebrating the beginning of our life journey together. But for Wills, it's all still a ruse. For me, it's everything I've ever wanted.

My high school hockey buddies start showing up, as well as Wills's student council friends who delayed their trip home so they could celebrate with us. Wills introduces them to the girls, and for a moment I sense her nervousness, but her Badass Babe Brigade always has her back, and her student council friends were always nice people who respected and appreciated Wills, so it makes sense that they all seem to get along.

My high school hockey buddies try to play it cool, but they're all Terror fans, so the energy gets a little frenetic. My brothers and sister arrive around noon with more food and coolers of drinks.

Paris caps a beer and surveys the crowd. "Where are the Sheep's Asses? Or are they too good to show their faces?"

I frown. "They should know better."

"That's putting a lot of their in them that they don't deserve." She tips her chin in Wills's direction. "Badass Babe Brigade?"

"They're Wills's girl squad," I explain.

Paris links her arm with mine. "She's so different than she was in high school, but the same, you know? This place was too confining for someone like her. She always had to fight to be herself, and now she's the center of everything, isn't she?"

"Yeah, she really is. She's a big part of the reason we're all as tight as we are."

"You did good, big brother. She's the perfect woman for you."

"Yeah. She is."

The loud whir of an engine momentarily makes conversation impossible. It's followed by a gust of wind that has people scrambling to keep their plastic glasses from toppling over. A seaplane passes above us, and suddenly Wills's moms are rushing to the end of the dock, arms waving over their heads.

"What the hell is going on?" Flip shouts.

"My brothers are here," Wills calls out. She excuses herself from the table to join her moms on the dock.

"Is Hemi's brother a pilot or something?" Ash sidles up beside me and Paris again.

"Or something," I say. "Isaac owns a massive company, and I have no idea what Sam does, but I would not be surprised if he was a secret agent or a fixer."

"Huh."

"I should probably go over there and say hi."

"Probably, yeah," Ash agrees.

But I don't make a move to join them on the dock. Mostly I'm preparing myself for the onslaught of unbridled energy. And I'm still a little terrified of her brothers.

"Holy crap. Is Sandy just tiny, or is Sam that huge?" Paris asks.

"He's that huge."

"He was kind of a legend." Paris twirls her hair around her finger.

"In what sense?" I give her the side-eye. "What is this?" I flick the back of her hand that's all tangled in her hair.

She drops it and shrugs. "He was the high school quarterback. Dorie's older sister went out with him a few times, and there were ru—" She waves that away. "He was just larger than life, and apparently he still is." She shoves me forward. "You should go say hi. He's going to be your brother-in-law."

I leave the safety of Ash and Paris and head for the dock. But the second Sam steps out of the plane—looking like a 007 agent of death with his groomed beard, aviator glasses, black suit, and black dress shoes—he's mobbed by our former classmates.

Isaac sidesteps him with a roll of his eyes. He's dressed for the occasion in khaki shorts, a polo, and Birks. Aside from the shoes, he looks like he stepped off the golf course. Wills's moms flank Isaac. He pulls me in for a hearty back-slap man-hug. "Great to see you, man."

"You too. Thanks for flying in. We appreciate the support," I say.

"As if we'd miss our baby sister's engagement party. It's a big deal." He glances over his shoulder and lowers his voice. "Plus, high school wasn't the easiest for her, so we'd planned to show up today anyway in case she needed us to bury anyone."

"No funerals to plan," I assure him.

"Funerals are for people who die. We'd just make them disappear."

I chuckle, but it kind of dies in my throat. Seriously, I can't tell if he's joking.

"Isaac, my man! It's great to see you!" Manning comes in for a hearty back pat.

"It's been some years." Isaac returns the man-hug.

"Let's grab a beer and catch up." Manning guides Isaac toward the food and drink tent.

Sam makes his way through the throng of excited partygoers, his arm slung over Wills's shoulder. She's tucked into his side, and despite the fact that she doesn't look like her moms or brothers, it's clear that they are the very definition of family.

"We need pictures now that we have everyone here!" Georgie says, clapping. "Both families. Everyone together!"

We assemble, my family on one side and Wills's on the other, and our friends snap photo after photo. Wills hugs my arm and smiles for the camera. I'm in my glory, but I worry about where she is.

Once we're done with the shoot, Sam insists on getting pictures with Roman.

I bend and kiss Wills's temple. "You doing okay?"

"Yeah. Good. Having all my people here is nice. And my brothers showing up was a great surprise, even if Sam always steals the show." She's smiling.

"I forgot he played football."

"Mostly he tried to knock people out." Her nails dig into my arm. "Oh shit. They came."

"Who came?"

"Who do you think?"

I scan the crowd and find Sean and Brooklyn on the edge of the party, looking a lot like they don't fit.

As if the girls can sense the arrival of Wills's nemesis, they appear, Shilps leading the pack. "Is everything okay?"

"She's here," Wills says.

Shilpa's lip curls in what almost seems like a snarl. She rolls her shoulders back. "The fucking nerve."

Hammer grabs Shilpa's arm. "They're coming this way."

"We got you, girl," Rix says.

I love these women.

Brooklyn looks like she's about to shit her pants as she grips Sean's hand and crosses over to us. "Hi-eee." She waves a maniacal hand in the air.

"It's so nice you could make it," Wills says through a tight smile.

I skim the back of her hand, then cross my arms and step forward, leveling Brooklyn and Sean with a glare. "No."

Brooklyn's eyes dart around and Sean looks confused. "No, what?"

"You don't get to be here. You don't get to talk to Wills. You don't get to celebrate with us. Not after all the shit you've pulled. All the shit you *continue* to pull. You are not welcome," I snap.

Brooklyn scoffs as her face turns red. "I didn't even want to come anyway." She grabs Sean's hand. "Let's go."

Sean puffs his chest out. "These are all our friends, too."

"Not today, they aren't. Today is about Wills, and our family and our friends. And that does not include you."

"Everything okay over here?" Sam's eyes narrow. "B and S. Well isn't this one hell of an unpleasant surprise. Who invited you?"

"They were just leaving," I tell Sam.

"Let me walk you two out." Sam slings one massive arm over their shoulders and steers them back the way they came.

Shilpa turns to me. "I really wanted to tell her off, but that was wonderful."

The Babe Brigade bursts into applause. Wills grabs the front of my shirt and pulls my mouth to hers. "I'm going to do filthy things to you later for being such a good boy...friend."

"I'm so excited for that."

Shilpa pries us apart. "Your parents are watching. Keep it PG for now."

"Fair. Thank you." Wills steps back and smooths her hands over her hips. "That was so gratifying."

"Let's celebrate with something fun to drink." Shilpa winks at me, and she and the girls head to the makeshift bar.

Knocking Brooklyn and Sean down a peg is one of my top-ten favorite things ever. As is seeing Wills surrounded by our friends and family, laughing and smiling and being her authentic, amazing self. She needed to be reminded that she's loved, that she has true, genuine friends who will always stand up for her. That we love her exactly as she is.

An hour later, she sidles up next to me. She drapes one of my arms over her shoulder, snaking hers around my waist and tucking her thumb into my belt loop. "Thank you for making this happen today."

I kiss her temple. "I'm glad it makes you happy."

"It does." She sighs. "It's just sad that it's not really real."

"Things are only as real or fake as you allow them to be." I tuck a finger under her chin and tilt her head up. My chest aches with the knowledge that I want this, all of this, and she's still just playing a part. "All these people here love you. We all adore you. Exactly as you are." I hold her gaze. "Everything about this is real for me. But it's okay if it takes time for you get where I am."

She squeezes me in a side hug and turns to survey the crowd. I take a deep breath as my biggest fear looms in my subconscious. *What if she never catches up? What if she never wants this, me, the way I want her?*

CHAPTER 33

HEMI

"We have a slight problem." Hammer appears in my office and nervously fingers the banana-print scrunchie around her wrist.

Shilpa sets down her coffee. "Slight?"

"On a scale of one to ten, how would you rate this slight problem?" I ask. This morning has been a giant clusterfuck. I should not have slept over at Dallas's last night. But he was so damn persuasive.

It didn't help that I spent the two-and-a-half-hour drive home telling him in excruciating detail all the dirty things I planned to do to him when I got him alone. I was just as amped as he was when he invited me in so I could make good on all my threats. I can function on too-little sleep for one night, but a whole weekend is another story. And my entire body freaking aches. Dallas is exceptionally skilled between the sheets, and his stamina is unparalleled. I could really use a soak in the hot tub to ease my aching thighs and a five-hour nap.

"Probably an eight."

"That seems like a significant upgrade from slight," Shilpa mutters.

"I was trying to downplay it." Hammer exhales a steadying breath. "The shipment is still sitting in the warehouse fridge."

"It's supposed to be there when the foodbank opens in"—I check the time—"three hours. I had it all organized. It was being picked up on Friday, before everyone left for the weekend."

"I guess the driver was running behind because there was an accident blocking the loading dock, so he was half an hour late," Hammer explains.

"And the office was closed," I finish for her.

"I would've come back if I'd known, but the driver called the head office and was transferred to Topher, so I didn't know about it until twenty minutes ago."

"Shit." And that explains why I didn't get a call or any information. This is blatant sabotage. Topher has gone too far. But before I confront him, I need a plan to manage this fuckup. "Okay. We should still have time to get everything to the foodbank before it opens and the women's team arrives." Is it ideal? Not in the slightest. But the foodbank is a half-hour drive away, and we can load everything into the back of my truck.

"Technically, yes, but we might need to make more than one trip, even if we drive there separately."

"Why? How much food is there?" Before I left on Thursday, there was enough to fill a cargo van.

"Fresh Foods delivered the fruit and veg on Friday morning. It's still in cold storage. But there's more than we expected."

"How much more?"

"Enough to fill my truck twice."

"Well, that's great and also a problem."

"I can call Hollis and my dad to help?" Hammer offers.

"And I'll call Ash." Shilpa already has her phone in her hand.

"I'll call Tristan and Dallas."

Once the calls have been made, Shilpa and Hammer head down to the loading dock, and I pay Topher a visit. "Do you have a personal problem with the women's team, or is it just me that's your issue?"

Topher purses his lips and looks like a perturbed Kermit the Frog. "Is this about the delivery?"

"Yes, Topher. It's about the delivery. You and every single other person in this office who deals directly with the teams who use this arena were aware of the foodbank promo I set up for the women's team. We talked about it in a meeting, and you were briefed in the weekly emails."

"I get a lot of emails."

"We all get a lot of emails. When you got that call on Friday, did it not occur to you at the very least to send an email to me and my team to let us know what happened so we could adequately prepare for what we were facing this morning?"

"It was after hours on a Friday," he says defensively.

"And yet I received an email from you on Friday night at seven o'clock about rink time. So that excuse doesn't hold a lot of water. I am trying to bring positive press to the Terror organization and demonstrate that we are wholly committed to inclusivity in the sport and support of our community, and this bullshit you pulled makes us look like a bunch of amateur assholes."

He tugs at his tie.

I'd like to strangle him with it.

"This event starts in less than three hours. And instead of things going smoothly, we're scrambling to get everything to the foodbank in time. Think about the headline on that one, Topher, and how it would reflect poorly on the Terror as a whole."

"I can call down to maintenance and see if they have a couple of trucks." He looks back at his computer and moves his mouse like he has better things to do than clean up his mess.

"I've already handled it. What you can do is call Denise and personally apologize for the miscommunication."

Half an hour later, Dallas, Ash, Hollis, Roman, Flip, and Tristan arrive at the warehouse loading dock with a huge moving van. Even Kai, the team photographer, has come to help, along with the two staff from media relations who the PR division sometimes collaborates with. We load everything and deliver the food with just enough time to unload and set up. I'm so grateful for the support, but I remain frustrated that Topher is set on making my life difficult, ruining good things for the community in the process.

Once everything is ready, everyone but me and Hammer takes off. Apart from the late delivery, no one would guess that we had any glitches, and the foodbank is incredibly grateful for the donation and the help of the women's team on what turns out to be one of the busiest days they've ever had.

Afterward, Hammer and I meet the rest of the girls at the Watering Hole.

"You look like you could use this." Shilpa slides a pint glass of club soda across the table.

"I'm parched." My phone buzzes with a message from Dallas, letting me know he's picking me up in an hour. "I hope whatever Dallas has planned includes lying on the couch and him watching a movie while I nap. I'm exhausted after this weekend."

"Sounded like you had a great time," Rix says with a smirk.

Essie points a finger at her. "People who live in glass houses shouldn't throw stones." Essie surprised everyone and moved back last week from BC. She's Rix's childhood best friend, making her an honorary member of our group whenever she's in town. And now she's full-fledged since she's living in the city again.

Rix raises both her hands. "I'm not throwing stones. I'm just saying he seems like a real giver, and he wants to make her happy."

"He strikes me as the kind of guy who will always make sure you come first," Hammer muses.

"Ten out of ten, every single time," I agree. At least that's how it's been since we started having sex two days ago. We've had a lot of sex over the past forty-eight hours, even with the engagement party and the two-and-a-half-hour drive home.

"But that stays between us. Dallas does not need his ego stroked."

Shilpa pats my hand. "Um, sweetie, everyone already knows. We heard it with our own ears."

I flick a straw wrapper at her. "Now everyone knows what my orgasms sound like."

Rix pats my arm. "More people than I'd like also know what my orgasms sound like, so we can be embarrassed together."

"I appreciate that." I hug her arm. "And thank you all for driving up to Huntsville for the engagement party. It was so nice to have you there, especially after the reunion."

"We wouldn't have missed it for the world."

I return the smile. "Is everything okay? Tristan seemed tense earlier. Nate too yesterday."

She nods. "He'll be fine. He just has some family stuff, and it's giving him feelings he doesn't know what to do with."

"Are his dad and brothers okay?" I ask.

"Yeah. We're figuring it out. Nothing to worry about."

I nod, leaving it alone for now, turning to Tally. "Have you started packing for your move into residence next month?" Her summer has been busy. She's dancing five days a week and working for me part time.

"Some stuff is in boxes. But the rooms are smaller than I'm used to, so I'm trying to be selective about what I'm bringing. And I found out my apartment is co-ed."

"How does your dad feel about that?" I ask.

"He's trying to be cool, but I heard him stressing over it to my mom. It's not like I'll hook up with one of my roommates. That seems like a disaster waiting to happen."

"Speaking from experience, I agree that it isn't the best plan to hook up with a guy you'll share space with for an entire year," Rix says.

"I know it worked for the two of you, but the guy I date in first year becoming the guy I end up spending the rest of my life with doesn't seem likely. I'm excited to have roommates, though," Tally says.

"It'll be great," I agree. She's disciplined, smart, and has a good head on her shoulders.

A waft of muggy July air sweeps through the Watering Hole as my new boyfriend walks through the door. Dallas looks gorgeous in a pair of khaki shorts, a dark blue T-shirt, and an open, button-down plaid short-sleeve shirt over top. The smile that lights up his face when his gaze lands on me makes my heart stutter.

He crosses the restaurant, and his fingers glide along the edge of my jaw as he tips my chin up and kisses me gently. "Hi. I missed your face."

I laugh. "You were with me a few hours ago."

"I know. But we had the whole weekend together, and I spent most of today *not* with you. I like this better. You should sleep over again tonight."

I arch a brow. "I wouldn't call what happened last night sleeping."

"It was fun, though. Especially the part where you—"

I press a finger to his lips. "Be a good boy and save it for later."

"Yes, ma'am." His eyes heat, and the way his lip curls makes everything below the waist excited. "Sorry to interrupt, but we have somewhere to be in fifteen minutes."

I hug the girls goodbye and leave the Watering Hole with Dallas.

"Any hints?" I ask as he links our fingers.

"You'll see soon enough." His lips find my temple. "Everything work out okay at the foodbank?"

"Yes. Thanks for coming to the rescue."

"Honestly, anytime. What happened with the initial pickup?"

"Topher happened. The loading dock entrance was blocked because of an accident, so by the time the delivery guy arrived, the office was closed. The call was routed to Topher, and he did nothing. Thankfully, we had enough time and people to help this morning to make it work."

"Why does Topher have it out for you?"

"Just because I'm me, I think." I hug his arm. "He and I have never really gotten along, but it doesn't help my case that I'm involved with you now."

He frowns. "I made your job harder, didn't I?"

I shrug. "Your heart was in a good place. You're a famous hockey player dating someone who works for the team. I'm the unscrupulous woman who seduced a player."

"Excuse me, I had to force you into a fake relationship to even get you to kiss me. And that was mostly under duress." He tries to make light of it, but his eyes drop to my lips, like he's remembering those kisses.

"Stop looking at me like that." I hold up a hand to shield my eyes. "Your thoughts are written all over your face, and they're obscene."

He pulls my hand away and bites my knuckle. "Want to get dirty with me later?"

"Only if you can behave while we're in public."

His lip curls in a salacious grin. "I can be good. But only for you." He stops in front of my favorite mani-pedi place and opens the door.

"You scheduled me a manicure?"

"No. You had your nails done before we left for the weekend. I scheduled us both for pedicures."

I smile up at him. I've never been with someone who pays this kind of attention to what I like. "Yeah, you did."

His answering grin melts hearts and panties. "You approve."

"I absolutely approve." I push up on my toes and kiss the edge of his jaw. He is terrifyingly amazing.

He laces our fingers as we enter the spa and they get us settled in two chairs. Anita, my usual technician, passes me a gossip magazine.

"What's that?" Dallas asks.

"You won't poke fun, if you know what's good for you." I arch a meaningful brow.

Paramita, another technician, sits in front of Dallas.

"Hi. I'm sorry my feet aren't as pretty as Hemi's. I'm Dallas, and she's the love of my life."

Paramita laughs. "I know who you are. My husband and son are Terror fans."

"Oh yeah? Who are their favorite players?"

"My son adores you, and my husband is a Hollis Hendrix fan."

"Hendrix has been with the team a long time."

Dallas settles in and keeps Anita and Paramita entertained by telling them how he's known me since kindergarten. "She was the first person to learn how to tie her shoes, and she spent all of play time teaching everyone else until they mastered it."

"That sounds like Hemi," Anita says. "So how did you two finally end up together?"

"I saw some guy making her uncomfortable and couldn't stand it, so I went over to make sure she was okay. One thing led to another, and I figured eventually I would convince her I was good boyfriend material, and now here I am." He props his chin on his fist and smiles at me. "With my favorite toe keeper. Always keeping me on my toes."

An hour later, I have blue toenails and Dallas has kept Anita and Paramita in stitches with stories of all his flubbed promo ops. We grab takeout and head back to his place. "I can't sleep over again tonight," I warn as we take the elevator to his penthouse.

He frowns. "Why not?"

I smooth the line between his eyes. "Because I slept like garbage this weekend, first from the sexual tension and then the actual sex. I need to sleep tonight so I can function tomorrow."

"What if I just spoon you all night?"

"If you get spoony with me, you'll get a hard-on, and then

you'll rub it on my ass, and we both know what that will lead to." I won't be able to resist Dallas or the D. I know this already.

"We can have early sex and be in bed by nine."

My eyes slide closed. "I can't believe you're trying to negotiate sex with me."

"Is it working?"

"No." *Absolutely yes, it is.*

He cages me against the mirrored wall and drags his lips along the edge of my jaw. "I'm desperate for the taste of you, honey. I need to be inside you, and I need the sound of my name on your perfect, pretty lips when I'm making you come."

"We're in bed by nine—nine thirty at the latest—and if you rub your hard-on on my ass in the middle of the night, I will make sure you regret it."

He backs off, eyes dark and smile full of primal satisfaction. "No rubbing my hard-on on your ass in the middle of the night." He gives me the Boy Scout salute. "I promise I'll make every orgasm worth your while." He steps back as the elevator dings, signaling our arrival at the penthouse floor.

I half expect him to get me naked the second we walk in the door. But instead, he cues up one of my favorite movies to watch while we eat takeout. It's already eight by the time we're done with dinner. He puts the leftovers in the fridge, and I excuse myself to the bathroom to freshen up.

Dallas is still in the kitchen when I return to the living room. I grab one of the crocheted peaches from the fruit basket on his side table as I browse his massive collection of graphic novels, then flop down on his oversized couch and tuck a plaid pillow behind my head. He returns a minute later and stretches out on top of me, resting his head on my chest and pressing me into the couch with his weight.

"What are you doing?"

"Snuggling."

"With my boobs?" I laugh and run my fingers through his hair.

"With all of you." He nuzzles in. "I can't get close enough. You feel so fucking good, Wills." His lips find bare skin. "I'm still hungry. You gonna let me eat you for dessert?" His eyebrows dance, his grin wide and so damn beautiful it scrambles my brain.

I burst into laughter.

"Is that a yes?" He kisses the end of my nose.

"Yes, you can make out with my pussy."

He drops his head, lips capturing mine as he edges a knee between my thighs. I sink into the kiss, into the softness of his lips against mine. He strokes the edge of my jaw as he rolls his hips, and I'm already panting and achy by the time he starts working his way down my chest.

He folds back on his knees, pulling his shirt over his head before he helps me out of mine, and then rids me of my pants and underwear as well. His hot gaze caresses my body, and he follows with his hands, smoothing up the outside of my thighs. He drops his head again and kisses a path from my soft belly to the apex of my thighs.

And then his mouth is on me, tongue swirling, fingers sliding inside me, pushing me toward bliss with every perfectly timed pump and curl. I can't take my eyes off him as he devours me, making desperate, greedy noises as he fucks me with his tongue and fingers.

I'm teetering on the edge, holding off, but his eyes lift, and he pins me with that look I know so well. Even with his mouth latched to my clit, his lip curls in a devious grin and one finger slides lower, pressing against my back door. As he pushes his fingers deeper, that single finger slides into my ass. My eyes roll up, and a full-body shudder rushes through me. The orgasm is gloriously intense, dragging me under and keeping me pinned there as I moan Dallas's name.

When I'm boneless and panting, he shucks off his shorts and boxers, grabs a condom from his wallet and rolls it on, then fits himself between my legs again.

"You don't want to finish this in the bedroom?" I ask as I drag my nails down his chest.

He shakes his head as he grips his erection and lines himself up. "I want the memory of being inside you every time I lie on this couch."

"You're a little obsessed, aren't you?" I've never been with someone like this.

"Wholly, unequivocally, unabashedly obsessed." He kisses the end of my nose. "I'm going to pound you into the couch now, honey."

"Bring it on, sweetheart," I taunt, digging my nails into the back of his neck.

His hips jerk forward, and he fills me with one hard thrust. I moan, hooking my leg over his hip as he pulls back, all the way to the ridge, before he fills me again. He frames my face with his wide, warm palms.

"Keep your eyes on mine," he demands. "I want to see what I do to you."

He keeps fucking me, the rhythm as intense as his expression. I see every emotion as it passes through his eyes, ending with the primal satisfaction that darkens his gaze when another orgasm rolls through me and his name tumbles from my lips on a low, desperate moan.

"I love that sound..." Dallas tucks his arm under my leg, changing the angle, going deeper and dragging the orgasm out. I can't stop coming, or moaning, or digging my nails into his back.

The chemistry is incendiary, the sex a revelation, and I'm already addicted to the feel of his body moving over mine, the way he fills me so completely. But the thing that I can't get enough of is his enraptured expression, the way he bares his feelings without apology. I've never felt this loved, this consumed, or this cared for before Dallas.

And I can't tear my eyes from his as he reaches his peak. His muscles are tight, neck straining, biceps flexing. For a moment I wonder what it would have been like if he'd asked me out the way he'd wanted to. Would he have been my first? Would he have made me feel this special, this wanted, the way he does now?

All those hard lines and cut angles suddenly soften, and he presses me into the couch, still bearing most of his weight as his lips find my neck and skim until they reach my ear. They move against my skin, and I instinctively know what he's saying without sound.

That he loves me.

That he's mine.

And so is his heart.

CHAPTER 34
DALLAS

"I can't believe training camp starts next month. Where did the summer go?" Hollis shakes his head as he loads up the squat rack.

It's already closing in on the end of August. This summer has turned out to be the best one of my life. So far.

"I know, man." Tristan grunts from the incline bench where he's doing sit-ups. "Bea is starting courses in a few weeks, and she's a mix of excitement and nerves." He's the only one who calls Rix this.

"Is she still stressed about not having a full paycheck?" Flip asks between one-armed pushups.

"Yeah. She's been making spreadsheets for monthly expenses. I keep telling her it's fine, and I've got this, but this is one of her hang-ups, so I'm letting her do what she needs to do."

"She'll get comfortable eventually," Flip assures him.

"I hope so. She's been seeing her therapist more, so that's been helpful," Tristan agrees, looking over at me. "How are things with you and Hemi?"

"Amazing." I choose a plate for a chest press and lie on one of the benches. "It's been nice not having to hide how I feel about her." She's been spending more nights with me lately. And she's been leaving clothes, too. It makes sense for her to stay at my place, where she doesn't have to worry about being quiet or someone interrupting when we're making out on the couch. Did I mention it's been the best summer of my life?

"I can't believe I didn't see this coming," Flip gripes.

"The rest of us did," Ash mutters, then frowns at his phone. "Shit. Give me a minute."

"Everything okay?" I ask.

"Shilps was feeling off this morning. I hope she's not coming down with something." He steps into the hallway to take the call.

"I hope she's okay." I watch the gym door close behind him.

We have a double date tonight. I love having Wills all to myself, but it's been nice doing couple things with Ash and Shilpa. Sometimes Rix and Tristan, and Hollis and Hammer join us too. It's the first time I've had a girlfriend since I came to Toronto, and the fact that it's Wills... It's like my life is complete. I have everything I want—great friends, a fantastic family, an awesome job, and the girl of my dreams. It doesn't hurt that she's adventurous in bed and the power balance is addictive as hell.

"She didn't feel well the other morning in the office, either," Roman says.

"Hopefully she doesn't pass whatever she has to Wills." Those two spend a lot of time together. And with Hammer and Tally working in the office, too, half our group could come down with something, if they're not careful.

Ash returns a minute later.

"She okay?" I ask.

"Yup. All good." He gives us the thumbs-up, but he still looks a little worried.

Ash and I finish our workout, grab a bite with the guys, and head home.

"Do you need to postpone the double date?" I ask as we

drive the short distance. Ash and Shilpa live in the building across the street from mine.

"It's nothing serious. She's just a little disappointed that the crimson tide came in. All the talk about starting a family led to a lot of practicing last month, and we stopped birth control. We know it won't necessarily happen right away, but she was a couple of days late and started to get excited. Going out tonight will be good for her."

"I didn't realize you were diving in with both feet," I say.

"We weren't, but we planted the seed, and now she wants me to plant my seed." He rubs his bottom lip. "Anyway, you and Hemi seem to know a little something about diving in with both feet."

"It's been the best summer of my life." I rap on the armrest.

"But..." he presses.

I sigh. "It's more of an *I wish* than a *but*. Everything's kind of backwards."

"Because of the engagement?" he asks.

I rub my chin. "Yeah. It's this thing that just sort of looms. I want her to want this the way I do."

"She'll get there." He pats me on the shoulder. "You've had a lot more time with your feelings than she has."

"I hope so." He's right. I've loved her for years. She's hardly had time to like me. But my feelings for her are like ivy, spreading, growing, and I worry she'll never have enough time to catch up.

"You're sleeping over tonight," I say later that evening as the elevator climbs to the penthouse floor. Wills is wearing a wrap dress that does an unbelievable job of highlighting her curves. One tug on the bow at her hip, and everything I want is at my fingertips.

She regards me with a half smile. "That sounds more like an order than a request." She fingers the end of my tie, bottom lip sliding through her teeth.

"So you want it quick and dirty?" I nip the edge of her jaw.

"You mean as opposed to torturing me with foreplay and keeping me on the edge?" She pokes me in the chest.

"Admit it. You fucking love it, Wilhelmina." I work my knee between her thighs and take her lobe between my teeth.

She makes a noise that's neither confirmation nor denial.

"You can always make it easy on yourself." I hover my lips over hers.

"How's that?" She tips her chin up, a silent request to kiss her.

I pull back an inch. "Be a good girl and let me have control this time." I stroke her cheek with gentle fingers. "I won't keep you on the edge. As soon as we walk through the door, I'll get on my knees for you. We both know I can make you come in two minutes."

She groans. "You're playing dirty, Dallas."

"Is that a yes, then?" I run my hand down her side and curve my hand around her ass, pulling her tight against my thigh.

She makes an annoyed sound.

"Last chance to get what you want without a fight. I'll do that thing with my tongue. I won't even make you beg for it."

She sighs. "Fine. Yes." She shoves her hands in my hair and tries to pull my mouth to hers.

"*Yes* what?"

She narrows her eyes.

"Say the words, honey."

"You can have control."

I grin.

She growls.

The elevator door dings, and I step back, lacing our fingers. Wills tugs on my hand, trying to make me walk faster. She rummages in her purse for the key fob I gave her weeks ago—as soon as she agreed to be my girlfriend. "Where is it?" she grumbles.

I pull mine from my jacket pocket and swipe it over the sensor. She gives me another withering look, grabs my tie, and pulls me inside along with her.

The second we're inside my penthouse, she starts undressing me. I lace my fingers with hers and crowd her until her back meets the door, pinning her hands over her head.

"You said you weren't going to torture me," she gripes.

"I'm not."

"I want you naked."

"That's nice." I capture her lips and stroke inside. She moans and arches against me, fingernails digging into the backs of my hands. My knee finds its way between her thighs again, and she rolls her hips. "But you gave me control, so I'll get naked when I'm good and ready." I kiss the end of her nose and smile when she makes an irritated sound.

I pull the bow at her waist and one side of her dress falls open. Next, I pull the tie on the inside and push the dress over her shoulders. I catch it before it falls to the floor and hang it on the hook beside the door. She's wearing a royal blue lace bra and matching panties.

"God, you're sexy, and you're all mine."

I kiss her again as I reach behind her and flick open the clasp on her bra. It slides down her arms, and her bare nipples brush my chest. On nights like these, when Wilhelmina hands me the reins, I want to worship every inch of her. I cup her breasts, thumbs sweeping over her nipples as I kiss along her collarbones. I stop to suck her nipples as I sink to my knees, and then I hook my thumbs into the waistband of her panties and drag them down her tanned thighs.

I press a kiss and inhale deeply. "All night long, Wilhelmina, I've been thinking about getting on my knees for you." I curve a hand around the back of her calf and bring it over my shoulder, opening her for me. "How long do you think it'll take to bring you to yours?" I lick up the length of her on a groan.

"Oh my fuck." She grips the doorknob with one hand and my shoulder with the other as the toes beside my knee curl.

She slides her fingers into my hair and rolls her hips in time to the swirl of my tongue. Her soft moans grow deeper, her nails press into my scalp, and her legs start to tremble. A minute later, a low keening sound tumbles from her lips, along with my name, and her knee buckles.

I rise in a rush, grip her ass, and lift her. She's uncoordinated as she wraps her arms around my neck and her legs around my waist, but she holds tight as I carry her to the bedroom.

I deposit her on my bed and stand at the edge while she kneels and struggles to get me out of my clothes, fumbling with the buttons on my shirt. But the second her palms connect with my chest, she sighs, like there's relief in finally being able to touch me.

"God, you're beautiful," she murmurs, fingers tracing the dips and curves as they trail down my stomach. She unclasps my belt, then unbuttons my pants. As soon as I'm naked, she gives me the coyest, sweetest smile. "Will you fuck me now?"

"Soon." I take her face between my palms and kiss her, then climb up on the bed with her and settle between her thighs. She tips her hips up, sighing once again as my cock slides over slick skin, but I don't make a move to push inside, don't give her the thing we're both so desperate for.

I push up on one arm, hovering over her, the head of my cock resting on her lower abdomen.

She frowns. "What are you doing? You're supposed to be in me."

"I will be soon." I lean down to kiss her. "On your stomach for me, honey."

Her eyes light up, and she flips over. I drop my hips, and my cock slides between her ass cheeks. Transferring my weight to one arm, I move her hair over her shoulder, exposing her back and the delicate curve of her neck. She turns her head, and I press my lips to her cheek as my weight settles on top of her.

She hums and wiggles under me, pushing her ass up as I shift my hips back. The head slides low, nudging her entrance.

Wilhelmina reaches back, her fingers pressing against the outside of my thigh. "Go bare for a minute, please, Dallas."

We've had the protection conversation. She's on the pill and has been for years. She has an alarm set on her phone and takes it at the same time every single day. Before her, it had been an incredibly long time since I'd slept with anyone. It was hard to engage in meaningless sex when the woman of my dreams was right in front of me.

I kiss her shoulder. "For a minute." I shift forward, sheathing myself in her.

"Oh fuck, thank God," Wilhelmina groans.

I press my face against the side of her neck, lips parting and teeth sinking gently into her skin as I work to control my desire to just thrust. *Fuck. Claim. Own.*

Her fingers find my hair, and she twists her head, lips seeking mine. "Please, Dallas."

I slip a palm under her cheek and cover her mouth with mine, meeting her lust-drenched gaze. I love every side of her, but this one is my favorite. She's always poised and in control. She's the master of her own domain, and she's unapologetically herself. But it's a rare and special gift to see her give herself over, relinquishing control. "Please, what?"

"Please fuck me."

"Such a good girl." I pull my hips back and push in again. "Such nice manners."

"Oh God, yes." Her fingers curl in my hair, gripping tightly as I give her what she wants. What we both want.

But I'm bare, and as much as I'd like to finish inside her, it's not a risk I'm willing to take. Not now. An unplanned pregnancy on top of a fake engagement isn't something I want to put on her.

I pull out, and she groans her displeasure. I kiss her shoulder. "I'll be back inside you soon. Just need a condom."

I grab one from the nightstand and fold back on my knees. I can't help myself, I slap her ass, then knead the spot before I press my cock between her cheeks and fuck the divide for a few strokes before I roll the condom down my length. I straddle her thighs as I push back in.

"Oh my God, thank you." She moans.

I keep kneading her ass as I kiss between her shoulder blades and roll my hips, staying deep. When it's not enough for either of us, I edge my knees between her thighs. "On all fours for me," I command as I grip her hips and pull her up with me.

I start fucking her again, long hard strokes that wring gasps and moans from her. I run my thumb along the length of my cock as I pull out, gathering wetness as I press against her puckered hole.

She looks over her shoulder, eyes alight with anticipation. "Yes, please," she pants.

I ease my thumb into her ass, and her head drops on a low expletive. She repositions herself, bracing her weight on one arm so she can reach between her thighs. Her fingers graze my cock as I pull out and push back in, sliding my thumb deeper into her ass. She strums her clit while I drive into her.

Sweat trickles down my spine, and I glance to the right, where the mirror above my dresser gives me a perfect view of her swaying breasts and my cock sliding in and out of her slick, tight pussy.

"Don't stop, don't stop, don't stop," she chants as she spasms around me.

I slide my thumb out and grip her hip, using my free hand to wind her hair around my fist. I pull her up, her back to my chest, and twist her head so my mouth is at her ear. "Look at you." I incline my head toward our reflection, bodies slick with sweat, her soft curves pressed against me, hair damp at the temples, cheeks flushed, nipples peaked. "Such a goddess." I bite the edge of her jaw. "So damn beautiful when you're coming on my cock."

"You're so good to me." She moans and reaches up to thread her fingers through my hair. "You feel so good inside me."

I slip my hand between her thighs and circle her clit as I continue fucking her, staying deep, lips at her ear, other hand still fisting her hair. "You're going to let me in this sweet ass with more than my fingers soon."

Her nails bite into my skin as she comes again. I stop holding back, taking her down to the mattress as I drive into her and find my own release. It gets better every time. It doesn't matter which of us is in control—being with her, being inside her, making her come, watching her at her most vulnerable—all of it is breathtaking. I can't get enough.

I pepper kisses along her shoulder and cheek. Then I roll to the side to lie next to her, removing the condom and tying it off before I wrap it in a tissue and drop it on the floor. I fold one arm behind my head and turn toward her. "Hey. How are you doing?"

She nuzzles my arm. "I am beyond good. Thank you for fucking me like you mean it."

"I noticed you didn't say no or try to bite me when I suggested anal." I've been obsessed with Wilhelmina's ass since high school. Pretty much any time she hands over control, I get her on all fours. Another favorite is reverse cowgirl.

She props her cheek on her fist. "I'll let you fuck my ass if you let me fuck yours first."

I blink, and blink again. She doesn't appear to be joking. The image of her dressed in black lace, wearing a strap-on pops into my head. Yeah. I'm definitely not opposed. "Okay."

Her eyes flare. "Wait, what?"

I let my gaze trace her naked body. "Do you have any idea how hot you are? The idea of you fucking me..." I roll on top of her and fit myself between her thighs. "Yeah. I'm into it."

CHAPTER 35

HEMI

"Have you ever slept on a twin bed before?" Hammer asks.

"At dance camp we slept four to a room and had twin bunk beds," Tally says.

"Of course you went to dance camp." Rix pats her shoulder, smiling.

Tally props her fists on her hips. "What is that supposed to mean?"

"That none of us are surprised you went to dance camp," Dred says. "How old were you?"

"I went every summer until I aged out at sixteen. I had my first kiss there." She tosses her purse on the bed and surveys the room. "I think my walk-in closet is bigger than this entire space." She cringes. "Oh, ew. I sound like a spoiled brat. I should not repeat that to anyone outside of this room."

Hammer gives her a side hug. "I get it. My room in my off-campus apartment was about the same size as this. It took a little getting used to, but I promise we'll make it yours, and it'll feel like home."

"Remember the two-bedroom apartment we lived in during second year?" Essie says to Rix.

"Two bedroom was a stretch. The twin bed took up ninety

percent of one room," Rix says with a smile. "But it was ours and it was fun. Minus the snow that came in under the crack in the front door."

"That sounds like an adventure," Hemi says.

"It absolutely was," Essie agrees. "And I wouldn't trade it for the world." Essie's living in a tiny bachelor apartment not far from the rest of us, making it easy for her to join in on moving day.

Rix pulls her phone out of her pocket and sighs. She types a message and slides it back into her pocket.

"Everything okay?" I ask.

"Tristan is on his way here and he's bringing Nate."

"I didn't know he was coming." When I told Dallas we were moving Tally into residence this weekend, he offered to help. Her dad was called out of town for an unexpected meeting in New York, and Tally's brother has a cello performance that her mom needs to attend, so we gladly stepped in. Flip decided to tag along. And apparently now Tristan and his younger brother.

Not quite the low-key entrance Tally was hoping to make, but she doesn't want to hurt their feelings and tell them no. Also, she has a lot of boxes.

"Yeah. He's been a bit needy lately."

"Is everything okay?"

"Brody's convocation is in September, and his mom is suddenly interested in attending. She called him last night, and he's having a hard time. Add in Nate staying with us until he gets his apartment at the beginning of the month, and it's been intense."

"Tristan doesn't have much contact with her usually, right?" Dred asks.

Rix nods. "She sends a card at Christmas, but he hasn't seen her in years. The whole thing has been really triggering for him. In the past, he would shut down, or be a dick, but he doesn't want to default to asshole mode now, so he's increased his therapy sessions. It's been good for him, but it also means feeling all the feelings and learning how to let them exist without taking over." She sighs. "With me going back to school soon, Nate moving to the city for a new job, and the start of the season, it's just a lot. And he wants more time with me, so he's on his way over. He's been showing up for himself and asking for what he needs, even when it's hard, and that's huge progress."

I bump her shoulder with mine. "It can't be easy, though."

"It's not, but we're supporting each other, and that's what relationships are about." She looks over at Tally. "I'm sorry another Terror player is helping you move in."

"It's okay. Anyone who knows hockey knows my last name anyway. It isn't like I'll be able to keep it a secret." Tally hugs Rix.

We all pile on.

Dallas appears in the doorway, followed by Flip.

"Uh, everything okay?" Dallas's forearms and biceps pop under the strain of the box he's carrying.

"Everything's fine. Just girl bonding," I assure him as I shamelessly eye-fuck him. I've learned recently that he and the guys often work out in the gym at his building. Occasionally, I'll poke my head in to say hi so I can get an eyeful of his sweaty hotness. Then I wait in his penthouse until he's done and jump him the second he's out of the shower.

He winks. "I'm all yours later tonight."

"You're always all mine," I retort.

"Wow, that's some heat coming off you two. Do you need a couple minutes alone?" Dred asks.

"He'll be fine for a few hours," I say.

"But will you?" Dallas kisses my cheek and sets the box on the floor. With eight of us crammed in here, there's almost nowhere to turn that doesn't involve bumping into someone.

"Aw, man, this reminds me of my freshman year." Flip sets his boxes on top of Dallas's and flops down on the bare mattress. "University was good times." His smile falls a little, and he points at Tally. "But you should definitely not do any of the things I did."

She rolls her eyes. "University is all about experiences, and I plan to have a lot of them."

"I'm with Flip that you shouldn't do any of the things he did in university. Yes to new experiences, but no to bad choices you'll potentially regret," Rix says.

Tally narrows her eyes. "Everyone raise their hands if they *didn't* go to a keg party during their university days, drink too much, vomit, and wake up with a horrible hangover."

None of us raises our hand. "Okay. Point made," I note. "But Flip isn't referring to the keg parties as much as he's referring to everything else."

"I'm going to grab some more boxes." Flip hops to his feet and heads for the door. I swear the back of his neck is red, like this whole conversation embarrasses him. I don't know how talking about his past makes him feel, but having his reputation for sexual exploits can't be easy.

"You Badass Babes can start unpacking. Flip and I will manage the rest of the boxes," Dallas says.

"Tristan and Nate are on the way over to help," Rix tells him.

Essie pulls out lip gloss and reapplies it.

"Cool. We'll be done in no time." Dallas kisses me on the cheek and follows Flip out of the room.

Rix pokes her head out the door before she turns back to us. "Was Flip blushing? I swear he was blushing."

"I thought the same thing!" I reply.

"Interesting," Dred muses.

"Why is that interesting?" Tally asks.

"Because Flip isn't known for feeling any kind of guilt or embarrassment over his past actions," Dred explains.

"I wonder what it was about that specific conversation that made him feel some kind of way." Rix surveys the room. "Where do you want to start?"

"My bedding is in that box over there, and that one has my

fall clothes, like sweaters and hoodies and stuff. We could start with those?"

We help Tally set up her room, make her bed, hang her posters, and get most of her clothes put away. Dallas and Flip bring up the last of the boxes, which contain Tally's books, and Tristan and Nate show up with pizza and cake.

Nate hangs back, looking a little unsure of himself. Tristan stands on the threshold of the room, eyes bouncing around as he nods his approval. "Nice work. Two thumbs-up, and I approve of your band posters. So does the rest of Canada."

"My dad loves The Hip." She makes the sign of the cross. "Rest in peace, Gord."

We all do the same. The Tragically Hip are a beloved Canadian band that lost their lead singer to cancer. I went to one of their last concerts during my university days.

"We have food and a cake," Tristan announces, like we can't see or smell it.

"We can eat in the dining room! Let me show you!"

We follow Tally down the hall to the common area she'll share with her roommates. A small dining table with six plastic chairs takes up one corner. There are also two love seats and two chairs that don't look particularly comfortable.

"Are you the first one to move in?" Tristan sets the pizza and paper plates on the table.

"One of the other girls was here earlier, but I think the rest of my roommates are coming this afternoon. Two of them are from Sudbury, and another one is from Ottawa, so it's a drive," Tally explains.

We gather around the table, and Tally hands out plates.

"Are you excited to meet everyone? The first week is the best," Dallas says. "Nonstop fun."

"And then classes happen," Flip says.

"And practices," Tristan adds.

"And studying," Nate mutters.

"I'm a little nervous but also trying to take it all in." Tally takes a bite of her pizza.

"You're going to have the best time," I assure her.

Tristan gives Rix a hug from behind and kisses her shoulder. She turns her head and kisses the edge of his jaw. He visibly relaxes with the affection. I don't know the full extent of his damage, but I can empathize. His mom left when he was nearly a teenager and Nate was even younger. That would leave scars.

I can't imagine what they've been through, as sometimes I struggle myself, and I have a wonderful family. Two parents who adore me, two brothers who always have my back, and some days I still question why I ended up being adopted. I was three months old when I was handed over to child services and placed with my moms only days later. Was I too much for some people even as an infant? Was I the consolation prize for my moms who wanted a third child but couldn't conceive on their own again? With that, my mind is a swirling mess of insecurity.

Dallas's eyes move over my face as he hands me a plate with pizza. "You okay?"

"Yeah." I smile up at him. "Thank you for wanting me."

"Every day. Wills, you're perfect." He drops his voice to a whisper. "And the other night, when you let me—"

I press my finger to his lips. "Stop now or I'll never let you do it again."

Dallas clamps his mouth shut and looks around, like he's suddenly remembered we aren't alone.

While we eat pizza, Tally and Rix talk about classes. Essie sits next to Rix and I'm not sure if I imagine it or not, but I swear she and Nate keep stealing glances at each other. Tristan sits on the other side of Rix with his arm slung over the back of her chair.

The cake is from Just Desserts and reads *Congratulations, Tally!* It's cherry chip, which is her favorite.

Two more students arrive, with parents in tow. One boy-man wears a Terror hat. Their smiles turn to shock when they realize there are hockey players sitting in their living room.

"Is this real or am I tripping balls?" The Terror hat wearer rubs his eyes.

A round of introductions follows, and I can practically feel Tally's anxiety. She's already the most popular girl in her residence, and not because she's nice, or fun, or sweet. My heart breaks for her a little—especially when Flip starts in on a dad-style inquisition. Tristan and Dallas have to step in and redirect the conversation.

We wrap it up quickly and promise to message her later, leaving her to settle in.

"I'm glad I'll be on campus this year so we can keep an eye on her," Rix says on our way out. "I think this transition will be an eye-opener."

"I can't believe Vander Zee let her live with guys. And one guy is on the freaking hockey team." Flip looks tempted to call her dad and confirm.

"She knows better than to date hockey players, or to hook up with her roommates," Dred says with a roll of her eyes.

"Just because she knows better doesn't mean she won't make bad choices," he gripes.

Hammer looks at him. "She's been insulated by the team her entire life. She needs the chance to spread her wings."

Flip does not look convinced.

Dallas and I drop off Flip and Dred on the way home, and because Dallas has no chill, and my hormones are always raging when he's around, I end up back at his place, underneath him. Tonight, I take the reins, but instead of climbing on top and riding him like a joystick, I pull him on top of me and revel in the feel of being surrounded, of the way his eyes never leave my face as he moves inside me, pushing me to the edge of bliss. Or how he laces our hands together and brings my ring to his lips— the ring I haven't taken off since that night. He whispers dirty words and sweet praise, and when he tells me he loves me, I let his words sink into my heart.

I want to say them back, because the warmth in my chest is

familiar. But I'm terrified to let it take root and become real. What if I fall for him and he walks away? My thoughts run to the darkest place, the one where I'm just a game to him. That once he has me completely, he'll be over it—and me.

My adoptive family are the only people who haven't bailed on me. Sure I have the BBB, but what if that changed? Dallas loves me now, but at some point, when all the sexy chemicals fade, when the fantasy has thoroughly morphed into reality, all the things he finds endearing could shift. What if he gets tired of how I'm all-in with work? That's how I operate. I pour all my energy into my commitments. I could lose myself to work instead of life. He'll walk eventually if I do that to him. And how could I blame him? So I keep those three words to myself. These are my most vulnerable fears. My soft underbelly.

We're snuggled on the couch, basking in the afterglow of amazing sex when my phone buzzes on the coffee table.

Dallas's arms tighten around me. "You should ignore that."

"It might be the girls." I tap the back of his hand, knowing full well it isn't.

He reluctantly releases me, and I grab my device, opening the email and scanning the contents. "Shit. No. What the hell?"

"What's going on?"

"Flip's endorsement campaign with Milk has been pulled. He's been doing so good." I stand and scan the rest of the email, trying to figure out what happened. I pull up Flip's contact and call him right away.

"I just got the email," he says through the speakerphone. "There were a few students in the elevator on the way up this afternoon, and they wanted pictures. That's normal. I didn't think anything of it, but one of them had coolers. I'm used to being in places where that kind of thing is controlled, Hemi. I've been off the radar for months, and now I look like the worst kind of douchebag."

"Did they post the pictures?"

"Yeah, and I'm tagged. I'm pretty sure they're underage, too."

"Are you at home now?"

"Yeah."

"I'm coming over so we can figure this out."

"Are you sure? I know it's late."

"I'm sure. We can make a game plan for tomorrow. I'll be there in a bit."

I end the call, already walking to the door.

Dallas's brow furrows. "Do you really need to deal with this right now? It's going on ten thirty, and you've been running all day."

"It's my job to figure out how to fix this. This isn't just a Flip issue. It's now a team issue."

"I know, but you need to rest." He follows me to the door. "What can you do about it now? All the offices are closed. People aren't answering their emails at this moment."

"I won't sleep tonight with this hanging over my head. And neither will Flip." I kiss him on the cheek. "I'll see you tomorrow."

"Please text when you get to Flip's so I know you made it safely. You've got this." He pulls me in for a tight hug and kisses me one last time before he lets me go.

As I walk out the door, I worry once again that I'm right. I'm powerless against my nature, and if I give in to the feelings that want to settle in my heart, it'll end up broken all over again.

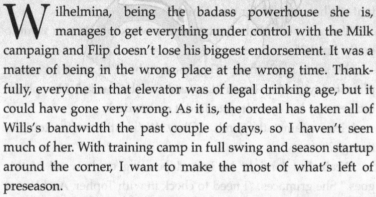

CHAPTER 36

Wilhelmina, being the badass powerhouse she is, manages to get everything under control with the Milk campaign and Flip doesn't lose his biggest endorsement. It was a matter of being in the wrong place at the wrong time. Thankfully, everyone in that elevator was of legal drinking age, but it could have gone very wrong. As it is, the ordeal has taken all of Wills's bandwidth the past couple of days, so I haven't seen much of her. With training camp in full swing and season startup around the corner, I want to make the most of what's left of preseason.

The team has just finished morning skate, and I have a two-hour break before we hit the gym for our workout. If the timing is right, I can get a little one on one with Wills and take her out for lunch. I peek my head into her office and take a moment to appreciate the fact that this woman is my girlfriend. Like most days, her hair hangs in loose waves over her shoulders. She's dressed in a bright blue blouse and black dress pants. She looks beautiful, and like the woman of my damn dreams.

I knock on the door, and she glances up from her computer, lifting a finger in my direction before she continues typing.

"I can come back later."

"Just a minute. I'm almost done."

She's in business mode, and I've interrupted her. But this feels a lot like how she responded *before* she stopped hating me and started letting me love her. *But she's not in love with you.* That niggling voice in the back of my head has gotten louder lately. Every time I say those three little words to her, and she doesn't say them back, it feels like a barb working its way under my skin. I question whether she'll ever feel that way. I want forever with her. I want this engagement to be as real for her as it is for me. But every time she puts off another discussion with her moms, or tells the Badass Babe Brigade that there's no rush to plan, it feels like reopening a wound that hasn't healed.

She finally stops typing and looks up, her expression expectant. "What can I do for you, Dallas?"

"I've got a couple hours before my workout. Do you want to go for lunch?"

Her smile is pinched. "That's sweet, but I've got a lot on my plate today, and a lunch date isn't in the cards." Her phone buzzes, and her eyes drop to find it on her desk.

I lean against the jamb. "Okay. We're still on for tonight, though?"

"Yeah. But I might be late, depending on how all of this goes." She grimaces. "I need to check in with Topher. And I need the scheduling conflicts with ice time to stop being a thing," she grumbles as she pushes her chair back. "I can walk you out."

"Is everything okay?"

"Let's hope so."

She meets me at the door, and we head down the hall, but she stops outside the staff break room to adjust her shoe.

"I wouldn't date a player, but you can't be mad at the paycheck," one woman says.

"She's set for life, isn't she?" adds a man I recognize from accounting.

"I don't get it. She's so high octane."

"Topher can't stand her," the guy says. "She's kind of a bitch, just like he says."

"Maybe he's known about this longer than we have. You know it had to be going on for a while," a third voice says.

"You think she took the job so she could get close to him?" the guy from accounting wonders aloud.

I take a step toward the room, but Wilhelmina's fingers lap my wrist, and she shakes her head. She tugs me down the hall, not sparing the group a glance, but her jaw tics and her posture is stiff.

She stares straight ahead as we wait for the elevator to arrive. It's empty when we enter.

I wait until the doors close. Keeping my cool is a challenge, but I don't want her on the receiving end of my anger. "How often does that shit happen?"

"Enough that I'm used to it. Before I was dating you, it wasn't quite as bad. But I'm still me."

"What does that mean?"

"I don't mince words, and I make things happen. Not everyone likes my style." She inspects her nails. "I'm head of PR, and I'm dating you, the team golden boy. People have a lot to say about it."

"They're shit-talking you behind your back." I can't believe she puts up with this garbage.

"It's nothing new, Dallas. It happened all the time in high school. I would love to be the office favorite, but then things wouldn't get done. It's obnoxious, but *Bitches get shit done* is true for a reason. And now we're a thing. Everything they're saying is exactly what I would think too if it was one of them and not me. Ugly or not." She shrugs. "It's why Hammer and I had more than one conversation about the logistics of her working for the team when her dad is a player and she's with Hollis." She taps the ring on her finger. "This is what I signed on for when I said yes to being your fiancée."

"But it's all bullshit." What I've done to her is hitting me in a whole new way. She saved my career and put her own in jeopardy. No one should ever treat her this way. And I don't like it one bit. Especially since the engagement part isn't something she wants the way I do.

She sighs. "What can I do about it, Dallas? Tell them they're wrong? They won't believe me. Why should they?"

I cross my arms. "But it's not true."

"Neither was the gossip about why you told everyone not to ask me to prom, but people still believed it. I believed it. You were and still are the popular hockey player, and I was and still am me. Too intense. Too bossy. Unlikable."

"You're powerful and exquisite." I remember what everyone said in school, but they were wrong. They just wanted to project their own shit onto her, tear her down to make themselves feel important. Wills has always been the most competent person in the room, but she wasn't unaffected by the petty things people said like she pretended to be.

"I don't have the softest touch, which sometimes doesn't go over well," she continues. "I'm better at it now than I was growing up." She pats my chest as the elevator doors open. "It is what it is, Dallas. Just let it go."

We step out of the elevator, and Wilhelmina says hi to a couple of women. They're polite, but their demeanor changes when they see me. Their smiles widen, and they stop to ask if I'm excited for the coming season. They're proving her exact point.

"I'll see you later." Hemi waves and heads down the hall without a backwards glance.

What we heard in the break room sits with me for the rest of the day. How often does that happen? How frequently is Wills the focus of water cooler chats? I did this to her. *Again.* I made her life difficult because I did what I always do—act without thinking through the consequences.

I'm distracted all through the workout with the guys, and I'm not surprised when Ash asks me if everything is okay once we're on the way home.

"I overheard a bunch of people shit-talking Wills in the office today."

He arches a brow. "Did you say anything?"

I shake my head. "I wanted to, but she was with me, and she shut me down before I could."

He nods. "Was she upset?"

"She brushed it off, but she's not immune." I tap my thigh. "This is my fault, Ash. I made it like this for her. Pulling the shit I did with one drunken mistake—I turned her work environment into the thing she never wanted it to be."

He glances over at me. "What are you really upset about? That people are saying nasty things about the woman you love, or that you can't protect her from it?"

"Both? It just makes me think of how she was treated growing up. I guess this explains why she wasn't super thrilled when I stopped by her office." I don't like the tightness in my chest. How can I make it worth her while to put up with that kind of office gossip?

"How so? What happened?"

"She just…didn't seem all that happy to see me." She seemed bothered by the distraction more than anything.

"It's a busy time of year in the front office. I usually message Shilps first, so she has a heads-up," he offers.

"Okay. Yeah. That makes sense. I probably wouldn't love it if I was focused on game tape and she tried to get me to take a break."

He inclines his head as he pulls up to my building. "You want me to come up for a bit?"

"Nah. It's cool. Thanks for the chat."

I get out of the car and head up to my penthouse. I should do something nice for Wilhelmina. Something to show her I appreciate her, and that I'm sorry for all the stress that comes with being in a relationship with me.

I pull my phone out of my pocket and find a new message from her.

WILLS

> Thank you for stopping by my office earlier. I'm sorry I couldn't make lunch work, but your smile was the highlight of my morning. We can compare schedules tonight and see if something would work later this week. I'm picking up supplies so we can make pizza for dinner. Xo

The weight in my chest lifts a little. I need to remember that work Wills isn't the same as the one I get to see when it's just the two of us.

When six o'clock rolls around, she appears on time, and we make dinner together. But when I try to bring up what happened in the office, she distracts me with her mouth. We end up having sex on the couch, and then again in bed. She stays the night when I ask her to, and I wrap myself around her, wanting this to be how every night ends.

I wake alone, which isn't a surprise. She tends to go in early to tackle emails before morning meetings. I shake off the vestiges of my dream. In it, Wilhelmina was pregnant, with a rounded belly and soft smile. She radiated total contentment. I want that with her. I want to love her, take care of her, spoil her, tell her every day how fantastic she is, watch her become a badass mother, teach her it's safe to show her softer side. I know it's there. When she's with her girlfriends and every time she's come to a church fundraiser or the retirement village, I see that softness. I want a family with her. Four kids and a house on the lake. And isn't it so fucking ironic that I can see this life unfolding with her, how amazing it could be if we can put the past behind us, but I'm the reason it sucked in the first place? I'm the reason for so much of the hurt, and I want to fix it, but I can't.

I've bound her to me with a promise of forever in the form of an engagement ring. But what if she can't ever love me the way I love her? What if the walls she built around her heart never come down? High school might be in the past, but it doesn't mean she's not still guarded. And how can she move forward when shitty office gossip has replaced all the crap she's tried to leave behind? Am I signing her on for a lifetime of people misjudging her? What if where we are right now is as close as she ever gets?

CHAPTER 37

HEMI

"Where is it?" I prop my fists on my hips and survey my bedroom. Now that I'm looking for the purse, I can't rest until I find it. It doesn't matter that I have a million other purses. Or that there are three perfectly acceptable options on my bed. I need this specific one. It matches my outfit precisely. And I picked that out for maximum Dallas enjoyment, so I don't want to change. I know he'll be extra touchy and desperate to get me back home and out of it later.

A spike of anxiety rushes through me. That's been happening a lot more lately, these little fears prickling like barbs under my skin. I realized after the fact that I probably came off as short and cold last week when Dallas stopped by my office unannounced. But I'd just dealt with another shitty email from Topher regarding double-booking one of the rinks. Couple that with all the preseason stuff on my plate and Dallas overhearing the office water cooler gossip, and I couldn't appreciate his effort until after he'd left.

I wonder, often, if one day his rose-colored glasses will break —the pedestal he's put me on will topple, and he'll see me the way other people do. Irritating. Overbearing. A lot.

But worrying about that won't do me any good. I refocus on

finding the stupid purse, though I know it's ridiculous. I can't let it go.

There's one more place it might be. I open my closet door and flick on the light. Swallowing past the lump in my throat, I strain to shift the box on the top shelf out of the way. The lid pops off, and the box tips when I push it aside. I catch it before the mountain of paperwork inside rains down on me, but anxiety makes my throat tight as I set it on the floor at my feet. It's been years since I've looked at that stuff.

In my first year of university, I dated a guy studying molecular genetics. He knew I was adopted and asked if I'd ever sought out my birth family—not because I wanted to connect with them, but so I could understand my genetic history. He made a good point, one that stuck with me. I had no idea what kind of genetic roulette I was playing. Shouldn't I know if I had some latent, recessive gene that could cause serious health issues down the line?

I did the search, but in the process, I realized that more than genetic details, I wanted to know why I'd been given up. There could be tons of reasons. Maybe I was loved. Maybe I wasn't. I loved my moms and brothers, but that question was a weight I couldn't shake.

I told my moms about it, and they supported me. But nothing really came from any of my searching since my adoption was closed. I did some genetic testing to better understand my potential health risks, but the unanswered questions sat heavier. What had led my biological mom to give me up and never want to find me again? Why didn't she want to know me?

Most of the time I can compartmentalize all those insecurities, but the past few months have made old wounds I thought had healed fresh again. All my hard edges are armor meant to protect me from more hurt. But in guarding my heart I'm also making it impossible to open up to Dallas the way I know he wishes I would.

"Get a grip, Hemi. Today is not the day to go down that

rabbit hole." My gaze snags on the purse sitting on the top shelf. I grab it, shove the box into the back of my closet, turn off the light, and shut the door. But the wound is already bleeding again, even with the box out of sight.

I press reset on my feelings and head to the Watering Hole to meet the girls. I need some Badass Babe Brigade time. They're my team. My soft landing and my safe place. Rix and Tally start classes next week, and preseason exhibition games follow soon after, so this night out feels necessary.

I meet Shilpa in the front lobby of my building, and we step out into the summer evening. It's the last weekend of August, and while the nights are steadily growing cooler, it's still T-shirt weather. Shilpa eyes me from the side as we walk the few short blocks to the bar.

"Are you okay?" she asks.

"Yeah. Fine. Why?"

"You seem stressed."

She's my best friend. If there's anyone I can talk to about this, it's her. "I'm just afraid that one day I won't live up to the hype in Dallas's head, and then he'll break my heart, *and* I'll be the butt of more gossip."

"That's fair, but it also discounts how special you are. Also, who's talking shit?"

"The usual suspects," I mutter.

"It's easy for people to sit on their thrones and judge, but they don't know you, and frankly, they don't deserve to. If you'd like to file a grievance, I'm here to help."

"That would make things infinitely worse."

"Don't rule it out as an option if things escalate. You shouldn't be dealing with this, no matter who you're dating."

I nod as we reach the Watering Hole. Tally and Hammer are already seated at our preferred booth. Dred walks in with Essie, a minute later. Rix messages that she'll be here in a couple of minutes. We've just ordered drinks when she bursts through the door. She glances over her shoulder as Tristan saunters past the front window, hands tucked into his pockets, looking exceptionally smug. She motions for him to hurry up and beelines it for our table. Her eyes are wide, her smile manic, and she looks like she might be on the verge of tears. The door tinkles as Tristan enters the restaurant.

"Are you okay?" I ask.

Essie's eyes are lit up with expectation, which makes me wonder what's going on.

"Yes. No. Yes." She looks over her shoulder at Tristan. "Can you hurry up, please? I'm bursting here."

"I pulled a hammy. I can't walk as fast as you. Plus, Nate is on his way in still."

"How'd you pull a hamstring?" Essie asks with a smirk as she fishes her lip gloss out of her purse.

"You don't want to know." Tristan rubs his bottom lip. He waves his brother over. "Come on, man."

"I'm coming." Nate shoves his hands is his pockets and stands next to Tristan as we all wait in anticipation.

Rix laces their hands together and thrusts her left one into the center of the table. "We're engaged!"

"Holy crap!" A chorus of feminine shrieks follows.

"Tristan just asked. Actually, he asked a few hours ago, but well—" She waves the comment away. "—and obviously I said yes, and look at how pretty my ring is, and oh my God, we're *engaged!*"

We slide out of the booth as happy tears stream down her face and offer hugs and congratulations to her and Tristan. He's beaming. Literally fucking beaming, like he just won the Cup. In all honesty, that's probably on par with how he feels right now.

"I'm so proud of you," I tell him. "You've come a long way in the past year."

"I just want to deserve the love she gives me, you know? She's my world." He's so earnest, looking at her with obvious adoration.

"I know." I squeeze his arm. "And so does she."

The guys show up, and suddenly it's a full-on party. Hugs and congratulations flow, and Flip orders a round of drinks, then hands over his credit card and orders food and prosecco since they don't have champagne.

"Tell us how he proposed!" Hammer says to Rix as the guys make Tristan do shots.

She slides into the booth beside Essie and begins with a little squeal. "It was so freaking romantic. He took me out for this beautiful picnic lunch on Toronto Island. He brought all my favorite foods, and it was just so perfect. Then he got down on one knee and asked me to marry him, and I said yes, and we went back to the penthouse. There were rose petals all over the bed and champagne, and you can all guess what happened next, and now I'm here." Her hands flutter in the air. "I'm just so excited." She turns her wide, elated grin on me. "This must have been how you felt when Dallas proposed to you!"

I fight to keep the smile from sliding off my face. Because it's not at all how I felt when Dallas proposed. I was shocked and angry. There hadn't been any room for joy. "Yeah. Exactly. You must be so thrilled. It's the beginning of your forever."

Rix grabs my arm. "We can go dress shopping together!"

"We absolutely can," I agree, even as my stomach flips.

"You're all going to be in my wedding party. We can do all the shopping and planning." Her smile is wide. "I'm so excited that we get to do this together!"

"It'll be so fun." And it should be. I should be ecstatic, and I am for Rix, but I'm missing that feeling for myself. Not because I don't genuinely care about Dallas. I do. But I didn't even like him when he asked me to marry him.

I glance across the room, feeling Dallas's eyes on me. He smiles, but I see the tension in his shoulders, and I worry it matches mine. He probably felt the same way Rix and Tristan do when he asked me to marry him. And it hurts my heart to know I didn't share that excitement with him. He was elated, and I was angry. How does that memory sit with him? Because right now, it makes my heart break.

Everything about us is backwards. Our engagement is a lie we've twisted into the truth.

Tristan raises a pint glass and shouts, "I have something I want to say!"

Everyone quiets.

He turns to Rix, his love written on his face. "Bea, you are the most incredible woman. I adore everything about you. I know I'm not easy, and I'm forever a work in progress, but I promise I'll work my ass off to keep deserving you for the rest of my life. I want to give you the world. I want to be the person who makes you smile, and laugh, and who gets the honor of loving you more than anyone else. Even though it was a shitty situation that brought you into my world and my apartment, I'm so grateful that you rage-quit your job. I love you more every single day, and I can't wait to make you my wife, so I can be at your side forever."

Rix launches herself into his arms, and everyone cheers and claps for them. Hollis gives Hammer a look that tells me she's next.

My heart aches with the knowledge that from the very beginning, all the bullshit I thought Dallas was spewing was the truth. He was honest the entire time. About everything. And I was just determined to hate him for what he'd allowed me to believe he'd done all those years ago. What a mess.

We should have had an engagement party like this, one where we were both genuinely happy about the possibility of forever. But I can't even bring myself to tell him how I feel about him.

Flip taps his pint glass with a spoon, and the chatter stops. "I'm so damn happy for you." He clears his throat and looks to the ceiling as he takes a deep breath. "You are two of my favorite people in the entire world." He coughs into his arm, like he's composing himself. "Love can be such a messy thing, but I see the way you love each other, the way you always stand up for and to each other. The way you have each other's backs. I know it's not easy. I know we had a hard beginning, Rix, and that you made a lot of sacrifices, but this guy..." He points at Tristan. "He'll love you until the world ends. You deserve the best of everything, and I know he will cherish you. And Tristan, man, you know." He taps his heart with his fist. "I support you. Both of you. It's an honor to celebrate you." He holds his glass up. "To love, and to my sister and my best friend finding it in each other."

We all toast and dab our eyes.

Essie stands next looking at her bestie. "Rix, I am so happy for you. I love that you found a partner who will go grocery shopping with you."

Rix laughs and says, "But no one will ever replace you as my price matching partner."

"Forever and always," Essie agrees. "Tristan, thank you for loving and supporting her. You've shown me that love is real. People can change. And if you hurt her, I will do unspeakable things to you with the help of Hemi's older brother."

Tristan laughs and wraps his arms around Rix. "Honestly, I expect nothing less. Samir is a scary motherfucker. I'm glad my girl has someone like you in her corner, Essie."

"Here, here!" Roman raises his glass. "To love!"

We all cheers again.

It's an amazing celebration. But it's a reminder of how different it is with me and Dallas. I know how he feels about me, what he wants, but I'm struggling to get where he is, and the engagement ring I'm wearing is a reminder of how it all started —with a lie we keep telling our friends.

So when he asks me if I'm coming back to his place, I tell him I can't.

It's not a lie.

I'm too raw. Too afraid of my own feelings.

And even more afraid of his.

A few days after Rix and Tristan's engagement, we plan a girls' afternoon. Rix is super excited about planning her wedding, and I wish I was in the same place emotionally. It sucks that she's so over the moon and I'm still over here, wishing it didn't feel like an anvil swinging.

"Where are we going?" I ask as I climb into the back of Rix's Mercedes SUV. Tristan bought it for her birthday like the giant, sappy, lovesick fool he is.

"It's a surprise!" Rix is practically bouncing in her seat.

Essie is in the front seat, and Tally, Shilpa, and I are tucked in the back. Dred is meeting us wherever we're going with Hammer, which is good because I don't think we could cram two more bodies back here unless they wanted to ride in the trunk.

"Any hints?"

"Nope, you'll see when we get there," Shilpa replies.

Half an hour and some harrowing Toronto traffic later, we're standing outside Just Desserts. "We're cake testing!" Rix announces.

"And then looking at bridesmaids' dresses," Tally adds. Her eyes go wide. "For Rix, since we're all in her wedding party."

"You'll all be in my wedding party, too." If I ever get married. I turn to Shilpa. "And you'll be my matron of honor."

She smiles and squeezes my arm.

Dred and Hammer meet us on the sidewalk. Hammer had a meeting off-site, and Dred is using her lunch break to join us.

We follow an excited Rix, Essie, Hammer, and Tally into the shop and spend the next half hour testing cakes. "I can't decide which one I love the most," Rix groans while rubbing her stomach.

"You don't have to pick just one. You'll have tiers, right? So each tier is a different flavor," Hammer says.

"That's expensive, though." Rix sinks her fork into her cake, despite already having said she's full.

Essie gives her an understanding smile. "You're marrying a professional hockey player who adores you. He'll want to order a ten-layer cake to make sure you get all your favorites."

"This is accurate," Shilpa says.

"I seriously love the way he loves you," Dred says with a smile.

"This," I agree.

"My top three are the banana cream, double chocolate fudge, and the lemon curd. How about you, Hemi?" Hammer asks.

"Probably the double vanilla, the German chocolate, and the peach custard. But I think Dallas would go for the carrot cake."

"Have you talked about dates yet? I think we're looking at early June next year, but I want to make sure we don't conflict with yours," Rix says.

"Oh, you don't have to worry about that. We'll probably wait until the summer after." I hate how easy the lies come these days. I want to love this the way she does. I want to share her excitement. But the fear that I'll never catch up to Dallas sits heavy on my shoulders, and so does the worry that one day, he'll change his mind. And then where will we be?

CHAPTER 38

DALLAS

W ills is tucked into my side, legs crossed, with her foot hooked behind my calf. My arm is slung over her shoulder, and I rub my thumb back and forth along the exposed skin of her arm. Her hand rests on my thigh, and every so often she digs her nails into my skin through my pants. Because she knows I love it. I press a kiss to her temple, and she smiles, side-eyeing me. Next week training camp starts, and our schedules are about to get busy as hell.

We both have a soft spot for The Hip. I have several playlists with their music, so she bought us tickets when they announced a date at an intimate outdoor venue and invited Ash and Shilpa to join us. I'm a huge fan of double dates with our best friends. The Practically Hip, a Tragically Hip cover band, finishes their first set, and we clap and cheer.

"Why don't we grab another round before they start the second set?" I say to Ash. "You want the same thing, Wills?" I tap her empty glass.

She tips her head up. "Please."

Her lips are too tempting to resist, so I bend to kiss her before Ash and I head to the bar.

"You and Hemi seem good," Ash says.

"Yeah." On the surface, everything seems perfect. Last week, she was a little off after Rix and Tristan announced their engagement. We both were. It was hard to see them so over the moon with real happiness. I want us to match. But we don't. And it hurts more than I'd like. I want it to get easier, for her to feel about me the way I feel about her. She's not there yet though, and it's a raw wound. I keep telling myself she just needs time.

She's stayed at my place the last few nights, and things have been explosive in the bedroom, so I'm taking that as a good sign.

We reach the bar and order drinks.

"You ready for the start of the season?" he asks.

"It's bittersweet with this being Roman's last one and Hollis's final contract year, you know?"

Ash nods. "Yeah. But they're in a good place about it. And it's great that they get to finish out their careers with Hammer working in-house."

"I hope Wills and Hammer travel with the team some this season." The idea of being away from her for longer stretches isn't appealing. I'd ask her to move in with me now if I thought she was ready.

Ash snorts. "You're such a goner for that woman."

"Yeah. I know."

He claps me on the shoulder. "I need to hit the bathroom."

I nod as the bartender sets our drinks in front of us, and I hand over my card. "I'll take these to the girls."

"You want to wait and I'll give you a hand?"

"Nah, I got it."

Ash heads for the bathroom, and I carry the drinks to our table. Shilpa and Wills's backs are to me, so they don't see me coming.

"Are you in love with him?" Shilpa asks.

"I don't know. Maybe?" She sighs and rubs her fingers over her lips. "I feel like I'm still trying to reconcile the past with the present. I know he's not that guy who laughed when my dress was covered in smoothie in grade nine. But this thing between us still doesn't feel completely real. His feelings for me are so certain, but for how long? It all feels a little lopsided."

"Does Dallas know you're struggling with this?"

She shakes her head and traces a heart carved into the top of the picnic table. "I don't want to upset him. So many things about being with Dallas are great. Truly. We have the most unreal chemistry, Shilps. The way we connect." She sighs and drops her head. "But then Tristan and Rix got engaged. I'm so happy for them, but their happiness... It shines a light on how excited I should be about my own engagement."

Her expression makes my chest feel like it's caving in.

"I didn't say yes because I was in love with him. I said it to protect the team and our careers. He did it to prevent me from being the laughingstock of our high school reunion. I never even thought I'd get married, let alone have everyone we know expecting me to plan a wedding. My moms have already created an inspo board. Dallas's mom has a literal binder filled with wedding things. All the reasons are wrong, and it just taints everything."

"Oh, Hemi, I'm so sorry. I wish it was different." Shilpa puts an arm around her shoulders and gives her a side hug.

"Me too. I don't know how to fix this. I'm not at a place where marriage is even a thought."

Ash startles me, and the girls turn around. I force a smile and take the seat next to Wills, but I'm a million miles away. Everything I've been afraid of is true. I'm in love with her, so ready to spend the rest of my life with her, and she doesn't know if she wants any part of forever with me.

"Is everything okay?" Wills asks as the band comes back on.

"Everything's great." I kiss her shoulder.

She gives me an uncertain look. "Are you sure?"

"Yeah, honey." The lie is covered by a guitar riff.

I don't hear the rest of the set. And I'm lost in my own head on the way home.

"We just passed your place." Wills thumbs over her shoulder.

I grip the steering wheel, my throat tight as I pull up to her building and put the car in park.

"Dallas? What's going on?" she asks, her voice unsteady.

"I overheard your conversation with Shilpa," I say.

"What conversation?"

"The one about not being excited to be engaged to me," I say to the windshield.

"Shit. Dallas—"

"I don't want to lock you into something you don't want," I say softly.

"It's not that I don't want to be with you—"

"We're not on the same page, Wills. We're not even reading from the same book." And there's a good chance we never will be.

"Can you look at me and say what you're going to say, please?" Her voice wavers.

I steel myself, aware that I'm hurting her in ways I never wanted to, not again. But I can't keep forcing her into a relationship she didn't ask for. "I love you so fucking much, Wilhelmina. With my whole goddamn heart. But I can't be engaged to you when I know you don't want to be engaged to me. It hurts too much."

"That's not—"

"Do you love me the way I love you? Like spend the rest of our lives together?" My question is quiet and without judgement.

Her silence drags between us in the car. "I just—"

I hate to argue with her, but I have to get this out. "I get it." I honestly do, especially with how ecstatic Rix and Tristan are. The person he loves returns that love. "I wish I could take so many things back. I shouldn't have proposed to you. It was reactive and shortsighted. I shouldn't have forced you into this with me. I should have owned what I'd done, regardless of what it did to my career. I got caught up in the same shit I did as a teenager, taking the easy way out, and I pulled you into it with me. And then I let you do what you always do and smooth my mistakes over. I won't do that to you anymore. It's unfair, and I've already hurt you enough."

"Dallas…" Her voice cracks.

I take in her sad, beautiful face, wishing I could be what she needs. "I want to be with someone who loves me the same way I love them. I've had all this time to be in love with you, Wills. All these years to want this with you. I can't force you to feel the same way about me." My eyes sting, and wetness tracks down my cheek. I scrub a hand over my face, swallow the pain, and push on. Because I need to do this. For her. For me. For the future I want but can't have. "This, the way *you* feel, it's my fault. I made it this way between us from the very beginning, starting when we were kids. I can't hold you hostage like this anymore, Wills, living a lie. I won't. I'm so thankful for the time we've had together, but I know I'm not what you want. You would never have chosen me. I pushed you into this, and I'm absolving you of it. And don't for a second think this is all about you, either. I'm protecting myself as much as I'm saving you from a lifetime of lying about who we are to each other." I fight not to look away, but God, it's torture watching her bottom lip tremble. "Loving you like this hurts, Wills. So fucking much. Knowing that I'm alone in the way I feel about you…" I shake my head. "I can't fall any harder than I have already. I'm not the right guy for you."

Her chin wobbles as tears track down her cheeks, and my heart cracks in two.

She nods as her eyes dart around, hands sliding up and down her thighs. Her voice is a broken whisper when she says, "Okay."

The silence in the car is deafening. The click of her seat belt sounds like a gunshot. She makes a soft, desperate sound as she opens the door and climbs out.

I don't try to stop her. Don't chase after her. Don't take back what I said, even though it hurts like hell to let her go.

She closes it and turns away, rushing up the steps to the front door, head bowed, hand at her mouth. She doesn't look back, but I catch her reflection in the mirrored glass door.

She looks just as devastated as me.

CHAPTER 39
HEMI

I can't even hold it together long enough to make it to my apartment. My shoulders shake as I stab the elevator button, willing it to be empty when it arrives. Thankfully, my plea is heard, and I step inside to press the button for my floor. As soon as the doors close, I break, tears streaming down my face, a horrifyingly loud sob bubbling up from my throat.

It feels like someone just ripped my heart out of my chest. I can't get the look on Dallas's face out of my head—how resigned he was.

If I'm so uncertain of my feelings for him, why does this hurt so much? Why does it feel like I'm dying? Like there's a gaping hole where my heart used to be? Like the best thing I ever had just slipped through my fingers?

It was too good to be true.

I'm grateful the hall is empty when I reach my floor. I'm crying so hard it's a struggle to find my fob again through blurred vision. I finally manage to get inside and almost knock my roommate over in my rush to get to my bedroom so I can break down in private.

She has rings around her eyes from wearing her virtual headset. She tips her head up—she's barely five feet, and I'm nearly five eleven. "Oh, hey. Oh wow, are you okay?"

"I'm okay, thanks." I disappear into my room and slap a hand over my mouth, but it doesn't muffle the anguished sob.

I grab a pillow to smother the sound. He just seemed so resolute, so certain that this was the right thing to do. Convinced there was no future for us. If I'd told him I was falling in love, would it have changed things? Would he have believed me?

Knowing him. Seeing Dallas as he is today and not a snapshot of a bad memory—he made me believe that maybe, just maybe, I could be loved forever. Worse, he made me believe it was safe to fall in love—to trust him with my scars and glass heart—that love wasn't fleeting, love was patient and gentle. Now I'm alone again, with different wounds under my ribs this time.

I sob myself to sleep and call in sick the next morning. I can't face the world, not like this. I'm a mess. And I can't stop crying. I woke up in the middle of the night having soaked my pillowcase.

I try to avoid a call with my moms this morning, but it's like they have a sixth sense for when I'm upset. After they've called three times in a row, I give up and answer.

"Is everything okay? I woke up this morning with a feeling," Mom says.

I immediately burst into tears.

"Hemi? Sweetie? What happened?" Mom asks.

"Deep breaths, baby girl. Whatever it is, it'll be okay," Ma says soothingly. "We're here to help however we can."

"I-I-I—" I gulp air. "Damn it!"

"It's okay," Ma murmurs. "Take your time. We're not going anywhere."

It takes another minute for me to get my tears under control. "Dallas broke up with me, and none of it was really real—not the dating, not the engagement, and I'm sorry I lied to you, and everything hurts." I'm sobbing all over again.

"We're calling you back on video," Mom says.

"I'm a wreck," I blubber.

"Sweetie, we're your moms; when you hurt, we hurt." She ends the call and a second later starts a video chat.

Seeing their faces through the small screen only makes things worse. I'm a real mess. But once I get things under control, I sob/word-vomit the entire story, starting with my braid being lopped off by Dallas's friend in grade three, my lost bike in middle school, to the prom fiasco, to the fake dating and the fake engagement, and finally to the real dating and the subsequent breakup.

"But you looked so happy together at the engagement party," Mom says softly.

"I was. We were. I mean, apart from the fact that the engagement wasn't actually a real engagement. The reunion was when things shifted. For me. He's had feelings for a long time."

"But you spent all that time together for the promo opportunities…" Ma seems to be just as confused as I am.

"Because he needed a babysitter." Or he acted like he did.

"And he knew you would always show up," Mom finishes.

"He's been in love with me all this time, and I don't match him yet. I thought I was falling for him. And now I never can. He said he can't keep doing this. That it hurts too much to love me the way he does and know I don't feel the same way."

"Oh," Ma says. "I see."

"Is that true? You don't love him?" Mom asks.

"I think I really actually do. I just couldn't own those feelings, and what if I do own those feelings and down the line he realizes I'm too much for him?" I'm spiraling, and I don't know how to stop. "Why would I let myself love him?"

"Oh my sweet, sweet Hemi. You've got that candy coating, but under that shell is a girl full of melty feelings." Her expression is soft and knowing. "I think you need to start looking at yourself through a different lens. We picked you because you were clearly a fighter. All of us picked you. Your moms, your brothers, the Terror, your Badass Babe Brigade, Dallas. We chose you, and we will always keep choosing you. The way things started with you and Dallas may not have been conventional, but he keeps picking you. If he's worthy of your heart, you can let yourself pick him, too."

"You make it sound so simple."

"Sometimes it is, sweetie. It's just our trauma that makes it complicated. If you love him, then love him."

"I love you both."

"We love you, too, Hemi. With all our hearts."

I spend the rest of the morning in bed crying. Shilpa messages at lunchtime, already aware of the breakup thanks to Ash. She was in meetings all morning, otherwise I know she would have been in touch earlier. She texts me twenty minutes later to tell me she and Hammer are standing outside my door with soup and won't leave until they see me. Dragging myself out of bed is an epic feat. Heartbreak isn't a good look for me.

Their eyes flare when I open the door to let them in.

"Oh God, you poor thing." Hammer sets the takeout bag down.

My nose is red, my eyes are puffy, I'm sure I'm blotchy, and I'm wearing the smiling peaches hoodie Dallas bought me, despite it being September and not quite cool enough for it.

She and Shilpa open their arms, and I fall into them as I burst into tears all over again.

They hold me and let me sob. I'm grateful my roommate is on day shifts this week so I can wallow in the living room.

Hammer and Shilpa lead me to the couch and sit next to me. "I don't understand why he broke up with you," Hammer says.

I wish her shock made me feel better, but it doesn't. It takes several minutes of sobbing and sucking in labored breaths before

I can get myself together enough to explain. By the time I'm done, the coffee table is covered in used tissues.

"But...he's obsessed with you. He's more obsessed with you than Tristan is with Rix, and that's saying something because that man is *obsessed*, all caps."

Shilpa smiles sadly and squeezes my hand.

"He said he wasn't the right guy for me." I hiccup.

"What in the actual fuck?" Hammer's brow furrows in confusion. "Why would he go to all this trouble to propose to you in an arena full of people and then tell you he's not right for you? Do you want me to set up a birthday party promo op for him? I can make him do balloon animals again. Or sign him up for some kind of sauerkraut festival detail. Or both."

I shake my head. "I don't want to do that to him." I've tortured him enough for several lifetimes. Making him miserable now will just make me feel worse. And these lies are too much to carry around. Hiding the truth from my friends has been a weight I can't bear anymore.

I look to Shilpa, who seems to read my thoughts. "Hammer is safe, and this is too much of a burden for you to carry around."

So I tell Hammer the entire ugly truth.

She exhales on a low whistle. "Dallas could have been traded for that."

"I know."

"Which is why you went along with it—at first, anyway," she muses.

I nod. "I'm sorry I couldn't say anything."

Her expression softens. "Don't be sorry. I hid what was going on with Hollis for months, and Rix was getting railed by Tristan for weeks before we knew. You were protecting the team, and Dallas, and yourself." She squeezes my hand. "I'm glad you at least had Shilpa and Ash to help you through this. And it won't go any further than this room."

"Thanks. I just don't want to make this worse than it already is," I admit.

"What can we do? How can we help?" Shilpa asks.

"I want this to stop hurting."

"Honestly, it must have been hard to wear his grandma's ring, and for him to see it on your finger, be so in love with you —and know he's alone in that feeling. Unrequited love hurts. It makes your heart feel like it's breaking a thousand times a day. Plus seeing Tristan and the way Rix loves him back, and being so happy about their engagement. I think it messed you both up." Hammer's voice is soft and gentle, even as each truthful word feels like a blow.

"Why did he let me see how good we could be and then take it all away?" My heart shatters, and all my deepest fears seep out. "Why doesn't anyone ever stay? Why am I always too much?"

They hug me from both sides. "Oh, Hemi, you're not too much. Other people's actions are usually about them, not us," Shilpa says.

Hammer squeezes me tightly, like she's trying to hold me together with love. "What if he just thinks he's not enough?"

I'm not surprised when the messages from my brothers start soon after Shilpa and Hammer leave. It seems that everyone I love is in tune with how big my feelings are today.

SAM

Moms told us you and the hockey player broke up. Are you okay?

The answer is no, I'm not remotely okay at all. But I will be less okay if my brothers take it upon themselves to come visit and bring all their high octane into my already overwhelmed world. They're dudes to the nth degree. They'll want to problem solve by filling my schedule with activities, and all I want to do right now is lie on the couch and cry. So I type out a lie.

> **HEMI**
>
> I'm fine. It just wasn't working out.

ISAAC

frowny face

SAM

That smells like a lie.

Do we need to fly in and take control of the situation?

I will go full Tonya Harding if I need to.

ISAAC

I second this.

> **HEMI**
>
> He's too important to the team.

SAM

There are lots of talented players out there. He's fully replaceable.

> **HEMI**
>
> I don't know if my friends will agree with that.

ISAAC

We'll source a replacement in case you change your mind.

Sam calls me five seconds later on video. I sigh, because not answering will just make things worse.

"What happened? What did he do?" he demands.

"I'm not as in love with him as he is with me." Sam can smell a lie a million miles away.

"So you ended things because he's too into you?" he asks.

"No, he ended things because he's too into me, and he doesn't think I'll ever be as into him."

Sam is silent for a moment before he admits, "I already siphoned the information out of Moms."

"Why am I not surprised?"

"They made a valiant effort to keep your secrets, but you know how good I am at getting the truth out of people. Plus, they're the worst liars. It's why we have a family no-lying rule. Which you broke and I'm disappointed about. I'll be honest, though, I'd already figured out most of it when we came down to visit after the surprise televised proposal."

"Why didn't you say anything?"

"Because you clearly had your reasons for doing it the way you did. This job means everything to you. You love this team, and I understand why. They love you right back. You are an integral part of what makes them work, and you're fiercely loyal and protective. You could have thrown Dallas under the bus, and maybe you should have, but you put the welfare of the team ahead of your own. Protecting other people shouldn't come at such a great cost to yourself."

Isaac pings repeatedly to be let in on the call. Sam pulls him in.

"What'd I miss?" He frowns as he takes in my face. "Shit. This is bad. You never cry."

"I don't normally get my heart broken."

"We should come down," Isaac declares.

I hold up a hand. "I love you, and I appreciate you, but I need some time to feel all the feelings. And apparently Sam knew all the things but sat on that knowledge until now." I rub my temples. "How come Moms didn't see this?" They were the ones I thought would see through this charade.

"Because every time Dallas came home to visit, he told everyone in town how incredible you are, and news travels in Huntsville, as you know. But then Brooklyn and Sean's engagement happened and tipped the scales," Sam says. "Though who knows how long those two will stay together."

"And Dallas—who, by the way, is a great guy with some

poor impulse control—saw an opportunity to protect you from the bullshit that would be the high school reunion. He's had a thing for you forever. It seemed like the win of all wins. Until he realized the engagement put unnecessary pressure on your relationship," Isaac adds.

"He said he's not the right guy for me." I fail to keep my voice from cracking at the end.

"Is he the wrong guy for you?" Sam asks.

"I don't know." But not being with him hurts more than I ever imagined it would.

"Don't you, though?" Isaac chimes in. They're the reason I was such a master debater. "He adores you. You adore him back. We all see it, Hemi. It might have started as a lie, but somewhere along the way it became the truth. Probably earlier than even you realize. Is it backwards? A little. But you've never looked as happy as you did at your engagement brunch."

"What if his feelings change? What if down the road he decides he wants someone more laidback like him?"

"He's loved you since you were kids. His feelings aren't going to disappear," Sam assures me.

"You are so loved, Hemi, by so many people." Isaac smiles softly. "We saw it at the party when all your friends showed up for you—not out of obligation, but out of love. Dallas doesn't want to be without you. Do you want to be without him?"

"No." I miss him so damn much. I love the way he always opens the door for me or brings me lunch. I love how kind he is to everyone he meets. I love that he would do anything to protect the people he cares about. But the three words *I love you* are terrifying.

"Have you told him that?" Sam asks.

"No."

Isaac jumps in. "Have you told him you love him?"

I sigh.

"So you're not being honest about your feelings. This all makes sense now." Sam nods knowingly to Isaac.

"Little sister, we love you to the moon and back," Isaac says.

"Truth," Sam agrees. "You were the best thing to happen to our family, Hemi. We still remember when Moms got the call about you. The second we met you, we all fell in love. I know our family isn't conventional, and that Isaac and I are a lot to deal with, but we needed you."

"You're going to make me cry again."

"We can handle it if you do," Sam assures me. "You are brilliant and beautiful and a badass, and you always have been. You're a fighter. But right now, you're letting fear win. Take the time you need to get your head where it needs to be, but tell Dallas how you feel. I guarantee it'll change everything for the better. And then you won't be sad, and Isaac and I won't have to hide a body."

I laugh. "I love you."

"We love you back, sis," Sam replies.

"Seriously, though, Sam and I have the perfect spot if we ever need it," Isaac adds.

"I know you do, and I adore you for it."

"We're here if you need us. For anything."

We end the call, and I sit there, holding my phone against my chest. They're right. I'm letting fear win.

CHAPTER 40
DALLAS

I can't deal with being in my penthouse. Everything reminds me of Wilhelmina, so I go home for the weekend. But before I do, I schedule my cleaner to come while I'm gone so when I return, I'm not slapped in the face by my failure.

Like an idiot, I leave on Friday afternoon, and the two-point-fiveish-hour drive takes four. My regrets are excessive by the time I arrive. Because now I have to explain why I'm here, looking wrecked.

"Where's Wilhelmina? When you said you were coming to visit, I thought you would bring her along." Mom frowns.

"We broke up." Saying it aloud feels like I'm being stabbed in the chest.

"What? Why? What happened?"

"I messed up," I admit. My eyes are hot, and my chest aches in a way I've never experienced before.

"Well, you can fix it, can't you?"

I shake my head. "I don't think so."

"Come on, sweetheart." She takes me by the elbow and leads me inside.

My younger sister, Paris, is already in the kitchen, helping

Mom with dinner. Her brow furrows when she sees me. "What happened?"

"Dallas and Wilhelmina broke up."

She drops the potato into the pot on the stove. "What did you do, Dallas?"

I flop into the chair and accept a glass of fresh-squeezed lemonade. I'd love a shot of vodka or seven to go with it, but I should probably be sober for this.

"Why do you assume it was me?"

"Well, was it?"

I word-vomit the whole horrible story, starting with all the things that happened when we were kids, down to every shitty little thing my friends did in high school, and all the ways I tried to make it better—like going to the custodial staff and secretly painting her locker when it was defaced after everyone else had gone home, or stopping one of the guys on the hockey team from ruining her student council president's speech, and ending with the breakup in my car and the shitty office gossip. Marrying someone who doesn't want to marry me was a future I didn't want.

Mom plants her hands on her hips. "Dallas Mattias Bright, what were you thinking?"

"About which part?"

"Any of it! All of it! That poor girl." She tosses her dish rag on the counter. "And to think, we just ambushed her! All of us showing up out of the blue, and she had to entertain us and *pretend* the engagement was real." She shakes her head. "I don't understand where your head was with any of this."

"In his ass," Paris mutters.

I glare. "You're not helping."

She gives me a look. "Well, you're sitting here, looking the part of the sad sack, so you're not doing much to help your case either."

I drop my head into my hands. "I'm such a screw-up."

Mom sighs. "You screwed up, but you're not a screw-up,

Dallas. Far from it. But the way you went about this whole thing didn't leave much room for it to go right. Why not be honest with her from the start? You could have taken her to prom and fixed it all years ago. Why wait all these years to tell her the truth? Why set it all up as *not* real when you want the opposite?"

"It just...spun out of control on me." I run my finger along the rim of the glass. "I thought I was protecting her after she protected me."

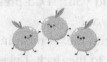

My mom and sister are more than happy to recount the horrible story to my dad and brothers when we all sit down to family dinner.

"It's pretty on brand for you," Manning says.

Ferris agrees. "I mean, you ratted out your friends and spent your own money on new student council posters but let her believe you were one of the ones who'd defaced them."

"I still don't get that," Manning muses.

"What right did I have to tell her? Because I let it happen in the first place. My friends were being dicks. She didn't deserve it. Like hey, listen I fixed this for you and stuff but also stole your bike once? She never owed me that opportunity. Just like she doesn't deserve the shit I've put her through these past months." That's ultimately why I ended things. She deserved better. That and being in love with someone who doesn't love me back hurts too fucking much.

"I think you need to give the seventeen-year-old version of you a break," Dad muses.

"The seventeen-year-old version of me knew better, though," I retort.

"Sure, but are you seventeen anymore? Have you allowed anyone to be mistreated since then?"

"No. Of course not."

"What if you tried to forgive yourself instead of beating your-self up about it? You've grown into a person to be proud of over the last ten years, son." Dad looks at me as though stating that should erase my shame. He taps the arm of his chair. "Did she want out of the relationship?"

"I want to be married to her," I tell them. "I wanted that ring on her finger. I want to spend the rest of my life loving her, but knowing she doesn't want the same...that's torture."

"Is that what she told you?" Dad presses. "That she's never interested in a life with you?"

"She's not in love with me." I push my chair away from the table. "I'm going down to the dock. I need a breather." I grab a bottle of scotch, a plastic glass, and the crochet bag from the living room and leave my family sitting at the dining room table. I need time to wallow.

Unrequited love is some shit. Why doesn't my family under-stand how hard it is to know my feelings aren't matched? I know I'm not entitled to her love. I'm not entitled to any part of her.

I'm good and drunk by the time my sister drops into the chair beside mine.

"What is that supposed to be?"

"A peach." It looks like a blob.

She picks up the bottle and gives it a shake. "Dude, you're a mess."

"I know." I just want to be sad and hate my life in peace.

"Was any of it real at all? Or were you so in love with the idea of having her that you forgot to consider the ramifications of what would happen when you made her yours?"

I blow out a breath. It's annoying that my sister can so succinctly lay it out for me in a few sentences.

"I'm not in love with the idea of her. I love *her*. Everything about her. She's everything. She goes after everything she wants and doesn't stop until it's hers. I don't care that she might not be for everyone. She's it for me." I take a deep breath. "Why am I such an idiot?"

"You're not an idiot. You're impulsive. You always have been. It works well on the ice, but it doesn't always translate in real-life situations. Like this one." She gives me an empathetic smile. "Impulsivity aside, you're a great guy. You're genuine and you do things not because it will look good, but because you actually care. Hemi obviously saw that, or she wouldn't have gone along with any of this nonsense."

"She didn't have much of a choice."

"Yes, she did. And she made it. She chose you, Dallas."

"She didn't want to ruin my career. She never wanted me."

"Did those words come out of her mouth?"

"No. But she doesn't date players. She dates smart, educated guys who don't do stupid shit, like propose in front of an entire arena."

"Your excuses are bullshit, big brother. The proposal could have backfired spectacularly."

"It did backfire!"

"So you say. But I'm pretty sure the reason she hasn't dated a hockey player before is because of the bureaucratic headaches and office politics. And smart isn't limited to people with PhDs, Dallas. She would not have agreed to be with you if she didn't find this package attractive on more than just a physical level." She motions to me. "She doesn't strike me as the shallow type."

"She's not."

"So let me ask you again, why are you sitting here, regretting your choices, when you should be figuring out a way to fix this?"

"What if there's nothing to fix? All she said when I broke it off was *okay*."

"Fucking hell, Dallas." She sighs and shakes her head. "Think about it from her perspective. For nearly a decade, she believed you sabotaged her life because you flexed your popularity. And when she joined the team you signed up for every promo known to man to spend time with her. But you never told her the truth. Instead, you pushed every last button she had, like you were back in high school all over again. Man. Child. Finally, you tell her you love her, and then you break up with her before she even has a chance to catch up, like it was all just another game to you."

"Fuck. It's not a game."

"You wanted her attention. And then when it got real, and hard, instead of saying, 'Hey, I messed this up. I want to be engaged to you, but now that we're in a real relationship, I realize maybe you would prefer that I propose when you're actually ready, whenever that is. So how do you want to move forward?', you just gave up on the love of your life. Like a saggy scrotum. You made the decision without consulting her, a-fuck-ing-gain."

"Why are you being so mean?"

"I'm not being mean; I'm being real. Don't be a baby. Hemi would have this exact conversation with you if she were in my position and not on the receiving end of this breakup. Your biggest flaw is that you don't think you're good enough, which is mind-blowing, considering how you don't have to be anyone other than yourself for people to want to be in your orbit. What if you are exactly the right person for Hemi? What if you're everything she actually she needed?"

"This pain is astounding."

"Welcome to falling in love and then fucking it up. It hurts. Love is the most powerful emotion. It makes us incredibly vulnerable, but when it works, when it's right and real, it's the most beautiful, wonderful thing." She sighs, and her expression turns sad. She's only twenty-three, and it makes me wonder what's happened to her heart while I've been off living my life. "You have the potential to be the best boyfriend, husband, dad, and friend Hemi could ever hope to have. But you didn't give her a chance. So this is where you are." She motions to the setting sun. "Now you have to decide if it's where you're going to stay."

I drive home the next morning after breakfast with the family. My place smells like lemon and cleaning supplies when I arrive, which is to be expected. I drop my bag in the laundry room and stop in my bedroom, frowning at the lack of nightshirt on Wills's side of the bed. I folded it and left it there out of habit.

My heart aches when I open the top drawer of my dresser, where Wills leaves her sleepwear, and find it empty. I move to the closet, already knowing what waits for me. But I'm unable to believe it unless I see it with my own eyes. Empty hangers greet me on the right side, where Wills's clothes used to be. The outfits I bought for her are all still there, though. Did she think I'd want her to give them back?

My bedroom is too depressing, so I move to the living room. The blanket she brought over for cuddle-on-the-couch nights is gone. She took everything that was hers.

The awful ache in my chest expands when I reach the kitchen. On the counter is an envelope, my apartment key, and her engagement ring. I pick it up by the band and curl my fist around it, the diamonds biting into my palm. I slide it onto my pinkie and pick up the envelope. My hands are unsteady as I break the seal. I don't know what I expect to find. A scathing letter? An admission that I was right all along, she would never love me the way I loved—*love*—her?

Instead, I find two tickets to a special event featuring my favorite comic book artist. They're VIP meet-and-greet tickets that sold out months ago. Wills went out of her way to get these for me, and still gave them to me, even though I broke up with her. She's such a rare, special person, and I don't know if she sees that the way the rest of us do. She always puts others ahead of herself. She did it with every single promo op she had to help me through, and again when I proposed, and even now, maybe without even realizing it. It's who she is at her core. She's the most loyal person I know. The glue. My heart and soul.

I didn't think it was possible to regret my choices more, but here I am.

CHAPTER 41

HEMI

Breakups suck. Work sucks. The little things I can usually ignore or let roll off my back now prick like needles. Topher Guy has become the bane of my existence. All I want to do is hibernate until the ache in my chest goes away. But it's the busiest time of year in the Terror office, so that's not possible.

On the upside, I set up a huge promotional opportunity for the women's team that will give them incredible visibility. I want to tell Dallas, but since we're not together anymore, I can't. I rub my bare ring finger and feel another debilitating wave of sadness. I breathe through it, trying to center myself so I don't get emotional at work. It was a knee-jerk reaction to leave the ring at his place when I went over to clear out my things. But it belonged to his grandmother, so I couldn't keep it. And looking at it every day was too heartbreaking.

Being honest with myself about how I feel about Dallas Bright has been devastating. I love him in a way I never thought I'd love someone. Every time I reflect on the past couple of months, I see more of the truth of who he is and who we were together. But now we're nothing.

I refuse to cry in front of work people. My friends are one thing, but I can't let the colleagues who love to gossip see me break down. So I hole myself up in my office as much as possible to avoid running into the people most likely to shit-talk me.

An hour later, I'm fading. Sleep has been horrible—I've spent the past few days tossing and turning and waking in the middle of the night, unable to settle again. I head to the staff room, too tired to even make the trek across the street for a latte.

I regret the decision as soon as I enter the room. Two people from Topher's department are sitting at the conference table, sipping coffees—Chad and Janessa. The room goes silent as I enter. I'm used to it, but it still stings every time. When I stopped wearing the ring, chatter followed. I could handle it when it was about me being too direct and blunt. This is so much worse. Being the center of office gossip because I was dating, then engaged to, and subsequently broken up with by a player is my worst nightmare.

I set the coffee to brew and busy myself with adding cream and sugar to my mug.

"I don't know how you do it."

I stiffen but don't turn around.

"I wouldn't be able to show my face in the office after being dumped by one of the players," Chad continues.

Janessa coughs to hide a chuckle.

High school feels like a skip in the park compared to this. When I don't fight back, they take it as an invitation to keep slinging shit.

"The whole thing is just so embarrassing." His chair creaks as he slurps his coffee. "There's a reason for the no-fraternization policy, and now you're basically the poster child for why it's there."

"Oh my God, Chad." Janessa snickers.

I drop my head, grateful that my hair provides a protective curtain, and struggle to stay in control. It doesn't matter what I do or say; they're just going to keep coming for me. Evidently, it's open season. I'm tired of having to fight for my position. It makes me feel so small—like that unlikable girl all over again, the one Dallas's friends would tease in the halls between classes. I don't feel like a badass anymore—not even here, where I always have. I feel broken and insignificant.

But I roll my shoulders back anyway. I can't just let them do this. It's not right, and that matters. So I turn to face them. Chad is leaning back in his chair, smirk firmly in place. Janessa is focused on her coffee cup. So predictable.

"It must be so fun for you, watching the wicked witch fall. Do you think your cruelty makes you important? Does it feel good to shit all over me when you think I'm at my weakest? Should we give you an award at the next staff event?" To my absolute horror, my voice cracks and my vision blurs.

"Aw... Need a tissue?" Chad scoffs. "Topher was right. Dallas finally saw you for who you are. You're an overbearing bitch who tried to sleep your way up the ladder, and look where it got you." He slow claps. "You're a joke now. Way to make the front of house look bad. What kind of precedent do you think this sets?"

I've just drawn a breath to rip him a new one when Dallas's deep voice comes from the doorway.

"You are out of line, Chad. Wilhelmina's relationship status is none of your business, and running your mouth the way you are makes you a douchebag. If you have a problem, you should take it up with management." Dallas positions himself between us. "Or me, since I'm standing right here. But you probably don't want to do that, since I'm likely to grieve you for harassment. Which is exactly what this is, if you were unaware."

"I was just—"

Dallas's fingers skim the back of my hand. "You were just what, Chad? You think you have a right to talk to your colleagues—your superiors—like this? To treat them like garbage because you don't approve of what's going on in their personal life? As I've already stated, that is none of your fucking business." Dallas steps to the side and wraps a protective arm around my shoulder. "Let's go, Wills."

I allow him to pull me close and lead me out of the room.

"Why did you defend me?" My voice cracks. The boy who was once my dragon just became my dragon slayer. I can't pretend their words don't hurt anymore—that I'm unaffected by other people's cruelty.

"No one talks to you like that. Especially not a douchebag asshole named Chad." He continues down the hall and stops at Hammer's office. "Wills is done for the day. She'll be back tomorrow," he announces.

I keep dashing tears away, but they won't stop falling.

"Is everything okay?" Hammer asks.

"She'll be okay as soon as people learn how to behave. I appreciate you handling things today," Dallas says.

"Yeah. Of course." Hammer nods, eyes full of questions. "Screw the assholes." She cringes. "You know what I mean."

"Thanks, Hammer," I croak. "I appreciate you." I let Dallas guide me to my office. I grab a handful of tissues and try, in vain, to stop the freaking tears.

Dallas is here, taking care of me like I'm still his. My Dallas who isn't mine anymore.

He gathers my things, pausing to glance at the bowl of crocheted peaches sitting on my desk before he slings my purse over his shoulder. He kept adding to them and of all the things he gave me, I couldn't bear to part with them. "Do you need anything else?" he asks. "And don't say your laptop. It's staying here until tomorrow."

"Why are you doing this?" I manage to ask.

"Because I care about you." He holds out his hand, and I lace my fingers with his.

We take the elevator to the parking garage, and he helps me into his car. I'm surrounded by his scent, and he's sitting right next to me. But he's not mine anymore, and I don't know how to handle any of this. And the freaking tears won't stop. Dallas turns to me, and the look on his face only makes me cry harder.

Why is he here? Why show me what I'll never have with him?

I'm so in love with him. So hopelessly, terrifyingly head over heels for this man, and I'm so confused. He broke up with me, yet he's here, taking care of me. He keeps seeing me at my worst, and still, he's here.

"It's okay, honey. I got you." His thumb sweeps the hollow under my eye. More tears follow. "I'm sorry I made your life harder." He kisses my forehead. "Now let me get you out of here." He sits back, flips open the center console, and passes me a small packet of tissues. The ones I'm holding are already drenched.

"Thank you." I dab at my eyes. I've cried so much over the past week, I could probably fill a bathtub. I hate feeling weak. As many times as Ma tells me crying isn't weak and emotions are strength, believing her isn't easy. Any crack in my armor has always meant vulnerability I couldn't afford.

I expect Dallas to take me home, but he heads in the opposite direction, away from my building and toward the lakeshore. He pulls up in front of the Windsor House, a swanky hotel with my favorite spa.

"What are we doing here?"

"Giving you the break you need from the nonsense. Stay here. I'll be back in a minute." He leaves the car running and hops out.

My phone is blowing up with messages from Shilpa. I let her know I'm with Dallas and that I'd had enough of being shit on by colleagues today.

Dallas returns a few minutes later, turns off the ignition, and comes around to my side, helping me out of the car. Once again, he shoulders my purse.

"I can take that."

"I'm man enough to deal with a purse," he assures me.

He hands his keys to the valet. We pass the front desk and head toward the elevators.

"What's going on right now?" I ask as I follow him into the elevator and he punches the button for the penthouse floor.

"First, we'll get you settled in your room, which you have until noon tomorrow. I've scheduled you a facial, massage, and mani-pedi." Dallas is so matter-of-fact. He glances at his watch. "But not for an hour and a half, so you have time to relax first."

"But...why?"

He tips his head. "But why what?"

"Why are you doing this?"

"Because you need to be taken care of, and I want to be the one who does that."

"But you broke up with me," I whisper.

"I'm still in love with you, though, Wills. That hasn't changed."

My heart stutters with that admission.

Before I can say anything, he adds, "We can talk about that later. I'm not going anywhere. Right now, your feelings are on fire. I'd like them to drop from an inferno to maybe a light smolder before we dive into that particular topic."

He makes a good point, and I almost manage a smile. The elevator doors open, and he ushers me into the hall. He passes the key over the sensor and holds the door as I step inside the one-bedroom suite. It's beautiful and romantic, and the waterfall behind my eyes threatens to spill over again.

He grabs a bottle of Perrier from the mini fridge and twists the cap off, handing it to me. "Drink this, please."

I sip the bubbly water. Staying hydrated has been a struggle the past few days.

"Settle in. Take a bath if you want. Lie on the bed. Watch TV. I'll text when it's time to go to the spa."

"You're leaving?" *Fuck.* I hate how paper thin my heart feels.

"I'm going to pick up a few things. I'll be back, though." He kisses my forehead and leaves me alone in the room. I do as he suggests and run myself a bath.

As promised, he texts when it's time to go to the spa. I head down and spend the next two and a half hours being pampered.

Dallas is in the room when I return. He's sitting on the couch reading a comic book. A pair of comfy jammies are laid out on the bed, a pair of slippers on the floor.

"What's all this?" I ask. The coffee table is covered in my favorite treats, even the ones Mom picks up from the Indian market, and my favorite gossip magazine.

"It should be everything you need for a relaxing night in." Dallas pushes to a stand. "Do you want some alone time?"

I shake my head, feeling fragile, like one wrong move will shatter me.

He crosses the room and stops with his toes an inch from mine. "Do you want me to call your girlfriends?"

Bottom lip trembling, I shake my head again. Trusting him feels like free-falling. "I'd rather have you, if you want to stay."

He strokes my cheek. "Of course I want to stay." He opens his arms, and I step into them. He envelops me in his embrace, and for the first time since he broke it off with me—which was less than a week ago but feels like a year—I'm where I'm supposed to be. But we're still in pieces.

He holds me while I break down. Again. Then he disappears into the bathroom while I change into the jammies.

After that, he sits in the corner of the couch, one leg stretched out, arms open as he invites me to cuddle with him. He's so beautiful and thoughtful, and he's right here, giving me all the things I need, showing me how he feels with actions. He's confirming that letting me go wasn't about not wanting me. I curl up against his warm chest, the steady beat of his heart calming me.

As he holds me, my favorite movie playing in the background, I'm finally ready to accept the truth. I'm just as in love with Dallas as he is with me. It's not just about the way he loves me, although that's certainly a factor. To be accepted so fully by another person—it isn't something I've experienced before. Not like this. Dallas has seen me at my very worst, time and time again. And he loves every part of me. He settles me like no one ever has. He's been constant since the moment I started working for the Terror. And as much as I made his life hell with some of the activities I scheduled for him, I can admit now that I loved the way he always stepped up and took on the challenge.

I shift and look up at him. "Dallas, I need to tell you something."

"I know." He strokes the edge of my jaw with the backs of his fingers. "But not today. It can wait until we're both clearheaded, okay? I'm not going anywhere tonight unless you ask me to. Right now, the most important thing is you. I need you to see that. Just let me take care of you."

CHAPTER 42

DALLAS

For the first time since I broke my own heart, I sleep like a damn baby. It helps that I get to spoon Wills all night long. I hated seeing her break down, but I wouldn't trade getting to be the person to take care of her.

I'm up early for ice time with the guys, so I have a fruit and muffin platter delivered to the room, and I leave Wills sleeping in the massive bed. I kiss on the forehead, and she hums, but doesn't move otherwise. Her eyes are still a little puffy from all the tears last night, but at least she's getting sleep, which she needs.

She told me about her childhood. Good things and bad. She told me about how she feels in the office and why fake dating me was the only real choice. She also shared what she wanted out of a partner, and that she never thought she'd have love. My heart ached as she let me in, one piece, one story, one vulnerability revealed at a time. I was selfish and impatient. But from now on, I'll be the man who puts her first in all things. Loving her is bigger than my fears, impulses, and dreams.

I make it to practice on time—barely. Tonight is our first exhibition game, and there's no way I want to be stuck warming the bench. It isn't until we're off the ice that Ash asks me how things are going. He knows what's up, in part because I texted him yesterday afternoon to bail on our evening yoga session with Hollis and Roman, but also because Hammer informed Shilpa that I took Wills out of the office yesterday.

Ash makes sure no one can hear him before he asks, "Does this mean you're back together?"

"Uh, not yet, no."

He frowns. "But you spent the night together?"

"Yeah. Nothing happened, though." Other than temple kisses and the one I pressed to the back of her neck when she snuggled against me in bed, it was a PG night. "We'll talk tonight. After the game. She needed to know she didn't always have to be strong alone, and I wanted her to know I would hold her when she needed someone."

He smiles and claps me on the shoulder. "Look at you, doing your best to show up for her."

"I hope it works."

"It will. She loves the way you love her. Shilps and I see it. Hemi is the strong one in most parts of her life, but falling in love is one of those things that doesn't allow much room for control. That can be scary."

After practice, I find messages from Wills thanking me for yesterday and this morning and a whole bunch of fingers-crossed emojis that I made it to practice on time. She has meetings this afternoon; otherwise, I'd be in her office, checking on her. I assure her I did and that I'll see her tonight. Regardless of how rough the past few days have been, she won't miss the first exhibition game of the season. Especially when we're playing against New York, and Flip's archnemesis, Connor Grace.

I'm feeling optimistic—not just about the game, but about me and Wills—as I suit up later that evening. We take the ice, and I scan New York's bench. Kodiak Bowman is impossible to miss. Despite being young, he's huge and imposing, and tonight he looks like he's on edge. Or more on edge than usual. I've heard rumors that he still pukes before games. It's hard to say if that's bullshit or not.

"Is Grace missing?" I ask Palaniappa.

"Looks like it. You think he got traded?"

I shrug. "Dunno. Last I heard he was holding out until New York offered him more money." At the end of last season, he became an unrestricted free agent. He didn't like the deal New York offered, so he was sitting on it. I thought he would take it eventually, but maybe he didn't.

Madden and Stiles take the ice, along with the rest of the starting lineup. We gain control of the puck right away and score a goal within the first five minutes of play. It doesn't matter that New York has the league's star player in their lineup; Bowman is off his game, and that gives us the advantage.

We wipe the ice with their asses, beating New York 5-1. It's a rough loss for them, and not a great way to start their preseason. When we hit the locker room, Hammerstein is feeling good about the near shutout, and Madden is practically floating on the high of scoring three goals. Stiles is all smiles over his two assists, as are Hendrix and I over ours. It's a hell of a preseason start.

I'm surprised when Flip suggests we go to the Watering Hole, once we're showered and dressed. Usually on a night like this, he'd suggest a club. But lately he's been more about low-key nights with the team. I want to ask Wills if she's coming, but I don't want to put pressure on her. I've done enough of that.

The girls are at their favorite table when we arrive, and I'm glad to see Wills is with them. She looks better. She's smiling, and the puffiness around her eyes is gone.

That smile is directed at me, real and genuine, when she sees us headed their way. The girls slide out of the booth, cheering and clapping along with the staff.

"Oh shit," Roman mutters. "Is that Tally?"

My gaze shifts briefly from Wills, and I fight to keep my eyebrows from climbing my forehead. "Uh, yeah. It appears that way." Gone is the sweet little Tally who wore jeans and hoodies to games and dress pants and blouses to the Terror office for her internship. Tonight, she's in a crop top and a leather jacket.

"Is she wearing makeup?" Roman asks.

"Yeah."

"Huh."

"At least she's out with us and not at a keg party," Flip mutters and heads for the girls.

Tristan skirts around me and heads straight for Rix. Hollis does the same with Hammer, but his greeting is more PG, because Roman is standing right here. Ash kisses Shilpa on the cheek. Wills takes a tentative step forward. Like magnets, we move toward each other, our smiles widening. When she's close enough, she winds her arms around my waist and squeezes. I do the same and drop my head so I can breathe her in like the balm she is.

"Thank you for yesterday. It was so incredibly sweet and thoughtful."

I lean back and brush her hair over her shoulders. "I'm sorry I had to go before you woke up."

Her palms settle on my chest. "You couldn't be late for practice."

"I could have, but neither of us needed that." I stroke the edge of her jaw. "And I felt you needed sleep more than you needed me waking you up just to tell you I had to go. But I didn't like leaving you."

She fingers the buttons on my shirt and adjusts my tie. "After we're done celebrating the win, can we go back to your place and talk?"

"Absolutely. We can go whenever you're ready." I'll leave now, if she wants to.

She pats my chest. "Celebrate the win with your teammates. I'm not going anywhere."

"Me neither. Not ever again. Not unless you tell me to. And even then, I won't go without a fight." I dip down and kiss her perfect lips. "Can I get you a fun drink?"

"I could be persuaded."

"I'll be right back." I reluctantly release her.

I step up next to Tristan at the bar as he pulls his phone out of his pocket. I glance at the screen.

"What's Bowman texting you about?" Me, Flip, and Tristan all went to the Hockey Academy, and he and Kodiak Bowman kept in touch, despite him being a few years younger. We all saw the talent in that kid, and he's proving to be one hell of a force on the ice.

"Dunno." He opens the message, and his brow furrows. "Well, shit."

"Everything okay?" I ask.

"Connor Grace wasn't on the ice tonight because he was traded."

"To what team?"

"Ours."

CHAPTER 43

HEMI

Dallas and I stay longer than anticipated, in part because the team is suddenly reeling. Flip is losing his mind after finding out that Connor Grace, the one player he can't stand, has been traded to Toronto.

"Did you know about this?" I ask Shilpa, but I already know the answer.

She gives me a look. "The paperwork landed on my desk yesterday. The whole thing was completely unexpected."

I glance around the room, my heart in my throat. "Who are we losing?"

"Spencer."

"Shit. He showed so much promise." Coach said he was out yesterday and wouldn't be at the game tonight because of a family emergency, but none of us realized it was permanent.

"I know. We won't have time to give him a proper sendoff, either. I don't have all the details, but Spencer has family in New York, and from what I understand, his mom has some health issues."

"Poor kid. I hope he's okay. I feel like this change might make this season more challenging," I say.

"Yeah, probably. And Flip was settling down."

I spot him sitting at the bar, with Tristan on one side and Dallas on the other.

We have a team meeting tomorrow morning, and I'm sure the official announcement will be made there. The evening remains mostly upbeat, despite this news, as it was an amazing win tonight. Shilpa and Ash are first to leave, and they offer to take Tally with them since they live closest to her on-campus apartment, but she wants to hang around for a bit longer. I talked with her a little this evening, and so far, she's really enjoying the whole university experience. But she's decidedly not a fan of keg parties. Thank the Lord.

On the walk back to Dallas's, my palms start to sweat. "How's Flip?"

"He's not drowning himself in women, so that's progress. But he's riled about Grace being traded," Dallas says.

"I wish I knew what the deal was there."

"They were pretty competitive at the Hockey Academy, but about halfway through the program, it stopped being a friendly rivalry." He holds the door open and follows me into his building.

"I hope they can figure out a way to get along or it'll be a rough season for everyone." My anxiety spikes as we step into the elevator. This is filler, small talk until we get to his place. There we'll hash all of this out.

I already know how Dallas feels about me. It's how I feel about him that I need to own.

He leans against the mirrored wall. "How are you doing?"

"Spinning, to be honest. How about you?"

His smile is soft. "Same, honey."

The doors slide open, and he motions for me to go ahead of him. We're quiet on the way to his penthouse.

"You showed up for me when we weren't even together," I say as soon as we're inside.

"No matter where we've been or where we go from here, I will always show up for you, however you let me."

"You could have just extricated me and left me with Shilps or Hammer. You could have taken me home and brought me ice cream and walked away, but you stayed and took care of me."

"I would do it a million times over," he says.

"I believe you," I whisper.

"I let you believe the worst about me for a long time," he says.

"You did. I thought I knew who you were, what you were about. But then your mom said something when we stayed with them during the reunion that had me questioning how clear my picture really was. How often did you come to my rescue, Dallas?"

"Not often enough. Not the way I should have," he says, looking at the floor. "But I tried. You were always so brave, and I wanted to be like that, but I couldn't do it out loud. Not back then. But when people tried to fuck with you, I stepped in to fix it."

"By painting my locker when someone defaced it?" I remember the day I came to school to find my locker still tacky with semi-dried paint.

He nods.

"What else did you do to protect me?"

"Whatever I could. I made new posters for your student council president campaign after the guys pulled them down and came to school early so I could get them up before you noticed." Dallas rubs the back of his neck. "You were so good at making it seem like it didn't affect you, but I paid attention, Wills. I saw what it did to you when you thought no one else was looking, and I hated myself for the role I played as a bystander."

I see the truth in his words, in the ache in his voice. With each revelation, our entire history rewrites itself. I'm not the nerdy girl who was tormented by the prom king. I'm the brave girl who stood up for what I believed in. Braver than he was.

"I couldn't undo the bullshit you went through, but I tried to fix things when I could. And then I realized I'd been focused on all the wrong things. I'd run out of time, and when I tried to buy myself a little more, I hurt you in a way that felt irreversible. I should have told you then—even if you didn't believe me, I never should have let you believe the lie. I'll never do it again, Wills. I love you too much to ever be anything but one-hundred-percent honest with you." Dallas tucks his hands in his pockets. "I'm sorry it took me this long to tell you."

My fractured soul knits itself back together, and I give Dallas my own truth. "I was so sure that one day you'd change your mind about me, that who I am would eventually be too much. And I know part of that feeling stems from where I started in life."

I have such a supportive, loving family, but for too long I've let that feeling of being too much govern my actions. I won't let it be the thing that keeps me from experiencing this kind of connection with another person.

"I have all these fabulous people who see me for me and love me because of it, yet I've been so focused on the ones who don't. I couldn't imagine someone wanting me exactly as I am. You've shown me that, Dallas. Even before I felt worthy of it. But I feel it now. I know it's taken me time to catch up, but I'm in love with you. Not just because of the way you love me, but because you're you."

The lens of the past has altered, and the real version of Dallas melts my heart. "You're amazing. You're the guy who signs up for everything, even the stuff that makes you uncomfortable, because the mission matters to you. You're always there to support your teammates. Look at tonight. I'm sure the last thing you wanted was to help manage Flip and whatever is going on with him, but you didn't leave it all to Tristan. You always show up. Every single time. For your teammates, for your family, for me."

I reach for his hand, needing the connection to ground me. "I was so scared of my feelings for you, and afraid that if I voiced them, they would somehow erase yours for me. I know that's my trauma talking, not logic. You're not just the *kind* of man I want to give my heart to, you're *the* man. I know you will always keep it safe. I adore you, Dallas, exactly as you are. So if you want to give this another shot, I'm in." My heart hammers in my chest, stomach twisting up. But the only way to show him he's not in this alone is to put my heart on the line, too, like he has this entire time. Without me even knowing.

His smile is soft as he presses his lips against my bare ring finger. "I'm always going to be your number-one fan, Wills. Any time you fall, I'll be here to pick you up. I'll do my very best to be what you need, and to love you the way you want and need to be loved. And I will one-hundred-percent fuck it up somewhere along the way, but I will never leave you. Not ever again." He squeezes my hand. "I've been in love with you since the third grade, Wills. You've always been the bravest person I know, and I will love you with my whole heart for as long as you'll let me."

"Does this mean you're my boyfriend again?" I ask.

"Do you want me to be your boyfriend?"

"I do. So much."

"Good." He smiles. "I love being your boyfriend."

I loop my arms around his neck. "And I love being your girlfriend." I whisper the words I've been holding sacred. "I love you."

His fingers drift along my cheek. "I love you. More than anything."

"I know." I take his hand and press my lips to his knuckles. "I know taking off the ring feels like a step backwards, but when I put it back on, I want it to be because we're both ready. I'd rather deal with the speculation than live a lie when I have someone and something so real right in front of me."

"I'll keep the ring safe, and when you're ready, I'd like to ask you to be my wife again. But I'll make sure my proposal is romantic as fuck, and not in front of thousands of people."

"That sounds perfect." It doesn't matter what everyone else

thinks. This is our story. No one else gets a say anymore but us. I curve one hand around the back of his neck and press my nails gently into the skin.

He drops his head and claims my mouth in a soft, slow, bone-melting kiss.

"Please take me to bed," I whisper against his lips.

He regards me with dark, lust-heavy eyes. "You're going to be my perfect goddess and let me worship you the way I want to, aren't you?"

My knees go weak, and desire rushes through my veins, settling between my thighs. "Absolutely."

His hands glide over my ass, and he grips firmly as he hoists me up. I wrap myself around him and lower my mouth to his as he carries me through his penthouse. We bump into a few things on the way, and he smacks his elbow on the doorframe and nearly drops me, but we make it to the bed, and he settles between my thighs, hips pressing firmly into the cradle of mine.

We're a flurry of impatience, tugging at clothing, fingers seeking bare skin. But as soon as we're naked, Dallas slows things down. His fingers drift down my side as he claims my mouth with a searing kiss.

"God, I missed you," he murmurs as he kisses his way down my throat and along my collarbones. "The way you feel under my touch."

When he covers my nipple and circles the tight peak with his tongue, I thread my hands through his hair.

"The feel of your hands on me." He devotes the same attention to my other nipple before he moves lower, past my navel to the apex of my thighs. His gaze lifts to meet mine. "The way you taste." He pushes my legs wide and lowers his head.

I whimper at the soft strokes of his tongue.

"That fucking sound." He growls against my skin as he sucks my clit roughly. I gasp and arch. "I'm the only person who'll ever hear you moan like that again."

"Only you," I agree.

He sends me careening into bliss with his mouth. I'm bone-less and panting as he kisses his way back up my body. I can't get enough of the taste of myself on his tongue, of the way it feels to be so completely worshiped by him. He keeps his mouth fused to mine as he reaches across to the nightstand. I expect him to grab a condom, but instead of a foil packet, he presses something silicone into my palm.

I break the kiss long enough to check it out. "Well, hello." My gaze returns to his. "When did you get this?"

Dallas's heated gaze turns molten, and his smile makes everything tighten. "After I told you you could fuck me."

"You were serious." I wasn't sure if that was a heat-of-the-moment declaration, but I can't deny how much I'd love to be the one to unravel him.

"Of course I was serious. I did some reading." He rolls his hips, his cock sliding between my folds. "It was educational."

"Oh? Fuck." Images of Dallas on the edge of orgasm have me tipping my hips up in search of him. "And what did you learn?" The head nudges my entrance.

"That I need some training first, but that's part of the fun." He pushes in an inch. "Do you want me to get a condom?"

I shake my head. "I want to feel you."

His eyes lock on mine as he shifts his hips forward, sinking into me. "You feel so damn good, Wills." My nails dig into his shoulders, and his lip curls in satisfaction. "I could stay inside you forever, and it would never be long enough."

"I can't get enough of you, either." I ease my hand down his back and dig my nails into his rock-solid ass, encouraging him to fuck me harder. I luxuriate in the delicious weight of him pressing me into the mattress, the way he fills me, consumes me, loves me. "Does this mean you want to start training now?" I ask as he grinds against me.

He pushes up on one arm. "I want what you want." He holds up a small bottle of lube.

I uncap it, and he pours a little on the tip of the thin, tapered plug.

"Be a good boy and stay nice and deep." I lift my head, and Dallas tucks another pillow under it as I look down the broad expanse of his back to the glorious globes of his ass. I slide the plug between his cheeks, and he sucks in a breath as I press against the opening.

I brush my lips over his cheek. "Look at me when I'm fucking you," I whisper.

His gaze meets mine as I ease the plug inside, slowly, a little at a time. His mouth drops open, and his brow furrows as I push it deeper. "Well, fuck me, honey."

"It's good, isn't it?" I keep going until the plug is fully seated inside him.

"Jesus." He drops his head and nuzzles my neck. "I need to start moving."

"Not yet, honey."

He groans, and his arms tremble with the effort it takes to hold off, to wait for my next command.

"On your back for me. I get to fuck you now."

One second I'm under him, and the next I'm straddling his hips. His chest heaves, his eyes on fire as his fingers dig into my skin. I fold back so my ass rests on his thick, muscular thighs and crook my finger at him. He obeys the silent command and sits up. His eyes flare, and his hold on my hips tightens. "Oh my hell."

"Even better now, isn't it?"

"So damn good," he agrees.

I run my hands through his hair and rest my forearms on his shoulders as I start to move, rising until I feel the ridge at my opening before I take him inside me again. Dallas's fingers dig into my hips and he helps move me over him. His eyes stay locked on mine, his expression fierce as he bounces me on his cock, fucking me, filling me, worshiping me.

Sweat trickles down my spine as sensation builds, every nerve ending alight with desire.

"Look at you, fucking me like the goddess you are." Dallas fists my hair and claims my mouth as a tidal wave of sensation sweeps over me. "Do you know how much I want you? How much I need you?"

I find myself laid back on the bed, Dallas's hips slapping against mine as he takes over, pounding me into the mattress like he's exorcising demons from my pussy. I slide my hand down his back and press on the plug as he slams into me one last time.

He tries to bury his face against my neck, but I grip his chin with my other hand. "Eyes on mine when I'm making you come, honey."

"Fuck, I love you." He groans against my lips as a shudder wracks his sweat-soaked body.

"And I love you." I kiss him softly. "With my whole heart."

He's mine, and I'm his. And this is just the beginning.

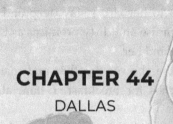

CHAPTER 44
DALLAS

I wake up wrapped around Wills. My hard-on is nestled happily in the crack of her ass, and I'm protectively cupping her right breast. A piece of her hair tickles my face, but I'm too content to do anything about it. She's the love of my life, and when she's ready, I'll make her my forever.

I lie there, basking in the glory of getting *the girl*. She's always been it for me. Everyone I've ever dated has been measured against her. She's the perfect woman. Bold, take-no-shit, and sweet as pie when she feels safe. And I'm the guy who gets to do that for her. Yeah, today kicks all the asses.

She hums softly and wiggles her ass. "Morning, Dallas. Morning, Dallas's cock."

I smile and kiss her bare shoulder. "Morning, Wills. Morning, Wills's ass."

"You should slide that a little lower and make it the best morning ever," she suggests.

I abandon her breast and shift my hips back. Gripping my shaft, I run the head past door number two. Wills moans, and then moans again as I pass door number one and rub over her clit before I line myself up and push inside.

"God, you feel so good." She groans.

"There's nothing better than being surrounded by you." I ease my hand down her soft stomach, and she parts her legs, giving me access to her clit. I stay deep and rub slow circles, murmuring soft praise and dirty promises as I send her over the edge, me right behind her.

We jump in the shower together and make pancakes with fresh sliced peaches for breakfast. I stare at her shamelessly while we eat.

She pauses with a bite of pancake on her fork. "What are you doing?"

"Watching you eat."

She covers my eyes with her palm. "You're ridiculous."

"Look, here's the deal." I grab her hand and kiss her palm. "I'm obsessed with you."

She props her cheek on her fist. "You don't say."

"And I'll be honest, I'm kind of disappointed that I can't track you the way Tristan tracks Rix."

"You mean with the phone app?" she asks, biting back a smile.

"Exactly. So if you just moved in with me, I'd feel a lot better. Then I can worship at your feet the way I want to. I mean, logically it makes sense, especially with the season starting and me being on the road half the time. Plus, you've been staying over a lot anyway, so it seems like the reasonable next step."

She leans in and kisses my cheek. "First, you can track me with the app, if you want. Second, I would need to give my roommate notice, and third, can we be girlfriend and boyfriend for like, a month or two before we take the next step?"

I nod knowingly. "Ah, I see how it is. You're being the toe keeper, keeping me on my toes by playing hard to get."

She rolls her eyes, but smiles. "Which is why I'm sitting in your kitchen, wearing one of your shirts and eating breakfast." She arches a brow. "And I have to give sixty-days' notice to move."

"But you'll sleep here when I'm not on an away series?" I press.

"Yes. I'll sleep here when you're not on an away series."

"And you'll move in full time sixty days from when you give your notice to your roommate?" I confirm.

"Yes, Dallas."

"Fantastic." I kiss her cheek. "Just for the sake of clarity, how soon will you give notice?"

She laughs and rolls her eyes. "Don't worry. I won't make you wait long."

"Okay. I'll check in with you next week and see how you feel then." I pop in the last bite of pancake, smiling my face off. "We should get ready for the meeting."

Wills's phone buzzes relentlessly when we leave for the head office half an hour later.

"Everything okay?"

"The Babe chat is blowing up. Apparently, Flip had a rough night. He almost fought some guy who was flirting with Tally. After Tally left with Shilpa and Ash, Tristan and Rix had to bring him back to their place and monitor. I guess he was a real mess."

"I wonder what management was thinking, bringing Grace to the team," I muse.

"He's an excellent defensive player when he's not being an antagonistic ass," Wills says. "And with Roman hanging up his skates at the end of the season and the new goalie being phased in, they probably wanted to make sure defense was strong."

"I see the logic, but I don't know how good this will be for team morale if one of our lead scorers is on edge all the time."

She shrugs. "I guess we'll see how it all plays out."

I pull into the Terror lot and back into my spot. Wills slips her hand in mine, and we take the elevator to the office floor. Shilpa, Ash, Hammer, Hollis, and Roman are all in Shilpa's office when we arrive.

"We're back together," I announce.

Wills pats my chest. "I'm pretty sure they already know that, considering we're holding hands, but I love you for feeling like we needed to state the obvious."

Roman, Hollis, and Ash give us the thumbs-up, and the girls hug Wills.

"Any word on what this meeting will look like, Shilps?" Wills asks. She's the only one who has unspoken permission to ask her that. We know she's the team's lawyer, not our lawyer, and can't say anything.

"There's not a lot I would be able to share. Even so, there have been some closed doors in upper management the past few days, so it's anyone's guess," Shilpa says.

"Let's hope Flip can keep his cool," Hollis grumbles.

"Ending up at Stiles's place is better than going out and potentially killing his endorsement campaigns, right, Hemi?" Roman asks.

"Yeah. That's real progress for Flip," she agrees.

Shilpa glances at the clock on the wall. "We should probably get to the meeting."

We're the first ones there. Usually Wills would be briefed early, but this time she's in the dark like everyone else. The table at the back of the room is loaded with pastries and fruit. I grab a plate while Wills doctors coffees for us as more team members arrive. Tristan accompanies Flip, who looks rough.

Flip, who never says no to free food, bypasses the breakfast spread and takes a seat beside Roman. After another minute, Jamie Fielding, the general manager, and Coach Vander Zee move to the front of the room, and everyone quiets down.

"Some of you might be aware of the news I'm about to share, but Dane Spencer had a family emergency last week, and after a lengthy discussion, we decided the best plan for him and the team was to send him where he's needed. He'll be moving to New York in exchange for one of their players. Connor Grace is excellent on defense, and he'll be a fantastic addition to this team. I know losing Spencer is a shock, but I expect you to make

Grace feel welcome. We are all professionals here and will be a united front." His gaze shifts to Flip, who's slouched in his chair, arms crossed, expression grim.

With that, Connor is ushered into the room. There's a smattering of applause, but it seems everyone is still in shock.

He smiles, but it looks smug more than anything. "Pretty sure some of you wish I was literally anyone else, but it's hard to argue with my stats." He looks around the room. "I'm looking forward to playing with most of you."

"We just got Flip to settle down," Wills mutters.

"I'll be here to help you work out your stress." I kiss her temple.

She elbows me in the side but fights a smile.

Flip looks like he's plotting murder.

"And we have another announcement to make," Jamie says after a moment, adjusting his tie.

Everyone quiets down. There better not be another trade. Or an early retirement. I glance at Roman as Jamie clears his throat.

"We'd like to introduce Alexandria Forrester, who will be joining us as an assistant coach. We're excited to have her expertise for the coming season."

"Oh, she's fantastic. This is amazing," Wills whispers.

"No fucking way." Roman's eyes go wide, and he slouches in his chair, hand covering his mouth as he crosses and uncrosses his legs. I don't think anyone but me heard him.

"Coach Forrester comes to us from the Ontario league and has a background in sports psychology and sports management," Jamie continues. "She is incredibly knowledgeable and will be a valuable addition to our coaching staff." He claps as a woman with long dark hair, streaked with auburn, who looks to be in her late twenties, moves to stand beside him.

Alexandria says hello to the team, and her eyes flare slightly when they find Roman. But she keeps on smiling and thanks us for the warm welcome.

Looks like things are shaking up this season. Maybe I should be worried, but right now, it all seems like details. Whatever comes our way, I have Wills, and she has me. Together we can get through anything.

CHAPTER 45
HEMI

DALLAS

What time will you be done?

HEMI

Probably around 5, maybe 5:30. I have a
meeting with management in an hour. Making
big plans for later?

DALLAS

You know it, sexy girlfriend. Tell me what you
need from me tonight and it's yours.

I smile, and everything below the waist tightens in the best
way possible. It's hard to believe a handful of months ago I
was hell-bent on making Dallas's life as miserable as possible.

HEMI

You're so good to me.

DALLAS

I'm your good boy, right? *winky face*

HEMI

Absolutely.

DALLAS

Tell me what you want when I get you into bed later.

HEMI

I'd like to sit on your face.

DALLAS

Fuck yes. Baptism by pussy is my favorite. What else?

I bite my lip as I compose the next message.

HEMI

🌙 How about a little training tonight?

DALLAS

I was hoping you'd say that. I'm ready to level up.

HEMI

I mean for me this time.

DALLAS

Oh, hell yes. I'm going to make you come so hard you see stars.

Sex with Dallas is an adventure I never want to end. He's all-in—one-hundred-and-ten percent, one-hundred-and-ten percent of the time.

HEMI

That's every time we have sex.

DALLAS

Whole fucking constellations then. I can't wait to get my hands on your perfect ass.

HEMI

That makes two of us.

DALLAS

Ash and I will meet you, Shilps, and Hammer at the office so we can go to the Watering Hole together.

HEMI

Perfect. I love you.

DALLAS

With all my heart.

I slide my phone into my pocket and fan my face. This probably wasn't the best conversation to have right before a meeting with upper management, but at least I have something to look forward to after the Watering Hole. Today has been all about the scramble with Connor Grace and Alexandria Forrester joining the team and Spencer having left for New York.

Communications has fed out the trade, and I've been tasked with liaising with New York's director of PR so we can make this transition as smooth as possible. I anticipate that this meeting has to do with the trade, so I'm surprised to find Fielding and Vander Zee sitting at the conference table alone. Normally their personal assistants attend to take notes.

"Is everything okay?" I ask as I slide into the chair across from them, my palms suddenly clammy.

"Yes, this is an information meeting only, no fires to put out yet," Fielding assures me.

I rap on the table. "Knock on wood."

They chuckle.

Jamie leans back in his chair. "We wanted to talk to you before we share the news with the rest of the team. We performed an internal review, and Topher Guy has been let go."

"I'm sorry, what?" I look between them, my shock impossible to hide.

"Topher is no longer working for the league. We've been building a case for a while. We're aware of his unprofessional conduct, and its escalation in recent months. I know you didn't come to us directly with this issue, and that you're very capable of handling yourself. You're used to managing problems. But you're a valued member of the team, and the reports regarding his unfair treatment and lack of cooperation were not something we could allow to continue. We hired you because you're smart, effective, and you don't deal in bullshit. We want you to be able to do your job."

"Who's taking his place?"

"We're looking at internal movement, and Odette in Office Operations is at the top of our list."

I nod. "She would be fantastic in that role."

"We think so, too."

First Alexandria Forrester and now this. Two more women in administrative roles inside the Terror is a huge win. Sure, it will be a little hectic with so much change at the beginning of the season, but there's so much potential.

After the meeting, I head down the hall to my office, feeling lighter. I stop in to formally introduce myself to Alexandria.

She pushes her chair back and rises, a warm smile on her face. "Hi. Hemi, right?"

"That's right. I wanted to pop in and welcome you to the team. Looks like you're getting settled." There are boxes in the corner, but she's already put art on the walls.

"I am," she agrees. "Everyone has been welcoming so far."

"The team is fantastic, and the head office is super supportive," I assure her. The one who wasn't is no longer working here, which is a huge bonus for all of us.

She nods. "I've heard great things. I'm looking forward to working with you and Shilpa. I really love what you're doing with the women's team."

"That's been such a passion project for me."

"Well, it's incredible. And last year's gala was out of this world with the money you raised for all those charities."

"I couldn't have done it without Hammer's help. She's my right hand."

"Hammer? Like Hammerstein?" I can see questions in her eyes.

"Yeah, that's the one. Aurora Hammerstein. She works with me in PR."

Alexandria nods slowly. "Right. Okay."

"She was in the meeting this morning, but you were probably overwhelmed with all the people. She's out at a promo op with her dad, but she'll be in tomorrow. I'll introduce you."

She looks like she might say something else, but then she smooths her hands over her hips. "I would love that."

"Some of us are heading to a local pub after work, if you want to join us. I could actually introduce you to Hammer, since she'll be there and so will Shilpa, plus a handful of the players, if you want to meet them in a more relaxed environment."

"Thanks so much for thinking of me. Can I take a raincheck? There's a lot to learn, and I'm just getting my head around things. Plus, I still have some unpacking to do." She motions to the boxes.

"Absolutely. Maybe next week would be better."

"That would be great."

I leave her to it and return to my office. My mood is buoyant and my relief is overwhelming. Topher was toxic to the culture, and while he wasn't the only person who made things difficult here, he was certainly the loudest and the worst of them. Knowing I don't have to deal with him anymore is a weight lifted.

Shilpa pokes her head in at ten after five, glancing over her shoulder and lowering her voice. "I hear a celebration is in order."

"What are we celebrating?" Dallas asks, appearing out of nowhere.

"You're early."

"Honey, my sweetness." He skirts around Shilpa with a quiet *sorry.* "Of course I'm early, I haven't seen you in six hours. It's too long. I need a fix."

"How are you going to deal when you have away games?" I tip my head up to accept a kiss.

"Video call you relentlessly. And I might have already ordered a body pillow in your likeness."

"You're kidding."

"Totally kidding." He shakes his head. "Anyway, what are we celebrating? Other than you being the badassiest badass."

"Topher got fired," Shilpa replies.

"Hallelujah. It's about damn time. That guy is a super dick. Like the most saggy dick of all dicks. That absolutely is a reason to celebrate."

My phone buzzes on my desk. I have a message from Shilpa. I look up to find her no longer standing in the doorway. "I agree. I can handle a lot of bullshit, but his was next level. Still, I hope there isn't backlash."

He takes my hand in his. "This is your team, and the Terror is your family. It's why you're still here and he's not. He was the problem, not you."

"I know. And I'm not sad he's gone. I just feel...I don't know...like I don't want to give anyone another reason to hate me." Which I realize is a stupid thing to be worried about, but I've spent so much time being the person people talk shit about, it's hard not to fall right back into the crap.

"Topher was a jerk and he inspired other people to be jerks. He was a bully, and he needed to go. He's an example that needed to be set a long-ass time ago, and hopefully people will learn how to behave now that he's gone. And I hope like hell he learns something from it, too. It's doubtful though since he's a narrow-minded prick. Now repeat after me: I'm a badass."

I give him a look.

"Say it."

"I'm a badass."

"Like you mean it."

I bite my lips together.

He arches a brow.

"I'm a badass," I say with absolute authority.

"That's my girl. I love you. Endlessly." He kisses the end of my nose and cups my face in his palms, slanting his mouth over mine in a sweet kiss. He doesn't deepen it though, likely because we're in the office and my door is still partly open.

"You are the definition of the perfect boyfriend," I say. "And I love you, too."

"Only took me a decade to earn that title. You ready to go? Shilps and Ash and the rest of them are already there."

"I'm ready."

Dallas shoulders my purse while I shut my computer down and pick up my phone. I frown at the new alert.

"What's wrong?"

"Brooklyn posted in the reunion group and whatever it is, everyone is commenting."

"Oh yeah. I saw that earlier." Dallas rubs his bottom lip.

"Is it concerning?" I ask, suddenly nervous.

"For us? No. Brooklyn called her wedding off. I guess she caught Sean cheating and thought the reunion group was the best place to share that." Dallas tips his head, like he's gauging my response.

"That's awful." She wasn't a good friend to me, but I still won't wish her ill will.

"It is. But I don't know that broadcasting it will make her feel better." He tips my chin up. "You okay?"

"Yeah. I am. And so thankful that I have you."

He brushes his lips over mine. "I feel the same way."

He threads his fingers through mine and we leave the office and walk to the Watering Hole to meet our friends. When we arrive, Hammer, Shilps, Rix, Tally, Essie, and Dred are already at a table with Tristan, Nate, Flip, Hollis, Roman, and Ash.

"You gonna tell us what the deal is with you and Grace now that's he on our team?" Roman asks.

"Nope." Flip slurps his Coke.

Dallas shrugs. "Some guys don't get along with each other."

"He was a douche back then, and he's still a douche now. If this is what we're talking about, I'm going home," Flip grumbles.

"Tally, how's university life treating you?" I ask.

"Good." Her lips pull to the side. "It's different. I keep getting asked out by the guys on the hockey team, though." She rolls her eyes. "It's annoying."

"Stay away from those guys. They're a bunch of walking hard-ons," Flip mutters.

"People who live in glass houses..." Dred counters.

Tally snorts an indelicate laugh. "I'm eighteen, surrounded by eighteen-year-olds. It's a giant pool of hormones."

"Facts," Tristan agrees.

"I'm getting something stronger." Flip slides out of his chair and heads for the bar.

Rix turns back to Tally. "Make good choices."

"Oh, I will. I'm not stupid." Tally rolls her eyes. "I know they want to date my last name, not me."

"I've been there," Hammer says.

"Same," Rix adds.

"And you two are both with hockey players now, so is that my destiny?" Tally asks.

She's all snark these days, like real life is hitting her hard. University is good for her, but it's a lot of change, and she's been insulated in this world for a long time.

We stay for dinner and hang out with our friends for a while before Dallas takes me back to his place, gets me naked, and worships every inch of me.

I've never felt so wanted. So needed.

So loved.

CHAPTER 46
HEMI

"What the—" I come to an abrupt halt in my office doorway. A massive banner has been strung across one wall, framed by an arch of balloons. How Dallas managed to get all this stuff up here without me noticing is a wonder. When he had time is another question mark. Between practice, away games, and my hectic schedule, fall has been a whirlwind. I moved in officially two months ago. Dallas is an incredible partner and roommate. And one day, he'll make an amazing husband and father.

I love waking up to him and going to sleep with him. And those away stretches make me fall even more in love. He leaves sweet little notes and smiling crocheted peaches all over the apartment for me to find. He's obsessed, and I love it. The current state of my office further confirms just how deep his infatuation runs.

"Oh wow." Hammer appears beside me. "This is…wow."

"That about sums it up."

"How did he even get in here? When did he get in here?"

"Your guess is as good as mine. Someone must have given him access." The team landed a couple of hours ago, while I was in a meeting with Denise, the women's team's head coach. He must have been planning this for some time. That he managed to set this up between landing and now is seriously impressive.

The banner strung across my wall reads WILL YOU GO TO PROM WITH ME? The balloon arch is a whole separate thing. It seems totally unnecessary, but also very much something Dallas would do just because he can.

I snap a photo with my phone and send it to Dallas.

HEMI

We're minus a time machine to make this happen.

"We don't need a time machine. Just say yes."

I spin around and find him standing behind me, looking too delicious for his own good. And mine. I haven't seen him in five days.

"Hi, Dallas. Bye, Dallas." Hammer spins and walks out of my office.

"Permission to close your door so I can do unprofessional things with my lips?" he asks.

"Permission granted."

He closes the door and takes my face in his wide, warm palms and drops his head. But he stops before his lips connect with mine. I pucker in an attempt to reach him. He backs off a little. I narrow my eyes.

He grins. "I missed you, honey."

"I missed you. Kiss me," I demand.

"Say yes."

"Yes. I'll go to prom with you. Even though it was ten years ago."

"Excellent." He kisses me. Soft. Sweet.

I try to deepen the kiss, but he pulls back. "I appreciate your love for my lips on your lips, but you have an appointment for hair, nails, and makeup in less than half an hour."

"What?" The whiplash is a lot, as is my desire to get him home and into bed.

"Hair, makeup, and nails. We need to get you prom ready."

"You're ridiculous."

"Ridiculously in love with you." He kisses the end of my nose and grabs my purse, slinging it over his shoulder. "Come on." He takes my hand and tugs me toward the door.

Twenty minutes later, I'm sitting in a chair with a woman expertly recreating the hairstyle I wanted nearly a decade ago. Essie is working on my makeup while a third woman paints my toenails.

"I can't believe he sucked you into this," I tell her.

"I mean, any excuse to bring back the mid-two-thousands and all that came along with them is a good excuse," she says with a smile.

"Where the heck did you find that picture?" I motion to the clipping from a magazine.

"I have your moms to thank for that." Dallas sits in the chair next to me, one leg crossed over the other. "Apparently, you had a whole scrapbook page dedicated to prom."

"They did not send you my high school scrapbook." My horror must be written on my face.

Dallas grins, and it's a devilish, panty-melting expression on his gorgeous face. "Oh, they most certainly did. I had no idea you were an expert scrapbooker."

"It was a brief phase."

"Not that brief. The book spans all of high school. I love that your debate club was featured prominently. Can't say I was all that surprised to see me with devil horns in several photos."

"They suited you back then," I note.

"They did. They still do, but for very different reasons."

I hold up a hand to block his face. "It's inappropriate to look at me like that in public."

"You two are adorable. Were you high school sweethearts?" Anna, my hair stylist, asks.

"Dallas had a crush on me in high school," I say.

"Oh, honey, I didn't have a *crush*. I was head over ass in love with you."

"You've been infatuated for a while."

"Unabashedly accurate." He winks at me and mouths *I love you*.

I make a heart with my hands back at him.

It's another half hour before I'm done at the salon.

I hug Essie. "I'll see you soon."

"For sure you will." She winks and sends us on our way.

We walk the two blocks to Dallas's, fingers entwined, and take the elevator to the penthouse.

"I need you to close your eyes when we go inside," he informs me when we reach our floor.

"You have more surprises?"

"I do." His smile is impish as he leads me down the hall.

"Eyes closed, honey." He kisses my forehead, and I do as he asks, letting him guide me through the penthouse. Music from our high school era plays in the living room. "Okay, you can open them."

We're standing in the walk-in closet and hanging in front of me is the dress I'd planned to wear to prom a decade ago. "Oh my...how?"

"Your scrapbook came in very handy. I had it made for you."

"I can't believe I wanted to wear this." It's strapless and royal blue taffeta with a huge, poofy skirt and a lace underlay. The best part is the zebra-print bodice. I'd been so in love with it. We bought it months before prom, and I'd tried it on almost every day leading up to the event. I press my fingers to my lips and fight the onslaught of emotion. "I can't believe you had this made for me."

"It's a little self-serving. I wanted to go to prom with you, and I didn't get to, and I didn't get to see you in this dress." He kisses my temple.

Even without a date, Brooklyn and I had planned to go. My moms had bought me the dress and everything. But they were the only ones who saw me wear it. "Can I try it on?" I finger the tacky, ridiculous bodice.

"I would love that. But first…" He passes me a gift bag tied with zebra-print ribbon.

I pull the ribbon free while Dallas leans against the doorjamb. Inside is a bra and panty set that match the dress. "Where did you find these?"

"I had them custom made, just for you. I'll leave you to change. Call me when you're ready; there's more." He kisses me on the cheek and leaves me alone in his bedroom.

I change into the lingerie and dress. And I don't even have to call for Dallas, because he meets me at the door to his bedroom. "Oh, wow. That suit is—"

"Fucking awesome. I know." It's made of the same shiny blue taffeta as my dress. He's paired it with a black button-down, zebra-print tie, and a pair of running shoes with the plaid stripe that's missing from the rest of his outfit. He points to the floor and extends his hand. "Your shoes."

Of course they match the rest of my outfit.

I bite my lips together and blink back all the feelings that want to leak out of my eyes. "You really went all out for this."

"I wanted it to be perfect." He cups my face in his hands. "Your feelings on fire, honey?"

I hold my fingers apart a fraction of an inch. "A little."

He kisses my forehead and wraps his arms around me. "Let me absorb those for you."

"I love you."

"And I love you. Every single part of you. Especially the parts that bite. Those are my favorite."

When I'm ready, he releases me and holds out his hand. I take it, slipping my feet into the blue heels with zebra-print bows.

"We can and should wear these next year for Halloween."

"I was thinking the office Christmas party, but Halloween works, too." He threads his arm through mine. "You ready to go to prom with me, Wilhelmina?"

"Absolutely."

My heels clip on the hardwood as we walk down the hall. I gasp as we step into the living room. It's been completely transformed. The furniture is gone, and a balloon arch—clearly Dallas is a fan of these—decorates one wall. There's a photo booth and a table complete with punchbowl and popcorn. But the thing that nearly undoes me entirely is the fact that all our friends and family are here, including our parents and siblings, and Granny Bright. Even better is that everyone is dressed for prom. My grip on his arm tightens as they holler and clap.

"You threw me a prom."

"I wanted it to be a night to remember, and I thought having all the people we both love would make it special."

"It's perfect. I love you." I pull his mouth down to mine. "You're the best boyfriend in the world."

I'm crushed into a huge group hug by our friends.

"Were you all in on this?" I ask my friends.

"Absolutely." Hammer is wearing another princess dress, likely bought for her by Hollis, who loves to dress her up.

Tally is wearing her prom dress from a handful of months ago; Dred is wearing the most beautifully ostentatious red, poofy gown; Essie is in a lavender satin halter dress; Rix is stunning in a green dress; and Shilpa looks like a queen in her gold, floor-length number.

Our parents and siblings converge on us next, hugging us, then dragging us to the photo booth. Sam keeps side-eying Dallas though which just makes Paris laugh. In the months Dallas and I have been together, we've made a point of going home to visit our families, and our parents adore each other. They were already friendly, but now they have dinner together once a week. I love how much our love has united the people most important to us.

We take silly pictures in the photo booth. We drink spiked punch and eat pizza and laugh and dance. It's everything I could have ever wanted for the prom I missed. And it means that much more because all the people I adore are here to experience it with us.

Dallas cues up one of my favorite slow songs from high school and holds out his hand. "One last dance."

I kick off my heels and clasp my hands behind his neck.

"This was amazing."

"You're amazing." He kisses the end of my nose and his wide palm settles on my low back.

"You love me."

"More than anything else in the world," he agrees.

"I love you," I whisper.

"I'll never get tired of hearing those words." His lips meet mine.

Falling for Dallas, being loved by him, has been surreal. The changes in the Terror office have been for the better, and the new additions to our team have been mostly positive, Connor aside. He's my new PR project.

But Dallas is such a rock and the best partner I could ask for. "I can't imagine my life without you."

"Me neither. Loving you is my favorite thing in the world."

It's humbling to be loved with such ferocity. To be revered and adored, and I feel the same way about him. I'm just as obsessed with Dallas as he is with me. "I'm ready," I blurt.

His eyes light up.

"Ask me again," I whisper.

We're surrounded by the people we love—our families, our friends, our support system. "I'm happier than I've ever been, Dallas. Because of you. You're my favorite everything."

His expression shifts, and his smile softens, and then he drops to one knee. Like he's been waiting for this moment.

Because he has. Patiently.

He fishes the velvet box out of his breast pocket.

My fingers go to my lips as the music stops. "Have you been carrying that around all night?"

"I've been carrying it around for months, Wills. I wanted to be ready when you were."

"Oh blessed day! Is he doing what I think he's doing?" Granny Bright yells at Dallas's dad.

"Yeah, Mom, he is."

"That's why you're my favorite, Dallas. Manning, Ferris, take some notes," Granny Bright calls out.

"You too, Sam and Isaac," Mom mutters as she straightens her dupatta over her shoulder.

"Everyone good now? I can proceed?" Dallas asks.

Apologies are murmured, and a hush falls over our friends and family.

But we're both grinning, because as ridiculous as it is, it's also perfect.

He flips open the box. "Wilhelmina Reddi-Grinst, I have loved you every moment of every day since you kicked everyone's ass in debate in third grade. You have my heart and soul, and it would be an incredible honor to love you for the rest of our lives. I want you to be the mother of our children. I want to cherish every single sunrise and sunset with you. I want to call you my wife and grow old with you. Make me the happiest man alive. Marry me."

"Yes. A thousand times yes. I'm sorry it took me so long to catch up, but I'm here with you now, and there is nowhere else I ever want to be. I want to spend the rest of my life loving you and being loved by you."

His smile makes my heart swell to bursting.

"I love you infinitely." He slips the ring on my finger and rises. "You're a goddess, and I will worship you until my last breath." He kisses me. With reverence. With the promise of our future.

And our friends and family swoop in, cheering, laughing, and shedding tears of the sweetest joy. I feel their love surrounding us. Enveloping us. And I know that regardless of how we started, this is exactly where we're supposed to be. In love with each other, and loved so wholly by the family and friends who will always stand beside us.

EPILOGUE
DALLAS

TWO YEARS LATER

I cradle the tiny bundle in my arms, mesmerized by her bright blue eyes and sweet face. "Let's go on a little adventure, shall we?" I head down the hall, my finger caught in the tiny iron grip.

I make sure Wills isn't on the phone before I barge into her office. The past two years have been the best of my damn life. My career is at an all-time high. The Terror are kicking ass and every day I'm more in love with my wife than the last. She's phenomenal and she's mine and I'm hers.

"One sec. I just need to hit send." Her fingers fly across the keyboard for a few more seconds before she looks up. "Hi, my amazing—oh my God, Dallas, what are you doing to me?" She gives me a put-out look and curves her hand around her ear. "Did you hear that?"

The adorable bundle of joy nestled against my chest sighs and smacks her lips.

"The baby is exasperated on your behalf."

Wills rolls her eyes as she pushes her chair back. "It was the sound of my ovaries exploding. You can't show up in my office in the middle of the day holding a baby and expect me to be able to focus."

I smirk. "Is that right?"

"Give her to me. I want to hold the sweetness."

"In a minute. First, I need a kiss." I pucker my lips and Wills crosses over and presses hers to mine.

"Give me the baby," she purrs.

"We can make one of our own, you know." I give her a heated look. "In less than a year, you could be holding our son or daughter. You say the word, honey, and I'll get to work putting a baby in that beautiful belly of yours."

"If you let me hold her now, I'll let you start trying as soon as we get home tonight."

"Seriously?" I figured it would take a little more persuasion on my part.

"Do you have any idea how hot you are right now? This big muscle-y hockey player holding this tiny little wrapped bundle of cuteness. I'm pretty sure I just ovulated." She assumes the "hold the baby" position. "Give her to me, please."

I carefully transfer the baby into my wife's arms. She smiles down at her as she strokes her cheek.

"Aren't you the most precious little thing?" Wills laughs when she gets a look at her onesie, which has the angry goose Terror logo on it. "You'll have so many honorary aunts and uncles. It'll be the biggest, most amazing family you could ask for. We'll probably be a little over-protective, and it might be a bit much in your teen years, but you'll grow to appreciate it."

"I like that you're already giving her pep talks."

"She'll need them with the number of built-in bodyguards she'll have. You're our new little team princess, aren't you?"

"She needs a bestie; we should give her one. What time is it? Can you leave now so we can get started?" I glance at the clock. "It's four thirty. You can kick out a little early today, can't you?"

She laughs. "Turn off my computer for me and grab my purse."

I rush around her desk, minimize her open tabs, and smile as I take in the screensaver of our wedding day. It's a picture of us surrounded by our friends and family. The people most important to us, who support us and love us and have been there with us through every up and down since we started down this road together.

Last year, Samir offered to do a deep dive and try to locate Wills's birth mom for her. After a few therapy sessions, and a couple that I attended with her, she decided against it. Her information is already in the database. If they're supposed to find each other, they will, but between the family who raised her, the one she married into, and the Terror team family, and she's not looking to fill spaces in her heart, but she's always willing to make room for more people to love and be loved by.

I shut down her computer, grab her purse, and tuck in her chair, leaving her desk the way she likes it.

"Let's go find your daddy, Princess Ariel," Wills coos.

We step out into the hall and don't have to go far to find him.

"How did I know you two would have my little girl?"

Ariel perks up at the sound of her dad's voice. Her little hand shoots into the air and she squawks and squirms. "Dallas would like to give little Ariel a best friend," Wills informs him.

He chuckles. "Not even remotely a surprise. I think Ash and Shilpa's baby needs lots of bestie's too."

"I'm so excited for them," I say.

Wills carefully transfers Ariel into Roman's arms. "My littlest princess is going to be well loved." He gazes down at her with an adoration that speaks to the deepest kind of love there is and kisses his daughter's tiny cherub cheek. "You two enjoy your evening, I'm going to take Ariel to see her sister."

Wills threads her arm through mine as we watch him walk down the hall to Hammer's office, cooing to his daughter all the way. "That man was born to love, wasn't he?"

"Absolutely."

I bend to kiss her. "Let me take you home so I can worship you with every part of me."

"That's my favorite," she sighs.

"*You're* my favorite."

"And you're mine."

She's my everything. My beautiful badass.

My sweetness with bite.

The woman of my dreams and the love of my life.

EXTENDED EPILOGUE
PROM NIGHT VIRGIN

DALLAS

Post "Prom" Proposal

"That was hands down the best prom ever." Wills slides her hands up my chest and links them behind my neck. "I can't believe you threw me a prom. I can't believe we're engaged again. For real this time." She pushes up on her toes to kiss me. "My moms are so happy. Again. And I'm just so in love with you and so excited to be your wife. This was the feeling I always dreamed of."

"It's exactly the feeling I wanted you to have." I brush a tendril of hair away from her cheek. "And I love you, too. But you know that." I wink, and she giggles.

It's one of my favorite sounds in the world.

"You know what would make prom night complete?" She drags her fingernails down the back of my neck.

It sends a shiver of delight along my spine. "Losing our virginity together?"

She laughs. "I think we're both well past that point."

I smooth my fingers down her arms. "You know I tried to wait for you, right?"

She tips her head.

"I really thought prom would be it for us. I built that up in my head for the whole freaking year. And honestly, it's probably better that it didn't work out the way I wanted it to, because my first time was not a five-star event. Would not recommend on Yelp."

"You tried to wait for me?"

"Yeah, but then after the fiasco, I went to university and figured I'd never be with you." I wet my bottom lip. "But one part of me is still a virgin."

Her eyes flare. "Oh you mean...are you—"

I raise a brow.

"For real?" Her nails bite into my skin.

"Only you can fuck me, honey."

She pulls my mouth down to hers, tongue gliding against mine. I pick her up and carry her across the penthouse to our bedroom.

I set her on the floor and struggle to pry her arms from around my neck and disengage her lips from mine. "Honey, we're not going to get very far if you don't press pause for a second."

"Right. Yes." She releases my hair and steps back. "I'm really excited."

I point to my erection. "So are we." I motion to a black box with gold ribbon sitting on the bed. "You should open that."

I stand behind her, kissing her neck as she carefully pulls the ribbon free and lifts the lid. Her breath leaves her on a whoosh as she reveals the contents. "I like that you planned ahead with different sizes."

"I figure we start small, pun intended."

"Good call." She rubs her ass on my erection. "Starting with what you're packing would be a little intense."

I drop my head and tug on the zipper at the back of her dress. "I'll understand if it never goes both ways."

"Oh, it'll go both ways, darling. It'll just take a bit more time, practice, and preparation before we get there. But we have lots of time for that." She turns and shimmies out of her dress, leaving her in her bra and panties.

We undress the rest of the way, savoring each other and the moment. Once we're naked, I do the honors and help Wills into the strap-on. I take my time, running my hands over her ass as I tighten the straps, kissing her neck and shoulders.

When I'm done, I step back and take her in. "Fuck me."

She bites her lip and strokes the "beginner" silicone cock. "Oh, I plan to, honey."

"You're gorgeous." Our swords cross when I take her face in my hands and slant my mouth over hers.

She moans, hands gliding down my chest, fingers curving around my cock, stroking gently, then squeezing.

She pulls back, eyes hooded with lust as she uses my cock to tug me toward the bed. "You gonna be a good boy and get on your hands and knees for me?"

I shake my head.

She arches a brow, and her nails press ever so gently against my shaft. I fucking love it.

"I want to see your beautiful face when you're fucking me." I hold her hips and spin us around, pulling her onto the bed with me. The strap-on jabs me in the stomach, and I move her to straddle my hips and capture a nipple between my lips.

Wills runs her nails across the back of my scalp as she settles over my erection. She cups my face in her hands and kisses me softly. Then she pulls back and kisses the end of my nose. "Let me get you ready, honey."

"Fuck, I love you."

"Let me show you how much I love you." She pushes on my shoulders.

I lie back, and she retrieves the supplies necessary to make this experience possible. Then she kisses a slow, torturous path down my body. Edging her knee between mine, she takes my cock in her hand and gives it a slow stroke as her lips skim the tip. They part as the head disappears between them. She does that thing with her tongue that makes my balls feel like they're levitating. Her mouth is the most beautiful bliss.

She moves my hands to her head, giving me control, and I take it, holding her still as I pull out to the ridge and push back in. Her eyes stay on mine, her hands sliding down my thighs, disappearing for a few seconds before she gently cups my balls.

And then I feel it, the tapered plug sliding between my cheeks, pressing against my ass. On my next thrust she slides the plug in. Intense pleasure zips up my spine, and my hands leave her hair as my eyes roll up.

She pops off my cock, wrapping her hand around the length and gripping firmly. But she doesn't stroke. Just holds me while I fight to control my body.

"Such a good boy," she praises.

She kisses up and down the length of my cock, teasing me, tasting me. I would do anything for her, give her anything she wants. And she's mine. This amazing woman who isn't afraid to give up control or take it.

Her lips brush the head of my cock as her gaze meets mine. "You ready to be fucked, honey?"

"Only by you."

"Only ever me," Wills agrees. She takes me in her mouth again as she removes the plug and tosses it over the edge of the bed.

She folds back on her knees and grabs the bottle of lube, pouring a thick stream on the silicone cock. She's damn well glorious as she moves into position. The inside of her thighs rest against my ass as I spread my legs wide.

She takes my erection in one hand and the strap-on in the other, lining herself up. And then she pushes inside. Just an inch, maybe two, stroking me as I adjust. She works me with her hand as she fills me. And I watch her with rapt fascination. With awe. With a primal, untapped desire.

There is no one else I would give up control like this for. No one else I can ever imagine being this vulnerable with. Only ever her.

"You're doing so good, sweetheart," she praises as she pushes the rest of the way inside, thumb smoothing over my crown.

I groan as the intense burn shifts and pleasure surges through me. Every thrust makes me feel like I've died and gone to heaven. The way she fills me, owns me, possesses me. It will never be enough.

"God, you're gorgeous." Her eyes move over my body. "My big, hockey-player future husband getting good and fucked."

I grab the back of her neck and pull her mouth down to mine. "Just you wait, future wife, soon enough I'll have you screaming my name, begging for more."

She grins against my lips before she hits that spot inside me that lights me up. "Me first, though."

She finds a rhythm, stroking me in time to the roll of her hips. She's just so damn beautiful, and sexy. All that power and confidence, and I get to be inside her orbit every day for the rest of our lives. I get to love her. I get to make love to her, fuck her, and be fucked and loved by her.

"I want to be inside you when I come," I grind out.

I'm already on the cusp. I grab her hips, and she pulls out. We quickly rid her of the strap-on, and I fit myself between her thighs and fill her pussy the same way she did me. "I'm going to pound you into the mattress now, honey."

"Yes, please, Dallas," she says softly. Sweetly.

I pull my hips back, and my restraint snaps with my first thrust. Like I promised, she screams my name and begs for more. "Don't stop, don't stop, don't stop," she chants as I drive into her.

We tip over the edge at the same time, clinging to each other. The orgasm seems endless, spinning out, expanding and consuming us.

We're both breathless, panting and sweaty as I roll us to the side. Wills's fingers sift through my hair, and she smiles up at me. "We're going to have a lot of fun together, aren't we?"

I can feel the grin stretching my face. "So much fun." I stroke her cheek. "I get to love you for the rest of my life. It'll never be long enough, but it'll have to do."

She settles her palm on my chest. "My heart couldn't have a better home than here, with you."

She's all I've ever wanted. And finally, she knows she's meant to be mine.

Join my Newsletter for even more Dallas and Hemi:

**Preorder IF YOU LOVE ME, Roman's standalone forbidden
romance:**

ABOUT THE AUTHOR HELENA HUNTING

NYT and USA Today bestselling author, Helena Hunting lives on the outskirts of Toronto with her amazing family and her adorable kitty, who think the best place to sleep is her keyboard. Helena writes everything from emotional contemporary romance to romantic comedies that will have you laughing until you cry. If you're looking for a tearjerker, you can find her angsty side under H. Hunting.

OTHER TITLES BY HELENA HUNTING

LIES, HEARTS & TRUTHS SERIES

Little Lies

Bitter Sweet Heart

Shattered Truths

SHACKING UP SERIES

Shacking Up

Getting Down (Novella)

Hooking Up

I Flipping Love You

Making Up

Handle with Care

SPARK SISTERS SERIES

When Sparks Fly

Starry-Eyed Love

Make A Wish

LAKESIDE SERIES

Love Next Door

Love on the Lake

THE CLIPPED WINGS SERIES

Cupcakes and Ink

Clipped Wings

Between the Cracks

Inked Armor

Cracks in the Armor

Fractures in Ink

Printed in the USA
CPSIA information can be obtained
at www.ICGtesting.com
LVHW032257291024
795138LV00005B/5